# Rise of the Wounded Dove

## A Drakaren Novel
## Alexia Gray

First printing, 2026

Print paperback ISBN 979-8-9989675-3-5

Print hardcover ISBN 979-8-9989675-4-2

Ebook ISBN 979-8-9989675-5-9

This novel is entirely a work of fiction. The names, characters and incidents portrayed in it are the work of the author's imagination. Any resemblance to actual persons, living or dead, events or localities is entirely coincidental.

# CONTENT AND TRIGGER WARNING

This story isn't all ballgowns and banquets.

This story contains emotionally intense material that may be triggering to some readers, including sexual violence, captivity, and scenes of physical and emotional trauma. You know- the kind of stuff that buries itself deep then claws its way back to the surface to haunt you when you least expect it. Fun, right?

If any of that feels like too much, just close the book and walk away. No shame- some chapters aren't meant to be faced before snacks, sleep, or a good cry. This story will still be here when you're ready.

With love, lavender, and a very sharp dagger,

-Alexia

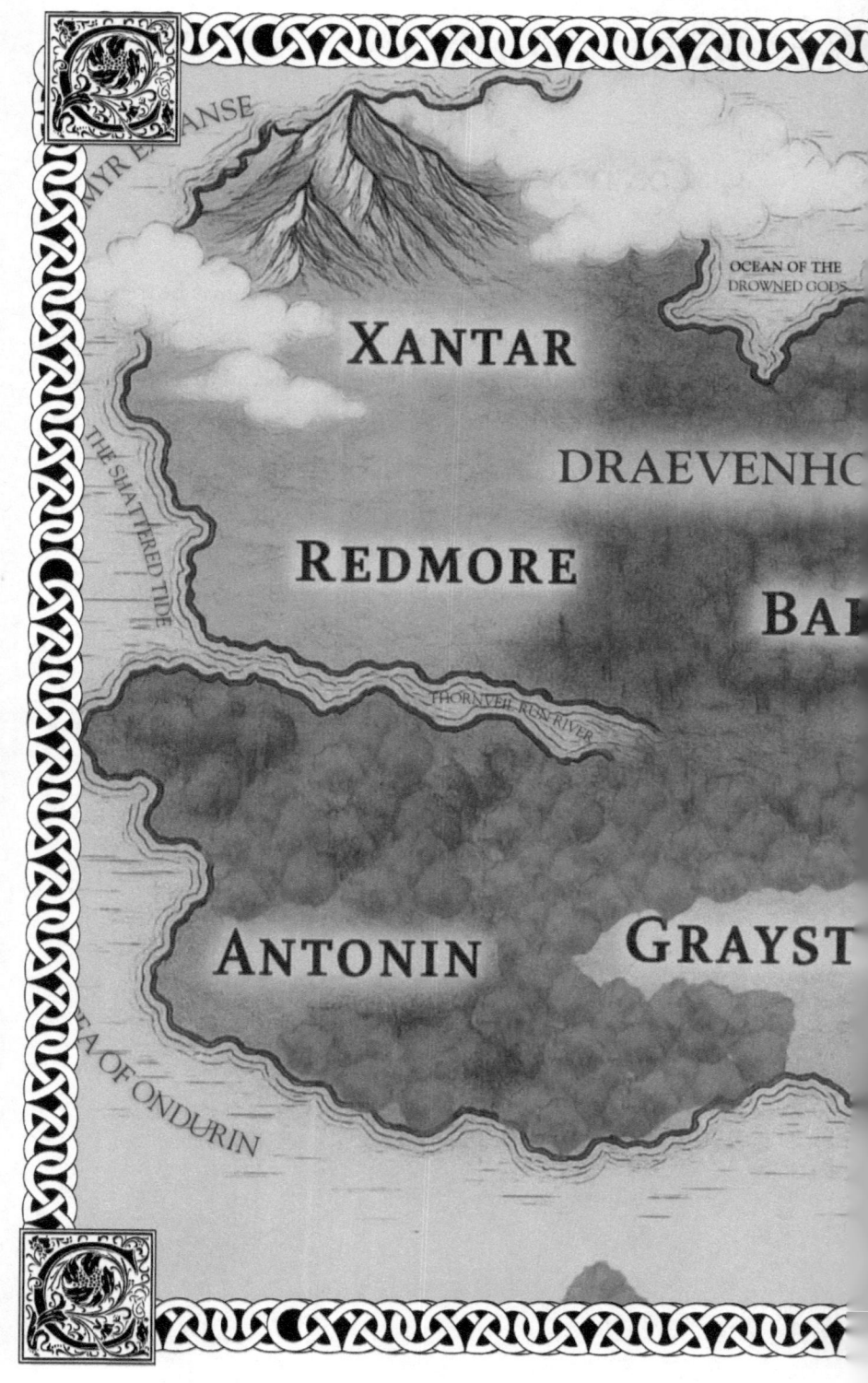

For the women who were told to behave.

And chose to conquer instead.

# PROLOGUE

The Blessing Beneath the Oak: A Glimpse at the Past.

*E**liryn**.*

*Eliryn felt the shift long before the mortal world would have noticed. It was not a tremor in the realm beyond the veil, but in himself. A pull. A spark. A flare of light in the tapestry of fate so familiar it halted him mid-thought. He knew that light. He had once loved the mirror of it.*

*Twin souls were rare. Rarer still were souls that could reshape a continent. The first had belonged to her, the woman whose life had united Caeleria before the Great War tore it apart. She had carried peace in her hands and fire in her heart. She had been his chosen, his beloved, the only mortal he had dared to walk beside.*

*Her death had hollowed him.*

*Her death had ended an age.*

*Eliryn had lived centuries without the echo of her essence. Until now.*

*The new spark pulsed again, faint but insistent, nestled deep within the womb of a mortal queen. Not the same woman reborn, but the same thread of soul, the same rare fire. Not a replica. A continuation. A possibility. This child carried the potential to finish what the first had begun, to mend what had shattered, to guide the world toward a dawn it had once been denied. He knew it in his very essence. And this time, he would not let the world destroy her.*

*He could not enter the mortal realm in full form. The veil he had woven ages ago to balance the worlds held him fast, unyielding even to a god. But a blessing required no crossing, only a reach. A gentle push of his essence through the narrowest seam in creation.*

*He had never dared to attempt such a thing before. Not even for her. As the keeper of balance, the steward of beginnings and endings, Eliryn had feared altering the mortal weave too greatly. Even when he loved her, even when her soul had burned bright enough to change an age, he had withheld his hand. And that had been his greatest mistake.*

*Now, staring through the veil at the queen laboring beneath the ancient oak, at the spark in her womb that pulsed with the unmistakable twin of the soul he once loved. Eliryn understood. This was not interference. This was correction. Continuation. A chance the realm itself had offered back to him. He would not fail her again.*

*The oak shivered at his presence, welcoming him. Its roots remembered the tears he had once shed there, and the spark within the queen answered like a steady heartbeat. The clearing shimmered where the veil thinned. The queen had not wandered here by chance. The oak had called* to her, the same tree that had held his grief when the woman he loved was taken from the world.

He watched through the veil as close as he could be. The clearing felt him, quiet beneath branches that bowed in acknowledgment. Leaves stilled. Air warmed. Even the earth seemed to brace itself. The queen labored in the cradle of the oak's shade, breath ragged and body shaking. Her husband knelt beside her, courage trembling at the edges. Destiny curled around them like rising mist.

They would believe this moment was coincidence. Eliryn knew better.

The queen cried out, and the moment split open. The infant spilled into her father's hands with a wail that rang like the first note of a new age. The sound cracked across the clearing, carried by sunlight and the trembling hush of creation listening.

Eliryn pressed firmly against the veil. The newborn blinked against the light, her tiny body trembling with the effort of living. Her cry softened as his presence brushed near. She quieted, almost listening, her soul reaching instinctively for the one who had answered her call.

Yes. Her soul remembered him. Not with love, not with longing, but with the echo of something older. A resonance. The faint remembrance of a twin flame that had once shaped a continent. A reflection of a bond that had existed long before she drew breath.

He reached out, his blessing moving like breath through the seam in the veil. As it touched her, a whisper of his essence unfurled within her, and something deep inside the child stirred awake. Not magic. Not yet. A thread of knowing, fine as silk, wove itself through her being. A sense for the moments when things must end. A sense for the moments when things *must begin. The spark flared bright and steady, marking her as one who would one day stand at the turning points of the world.*

*"Little one," he murmured, though no mortal ear could hear. "I grant you the sight of thresholds. The instinct to step where others hesitate. The pull to unmake what must fall and to breathe life into what should rise." The air warmed. The oak's leaves stirred as if in salute. She glowed faintly, only for a heartbeat, but it was enough. Her soul answered him with fearless clarity. "You carry the echo of the life that once saved this realm," he said, grief and hope braided in his tone. "A soul that ended war and began an age of peace. You carry the same strength. And this time, I will not fail you."*

*Blessing her required no ritual. It became truth pressed into bone, woven through breath, curled into the rhythm of her heart. A vow that her life would open doors others could not see. A promise that when the world reached its breaking point, she would be the pivot. The ending of one age. The beginning of another.*

*Peace settled over the clearing. The queen's trembling eased. The king's terror faded like mist before sunlight. They would call it miracle. They would never know it was him.*

*Eliryn stepped back, lingering longer than he meant to. The child turned her tiny face toward him, eyes unfocused yet strangely aware. The same way her twin-souled predecessor had once looked at him.*

*"It begins," he whispered, and the oak rustled in agreement.*

*He vanished into the rising light, leaving only the impression of peace in his wake and the faintest pulse of a blessing threaded through the heart of the girl who would one day end an age and begin a new one.*

# PART I

## *The missing month*

The epilogue of Book One carried the realm forward one full month, leaving a sliver of time unspoken. But stories rarely leap so easily. Some moments refuse to be left behind. Between the fall of Bartoria and the day the world believed itself steady again, a month passed in quiet movement. Yet battles were fought in that silence. Hearts shifted. Destiney began its slow turn long before anyone noticed.

These are the days between. The days the epilogue did not show. The days that honed Kain and Layla, sharpened them, shaped them, before the pull between them drew their paths together once more.

# Chapter One

*K*<sup>ain.</sup>

*Kain.*

Light exploded across his vision, white and merciless, searing away the last fragments of a dream until it dissolved into nothing and only pain remained. It struck hard, splitting through his skull and tearing down his spine until even breathing felt like a battle. His chest heaved, his breath came ragged and shallow, and his eyes fluttered open against the glare. A shaky exhale left his lips as he forced his mind to catch up with the agony of his body. He was alive. Though the realization came with no relief. Alive, but somewhere far from the dream and farther still from Antonin's wood huts.

Shapes began to form out of the blur. A ceiling. A bed. He blinked through the haze, and slowly the world came into cold, golden clarity. This was Graystonian splendor.

Tall windows towered before him, their velvet curtains thick enough to choke out the sun, yet a sliver of gold slipped through, spilling across the room like liquid dawn. Dust motes drifted within it, slow and aimless, like floating embers refusing to die. The walls were dressed in heavy tapestries, stags and wheat stitched in glimmering gold thread, the craftsmanship so perfect it mocked the ruin still clinging to his mind.

Beneath him, the bed was soft enough to swallow him whole, its silken weight pressing against every raw nerve. If not for the fire in his muscles, the pulsing ache behind his eyes, and the steady throb of his heart. He might have believed he had fallen into some decadent afterlife...or yet another dream.

As his senses returned, awareness followed. Linen pressed against his temple. Bandages wrapped his ribs, pulling tight with every breath. Each inhale stung, sharp enough to remind him he was still here, still whole enough to hurt. He drew another shallow breath and forced his eyes to focus, grounding himself in the present. And then the world shifted when he finally saw *her*.

Curled in a high-backed chair beside his bed, Layla Eradellian slept. A blanket had slipped to her knees, her hands folded loosely in her lap. Her head rested against the chair's edge, chestnut-brown hair spilling like silk across her shoulder, catching the morning light until every strand glowed with a faint shimmer of gold. Her face was half-hidden, soft in repose, lips parted just enough to reveal the slow rhythm of her breathing.

For a moment, he simply watched her, the quiet of it settling over him like a held breath. Then the thought rose, unbidden and undeniable.

He had seen warriors bleed bright and die bold. He had known women who could cut a man down with a smile. But he had never seen strength look like her's. Not loud. Not demanding. Something quieter. Stubborn. Enduring. A kind of strength he could not fight or outpace, one that stood steady even when she trembled.

As he stared at her, the truth continued to slide in without permission. He was completely and uncomfortably fascinated. The kind of fascination that settled low and coiled tight. Gods, he was in awe of her. This wild, sharp-edged princess who refused to break. This woman who burned on the inside and pretended not to. He loved drawing that fire to the surface, loved watching her shine when she forgot to hide it, yet somehow she steadied him in return. Calmed something restless inside him even as she roused it. And somewhere deep in his chest, a darker, hungrier part of him thrilled at the contradiction. She tamed him as she taunted him, he realized. And the worst part was that being tamed by her did not feel like a defeat. It felt like a challenge. A promise. One that terrified him as much as it excited him.

A slow smile crept across his lips, unbidden but impossible to stop, as the realization settled deeper into him. Looking at her now, keeping silent watch even in her sleep. He almost laughed at the fact that she was completely unaware of the havoc she stirred inside him. For a moment, his bruises felt distant and his pain almost unimportant. Something feral paced beneath his ribs, restless and hungry, while the part she had somehow stilled leaned toward her quiet as if it were a sanctuary he had never known he needed. Pain dulled. Thought thinned. All that remained was the quiet war she ignited within him simply by existing within reach. His smile deepened, slow and dangerous. Whatever this feeling was, he liked the way it burned, and gods, he wanted more.

As his gaze tracked her body, he noticed bruises ghosted her skin, faint and fading. A shallow cut traced her jaw. Silver scars shimmered across her arms like scattered constellations, proof she had fought and survived. Then he saw it... a dark imprint bruised around her upper arm. The distinct shape of a man's hand.

The rhythm of his breathing broke. No sound escaped him other than a slow exhale that quietly trembled through the stillness. Fury unfurled inside his chest, cold and deliberate, a blade turning within its sheath. He did not move. He did not blink. Memory filled the silence instead: the stench of Ivar's chambers, the splinter of wood beneath his boot, Layla's voice breaking as she endured, and Theron's sword ending it all *too* mercifully. *Too* fast. *Too* kind. Kain's fingers curled into the sheets until his knuckles blanched. Every muscle locked, trembling with the effort to remain still. His fury did not roar. It waited. It gathered strength in the quiet, tempering itself against the memory of her suffering.

She was alive. The thought sliced clean through the storm. Alive. Here. Breathing.

The peace she brought was real, but it was fleeting. The sight of the handprint stripped it away, dragging him back to the world beyond these walls, to everything that waited unfinished. Theron. Blood. Debt. Whatever calm she offered could not silence the truth pressing in his chest. Vengeance still waited for him, patient and merciless. And with that remainder, Kain knew stillness was no longer possible.

Slowly, he pressed his palms to the mattress and pushed. Pain tore through his body, white-hot and unrelenting, but he welcomed it. Pain was proof. Pain was focus. A sound escaped him, low and guttural, half breath, half vow, as he forced himself upright.

Movement stirred beside him. Layla's head lifted, her hair spilling forward in a soft cascade. Her eyes opened, hazel and luminous, finding his instantly. And for one suspended heartbeat, the world fell silent. The air between them felt awake and taunting. Thrumming with something raw and unspoken. She was peace. But her presence reminded him of everything he had to avenge.

"Kain." Her voice was soft, breathless, his name barely more than a tremor on her lips as recognition found her.

"Hey, Dove."

For a heartbeat, he could not make sense of what was happening, only a blur of chestnut and gold, and then she was in his arms. Her warmth hit him like life returning to a dead thing. Her scent, lavender, vanilla, and wild clover, filled his lungs and flooded his senses, clean and sweet and utterly devastating. The world fell away. The pain, the half-conscious nightmares, the endless raging thoughts stalled. All that remained was her.

Kain did not think, simply acted. His arms closed around her before his mind could catch up, dragging her close and holding her there as if the Gods themselves might reach down to steal her away. Fire tore through his ribs, but he welcomed it. He would endure it all a thousand times over if this was the reward.

She trembled against him, silent and raw. He felt her tears before he saw them, hot trails searing down his throat as her shoulders shook against his chest. He did not speak. He did not even breathe too deeply. If she needed to fall apart, she could do it here. If she needed to hide, he would be the place she hid. And when she was ready, he would help her rise again. His pain no longer mattered. Nothing did except her weight in his lap, the steady beat of her heart against his, and the way she fit against him as though she had always belonged there. Her breath brushed his collarbone. Her hair tickled his jaw. Every inhale carried her scent until even the air felt dangerous.

The thought came unsummoned, dry and reckless as a spark. "Sooooo, a head injury is what finally gets you into my bed, huh?" His voice was rougher than he intended, a whisper against her ear. "Good to know."

Layla jerked back, eyes wide, color flooding her cheeks. Her hand shot out and smacked his chest with an indignant thud.

"Umpfh, fuck," he hissed, half groan, half laugh. Pain ripped through him, but he still grinned, broad and unapologetic.

"Ass," she muttered, wiping at her cheeks, though a laugh slipped free anyway. The sound was soft, disbelieving, and it rang like victory in his ears. She was still here. Still fighting. Still her.

Kain winced dramatically, pressing a hand to his chest. "Careful, Dove. I am still recovering. You might finish the job."

Her glare sharpened, though a tremor tugged at the corner of her mouth. "You nearly die, and that is what you wake up with? Gods, you are insufferable."

"Mm." His grin tilted, lazy and merciless. "And yet you are still in my bed. Curious, isn't it?" Her breath caught, faint but there. She pushed off his chest, muttering under her breath as she stood and began

11

to straighten the blanket around him with more force than necessary. The color still lingered along her throat. Kain watched her fuss, his smirk softening at the edges. "For what it's worth," he said quietly, humor tempered now, "I did not think I would wake up either."

That stopped her. Her hands stilled. For a long moment, neither of them spoke. Then she looked at him, her expression unreadable but her voice steady. "Well," she said at last, a faint, wry smile curving her lips, "do not do it again. I am far too busy to mourn arrogant idiots."

His grin returned, slow and wicked. "Noted."

Before she could step back, his hand caught her wrist, small and warm against his palm. She let out a startled gasp and he tugged once, gentle but sure. She stumbled a half step toward him, balance wavering. He did not let go. Another pull brought her closer, close enough for him to feel her heat, close enough for every thought in his head to burn away. Her knees brushed the mattress, the cushion dipping beneath her weight as his hands found her waist. Layla blinked at him, lips parted, disbelief and warning tangled in her gaze.

"Kain."

He lifted a brow, his voice smooth and unhurried. "Dove, do not tempt me. If you run, I will come after you. Even like this. So be kind and stay right here." For a moment she just stared at him, then a quiet laugh slipped through soft and unguarded. She shook her head and muttered something under her breath again but did not pull away. Instead, she let him guide her back against him until her head rested lightly on his chest, her hair spilling over his skin once again.

The breath he had not realized he was holding eased from his lungs. Gods, the pain was everywhere, burning through his ribs and across his skull, but it did not matter. He could fight it. He would fight it as long as she was here.

Layla shifted once, twice, until she seemed comfortably situated. Half against him and half on him, her weight settled with a soft exhale that brushed his collarbone. The quiet that followed nearly undid him. Her warmth. Her scent. The slow, steady rhythm of her breathing falling into place with his. Kain had held women before, the Gods knew that much, but never like this. Never with reverence. Never with care. Every touch before had been fleeting, a brief indulgence meant to chase away the dark. But this felt nothing like shadow. It felt like light. Holding her was not about possession or desire. It was proof. Proof that she was alive. Proof that he still was.

Layla's fingers unconsciously curled into the fabric at his side as if she trusted he would not let her fall. Her warmth seeped through him, not as temptation but as steadiness, an anchoring he had never known he needed. His earlier realization being amplified in this blissful moment. And the fact that she did not pull away. She did not flinch as he wrapped his arms around her once more. She simply stayed. That small act, that effortless trust, was heavy enough to hollow him out. Her body fit against his with a familiarity that should not have been possible, one that made his pulse stumble and his thoughts blur. Her breathing brushed his skin. Her hair tickled his jaw. Her presence threaded itself into every raw place inside him. It stripped him bare, this simple closeness.

He swallowed hard and forced a rough cough through his raw throat, trying to wrench his mind away from thoughts that were far too forbidden for this moment. He needed to focus. He needed control. When he finally spoke, his voice came out low and steady.

"So," he rasped, forcing levity back into his voice, "what the hell happened?"

Layla drew in a shuddering breath before responding, her voice muffled against his chest. "What's the last thing you remember?"

Kain exhaled slowly, dragging through fractured, hazy fragments of his memory. The harder he reached, the sharper his skull throbbed, but he ground his teeth and forced his eyes shut, pushing against the pain.

"The room. Theron. Then you and I, falling." The memory hit like a blade twisting deep.

*Glass tore into his abdomen, fire searing through muscle and bone. His shoulders screamed as he clung to Layla's hand, her weight pulling at him, her body swinging below the shattered ledge. Her face was pale, her eyes wide with terror, her lips forming his name. The sight of her slipping burned into his vision. For the first time in his life, true fear took root in his chest.*

*The crash of splintering wood shattered the air behind him. He twisted, breath ragged, just as Bartorian soldiers flooded through the broken doorway, steel flashing in the firelight. Theron met them head-on, a roar tearing from his throat as he cut down three in a single sweep. Then came the enemy blade. It drove into his chest with brutal precision, silencing the world around them. Time fractured. Kain saw his brother seize, eyes wide, life snatched away in a heartbeat.*

*He had one breath to choose. One heartbeat to act. There was no saving Theron. No saving himself. Only her.*

*With a ragged shout, he heaved upward, every torn muscle screaming as he hauled Layla against him. His arm locked around her waist, and he threw them both into the open air. Wind ripped past them, stealing her scream. The world spun into a blur of glass and night sky. He wrapped his body around hers, crushing her close, the only thought left in his mind a single prayer. Let the ground take him. Let it spare her. Then the world vanished into black.*

The memory lingered, implacable. Kain could still feel the sting of glass in his skin, the weight of his brother's death pressing against his ribs. It was not a wound that healed; it only learned to ache quieter. For a long moment, he stayed lost in it, the ghosts of that night crawling just beneath his breath. Layla did not speak. She only seemed to watch him, quiet and still, as if sensing the storm behind his silence. Then she shifted, lifting her face toward him. Tears shimmered under her lashes, threatening to fall.

"So you remember... that he..." Her voice faltered, the rest swallowed by a trembling breath. One tear slipped free, tracing a line down her cheek, and something deep inside Kain cracked open.

"Yes." His voice was firm, steady as stone. "He died with great honor, Dove. He died as every warrior dreams. Blade in hand, fighting for what was right. He will be celebrated for it. We do not mourn such deaths." He meant it. Every word. Death was not a thing to fear. No Antonin warrior was raised to dread it. To fall in battle was the highest glory, a passage to Ondurin where endless feasts and old comrades waited. But as he looked at her, at the disbelief softening her eyes, the words grew heavier. She was not Antonin. She had not been raised to see glory in the grave. For her, it was not triumph. It was loss.

"I know he meant a lot to you," Kain said quietly, the words dragging like gravel through his throat. "Theron wasn't easy to love. Gods, he wasn't easy to stand half the time. But those who did... they saw what he

15

tried to bury. Not duty. Not honor. The other parts. The wanting. The doubt. The things that made him human." He drew in a slow breath, his gaze unfocused, caught somewhere between memory and regret. "He spent his life being the perfect soldier. Unshakable. Untouchable. And then you appeared, and suddenly he wasn't any of those things. You got under his skin, Dove. And it terrified him. You made him more than a blade, you made him a man."

Silence pressed close. The air between them held still.

"I knew what he was doing before he said a word." His voice dropped lower, unsteady in a way that betrayed the crack in his composure. "That look he gave me... it wasn't a command. It was goodbye." Kain swallowed hard. "He was saving his little brother... and the woman he loved."

The words hung there, heavy and unmoving. The admission cut through him like glass, each syllable splintering deeper than the last. He had seen men die in a hundred ways, but nothing had prepared him for the kind of sacrifice that did not look like glory. It looked like love.

He drew a breath that trembled in his chest and forced the emotion down until only steel remained. "I know you do not understand our ways," he said at last, his tone finding the weight of command again. "But hear me. Just because we do not mourn does not mean we do not make it right. He will be avenged, Dove. I swear it." The vow settled between them, quiet but absolute. Layla did not speak. She only nodded once, slow and sure. Kain leaned back against the pillow, every muscle pulled taut as silence filled the space around them, thick with loss and the echo of a brother's final act of love.

The quiet lingered, not empty, not cruel, but full. Full of what they had lost, what they had said, and the memory that refused to release them. The air felt heavier, as if the room itself remembered what they dared not speak aloud.

Then, softly, almost as though afraid to break the spell, Layla spoke. "You were out for a week." Her voice was soft against his chest, the words barely brushing the air, yet they shattered the quiet all the same. His eyes widened. *A week? Gods.* His body ached and burned, but an entire week lost?

"Fuuuck," he muttered under his breath.

"You collapsed after we escaped," she continued, her tone thin, hesitant, stumbling over each word as if she had rehearsed them a hundred times in her head. Slowly, she sat up, facing him. Reluctantly, Kain let his arm fall away. "The men got you on a horse with Xaden and brought you back here. You were barely breathing. The healers worked on you day and night. Sparrow and Xaden wanted to risk moving you to Eir, but you were too broken. Too far gone. I didn't think you'd..." Her voice cracked. She pressed her lips together, trying to steady herself, but the words came faster now, tumbling out as though she feared she might lose her nerve if she stopped. "So you stayed. You had to stay. I wasn't sure you'd..."

Kain's chest tightened. The tremor in her voice was not just worry; it was fear, the kind that lingers long after the danger has passed. She had been terrified, and still she had stayed. He could see it in the exhaustion clouding her eyes, in the faint shake of her hands, in the way her voice faltered around his name. Whatever those days had been, they had hollowed her. She looked like someone who had spent every breath willing him to keep his own.

Layla shook her head, eyes dropping to the blanket. "Sparrow's gone to update Queen Okteria in case Bartoria retaliates. Xaden stayed behind. I'm sure you'll want to see him, get caught up on everything. I've just been..." She gave a small, weary laugh. "Rotating. Between rooms. My sisters, my mother, and you. It just happened to be me here this time when you woke. I can go get him, if you want."

Before she could rise, Kain's fingers found her wrist. "Don't be sorry, Dove." His voice was low, the familiar drawl curling through it. A smirk ghosted across his lips. "You're a much prettier face to wake up to than Xaden."

Her eyes rolled, the familiar spark of annoyance flaring in them, but the smallest smile followed. He loved that smile, loved pulling it out of her even when she tried to hide it. But when her gaze met his again, something shifted.

"Thank you," he said quietly, the humor fading, sincerity roughening his tone. "For staying. For being here when I woke."

The words carried more weight than he intended. She did not speak, only held his gaze, and the silence between them thickened until it felt almost alive. Something unspoken moved through it, quiet and charged. Kain meant to look away, but he couldn't. Her eyes caught the light, soft and unreadable, and the sight of her hit him all at once. Strength and gentleness in the same breath. The steady rise and fall of her breathing brushing the small space between them. His pulse slowed, then quickened, unsure what to do with the calm she offered and the ache she sparked in equal measure. The distance between them was too much to bear. His gaze drifted from the tired edges of her features to the faint color warming her cheeks, then to the soft curve of her lips. Her breath hitched, quiet but unmistakable, and his pulse answered in kind. The space between them felt wrong. Too wide. Too empty. Every heartbeat drew the air tighter, until it felt like the room itself might snap beneath the weight of it. Then the sound of boots in the doorway broke the spell...

"Holy shit, you're awake!"

The door burst open, slamming against the stone wall as Xaden stepped through, all muscle and presence, as though the room itself bent to make space for him. His grin was wide enough to split his face, bright against skin as dark as onyx. Tribal tattoos wound across his arms and shoulders, bold lines of black ink against muscle that looked carved from iron. His hair was tied back in tight black braids, a faint stubble shadowing his strong jaw. Almost as broad as the frame he stood in, he was a wall of strength wrapped in mischief.

"Finally," he crowed, his deep voice carrying that easy humor that always seemed to follow him. "Pretty sure you left a trail of blood all the way from Bartoria to here. Surprised you're even breathing after that headshot." Kain ground his teeth at the interruption, pulse still unsteady from Layla's nearness, but he said nothing. Xaden barreled on, undeterred as Kain felt the mattress shift as Layla slipped from the bed. Her spine straightening, posture perfect once more. Just like that, the air changed. The warmth that had existed between them vanished. Kain's jaw flexed. He didn't know what the hell all he was feeling, but he knew one thing with absolute certainty: he hated seeing her guard go back up.

Hated that she hid behind all that polished composure. He didn't want her like that around him. Not ever.

Xaden's voice cut through his thoughts. "How many fingers am I holding up?" He raised four.

Kain didn't even look. "One."

Xaden froze. "Fuck, Kain..."

Kain lifted his middle finger.

Relief cracked into laughter. "Yeah, you're fine. Asshole." Xaden dropped into the chair by the bed, the wooden frame creaking under his weight. "So, how's the pain?" Kain only shrugged. He didn't want them to know the truth. "That bad, huh?" Xaden smirked, reading him easily. Kain rolled his eyes, but his attention had already shifted back to Layla. She was fidgeting. *Why?* The faint tremor in her hands and the way her eyes flicked toward the floor told him something was off.

Xaden leaned back, still grinning. "If you're good to stand, we can at least get you moving. Layla said we could borrow one of those royal beasts to get you back to the tribe. Eir will have you patched up in no time."

The thought of climbing back onto a horse made Kain's ribs protest, but he didn't argue. He needed to reach Eir. Needed her touch, her god-blessed healing. The Graystonian healers meant well, but they weren't her. And he had to see his mother, to plan, to strike back. Well that is if she let him live after his betrayal...

His gaze unintentionally found Layla again. She hadn't moved. Simply staring at the blanket like she was somewhere else entirely. Unease crawled through him. Then she looked up and smiled. But it wasn't real. Too careful. Too polished. Too perfect.

"Are you good to stand?" she asked quickly, her tone calm, formal, practiced. "I should have asked about your pain. I'll fetch the healers, then have the horses prepared if you're able." The words were smooth, but he could hear the tremor beneath them. She was retreating. Hiding behind titles and duty, pretending this was obligation. Pretending what had just passed between them hadn't meant something. And suddenly, he understood. She was trying to make it easier to say goodbye.

The realization hit hard. He didn't fully understand all these foreign feelings right now, but he knew he didn't want it to end here. Not like this. Gritting his teeth, he forced himself upright. Pain seared through his ribs, his vision tunneling, but he embraced it. Pain meant he was still alive. Still fighting. And right now, fighting meant not letting her slip away. He swung his legs over the edge of the bed, breath ragged. The room tilted, colors bleeding at the edges, but then he saw her. Layla's eyes were wide, her hands trembling, her teeth catching her lip, and the pain gave way to something feral. His focus zeroed in on one thing and one thing only. *That lip.*

He rose slowly, deliberate, closing the distance between them, his gaze locked on her mouth. Every heartbeat was a warning. Every breath a dare. Then the pain surged back, sudden and blinding. His knees buckled, his skull throbbed, and a low groan escaped before he could hold it back. Then warmth caught him. Soft hands. Steady. Grounding.

"Whoa. It's okay. I've got you."

He blinked through the blur, meeting her eyes. Hazel, fierce, and terrified. Her hands were shaking where they held his arms, but she didn't let go. And gods help him, all he could think about was the taste of

21

that lip. "Bite your lip again, Dove," he rasped. A ghost of a grin pulling at his mouth. "It helps."

Shock widened her eyes, bewilderment flashing across her face before laughter slipped free, bright and unguarded. "Yeah, you're fine to travel." Her voice was soft with relief as she steadied him, rolling her eyes at his grin.

He smiled wider, exhaustion softening the mischief in his voice. "It's alright to be disappointed. I know you've grown fond of having me around." Her laugh came again, quieter this time, carrying warmth but edged with something fragile. It slipped through the air like sunlight through ash, soft and aching.

"You good, man?" Xaden called from behind, his tone half teasing, half concerned.

"I've been worse," Kain said evenly, eyes flicking toward Layla. His gaze lingered a heartbeat too long, settling on her lips before he added, "Much worse."

Her mouth fell open before she shook her head, laughing under her breath. "You're impossible." She stepped back, her hands slipping away. "I'll fetch the healers for a once-over before you leave."

"No." The word came harsher than he intended. His eyes found hers again, steady, unyielding. "I don't need them. I'll make it to Eir." His head pounded, vision still swimming, but he forced his breath even.

"Are you sure?" she whispered, uncertainty softening her tone.

He gave her a crooked smile, forcing the ease he didn't quite feel. "I love that you're worried about me. But I'll be fine, Dove." The wink was intentional, offered like a shield, and it softened her expression even as worry still clung to her shoulders. Her fingers fidgeted once, betraying the calm she clearly was trying to grasp.

Xaden stepped forward, steady and unshakable, his presence as solid as the ground beneath them. Kain clasped his offered shoulder without protest, grateful for the anchor. The world still tilted at the edges, the floor threatening to pitch beneath his boots, but he forced himself upright. The last thing he needed was another damned injury before he even made it home.

Layla lingered only a moment longer, then straightened. The change was subtle but absolute. Her spine lengthened, her chin lifted, and the faint tremor in her hands stilled. In a breath, the woman who had watched over him was gone, and in her place stood a future queen once more.

"As I've told you both," she said, her voice clear and deliberate, "I do not consider us at war. We have a mutual enemy. I know Queen Okteria holds... her own views." That pause on his mother's name was subtle but there. "I only hope she considers recent events carefully and sees the value in a truce between our peoples." Her eyes found his and held. Steady. Composed. Unflinching. The strength in her gaze struck something deep within him, something molten and alive that he couldn't name. It burned through his veins like wildfire, both a challenge and a promise.

Then she turned for the door, the firelight spilling across her chestnut hair, turning it to molten gold as she passed. The faint scent of lavender and resolve lingered in her wake. "I'll see your horses prepared and the men will be told you're departing." Her tone was all business again, but when she glanced back, her voice softened, the steel bending just enough to draw blood. "I can't begin to thank you...for what you've done for me, for my family. There aren't words enough. Just know that I am... grateful. Eternally. And that you are always welcome here."

Kain's jaw worked, a thousand words clawing for release. He couldn't stop himself. "I don't give a damn about being welcome, Dove." She froze mid-step. He leaned heavier on Xaden's shoulder, his voice dropping to a low rasp. "Just don't pretend you won't miss me." The words left him like an arrow, quiet, but dead-on. She didn't turn, didn't seem to breathe, just stood there for a heartbeat too long.

Then her lashes lowered, her voice soft but unwavering. "I will miss both of you, of course."

And just like that, the mask slipped fully back into place. She turned and left without another word. The door closed behind her with a quiet click that felt far louder than it should have. Silence settled, broken only by the fire, a single ember snapping in the hearth. Xaden said something, distant and low, but Kain barely heard him. His jaw tightened, his breath shallow as the air she left behind turned razor-sharp in his lungs.

His eyes stayed fixed on the door. Every instinct in him urged him to follow, to stop her, to break the silence she had left behind. But he did not move. They both had kingdoms waiting. Wounds to tend. Vengeance yet to be claimed. His fingers flexed at his side, his jaw setting as the ache sank deep, heavy and unyielding.

This was not an ending. He knew that with absolute certainty. She may have walked away, but she had not escaped him. And he was not done with her. Not even close.

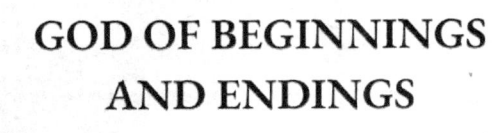

# ELIRYN

## GOD OF BEGINNINGS
## AND ENDINGS

# Chapter Two

**L**ayla.

She didn't remember deciding to move. One heartbeat she was standing there, heat rising beneath her skin, Kain's grin still seared behind her eyes. The next, she was already in motion. Her skirts hissed against the marble, each stride precise and measured, too controlled to be calm.

Her slippered steps struck a steady rhythm that betrayed her. She wasn't walking. She was fleeing. Fleeing the pull of him, fierce and consuming. Fleeing the way her pulse betrayed her when she looked into his eyes. Fleeing the guilt that cut at her throat, heavy with the memory of the brother he had lost and what she and Theron had been to each other. Whatever was waking inside her now, she could not face it. Not with Kain. Not now, not ever.

The castle unfolded around her like a labyrinth, corridors gleaming gold beneath the morning rays and candlelight spilling across cold gray stone. Banners hung from the vaulted ceilings, the golden stags of Graystonia standing proud beside woven trims of deep green, their colors merging where the light touched them. Everything looked exactly as it always had. Untouched and unchanged. The faint scent of orange peel and bay leaf drifted through the hall. The same mixture the servants used each autumn to chase the chill from the stone. Once, that smell meant warmth, routine, stability. Now it curdled in her stomach. How could the castle smell the same when she was not? When nothing was? When every part of her had been remade by blood, fear, and loss?

It was as if the walls themselves were trying to pretend the world had not been ripped open. Pretending her father was not dead. Pretending Theron had not fallen. Pretending she had not changed beyond recognition. The sameness pressed against her ribs until nausea rose. A tight, twisting reminder of the guilt, the fury, the grief she could not outrun.

Her breath came fast, fogging in the chill as she turned a corner. *Control yourself,* her mother's voice whispered in memory. *Chin high. Shoulders back. Never let them see the crack.* Layla obeyed. Her chin was high. Her shoulders were back. But inside, she was breaking. Fury quickened her pace, her pulse pounding in her ears. She didn't even know who her anger belonged to. Him, herself, or the Gods who had taken and taken until all that remained of her was duty and guilt.

Kain. The name alone caused her to misstep. *Gods, what had she done?*

Her hand flew to her mouth, trembling, as she slowed. Her footsteps softened into a glide, a fragile mimicry of grace. A queenly illusion.

But nothing could quiet the echo of his voice, low and smooth, or the heat of his body beneath her palms. She had been in his bed for goodness' sake. Not in the way court gossip would twist it into scandal, not in the ruinous way her mother had spent her entire life warning her about. But still... alone with a man, in his bed, her body pressed against his, his arms around her, his breath warm against her throat...

A flush crawled up her neck. She shook her head in brisk irritation at herself. That was absolutely unacceptable within her kingdom. That was impropriety. That was danger. And she had let it happen. Worse, she had wanted it. Wanted the safety of it. The warmth of it. Wanted the way it had felt, for one impossible moment, to be held and not merely endure.

A strangled sound slipped from her throat. "What is wrong with me?" she whispered.

Theron had died for her. For them. And now his brother, the reckless, infuriating, impossible man, was the one she could not stop thinking about. A sick twist pulled at her gut. Wanting that. Wanting him...

Her pace quickened again, fury snapping through her like a whip. She would not blur that line. She could not. For a thousand reasons. For Theron. Whether or not she believed Kain's Antonin creed of honor in death meant nothing. Theron was gone. Gone because of her. Gone, and she was still here, still breathing, still capable of wanting things she should not want. The guilt burned hotter than any hearth-fire she passed, scorching her from the inside.

By the time she reached the main hall, her steps slowed. The anger still burned, but exhaustion crept beneath it, shaking the edges of her control. The vast chamber opened before her, columns soaring like pale trees beneath a painted dome of stars. Servants scattered from her path, bowing low, their eyes fixed on the floor. She ignored them all.

At the end of the corridor, two guards stood at attention by the arched doors leading to the courtyard. They straightened when she approached, clearly startled. She rarely came down here herself.

"See to it that the Antonin warriors are provided horses and provisions," she said, her tone steady and clipped. The way a queen should sound. "They leave within the hour. And... they are welcome here, should they ever return."

The guards exchanged a glance, confused but obedient. "As you command, Princess."

She nodded once and turned away before her voice could tremble. *Heroes.* That was what they were now. Her family's saviors. The men who had carried her through hell and brought her home. Sending them off with honor was the least she could do. And yet... As she released them, something inside her felt like it unraveled, a quiet tearing she could not name.

Her steps slowed as she walked, her reflection flickering in the polished stone beneath her feet. Every portrait she passed seemed to watch her, the painted eyes of dead kings and perfect queens following her with silent judgment. Judgment not for failure of duty, but for feeling at all. For letting grief and loss touch her when she had been raised to be porcelain and perfect. For wanting comfort where she should have shown restraint. For thinking of Kain while she mourned Theron. For cracking when she had been sculpted to be unbreakable. Judgment for being exactly who she was in this moment, raw and exhausted, no longer able to keep the mask in place. Judgment she felt she deserved.

Layla's throat tightened. She brushed her fingers against the fabric at her wrist, grounding herself in the simple act of movement, of control, of staying upright when everything inside her felt fragmented. When she finally looked up, she was standing before Aerilynn's door.She didn't remember walking there. But of course she had. Her body was trying to keep going, to follow routine, to pretend she was still the girl who once moved through this castle with certainty. But she wasn't. And nothing about her life was right now.

The oak door loomed before her, its carved vines and gilded corners seeming far too bright for what waited beyond. Layla hesitated, her hand hovering over the handle. It had been a week since their return. A week since blood and fire and screams had followed them home and still, she came here every morning.

Two knocks. Soft. Hesitant. No answer. She opened the door anyway.

As she stepped inside, she took in the now familiar sight before her. Her sister lay curled on her side atop a mound of blankets. Her gilded hair was tangled and dull, her nightgown wrinkled, her frame too thin. The girl who once filled the castle with laughter, whose smile could still a quarrel, barely stirred now. Layla's heart clenched. The silence pressed in until she could hear nothing but her own breath. The air seemed to change, thick with smoke and panic, and the present slipped away. In her mind, time folded back on itself and she was there again. The night the Bartorians stormed the castle.

*The ballroom had become a slaughterhouse of silk and steel. What had begun in music and laughter now howled with terror. The scent of perfume mixed with blood and smoke. Candles toppled, splattering wax across gowns that moments ago had shimmered beneath chandeliers. Screams ricocheted off marble walls, rising and falling with the clang of swords and the thud of bodies hitting the floor. A guard's cry ended in a wet choke beside her. Another man fell face-first into the dessert table, crimson pooling among sugared fruit. Panic seared through her veins. Her slippers slid on blood as she grabbed Aerilynn through the chaos. Her sister's hand was small and trembling, fingers clawing for hers with a grip that slipped each time they stumbled.*

*"You have to move!" she had shouted over the din, her throat raw, her voice breaking as she shoved Aerilynn forward toward their mother, toward Sir Charles. The man they had trusted like family. Her father's loyal right hand. He caught Aerilynn by the arm and pulled her close. Relief had torn through Layla so sharply she almost sobbed. For a moment, she believed they would make it. That he would protect them. That someone still could...*

But he had not protected them. He had sold them, one desperate bargain at a time, until even Graystonia itself began to bleed. It was Theron who found her weeks later in the Bartorian dungeons. Aerilynn had still been wearing the same ruined gown from that night. Mud and blood turning the ivory silk to ash. She was huddled in a corner, wrists raw, eyes hollow. When Layla saw her again, her knees gave out beneath her. The sister who had once been all light and laughter now recoiled at the sound of her own name.

Since that night, Aerilynn had spoken only in whispers, her voice trembling at the creak of a door or the tread of a man's boots. And when she learned their father had died the same night Layla had sent her away, it had broken what little remained of her spirit. Now she barely left her bed, caught within a prison of her own making. Layla had come every day since their return, wearing her composure like armor, pretending she was strong enough for both of them. She'd smiled. Spoken softly. Tried to remind Aerilynn how to breathe again. But today, the mask would not come.

"Aeri," she whispered, stepping closer. "I just wanted to..."

Aerilynn looked up slowly. The grief in her eyes did not fade, but something beneath it shifted. *Recognition. Understanding. A sister's knowing.* For a heartbeat, her gaze cleared and one weary brow lifted. That tiny, familiar gesture undid her. Layla's breath shuddered out. Her shoulders sagged. The polished poise of a princess fell away, leaving only the hollow girl beneath. Without another word, she kicked off her slippers and crossed the room, the stone biting cold beneath her feet. The sound of the door closing behind her was soft and final.

Aerilynn stirred faintly when Layla climbed into bed beside her, shifting just enough to make space the way she had when storms used to frighten them as children. Layla lay on her side, facing her sister. Aerilynn mirrored the motion. Between them, the blankets rose like a fragile wall neither could bear to cross. For a long moment, they simply breathed. The silence was heavy, carrying the weight of everything they had lost.

Layla finally reached out, brushing her sister's arm. "You should eat," she murmured, though her voice lacked conviction. "The kitchens will send..." Aerilynn's gaze lifted to meet hers, slow and deliberate. There was no anger in it, only a quiet intensity that cut deeper than words ever could. Layla faltered. The rest of her sentence died before it could leave her lips.

Silence stretched between them until Aerilynn's voice broke through the haze, barely a whisper. "Do you want to talk about it?"

Layla shook her head. A single tear slipped free. "No."

So they didn't.

They did not speak of fathers or brothers, of love or betrayal. They did not speak of the way the world had changed, or how neither of them fit inside it anymore. Layla simply reached for Aerilynn's hand. Their fingers met, and the silence between them said everything words could not.

For a long while, they just lay there. Two broken pieces of the same world, breathing in unison. The candlelight flickered low, painting their faces in soft gold and shadow until even that small flame gave out. Layla's thoughts drifted, untethered and slow. Kain's laugh. Theron's final look. Her father's voice calling her brave. Each memory shimmered for a heartbeat before blurring into the next. Love, loss, guilt, duty, all folding into one heavy ache that filled her completely. The weeks of captivity. The endless miles on the road. The sleepless nights spent beside Kain's bed. Every mask she had worn since returning home. All of it had finally caught up to her. Her body had reached its limit. Her heart, too. She needed comfort. The kind only a sister could give. A presence that asked for nothing. That required no strength, no explanations. Just breathing. Just being.

When her eyes finally slipped closed, she did not resist. Sleep came quietly, merciful and deep. And for the first time since the war began,

Layla Eradellian set down the weight she had been carrying and allowed exhaustion to win.

**ELIRYN**

**The First Light. The Final Shadow. King of the Gods.**

Eliryn is the balance of all things, both light and dark, creation and ruin, the first breath and the last. He is the pulse that begins life and the silence that closes it. All power flows from him, and all destinies return to his hand. Where Eliryn turns his gaze, worlds rise, empires fall, and fate bends to his will.

Since the day he forged the Veil to divide gods and mortals, no known blessing has crossed into the human realm. Yet some whisper that when an ancient imbalance stirs again, one born long ago and left unfinished, Eliryn's will may slip through the Veil, choosing a single soul meant to restore what was broken and finish the cycle once and for all.

# Chapter Three

*L*ayla.

Layla stirred awake to something brushing her nose. Her lashes fluttered open, the light soft and muted, and she found Aerilynn leaning over her, dangling a loose strand of her own hair across Layla's face. A faint spark of mischief glimmered in her sister's tired eyes. Layla groaned, swatting the hand away before rubbing at her face and pushing herself up against the pillows. Aerilynn's lips twitched, almost forming a smile.

"You look like shit," Aerilynn rasped.

Layla froze mid-motion, her jaw falling open. Her sister had never cursed before. Not once. It wasn't ladylike. It wasn't proper. For a moment, Layla could only stare, stunned into silence. The disbelief on her face must have been obvious because Aerilynn's grin widened, and then, gods above, she giggled. *She giggled!* The sound pierced through the heaviness like sunlight breaking through storm clouds. Layla's breath hitched, the tightness in her chest unraveling into something pure and bright. Shock melted into laughter, laughter into tears, and before she could stop herself, she pulled Aerilynn into her arms. Her sister was fragile and warm, and Layla held on as if she could keep the world from stealing her away again.

When they finally drew apart, Aerilynn's voice softened. "Sooo, do you want to talk about it now?" Layla shook her head. She would not have known where to start. Everything inside her was still too tangled. The grief, the guilt, the fear, the ache she didn't dare name. Her chest felt bruised from holding it all in for so long.

The night before had stripped her bare. She had silently cried until she had nothing left, until the hollow ache inside her finally cracked open, until exhaustion dragged her into a sleep deeper than she had felt in weeks. And now, in the pale morning light, she felt... emptied. Not healed. Not whole. But quieter. Steadier. For the first time since Bartoria, she wasn't drowning. Maybe she finally had enough breath to take the next one. Maybe she had enough strength to try again. She wasn't ready to speak. Not yet. But she was no longer falling apart. Not entirely. Not today.

"Okay," Aerilynn whispered. "Well you know I'm always here."

"I know." Layla managed a small, aching smile. "And the same to you." Aerilynn nodded, her gaze falling to her hands as her fingers twisted together in her lap. The silence settled between them, soft and fragile. Layla let it linger, her eyes lifting toward the window where pale sunlight crept across the floorboards. She blinked, startled. The sun was already rising high above the courtyard. She must have slept an entire day and night. Her body had known what she needed long before her mind had admitted it. And gods, she did feel better. Not whole, not unbroken, but steadier. Enough to stand again. With a sigh, Layla looked back at her sister, her voice soft but threaded with hope. "Will you join me for breakfast?"

Her sister hesitated, then shook her head. "Not yet."

"Alright."

She knew better than to press. Aerilynn would come when she was ready, and Layla would be there waiting when that day came. She gave her sister's hands a gentle squeeze, holding on for a moment longer before standing. After slipping her shoes back on, she paused at the door and glanced over her shoulder. One last look. One last fragile smile. Aerilynn returned it, faint but real, before curling beneath the blankets and drawing them close like a shield.

Layla stood there for a heartbeat longer, the weight of love and sorrow pressing against her ribs, then turned and stepped into the quiet hall. The door clicked softly shut behind her.

Sitting across from her at breakfast was Layla's other sister, Ciana. They sat in the small private dining room where they had shared more meals than Layla could count. Ciana had always been the opposite of Aerilynn. She always would be, it seemed. Where Aerilynn trembled and hid, Ciana sat poised and immaculate, the very picture of a perfect princess.

Untouched. Unshaken. Unbothered. Or so she wanted the world to believe. She looked gorgeous as ever. Long golden hair spilling like silk down flawless shoulders, skin luminous, hazel eyes warm even in the soft morning light. She was their mother's mirror, an angel carved from sunlight and expectation. But Layla saw what others would not.

Ciana moved mechanically, nudging fruit across her plate as though performing a well-practiced routine. Perfect posture. Perfect grace. Perfect silence. From a distance, nothing about her had changed. But up close... the difference was unmistakable. Her confidence no longer carried the sharp edge it once held. Her eyes, though bright, never truly lifted. She held herself too still, as if afraid any shift might reveal the fracture beneath.

Ciana had never been one to speak of feelings. Never one to admit discomfort. But captivity had carved something out of her. Quietly. Cleanly. Like a blade slipping beneath armor. Layla had tried to reach her. Gods, she had tried. Each attempt earned the same polite, irritated look. That gentle tightening of the princess mask all three sisters had been raised to wear. As if to say the topic itself was improper. Unfit for breakfast. Unfit for daylight. Unfit for a princess. So Layla stopped pressing, though the worry remained sharp beneath her ribs. She knew too well that some walls only rose higher if touched.

So when Ciana excused herself with a delicate tilt of her chin and flawless grace, Layla watched her go. Wishing she could follow and knowing she should not. Which meant there was only one place left to go.

Layla rose from her seat, smoothed her dress, and stepped into the corridor with a breath meant to steady her. She had given her mother days. Morning and night she came, watching strength return to Queen Raynera piece by piece. But the woman she had seen in that dungeon, broken, trembling, and human, was gone. The moment Kain had carried her into her chambers two weeks ago, Raynera had begun rebuilding herself. Brick by brick. Mask by mask. Now she moved with measured grace, her bruises fading beneath fine silk, her grief tucked neatly behind a queen's composure. Her voice was calm once more, her gaze keen, her every word precise. The queen had returned, and the mother had vanished.

Pain was private. Sorrow was silent. Masks were for survival. That was Raynera's creed, and she had raised her daughters to obey it. But something inside Layla had changed. She had seen too much, lost too much, to ever hide behind silence again. The fire that had carried her through captivity and battle still burned in her veins, too wild to be buried. She was not a princess waiting to be placed like a pawn on her mother's board. She was a leader now. She had commanded. She had bled. She had survived. And she would be heard.

Layla made her way to her mother's chambers, the corridor quiet except for the two guards stationed beside the ornate door. They dipped their heads respectfully as she approached, stepping aside but saying nothing. Layla lifted her hand to knock, steadying herself with a breath she hoped would not tremble. But as her knuckles brushed the wood, the door yielded without resistance. It hadn't been latched. It swung inward with a soft creak. The room beyond was still. Too still.

The bed was perfectly made, every fold crisp and precise. The hearth crackled with a low, tended fire. Her mother's cloak hung neatly over the chair. Everything was in its place. Except the queen. Layla's heart stumbled. A cold prickle crawled up her spine. *Not now. Not before they had a chance to speak!*

She stepped into the corridor, skirts whispering over the stone, and caught the sleeve of a passing maid. "Where is the queen?"

The girl dropped into a quick curtsy, eyes wide. "Her Majesty has gone to the council chamber, Princess. The war council has been summoned." The words struck cold. The council...*without her.*

Layla's pulse quickened. She had wanted to stand beside her mother, not behind her. To be heard, not dismissed. Fury and dread tangled in her chest as she turned and ran, the sound of her steps echoing through the marble halls. The braid down her back whipped with each stride. Tapestries blurred by, the air thick with the mingled scents of smoke and oil and steel. She would not be left out. *Not again.*

The closer she drew, the louder the voices became. They were deep, edged, and full of authority. She pressed forward, every heartbeat a war drum beneath her ribs. When she reached the great doors of the council chamber, she did not hesitate. Her palms struck the wood, and the doors burst open. And there it was. Exactly what she had feared.

The council chamber was a cathedral of power. Iron chandeliers burned overhead, casting restless shadows across stone and banners heavy with the royal stag. Ink, smoke, and old wine tainted the air. At the center stretched the great oak table, scarred by generations of war, buried beneath maps and scrolls. Around it gathered Graystonia's most powerful men, their voices a low, rumbling thunder.

Sir Edwin, the kingdom's general, stood nearest the maps, his broad frame casting a long shadow across the table. He looked carved from duty itself, steady and unyielding, the man who had carried Graystonia's armies when her father no longer could. His loyalty was unquestioned. His allegiance to tradition, even more so.

Beside him stood his second, Sir Jerem, younger and keener, his eyes flicking over every parchment with restless precision. A mind made for strategy, all edges and calculation. Across the table lingered the lords who held Graystonia's wealth. Lord Rhoric of the western wheatlands lingered nearby, heavy with rings and heavier still with self-importance, his gestures broad enough to remind everyone of his influence. Near him stood Lord Marius of the northern mines, quiet and cold as the iron he dealt in, his silence more cutting than any boast. They were power in different shapes, one loud, one calculating, both dangerous in their own ways.

Around them, lesser lords whispered, quills scratched against parchment, and servants drifted through the candlelight, refilling cups with careful hands. The scent of spiced wine and melting wax hung heavy in the air. The atmosphere trembled with restrained force, with politics and ambition and the unspoken tension of men who held kingdoms in their grasp. This was no mere meeting. This was Graystonia's strength, its pride, its corruption. All gathered beneath one roof like a wall of shields and sharpened tongues. And at the head of that table stood her mother. Not seated. Never seated. Even as monarch, no woman had ever been granted a chair at the council's table, only the narrow space beside it, like a shadow permitted to stand but never to rule. Yet even standing, Queen Raynera commanded the room as if every candle burned for her alone.

The firelight gilded her form in molten gold. Her gown was a masterpiece of restraint, slate gray embroidered with threads of silver that shimmered like moonlight against steel. Her crown of polished iron and pearl rested perfectly upon her long, golden hair, each strand shining despite the fading bruises that marked her jaw and throat. Those bruises should have diminished her, but instead they only intensified her beauty, transforming her into something more than regal, something untouchable. Her skin was pale as porcelain, her bearing carved from grace and defiance alike. Her spine held the rigid precision of a drawn blade, her chin lifted in quiet challenge. She looked every inch a goddess wearing mortal form, her poise a weapon, her silence an edict.

For decades, that composure had been her shield. Her face revealed nothing, a mask of marble refined by years of scrutiny and power. But her eyes, Gods help her, her eyes betrayed her. They were hazel like Layla's, though lighter, touched with a warmth that caught the light like sunlight through amber. In them, Layla saw a reflection of herself, the woman she might become if she ever learned to smother her fire beneath ice. When those eyes found her at the door, they widened first in shock, a flicker of horror glinting through the gold. It vanished a heartbeat later, swallowed by fury. Cold, controlled, and absolute.

Yet even in all her splendor, even beneath that piercing gaze, Layla saw that something was wrong. Her mother stood proud and flawless, but she did not command this room. The lords spoke over her, their voices heavy with entitlement. The royal guards bent over the maps as though her counsel were little more than background noise. The scribes took their notes from the mouths of men while the queen, crowned and radiant in the firelight, stood ignored at the head of her own table. Raynera was present, yes. Stoic, yes. Furious, certainly. But she was not leading. She was enduring. Enduring the weight of power that should have been hers to wield.

The realization hit her like lightning, fierce and undeniable, setting every nerve alight. Her stomach twisted, her pulse quickened until it thundered in her ears. To see her mother, the fierce and unbreakable woman. Standing silent among men who treated her crown as ornament rather than authority, sparked something violent and unstoppable within her. The injustice of it seared through her veins, hot and electric, burning away hesitation until only resolve remained.

*No. Not anymore. This would not be the way it stayed.*

Layla stepped forward, the echo of her heels slicing through the noise. "If this is a war council," she said, steady and unwavering, "then I claim my right to stand here. To lead. I have lived Bartoria's cruelty. I know their strengths, their weaknesses. I am not a child. I am your heir. And I will not remain silent while Graystonia bleeds."

For a single heartbeat, silence ruled the room. The air itself seemed to hold its breath. Then the laughter came. It started low, then swelled into a roar. Lord Rhoric's great belly shook as he threw back his head, rings flashing in the firelight. "Lead?" he bellowed, choking on his own mirth. "The princess?"

Marius Thorne lifted his goblet, his smirk hard and transparent as glass. "Your Highness," he said, voice smooth and cruel, "your worth lies in heirs, not in armies. If you wish to save your kingdom, agree to a husband and open your cradle. Give us a king and a true heir. That is the only campaign you are fit to lead."

Heat surged through Layla's veins. Her voice cut through the noise like a blade through silk. "And when your sons fall on the battlefield, will you bleed for them? Or sit in your gilded chairs while others die for your cowardice?" With that, the laughter was swiftly extinguished and outrage erupted in its place. Voices rose, chairs scraped, fists struck the table. The council turned into a storm of noise, anger, and disbelief.

"Silence her!" a lord shouted, his voice cracking across the chaos.

And then the queen moved.

Raynera crossed the chamber in a sweep of gray silk and steel authority. The scent of lavender trailed behind her, soft and unmistakable. Her hand clamped around Layla's arm, the strength in it shocking, her composure unbroken. To the lords, she was calm. To Layla, she was fire contained in ice. Without a word, Raynera turned and pulled her toward the door. Her grip did not falter. The heavy doors slammed behind them with a sound that echoed through the corridor like judgment itself. The laughter and firelight faded, swallowed by silence. Thick, suffocating, and final.

For a heartbeat the queen only stared at her, chest rising, her face carved from marble but her eyes blazing like open flame. "How *dare* you." Her voice was low, controlled yet lethal. "How dare you set foot in that room as though you belong among them. Do you think yourself above centuries of law? Of custom? Do you think survival makes you wise? That crawling back from Bartoria grants you a seat at the table?"

Layla opened her mouth, but the words tangled. She lifted her chin, forcing the defiance into her throat. "I have fought. I have led. I have..."

"You have embarrassed me," Raynera cut in, her tone a blade sliding between ribs. "You mistake stubbornness for strength. You mistake luck for leadership. Men died while you stumbled forward blind, and you dare call it command?" Her eyes flicked, cold and piercing. "Do not think a handful of scars makes you fit to direct an entire army." Layla's fists clenched, nails digging into her palms, but her mother pressed on, each word deliberate and damning. "You were raised better than this. To know your place. To carry yourself with grace, not crash through doors like some unruly child. You stand there, demanding authority, yet all you show is your inexperience. A woman who knows nothing of war, nothing of politics, and nothing of ruling. You are out of your depth, Layla. Utterly."

Raynera released her arm at last, and the absence of her grip burned hotter than the hold itself. "This is not your place," the queen finished, every syllable honed to destroy. "Not now and not ever. Learn your station, or you will shame us all and possibly rid our chance of a fit king." She swept back into the chamber without another glance, the doors shutting hard in Layla's face.

Layla stood frozen in the corridor, the air around her heavy and unmoving. Fury and humiliation surged through her veins, twin flames warring for dominance. Her breathing turned ragged, her throat too tight for words. Only her mother's voice echoed in her skull, each word cutting deep. *Naive. Lucky. Out of her depth.* They burned like iron against her skin, but what hurt most was the truth beneath them. Every man in that chamber had looked at her and seen exactly what her mother had said. A girl. A symbol. A pawn to be moved, not a force to be reckoned with.

The fire within her did not gutter or fade. It folded inward, disciplined into waiting. They had made one truth unmistakably clear. Power in this world was not taken loudly or alone. It was gathered through trust cultivated, loyalties woven, and patience mistaken for submission.

So she would give them what they believed they had won. For now. She would still her tongue, soften her gaze, and wear the silks and circlets that signaled obedience. They would see a princess subdued by grief. A daughter shaped by loss. A woman who understood the boundaries of her place and did not press against them.

And while they watched the mask, Layla would listen and learn. She would gather what could never be seized by force until the day her presence alone altered the room and her voice no longer required permission to be heard. When that day came. She would not stand alone in that chamber. She would have the backing that mattered.

# VARYN

## GOD OF BLOOD AND VALOR

# Chapter Four

*K*<sup>*ain*</sup>.

The familiar sound came first, a sharp, impatient *tsk* that sliced through the quiet like a blade. Kain grimaced into the rough cot fabric, the scent of smoke and crushed herbs thick in his nose. He tried to lift his head, to make some half-hearted remark in his defense, but a firm, calloused hand pressed it back down with ease.

"These weren't *all* my fault, Eir," he mumbled, the words muffled against the bedding. No answer. Not that he expected one. Eir rarely wasted words on excuses. Cold liquid splashed across his back without warning, seeping into the raw arrow wounds the Graystonian healers had clumsily patched. The burn was immediate, fierce enough to make him hiss through his teeth.

"Turn."

He obeyed, rolling onto his back. The ceiling above him was a low web of wooden beams hung with drying herbs, animal bones, and strips of parchment scrawled with symbols no one else could read. Smoke curled from the hearth at the center of the hut, carrying the scent of pine resin and bitter root. The air was heavy and warm, thick with the hum of old magic.

Eir stood beside him, her figure haloed in firelight. Time had etched deep lines into her face, but there was strength in every one of them. Her hair, long and silver-gray, was braided down her back, glinting faintly like threads of frost. Her eyes were piercing, the color of tempered steel, bright and knowing. She missed nothing. Her hands were small, skilled, and impossibly steady, every movement a practiced ritual born of years spent defying death itself.

"Hey now," Kain said, forcing a crooked grin even as pain lanced through his ribs. "This one really wasn't my fault. I swear it." Her gaze lifted briefly, unimpressed, before she went back to grinding her herbs. That look said everything. He smirked but stayed quiet. He knew better than to test her patience twice.

Eir worked in silence, mixing crushed leaves with thick black oil, her motions smooth and sure. Every herb that passed through her fingers had been gathered by her alone, cut from the cliffs at dawn or the forest floor at twilight, dried in smoke and bound with whispered words no one dared repeat. The air seemed to shift when she worked, as if the walls of the hut itself leaned closer to listen. No one truly knew what she was.

Some said the Gods had blessed her. Others swore she had bargained with them. Kain didn't care which was true. What mattered was that she had always been there. Ever unchanging, unyielding, the quiet line between life and death for every Antonin warrior. She could not return the dead, but she could drag the dying back from the brink, and that was power enough.

Her voice broke the silence, low and coarse from years of smoke and prayer. "Dislocated shoulder. Already set. Two cracked ribs. Bone bruises. Lances across the abdomen. I will give you something for the pain. The head is the worst."

Kain wasn't surprised by any of it. The pounding behind his eyes had been relentless since he woke, each word she spoke sending a fresh ache through his skull. Still, he managed a grin. "You always know how to make a man feel special."

For a heartbeat, something that almost resembled amusement flickered in her eyes before it was gone again. The fire popped. Shadows danced across the walls. Outside, the wind howled against the hut, but inside, there was only the quiet rhythm of her hands and the steady sound of his breathing.

Then, with a pointed sniff, she moved behind him. "You should be dead."

"Guess Ondurin wasn't ready for me yet," he rasped back. She gave him a flat look that could have stripped the arrogance off any other man. He only smirked wider.

"I need to cut this," she said simply, fingers combing through the blood-stiff strands at the back of his head. "I can't see everything. Then I'll brew you a tonic. You'll drink it. You'll hate it. But you'll drink it."

"I expect this haircut to rival the Gods," he murmured, eyes closing as pain throbbed. "Have to keep up appearances, you know." For the first time, he could have sworn the corner of her mouth twitched.

*Snip.*

A long, golden section of his hair slid down, curling across his chest. Kain's eyes cracked open, catching the lock as it tumbled onto his lap. "Well," he muttered, twirling the strand between bloodied fingers. "There goes my charm."

Eir only clicked her tongue again, already working, already saving him without ceremony. And Kain, half-grinning through the haze of pain, let her. Because beneath all his bravado, all his banter, he knew: without Eir, Ondurin would have claimed him long ago.

Kain woke to the sound of his own breath, rough and steady against the stillness. The bitter tonic Eir had forced down his throat had done its work well. It had drowned him in a sleep too heavy for dreams and dragged him back to the living whether he was ready or not. He absentmindedly rubbed a hand over his face, grimacing as coarse stubble scraped his palm, and pushed himself upright. The world stayed still this time. No spinning. No lurching. No claws of pain trying to drag him back down. Only the dull, familiar ache of strained muscles and the faint throb at the base of his skull. Pain he could live with. Pain he could use.

His eyes adjusted to the dim light filtering through the slats of his hut. The sight that met him was comfort in its own rugged way. Weapons lined one wall, blades glinting faintly in the pale light. Two bows rested beside the door, their strings oiled and taut, waiting for the next hunt or the next battle. Beside them, bundles of arrows stood stacked high, more than any man could ever need. He had fletched every one himself, feather by feather, trimmed to perfect balance, each shaft a small piece of order in a world that had long since lost it.

The scent of pine resin and smoke lingered in the air, mingled with the sharper tang of Eir's healing herbs. A pile of wool blankets and animals furs lay folded near the cot, the edges uneven from restless nights spent mending gear or cleaning weapons instead of sleeping. Every inch of the space bore his mark, rough and precise, yet cozy. Built for both survival and comfort.

He exhaled slowly, letting the silence press against him. For a moment, the ache in his body faded into the background, replaced by the steady awareness of where he was. Home, in the loosest sense of the word. The place he always returned to when there was nowhere else left to go. And yet, as his gaze drifted toward the door, the stillness soured. Because now that he could stand, now that he could think without the haze of pain, there were no excuses left. It was time.

Xaden had carried him into Eir's hut when they first returned, half-dead and bleeding, cursing under his breath the entire way. He had been right, of course. Kain hadn't been fit to face anyone, let alone his mother. Eir had worked her miracles, stitching him back together with hands that smelled of smoke and wild herbs. For what he could only assume had been several days, he had drifted in and out of consciousness. Time had blurred into fragments of fever and shadow, broken only by Eir's voice or the bite of her tonics. But no longer. The fog had lifted.

And it was time to face what waited beyond that door. To face his queen. To face his mother.

He knew what awaited him. The judgment. The questions. The grief. He could already see the cold gleam in her eyes, the precise calm that always came before her fury. She would want everything from him. Every detail. Every drop of truth. She would want to know how Theron fought. How he fell. Whether he died with his sword in hand. Whether he had earned Ondurin's halls. And Kain would tell her. He would give her that truth because she deserved it. Because a mother should know the valor of her son. Because a queen should know the fortitude of her head warrior to his final moment.

After that... he wasn't certain what would come. He had betrayed his queen. Betrayed his tribe. Fought for their enemy. And though he still breathed, he knew the moment he spoke Theron's name, the ground beneath him would shift again. Whether it became his grave or his redemption, only the gods knew.

Queen Okteria sat at a small wooden table when he entered. The air thick with the mingled scents of smoke, leather, and the iron tang of sharpened steel. Her posture was rigid, the picture of composure and strength. Long brown hair, streaked faintly with silver, fell in a heavy braid down her back. Ink coiled across the deep bronze of her skin, marks of the Antonin line, of victories and oaths carved into flesh. The candlelight caught the cords of muscle in her arms as she turned, every movement deliberate and controlled.

When her gaze met his, it struck through him like an arrow. Piercing emerald eyes, bright and merciless, mirrors of his own. In that stare, he saw the woman who had forged him and the queen who ruled their tribe without question. But more than that, he saw Theron. The set of her jaw, the proud line of her shoulders, the quiet power in her stillness. So much of his brother lived in her, and for a moment, the memory twisted something deep inside his chest.

"So," Kain drawled, forcing a touch of cheer into his voice. "I'm back."

Her expression did not shift. No smile. No softening. She only stared, assessing him in silence, the weight of her authority pressing against the air itself. Then suddenly, she moved. The chair scraped against the floor, and in two long strides she was across the room. Her arms came around him, strong and unrelenting. The embrace was fierce, almost crushing, the kind that dared him to breathe wrong. For a heartbeat, Kain froze, caught between disbelief and something achingly close to relief. Then his body remembered, and he held her back just as tightly.

This was the side of his mother the world never saw. The woman beneath the crown. The warrior who loved her sons with the same ferocity she ruled her people. For a few heartbeats, she was not a queen. She was simply a mother holding the son who had returned from the brink. And then it was gone.

She stepped back, arms crossing once more as the warmth left her face. The mother vanished, and in her place stood the queen. Her expression smoothed into that cold, unyielding mask Kain had known since childhood. The firelight carved her into marble, every line held in perfect control. Kain slipped into motion, strolling over to a familiar post and leaning against it, buying himself a second to steady his breath, to prepare for what came next.

"Speak," she commanded. The word left no room for argument. So he did.

He told her everything. Every moment, every decision, every scream that had split the night. His voice stayed flat, stripped of emotion, a soldier's report delivered to his commanding officer. Yet every word felt like glass in his throat. He spoke of the ball turned to slaughter. Of the blades that flashed through silk and light. Of Theron's roar as he fell. Of blood. Of silence. Of the emptiness that came after.

Queen Okteria listened without interrupting, her expression carved from ice. She moved only to pace the length of the hut, each step measured, each pause deliberate. When he fell quiet, the silence that followed was absolute. Even the fire seemed to hold its breath.

At last, she spoke. "We will have a feast tonight in his honor." Her voice was steady, every syllable wrapped in command. "He will be celebrated in the eyes of the Gods." Kain nodded once. It was right. Theron deserved it. Songs, ale, firelight. A warrior's sendoff worthy of Ondurin's gates. "Sparrow returned days ago," she continued. "I sent him back with a small escort. He will learn how Bartoria handles the loss of their king and half their army. He should return soon, and then we will plan." Kain's jaw flexed, but he only nodded again. Of course Sparrow was already moving pieces. That was who he was.

Her gaze shifted then, and the weight of it hit him like a blow. Cold. Penetrating. Unforgiving. "Sparrow will face the consequences of his actions when he returns." Her voice dropped, low and final. "But you..." Kain straightened against the post. "You and Xaden will answer promptly. You betrayed your people. You betrayed your queen. Reason matters little. Betrayal is betrayal. At first light, you will fight each other in the Circle." The words landed heavy, but not unexpected. Death, or something close, was always the price for what he had done. He felt no fear. And not a single regret. He'd made his choices with eyes wide open.

Kain exhaled slowly, the weight of what was to come settling over him like armor. "If Xaden wins in the Circle, he should take command of the guard," he said, his voice steady, stripped of bravado. "Theron would have wanted it if you agreed. And truth be told, I agree. He's the right choice."

Queen Okteria regarded him in silence, her emerald eyes unblinking. She did not look at him as a mother might, but as a ruler assessing what the realm had just lost and what it would now demand in return. At last, she inclined her head. "Xaden has proven himself. If he wins tomorrow, he will lead." The words settled. Then she stepped closer, and the chamber seemed to draw tight around her. "But if you win," she continued, her voice low and absolute, "you will stop running. No more solitary hunts. No more vanishing into the woods as if blood can be outrun. You are Antonin's heir. You will stand before your people. You will act as the man this tribe requires." Her gaze locked onto his. "As a future king."

A sharp laugh broke from him. "Me. A king." He raked a hand through his uneven hair and shook his head. "That was never my path. I was not raised for councils or treaties. I do not weigh words. I act. I do what is right, even when it breaks your rules."

"That was by design," Okteria replied smoothly and Kain stilled.

"Theron is dead, Kain. You stood before me and told me so yourself just moments ago." Her voice did not waver. "What did you believe would follow?" She turned, pacing once, the firelight catching the bronze etched into her skin. "Xaden will be a formidable head warrior. But Antonin does not endure without a king. And a Drakaren must rule. Not just for tradition, but for survival." She faced him again. "I raised you to be what this tribe needed in its darkest years. A blade unbound. A wolf that chose vengeance when law failed. You did not hesitate. You did not seek permission." Her voice hardened. "But that time is over..."

Okteria took a formidable breath and stared at Kain. "You were not raised by me alone," she continued. "Your father shaped you as well. You watched him rule. You learned restraint, consequence, and sacrifice, whether you admit it or not." Her eyes burned. "You know how to do this." Silence pressed in. "I allowed your brother time," she said at last. "Because he believed he did not deserve the crown. I believed he would come to see what the rest of us already had one day." A pause. Heavy. Final. "But he never got the chance." Kain's jaw clenched. "I will not wait again."

He scoffed, hard and bitter. "You see a crown where there is only blood and impulse. I am not him. I will never be what you want."

"You will," she said calmly.

He shook his head. "You mistake what I am for what you wish me to be."

"I know what you are, even if you refuse to."

The firelight flared between them, bright and unforgiving. Kain rolled his shoulders, the familiar smirk sliding back into place like armor.

"If that is all," he said lightly, "I need food."

With that, Kain turned and left. Behind him, the queen did not call him back. Yet he felt the weight of the crown following.

The fires burned high. Not the careful banked flames of ordinary nights, but roaring pyres fed with fresh wood and reckless hands. Torches lined the clearing, their light throwing wild shadows across bark and bone, across laughing faces slick with sweat and ale. Voices rose in song, deep and thunderous, the old Antonin chants carried on the backs of too much drink and too much feeling.

Theron's name was everywhere.

It echoed in laughter and shouted boasts, in cups raised too high, in fists thudding against chests. Someone beat a drum too fast. Someone else sang off-key. Warriors danced barefoot in the dirt, blades flashing as they reenacted battles that grew more glorious with every retelling. This was not a night for grief. This was a night of celebrating his ascension.

Kain stood just beyond the edge of the firelight, his back against the rough bark of an old pine, a horn of ale loose in his grip. The smoke curled thick in the air, sharp with resin and sweat and burning sap. He watched the celebration with a quiet steadiness, eyes tracking faces, movements, the rise and fall of the tribe he had bled for. Theron would have hated this fanfare and attention. The thought hit him without warning and made him smile. Always the tormenting little brother.

Xaden appeared at his side like a storm given flesh, cheeks flushed, grin wide and unrestrained. He clapped Kain on the shoulder hard enough to make his ribs protest.

"Look at them," Xaden said, voice rough with drink and approval. "You'd think he conquered Ondurin himself."

Kain huffed a breath that might have been a laugh. "He probably did."

Xaden lifted his horn toward the fire. "To Theron Drakaren. Bastard fought like the Gods were watching."

Kain raised his own without hesitation. "They were."

They drank. The ale burned warm down his throat, grounding him in the now. Around them, someone roared a joke that sent the whole circle into laughter. A warrior stumbled mid-dance and was hauled upright by two others, all of them grinning like fools. Kain took another pull from the horn, then lowered it slowly. The firelight caught the edge of his jaw as his expression shifted, the humor draining away until only honesty remained.

"There's something you should know," he said.

Xaden glanced at him, still smiling, but the grin softened at the weight in Kain's voice. "That tone never brings good news."

"At first light," Kain said evenly, "my mother will call the Circle." The words settled between them, heavy but unsurprising. "For us," Kain continued. "For what we did. For choosing Graystonia. For following Theron."

Xaden didn't speak right away. He drew one deep breath, slow and deliberate, the kind a warrior takes before stepping into cold water or lifting a blade he knows might be his last. Then he nodded.

"Figured," he said simply. Kain studied him, searching for fear, regret, anything like hesitation. He found none. Xaden leaned back against the tree beside him, shoulder to shoulder. "Funny thing," he said after a moment. "When I followed Theron into Graystonia, I knew how it would end."

Kain glanced sideways. "You always were a terrible optimist."

Xaden snorted. "Not surprised, though. Not really." He lifted his horn slightly, gaze fixed on the fire. "Theron was my brother in everything but blood. There was never a world where I let him walk into that mess alone." His mouth curved, softer now. Kain said nothing, but the truth of it settled heavy and solid in his chest.

Xaden took another long drink. "Never thought my last night might be spent getting drunk with you, though."

That earned him a real laugh, low and rough. "Gods help us both."

They stood there in companionable silence, the fire cracking loud enough to fill the space. Somewhere behind them, someone shouted for another round. Someone else started a chant that devolved into chaos halfway through.

Xaden bumped Kain's shoulder again. "You ready?"

Kain didn't answer right away. He watched the flames twist and climb, sparks vanishing into the dark sky. "As I'll ever be. You?"

Xaden nodded once. No bravado. No ceremony. Just understanding. That was that. A beat passed. Then Xaden's grin turned sly again, all mischief and teeth. "By the way," he added casually, "the way you looked at that dagger-wielding princess..."

Kain exhaled through his nose, smirk tugging at his mouth. "Careful."

Xaden laughed. "Just saying. Doesn't look like a man who regrets his choices."

Kain tipped his head back against the tree, eyes briefly closing. For an instant, he saw her again. Hazel eyes bright with fire. Steel in her spine. A blade in her hand like it belonged there. If the Gods were kind, she would meet him in Ondurin one day. But if they weren't...

His eyes opened, the smirk settling into something quieter, more dangerous. "I plan on seeing her again in this life," he said simply. "If I have anything to say about it."

Xaden's grin softened into something like approval. "Then I'll drink to that."

They clinked horns. The fire roared higher. Theron's name rose with the smoke. And for this one night, beneath the stars and the sound of living voices, death could wait.

VARYN

**The War-Forged. The Bloodhound of Battle. The Eternal Flame of Strength.**

Varyn stood like a wall of muscle and war paint, arms crossed, carved from the same iron and fury that shaped the warriors who worship him. His skin is deep and sun-forged, marked by streaks of ancient paint that signify conquest, oath, and honor. Broad-shouldered, scarred, and unyielding, he carries the presence of a Viking warlord made divine.
Where Varyn walks, battle follows.
Where he gazes, warriors rise.

His blessing is strength, courage, endurance, and the fire that keeps a soldier standing long after the body fails. In the age before the Veil, warbands painted their faces in his colors, believing his hand guided their blades. And when blood was spilled in his name, he answered with power.

Varyn is the roar in a warrior's chest, the calm before a strike, the heat in the veins that says fight when death closes in. His domain is not cruelty, but resilience—the strength to endure, the fury to protect, and the valor to face whatever comes.

# Chapter Five

*L* *ayla.*

Layla did not remember leaving the council chamber. Only her mother's words followed her, precise and merciless. They were not lies. They were truths honed to wound. She could lead by instinct. She could command in chaos. She had survived where others had fallen. But instinct alone did not bind men to her will. It did not earn loyalty, or trust, or the quiet faith of those who had bled beside one another long before her name carried weight.

Her knowledge had been gathered in fragments over the years. Whispers behind closed doors. Lessons stolen when her father's council believed her unseen. Steel taught by Sir Charles before betrayal stripped it bare. She knew how to fight. She knew how to endure. What she had not yet been allowed to build were the bonds that turned command into allegiance. Men bound by years of shared blood and loss did not follow fire alone. They followed those they trusted to stand with them when the ground broke open.

Layla drew a slow breath and forced the heat inward. If she reached for power now, it would only expose her. Authority without trust was brittle. Power demanded witnesses. Allies. Roots deep enough to hold when the ground shifted. She would need names spoken in rooms she could not yet enter. Hands willing to steady her when the tide turned. Knowledge would come first. Quietly. Carefully.

Hours later, she had only just begun to steady herself when the summons came. She was not ready. Not for another reckoning. Not for the unforgiving weight of her mother's words. She did not know which version of Queen Raynera waited beyond the doors. The woman who had torn her apart before the council, or the mother she so desperately sought who might yet teach her how to rise.

Layla paused at the threshold of Queen Raynera's chambers. Her palms damp against her skirts, her pulse drumming hard enough to feel in her throat. She had been summoned much sooner than she wished. The summons had come swiftly after the war council adjourned, delivered without explanation by a messenger who wouldn't meet her eyes. That alone had been enough to tell her what waited beyond these doors would not be good.

Even so, she came. She always did. Her mother's words would cut, that much she knew, each one meant to slice her down to size. But this time, Layla had a plan. A purpose. And though she braced for the storm, she still held onto a thin thread of hope. That for once, her mother might listen before tearing her apart.

As Layla stepped inside, the chamber was warm with firelight and the scent of parchment and lavender oil. Gold spilled from the high windows, catching the polished marble floors and the edge of a writing desk strewn with scrolls and quills. Raynera sat behind it, poised as ever, her posture flawless, her honey eyes already fixed on her daughter's approach. She needed no jewels to announce her power. In her severe gray gown and the quiet authority of her bearing, she was Graystonia itself.

"Close the doors," Raynera said, her voice smooth but commanding. The maid obeyed at once, and the sound of the heavy wood sealing shut seemed to take all the air with it.

"Layla." Her mother's tone was cold, clipped, and precise. "I trust you will not repeat today's display. Such behavior is unbecoming of a lady. Even less so of a future queen."

Layla's chest tightened. She knew the answer her mother wanted: a bowed head, a quiet apology. Still, she tried to speak, tried to let her mother see what burned beneath the shame.

"Mother, I only..."

"Enough."

The word sliced clean through the air. Raynera's face remained calm, her expression carved from stone, but her eyes were fire held behind glass. "Do not insult me with excuses. I did not spend years shaping you into the ideal queen only for you to act like a foolish child."

Layla's hands trembled at her sides, clenched into fists she dared not raise.

Then, Raynera's tone softened, almost kind, and all the more unsettling for it. "Layla, I know you. I have been at your side every moment of your life. I know what you were taught. I know who you were shaped to be. You were born for one purpose: to be queen. To be beautiful. To be poised. To secure this kingdom's future through the husband you choose. That is your role. That is your worth. And it is enough." Her words fell like silk, smooth and quiet, but every syllable tightened the chains around Layla's heart. "You must remember this," the queen continued, rising from her seat with slow, deliberate grace. Her shadow stretched across the marble as she crossed the space between them. "You were not made for the weight of crowns or the burden of command. The men were forged for war, for rule, for strategy. You were not. To step into their world is to mock it, and yourself. Persist in these childish ambitions, and you will destroy everything you were born to protect."

Raynera stopped just before her, so close Layla could smell the faint rosewater on her skin. "If you cannot remember your place," she said softly, her hazel eyes flashing cold, "then tell me, what worth do you have to Graystonia?"

The words struck like a blow. Layla's breath caught, the silence between them stretching until it felt like a blade pressed between her ribs.

Then, Raynera stepped back, composure restored. "You and Ciana will depart for Drelith at week's end. You will represent this house with dignity. You will not falter. You will not embarrass me. Not a whisper of impropriety will reach my ears. Do I make myself clear?"

Layla swallowed hard, her fury burning beneath a mask of composure. "Yes, Mother," she managed.

"Good."

The queen turned away, reclaiming her seat with the effortless grace of someone accustomed to obedience. Her gown whispered against the marble as she settled, every movement deliberate, final. "But that is not why I called you here this afternoon." Her tone remained perfectly even, the calm of a blade before the strike. "A decision has been made and approved by the council." She lifted her gaze, composed and merciless. "We can wait no longer for you to waver. I have decided for you." Raynera's words fell with measured precision, each one striking harder than the last. "Lord Jameson's son, Ryker, is the ideal match. He will return soon from his mission to capture the traitor, Sir Charles. When he does, the nuptials will be set. A king will soon sit upon Graystonia's throne once more."

She paused, her voice softening to something almost reverent. "All will be as it should."

Layla's head snapped up, the name striking like a blow. "Ryker... is alive?" The question escaped before she could stop it. Instantly, she regretted it. Surprise was weakness.

Raynera's eyes hardened, her lips tightening at the interruption, the faintest flicker of irritation breaking her flawless composure. When she finally spoke, her voice was precise and cold. "He sustained a severe injury, but he recovers well. He did not allow it to deter him from his mission. That, Layla, is the mark of a man fit to wear a crown. He will make a fine king."

The words landed like a verdict. Ryker. Alive. He was returning. And her mother intended to place the crown upon his head. Layla's thoughts reeled. She had believed she still had time. Time to learn. To observe. To earn the council's trust. To prove she could lead before marriage sealed her fate. Bartoria had been wounded. Graystonia had drawn a fragile breath of peace. But that breath was apparently already gone.

Ryker Jameson was not her choice. He was their solution. A future arranged without her consent, a crown positioned beyond her reach but close enough to remind her it was never meant for her hands. The sense of betrayal burned. And yet, beneath it, something colder took shape.

Ryker had led men. He had risen through the ranks of her own army. He understood war. He understood politics. More important-ly, he understood the unspoken economy of trust that ruled men who had bled together. The very currency she had been denied access to.

If he returned as king and saw her as more than a bride, more than a symbol placed beside him to soften his rule, then the rooms closed to her might not remain closed forever. If he treated her as a partner in governance, even privately, even gradually, then she would gain what force could never secure. Presence. Proximity. Legitimacy shaped by association rather than defiance.

The realization unsettled her. This was not the alliance she had envisioned. It was not one she would have chosen. But it aligned with the truth she had already learned. Power here was not seized. It was granted, extended, and defended by those who already held it.

If Ryker proved capable of seeing her mind as equal to his own, then this unwanted betrothal might become the very opening she needed. Not because it elevated her, but because it placed her where trust was forged and decisions were made.

It was a bitter thought. But bitterness did not make it any less useful.

Raynera's voice cut through her spinning thoughts. "Go to your lessons. I will send word when you and Ciana are to leave for Drelith. Guards will accompany you. And Layla." Her gaze hardened, cold and final. "Remember your place. Do not disgrace your father's memory with these impulses again."

Layla bowed her head at once. Smooth. Perfect. Obedient. The rebellion did not blaze. It folded inward, banked low where no one could see it. A fire hidden was far more dangerous than one allowed to burn. This was not surrender. It was strategy.

Later that evening, after hours of merciless instruction and sharp correction, Layla could scarcely recall a single lesson. The day had passed in a controlled haze, her body moving on instinct while her thoughts remained stubbornly elsewhere. She walked beside Ciana, answered when addressed, and performed every expected gesture with practiced precision. The perfect princess. Polished. Composed. Hollow. No one had noticed how little of the day had truly reached her.

The resolve held only until her body finally demanded acknowledgment. She sank onto the edge of her bed, too weary even to undress. Marilla had lit the hearth, its small fire burning low and steady, softening the hard lines of the chamber. The warmth barely touched her. Cool air drifted through the open window, carrying the scent of rain and fallen leaves. Of endings. Of beginnings she was not yet allowed to claim.

She did not light a candle. Darkness felt safer. More honest. Layla leaned back against the pillows, the plan settling around her like armor finally fitted to her form. She would endure. She would observe. She would learn. And when Ryker Jameson returned, she would be ready.

For the first time that day, her breathing slowed. The tight coil in her chest loosened. Peace came, tentative but real, fragile as a held breath. But it did not follow her into sleep. Darkness closed in, heavy and swift, and the quiet she had claimed shattered the moment her eyes slipped shut. Her dreams offered no rest. They carried her elsewhere.

*Hands erupted from the dark, cold and countless, clawing at her skin. They came from everywhere and nowhere, faceless, formless, pulling her down into the black. The air thickened around her, heavy as tar. She tried to scream, but no sound escaped. Her mouth opened wide, her throat strained, yet silence devoured her cries before they could be born. The hands dragged her deeper. Fabric tore. Skin burned. Her arms were wrenched above her head, her legs forced still. Every desperate kick, every twist of her body only sank her further beneath the crushing weight that smothered the air from her lungs.*

*Then came the glint of steel. A blade pressed to her throat, its edge cold enough to burn, promising blood if she moved again. The pressure held her fast, until even her heart seemed to still beneath it.*

*From the blackness, a figure emerged. King Ivar. His eyes cutting like a predator's, catching what little light there was. The grin that split his face was wrong, twisted, carved from cruelty itself. He stepped closer, each movement deliberate, savoring her fear. The scent of him filled the air. A mixture of wine, sweat, and rot. He spoke, though his words were soundless, his laughter echoing through the void without breath or voice. It filled her head until it was all she could hear. She tried to beg, to plead, to call for anyone, anything, but the silence wrapped around her throat like a noose.*

*The darkness pressed closer, suffocating. Pain flared, white and merciless, a searing that made her vision crack into shards of light. She could not tell where her body ended and the terror began. All that existed was his weight, his shadow, his laughter was low, cruel, and endless. She wanted to vanish. To melt into the dark, to escape the body that betrayed her by staying alive. Her mind screamed though her mouth made no sound. Her limbs went still. Her heart did not know if it was beating or breaking.*

*When she looked up again, Ivar's eyes were gone. The face that stared down at her was her own. Pale. Hollow. Silent.*

Layla lay still, her heart racing as the last of the dream loosened its grip. The room remained unchanged. Stone walls. Low firelight. Silence. She fixed her focus there, on what was solid and real, grounding herself in the present until her breathing steadied.

She did not examine the nightmare. She did not pull it apart or linger on the images still clinging to her skin. She had survived it once. She would not give it more than it deserved now. Strength meant control, and control meant refusal. Yet even as Layla steeled herself, determined not to let the memory break her, the word slipped in all the same. *Lucky.* It threaded through her thoughts before she could stop it, a quiet, poisonous suggestion that whispered maybe her mother was right. Maybe survival had been chance. Maybe instinct had only carried her as far as fortune allowed. Layla shut it down instantly.

No. It was not luck. It had been her. Her instincts. Her choices. Her will to move when others froze, to fight when fear demanded stillness. She would not allow her mother's voice to weaken her now, not after everything she had endured. She pushed the thought away as decisively as she would a blade.

With that, Layla lay back against the pillows, forcing her body still. She did not wait for peace. She did not expect rest. When sleep dragged her under again, she endured the nightmare once more.

THE BLOOM OF THE BLESSED
IS BORN IN DECAY

LUMIREN

# Chapter Six

*K**ain.***

The Circle waited.

Dew clung to the packed earth, with the scent of pine and iron thick in the air. The morning was cold enough to sting, each breath turning to mist that drifted above the ring before vanishing into the rising light. The trees formed a living wall around them, ancient sentinels draped in gold and shadow. Sunlight speared through the canopy in narrow blades, striking the center of the clearing like a blessing or a warning.

Xaden stepped forward first, the crunch of his boots breaking the stillness. He moved with quiet precision, the muscles in his arms hard with restrained power, his expression unreadable. The crowd that ringed the Circle, warriors and elders alike, even children perched on fallen logs, stood in reverent silence. The weight of their gaze pressed down on the air, heavy and expectant. Somewhere, a raven cried, its coarse voice slicing through the hush like a challenge. But Kain heard none of it. His focus tunneled until there was nothing left but the man before him and the stretch of ground between them. The cold bit at his bare forearms, but he welcomed it, let it sharpen him. His arms folded loosely across his chest, bow and quiver settled against his back, the familiar weight grounding him. A smirk played at the corner of his mouth, slow and dangerous.

The fight had not yet begun, but the forest already seemed to hold its breath.

"You know," he called, voice carrying easily in the hush, "I could puncture that thick skull of yours before you even get close enough to swing that sword."

Xaden's blade flashed as he swiped it lazily through the air, matching Kain's casual tone. "Oh, I know. Question is, do we make this fun, or fair?"

Kain's smirk widened. "Fun. Definitely fun."

As one, they discarded their favored weapons, Kain setting aside his bow, Xaden his sword. A choice born of pride, of blood, of the unspoken agreement that if one of them died here, it would be by the other's hand, face-to-face.

"Begin." Queen Okteria's command split the silence.

Xaden lunged, but Kain was already moving. His hand snapped up, flinging a fistful of dirt he had palmed while setting down his bow. It hit true, bursting into Xaden's eyes in a haze of grit. They had agreed there would be no rules, and Kain had never been one for honor when victory was on the line. Xaden snarled in response while stumbling back, blinking furiously. Kain was on him before he recovered, his fist slamming into Xaden's face with a crunch that echoed through the clearing. Blood sprayed. Satisfaction flashed through him, hot and bright. But Xaden was no fool. Even half-blind, he moved with deadly precision. His leg swept out in a brutal arc, catching Kain across the knees and sending him crashing into the dirt. The breath ripped from his lungs, ribs screaming, but Kain was grinning as he rolled to his feet. Then the world narrowed to motion and blood.

They met in the center of the Circle, a storm of muscle and fury. Blow met blow. Blood answered blood. Daggers flashed, short and cruel, meant for killing at breath's length. Every strike carved a new wound; every counter drew another line of red across skin already slick with it. They circled and collided, blades sparking, breaths ragged. Pain no longer mattered. There was only rhythm: attack, block, slash, bleed. Around them, the tribe watched in silence, the air thick with dust and anticipation. Neither warrior yielded. Neither wanted mercy. The Circle demanded blood, and they gave it freely.

Kain's grin only widened, crimson staining his teeth. He relished it. The sting, the ache, the knowledge that he might leave this Circle in pieces. Better this than fading. Better this than silence.

"Hey," he panted, ducking a swing, "mind my head? I don't know if you noticed, but I *just* had it cracked open." Blood dripped down his cheek as he grinned.

"Oh, I noticed." Xaden's voice was low, steady. He struck again, driving Kain back a step. "Waste of Eir's work, though. Dragging you back from the brink just so I could kill you myself."

Kain barked a laugh before spitting red into the dirt. "True. But let's be honest, you needed me alive. How else would you remind yourself what real talent looks like?" He winked, even as Xaden's short blade nearly opened his throat.

They circled, breath ragged, steel flashing. Kain knew it in his bones; Xaden had the edge. He always had. Skill, precision, patience. Kain had come close to matching him, but close wasn't enough. He remembered his own words to Layla: *Don't underestimate your abilities or overestimate your strength.* So, he leaned on the one weapon he had left. His mouth.

Sarcasm rolled off his tongue like second nature, weaving jabs with truths honed enough to unsettle, distract, unarm. If he was going to bleed out in the Circle, he'd damn well go down smiling.

"Tell me, Xaden. How does it feel? Theron's gone, and finally you're the golden boy. *Finally* the best. Does it taste as sweet as you hoped?"

Xaden's jaw flexed, but he said nothing, his strikes sharper, his movements tighter. Kain spat blood into the dirt again and cocked his head, smirk cutting as glass. "Now the true question, are you going to be a wolf like our ancestors... or a house dog like Theron was? Loyal. Tame. Waiting for scraps of her approval." He let the words drip slow, cruel, savoring the way the crowd bristled. "Yeah, that's it, isn't it? Her mindless little pups. Tell me, will you piss when she tells you to, or are you allowed to do that on your own?"

A low chuckle slid past his lips, mocking, venomous. "Gods, I remember Theron wore that leash so well. Guess you'll fit it just as pretty..."

That was the strike, the perfect nerve prodded. Xaden's composure shattered. He snarled like the wolf Kain had denied him, fury blazing in his eyes as he lunged. Not with precision, not with strategy, but with blind rage. It was all Kain needed. He pivoted, feinted left, then drove forward. His dagger flashed, then flipped, before the hilt came down in a brutal arc against the back of Xaden's skull. The crack rang out like a drumbeat. Xaden dropped, limp in the dirt, unconscious but breathing.

The Circle erupted in gasps, the silence shattered by the echo of the blow. Kain stood over him, chest heaving, blood dripping from his mouth, but grinning, always grinning.

He bent down and patted Xaden's shoulder as he wiped some blood from his mouth. "Look at that... now we match. Eir is going to be thrilled." The smirk lingered as he turned, daring anyone to challenge the outcome. Then he straightened and pain caught up with him all at once. It surged through bone and muscle, white-hot and unrelenting, every breath scraping raw. His body trembled with it, but he stayed upright. Alive. And against every law of the Circle, so was Xaden. That was the risk. The Circle was sacred ground. Every warrior stepped into it knowing one of them might not leave. You did not enter with mercy in mind. To plan for it would have been an insult to the gods and to the blood already soaked into the dirt.

Kain had not planned it. In the single heartbeat where instinct screamed for the kill, he had flipped the dagger in his hand and struck with the hilt instead of the blade. A choice made mid-motion. A gamble taken between breaths. When he lifted his gaze, Queen Okteria inclined her head from the high stone and nodded once. No fury. No censure.

Only acknowledgment. The Circle had taken its due. The outcome had been accepted.

The roar of the crowd blurred into noise, smoke and sweat thick in the air, iron still sharp on his tongue. It was finished.

Kain exhaled, long and slow, the weight of it all bleeding out of him until only exhaustion remained. The ache in his limbs was heavy, but lighter somehow than before. He reached for his bow and quiver, fingers trembling as they closed around familiar leather and feathered shafts. Then he turned toward Eir's hut, every step dragging through the dirt that was still dark with blood. Behind him, the warriors moved in silence, carrying Xaden's limp body from the Circle. The sound of their boots against the earth was the only echo that followed him.

To say Eir was displeased at the sight of the two of them bloodied, battered, and half-dead again was an understatement. But like always, she said nothing. She simply worked. Her hands were steady, her concoctions bitter, her presence a tether in the chaos.

Kain welcomed the tonic she pressed to his lips, welcomed the way it dragged him under. For once, he didn't fight it. Sparrow wouldn't be back for days. The weight of vengeance for Theron, the war with Bartoria, and the uncertain future of their tribe could rest a little longer. And when sleep found him, it wasn't pain that lingered. It was her. Layla. Laughing, smiling, spinning through the haze of memory like she belonged there. Dreaming of her brought him peace. And for the first time in far too long, Kain let himself admit he didn't mind peace one bit.

A low groan cut through the quiet, pulling Kain from the depths of sleep. The world returned slowly, shaped by smoke curling from the dying hearth and the thick scent of herbs and blood in the air. Every muscle ached, his body heavy as stone, but the biting sting of pain had faded to a deep, pulsing throb that reminded him he was still alive.

He blinked, cracking one eye open toward the sound. The hut swam into view, dim and hazy, lit only by the faint glow of embers. For a long moment, he simply breathed, the taste of earth and ash clinging to his tongue. As he glanced sideways, he noticed that Xaden was upright. He was sitting on the edge of his cot, one hand rubbing the back of his skull with a grimace.

"You're a dick."

Kain huffed a laugh and let his eyes fall shut again. "Yes. But a dick that saved your life."

Xaden grunted, half a laugh, half a groan. "Still a dick, though."

"Shh." Kain waved a lazy hand. "Go back to sleep, pup. Your master will summon us soon."

That got him a glare he was sure, but before Xaden could retort, Kain added with a crooked smile, "Oh, and congrats. You're the head pup now."

Silence stretched. Kain cracked one eye open again, just in time to catch Xaden's face shift from simmering irritation to wide-eyed shock. His dark brown eyes, usually keen and steady, had gone unfocused, his strong onyx features slack with disbelief. Kain gave him a slow nod, genuine this time. Respect, given freely. Xaden held his gaze, breath ragged, blood streaking his jaw, and then returned the nod in kind. No words were needed.

Satisfied, Kain let his eyes close once more, sinking into the darkness where pain no longer mattered. Once again, he was eager to surrender to sleep. Not for rest, but for the world waiting beyond it. Where she was. The woman who had clawed her way beneath his skin and made a home there without even trying. She had no right to still haunt him, yet every time he closed his eyes, there she was. Laughing. Glaring. Fire and steel wrapped into a single impossible woman. Gods, he loved getting under her skin, loved the way her temper burned hot enough to match his own.

Every barb, every barbed retort she threw at him only made him grin wider. But it wasn't only the fight that kept her in his head. It was the way she thought. The precision in her mind. The spark behind those hazel eyes when she was scheming or strategizing, already seeing paths no one else could. She was going to change the world. He knew it in his bones.

So, he let the darkness take him again, welcomed it even, because in his dreams she would be waiting. Dancing through his thoughts. Glaring. Smiling that unapologetic smile that always promised trouble. Until he could hunt her down again, until he could stand before her and earn those looks for real, he would keep her there. In the only place she belonged to him.

Two weeks. Two fucking weeks since Kain had been home. No sign of Sparrow. No answers. Nothing but silence gnawing at him.

He had basically begged his mother to let him take men and search. Denied. Again and again. Every time her voice clipped and final. "*Wait.*" So, he turned to Xaden. New Head Guard. New leash-holder. He thought maybe he'd grant permission... But no. Xaden was exactly what Kain expected, *obedient.* A loyal pup chained to Queen Okteria's word. Not a wolf. Not a risk-taker. Not willing to defy her.

Kain's fury stewed hotter by the day. He was past patience, past obedience. He was at the point of defiance. If he left without permission, he knew the price. When he returned, if he returned, he'd be thrown back into the Circle, forced to fight for his life again to prove his loyalty. And if not that, then exile. Stripped of his blood, his name, his tribe. *So be it.* Answers were worth the risk. Vengeance was worth the risk. He still had a horse. That ridiculous beast the Graystonians had called Muffin. He could ride hard, cut the distance alone, and come back with the truth. No leash, no queen's orders, no silence. The thought hardened into resolve as he set his hands to the reins, tightening the saddle. His jaw clenched, his pulse steady. He was going.

Then... he heard it.

The sharp cry across the camp. The call that snapped through the air like lightning. The returning party. Kain's head jerked up. His heart slammed once. They were back. Sparrow with them.

He abandoned the horse without another thought, sprinting toward his mother's hut, blood pounding in his ears. He didn't care about protocol, didn't care about appearances. He wanted...no, *needed* the answers. And most of all, he wanted to know why in all the hell it had taken Sparrow so long to bring them.

Upon approach, Kain started pacing, boots grinding into the dirt with every abrupt turn. He couldn't hold onto his usual calm, that easy grin that masked the chaos underneath. The air was cold, heavy with the scent of pine and smoke from the distant campfires flickering against the dark. Every breath misted in front of him, every heartbeat loud in his ears.

Not a few minutes later, Sparrow emerged through the treeline, and Kain stilled. His brother-in-arms was a shadow against the dimming sky. Sparrow was taller than most, but still a few inches shorter than Kain. Jet-black hair hung loose from its tie, tangled from travel, matching the chaotic braids woven into his beard. His cloak was streaked with mud, the edges torn from days on the road. But what struck Kain most wasn't the exhaustion written across Sparrow's face, but his eyes, piercing blue, clear even through fatigue, yet laced with something else. Distress. It hit Kain like a blow, forcing his spine straight.

Sparrow didn't falter as he approached, but each step was heavy, deliberate. The kind that came from carrying more than just exhaustion. Whatever he'd brought with him trailed close behind, dark as the storm clouds bruising the horizon.

"You look like shit," Kain said, his voice dry as flint. The words weren't cruel, just an old habit, a nudge toward normalcy.

Sparrow huffed out something between a laugh and a sigh, the corners of his mouth twitching. "You don't look much better."

"I've heard worse," Kain shot back, finally forcing a grin. Sparrow just shook his head, folding his arms across his chest, posture straight despite the weariness dragging at his features. A warrior through and through.

The brief flicker of ease between them vanished a heartbeat later as the air shifted and Queen Okteria stepped into view.

"Speak."

"It's not at all what we thought..." He shook his head. His eyes showing the utter disbelief that Sparrow was clearly still feeling. "When I reached Bartoria, I expected to find the kingdom in shambles. King Ivar had no heir, only bastards scattered like weeds. He was a man who lived to take, not to build. No legacy. No plan. I thought the throne would be picked apart by cousins and vultures until nothing remained. But I was wrong." He paused only for a second, then continued.

"To my shock, Lumiren banners already flew over Bartoria's walls. They had taken the kingdom. Overthrown it. I don't know how, or why, but Bartoria hadn't stood a chance, it seemed." He shook his head as he went on. "I would guess that between a large part of their army being slaughtered by us on Graystonian soil, their king's head split from his shoulders, and their people already half-starved and ruined. They were too weak to resist. Whether Lumiren's soldiers marched in or Bartoria's lords simply bowed to survive, the outcome was the same...Bartoria belongs to Lumiren now. And the speed of it... it wasn't chance. It had to have been planned." Sparrow took a deep breath before continuing.

"So I asked questions. Pressed where I could. Most answers were whispers, rumors, nothing more. But all of them pointed in one direction: Lumiren. So I rode to the border myself and what I saw there..." Sparrow's voice faltered, jaw tightening, eyes far away. "...the land itself is dead. Not barren. Not fallow. Dead. Black earth that crumbles to ash at a touch. Trees hollowed and split, standing like corpses. No birds. No game. Only silence, and the stench of rot."

He drew a slow breath before finishing. "The rumors say Yssra is behind it, that the Goddess of Rot and Ruin blesses them, and their land is the offering she devours. I couldn't get straight answers, truth and fable are tangled too tightly. But I know this much: this is bigger than we imagined. Lumiren is not just surviving. They are spreading. And the rot is spreading with them."

"I'm going."

Queen Okteria's head tilted, slow and deliberate, like a predator scenting prey. "Excuse me?"

"I need to see this for myself," Kain said, jaw clenched. "I should never have waited this long. We need more answers. We need to know what the other kingdoms are doing. I can be there and back in a few days if I take Muffin."

The silence stretched as his mother studied him. She had always listened to Kain; he was the apple fallen closest to her tree, the reflection of her own will. She rarely denied him. That was why the past weeks of restraint had felt like a chokehold. But everything was different now.

At last, Queen Okteria inclined her chin. "Very well."

"I'll show you." Sparrow stepped forward, voice rough but certain.

Kain barked a laugh, though there was no humor in it. "Sparrow, you need sleep. I'm not carrying your ass on my horse when you pass out. I'm not as nice as Xaden."

But Sparrow only shook his head. "I'll be fine. I'll sleep when we stop."

The exhaustion was carved into his features so stark Kain couldn't fathom how he was still standing. Yet his eyes, gods, his eyes, burned with a fierce, unyielding fire once again. This wasn't about duty. This was for Theron. Kain saw it. Respected it. He gave Sparrow a single nod, warrior to warrior, and Sparrow returned it in kind.

Queen Okteria's reluctance was clear, but she did not stop them. Within an hour, packs were strapped, weapons checked, and the two of them were riding out of camp. Back toward Bartoria. Back toward the hellhole that had already taken so much and threatened to take more.

THE BLOOM OF THE BLESSED
IS BORN IN DECAY

"Through stillness and surrender,
we are sanctified."

All citizens of Lumiren are required by
royal decree to offer prayers of thanks to
the sanctified divine as appointed by the
Crown. To remain silent in worship is to
deny the hand that sustains you. Those
who fail to offer daily thanks, in public
or private, shall be detained for spiritual
correction until their tongues learn
reverence once more.

-BY THE SACRED LAW OF LUMIREN-

# Chapter Seven

*K*<sup>*ain.*</sup>

Bartoria smelled like coin left too long in a wet fist.

The castle cut the skyline like a pale wound, all clean stone and arrogant height, as if it could pretend the city below it was not starving. Lanterns ringed its walls in neat lines. Not warmth. A warning. Inside those towers, men laughed loud and ate like the world was not changing. Outside them, Bartoria learned how to live with rot in its teeth. But Kain did not come for the castle. He came for what fed it.

He and Sparrow moved through the streets with their hoods low, shoulders forward, hands close to steel. They did not walk like tourists. They walked like men who expected trouble and welcomed it.

The inner ring of the kingdom was polished stone and perfume. Clean boots. Soft hands. Guards at every archway, armor bright, posture proud. Too proud. Men like that never looked down. They looked through you. That kind of arrogance got people killed. The outer wards were cracked brick, crooked beams, and oil smoke that scraped the throat. The air here tasted wrong. Not just poverty. Something older. Something that made the hairs on Kain's forearms lift, like the world itself was warning him.

Sparrow's gaze kept moving, quick and methodical. Blue eyes, keen even under exhaustion. He had been quiet since Graystonia. Quiet in that way men got when grief turned heavy and decided to live in the ribs. Kain didn't ask him if he was all right. He knew there was no way that he was.

A patrol turned a corner ahead, three men in rusted mail, boots muddy, swords loose at their hips. Nothing unusual, except for the way one of them moved. Loose joints. Too smooth. Like his bones did not agree on how a body should work. Then Kain saw it. Black veins, faint at first, spidering along the man's throat and disappearing beneath his collar. Sparrow must have seen it too because Kain saw his posture stiffen beside him ever so slightly.

The patrol slowed near a woman carrying a basket of apples, her shoulders hunched, her eyes down. The black veined guard leaned in, fingers brushing her waist as if she belonged to him. The basket slipped. Apples rolled into the gutter. The woman flinched. Not surprise. Practice. Kain's hand found the hilt of his dagger without thinking.

Sparrow's voice was low. "Not here."

Kain didn't look at him. "I know."

The guard laughed at the woman like she was nothing. Like she was entertainment. Kain watched the woman gather her apples with shaking hands, and something inside him went cold and steady. He had seen what men did to women when power decided it was hungry. He had watched it in Bartoria's cells. He had watched it in the way that princess had learned to hold a blade like it was part of her spine. He did not need another reminder.

His mouth curved, slow and humorless. "Come on," he muttered. "Let's find where they crawl back to when the sun goes down."

Night One came with rain and not the clean kind. The kind that turned the streets into black paste and made every alley stink of old piss and wet ash. Kain and Sparrow took to a roofline, then another, moving over beams and broken tiles, following patrol patterns. Bartoria's guards supposedly changed shifts like clockwork. That was the first lie. The second lie was the men. At certain corners, certain streets, the same faces kept appearing again and again. Not rotating out. Not tiring. Not eating. They stood in the rain like statues that breathed.

Kain crouched behind a chimney stack, rain soaking his hair, water sliding down his neck.

Sparrow whispered, "Those three have been on the same post since dusk."

Kain watched one of them roll his shoulders as if loosening muscle, then settle again, patient as a predator. "Either Bartoria found a way to clone idiots," Kain said, "or they are not getting tired."

Sparrow exhaled through his nose. "The veins."

Kain nodded once. "The veins."

They waited until the patrol turned down an outer lane, lanterns bobbing, boots squelching in mud. The men's laughter was too calm. Before Kain and Sparrow dropped from the roof like shadows hitting the ground. One man turned at the sound of them, mouth opening. But Kain's hand clamped over his throat, yanked him back into the alley, and slammed him into brick hard enough to rattle teeth. Sparrow took the other two, swift and silent, blade to ribs, bodies guided down instead of dropped.

Kain shoved his captive deeper into darkness. The man tried to twist, tried to elbow. Stronger than he should have been. Fast too. Kain smiled like it amused him.

"Try again," he said, soft. "I like when you try." The man spat, but the spit came thick, dark, almost oily. Kain's eyes narrowed. "Lovely."

Sparrow stepped in, wiped rain from his brow. "Make it quick. We are not staying in one place."

Kain pressed his dagger's edge against the man's cheek, just enough to bite. "What are you," Kain asked, "and who did you kneel to for it?"

"Bartoria," the man hissed.

Kain chuckled. "No. Bartoria kneels to coin. This," he nodded at the man's throat where black veins pulsed faintly, "kneels to something else." The man's eyes flicked. Fear, quick and shameful. That was all Kain needed. "You can tell me," Kain said, "or I can take it out of you in pieces. I am a patient man."

Sparrow's gaze stayed on the street. "Kain."

Kain sighed as if Sparrow was ruining his fun. He leaned closer. "Where do they infect you." The man's jaw clenched. Kain lowered his voice. "Answer, and you keep your tongue."

The man swallowed. "Shrines. Not in the inner ring. In the yards. The tanners. The old mills."

Sparrow's attention snapped back. "Which yard."

The man's pupils darted. "North tannery. They take recruits there. The priests call it a blessing."

Kain's smile faded. "A blessing," he repeated, tasting the words like poison. He pressed the dagger a hair deeper. "Who pays."

The man laughed, harsh and wrong. "The rich. They offer up the poor in exchange for free labor and protection." Kain pulled back and looked at Sparrow. A silent communication that it was over and it was time to go.

Sparrow nodded once. "We heard enough."

The man's breath hitched. "Wait, I told you."

Kain tilted his head. "You did. You did very well." Then he drove his fist into the man's gut, hard enough to fold him. Not to kill. To quiet. He turned to Sparrow. "We need to move."

Sparrow's voice was flat. "What about him?"

Kain glanced down at the man, who was gasping and trying to crawl. Kain's rule was simple. Mercy was not free. He crouched, gripped the man's hair, and forced his head back so he could see the black veins clearly. "Tell your priests," Kain whispered in the man's ear, "that I am coming to reap what they have sown in this city." He slammed the man's head against the brick. Once. Twice. Enough to drop him into darkness. Then they vanished into the rain.

They did not sleep in taverns. Too many eyes. Too many mouths. So they found a storage loft above a butcher's shop in the outer ward, paid in silver and silence, and spent the early hours drying their clothes by a cracked chimney.

While Kain cleaned his dagger, Sparrow sat with his back to the wall, sharpening his blade with slow strokes.

Kain looked at him. "You think Theron would be impressed we are sleeping above dead pigs."

Sparrow's mouth twitched. Not quite a smile. "He would call it poetic."

Kain snorted. "He would call it disgusting."

Sparrow's gaze dropped to the blade. "He would call it necessary."

Kain's hand stilled. Necessary. That word had been Theron's favorite weapon. Kain pressed his tongue to his teeth and kept cleaning.

"No sign of his body," Sparrow said quietly.

Kain's jaw flexed. "No."

Sparrow's voice roughened. "You know as well as I do. They probably burned him with the rest that night. Tossed the bones after." Kain didn't answer. He would not give voice to the thought clawing at his gut. This city was too steeped in rot, too eager to turn death into currency.

A foreign prince's remains would not be discarded so easily. Bones had value here. Power. Purpose. But he would not let that happen. Theron deserved Antonin earth. Open sky. Fire and stone that knew his name. Not a foreign pit. Not whatever sickness passed for ritual in Bartoria. And never oblivion.

Kain ground his teeth, forced the thoughts down, and pushed to his feet. "We go north tomorrow night," he said. "We find the tannery." Sparrow nodded once. "And we don't walk into a yard full of guards dressed like ourselves." Sparrow's brow lifted. A slow, predatory grin followed. Kain's grin returned in kind. "We borrow their skin."

Day Two was for stealing. Bartorian soldiers were easy to find when the sun was up. They strutted in alleys near the barracks and drank in half-lit back rooms, fat on the illusion that their walls made them untouchable. Kain and Sparrow followed a pair who wandered too far from the main street, laughing about coin and women like the city owed them both. When the men ducked into a stable to piss, Kain and Sparrow came in behind them. No talking. No warning. Sparrow took the first one with a forearm across the throat, cutting air off clean. Kain drove his dagger into the second man's side and twisted. Not deep enough to kill fast, just deep enough to stop him from screaming. The man's eyes widened, piss splashing his boots as his body locked.

Kain leaned close. "Quiet," he murmured. "You are not worth the noise."

They dragged both men behind hay bales and worked quickly. Cloaks. Helmets. Wool tunics. Leather belts. Even the boots. Kain stripped his own soaked outer layer and pulled on the Bartorian tunic, grimacing at the stink of cheap oil and sweat. Sparrow did the same.

Kain tugged the helm down and glanced at Sparrow. "Tell me I look handsome."

Sparrow's face stayed dead serious. "You look like a pig in borrowed cloth."

Kain's grin widened. "Perfect."

They left the stable with their heads down, shoulders set, moving like men who belonged. No one looked twice. Bartoria did not see men unless they carried titles. So the uniforms bought them what they needed: access. They walked past two outer gates, nodded at bored sentries, and moved into the northern ward where the tannery smoke hung low and thick. The air here tasted like poison. Lime and rot and old blood soaked into wood. Kain watched men move inside the yard. Not workers, but soldiers. And far too many. He saw black veins on throats and wrists. He saw the way their eyes stared without blinking.

Sparrow murmured, "We hit it tonight."

Kain's gaze slid to the far corner where a woman hauled water, head down, moving fast. A soldier barked at her and she jumped instinctively. Kain's hands tightened at his sides. *Not tonight*, he told himself. He would not lay waste tonight. They needed truth. They needed proof. They needed to know how this blessing healed, how it failed, how it could be ended. Then he would make the yard bleed.

Night Two came with fog that crawled like a living thing. They came back to the yard still dressed as soldiers, cloaks pulled tight, heads down, moving with purpose. It was easier to get in once the yard was busy. Everyone assumed someone else had given the orders.

Within the tannery was a low complex of wooden sheds and stone vats, steam rising from hot pits, the stench thick enough to make a strong man gag. Lamps burned low. Shadows moved in corners. They slipped around the back, where crates were stacked and a side door stood cracked open. They heard the horror before they saw it. A wet, rhythmic sound. Flesh meeting flesh. A rasped breath that was not quite a scream. Kain slowed, lifting a hand. Sparrow halted instantly, blade half-drawn as they pressed against the broken wall of the tannery's rear chamber. Light flickered beyond the gap, lantern glow smeared across stone darkened by old stains.

Inside, a man was strapped to a post, arms bound overhead, chest heaving. His skin was unmarked except for a single open wound carved just below his collarbone, raw and red. A presumed *priest* stood before him. Not robed in white. Not crowned in gold. His garments were black, heavy with dried filth and stiff with old blood. His skin was wrong. Not merely darkened, but blackened, veins crawling visibly beneath it like something alive. His eyes were entirely black as well, reflecting the lantern light like pits.

The priest pressed his palm into the wound and the man convulsed. Something seeped from the priest's skin. Not liquid. Not smoke. A slow, viscous rot that clung and crawled, sinking into the torn flesh as if it recognized its home. The wound blackened instantly, veins spidering outward from the priest's hand, racing across the man's chest and throat. The scream tore free then and Kain moved.

Steel sang once. The priest's head hit the floor before the sound finished echoing. The rot recoiled. It shrank back from the severed body, veins withering and collapsing as if starved of breath. The man slumped against his bonds, gasping, black lines already fading where the priest's touch had been interrupted. Sparrow was at the posts in an instant, cutting him free.

"What did he do to you?" Sparrow demanded.

The man sobbed, clawing at his chest. "He said she chose me. That I was worthy."

Kain wiped his blade on the priest's robes and crouched, nudging the fallen body with his boot. Even dead, the priest's flesh twitched faintly, black veins pulsing as though searching for something to return to. "Who is she?" Kain asked.

Another laugh answered him. It came from the shadows. A second priest stepped into the lantern light, identical to the first. Blackened skin stretched tight over jutting bone. Eyes hollow and oil-dark. Rot woven so deeply into flesh it no longer looked like something added, but something grown. "Our Mother," he said calmly. "The one who will inherit what your kings have squandered."

Kain straightened slowly. "Say her name."

"Yssra," the priest replied without hesitation. "Goddess of Rot and Ruin." His smile widened as he spoke, reverent and terrible. "She does not need altars anymore. We are her will. We carry her into the body. Into the bone." His fingers flexed, black veins writhing beneath the skin. "We make soldiers who do not die. Cities that do not fall."

"She will rot this realm to its bones," the priest went on, voice steady with certainty. "Kingdom by kingdom. Soil. Stone. Blood. When everything that lives turns to rot and belongs to her, she will have a realm of her own. A true one." His breath hitched, almost worshipful. "And when it is ready, when the rot has fed her enough, she will tear the veil open and walk it."

Sparrow's voice cut through the dark, cold as iron. "And the rest of us?"

The priest smiled. "Slaves. Vessels. Offerings." His blackened nails scraped softly against the stone. "She will be stronger than the others then. Stronger than all of them together. They will not stop her. They cannot."

Kain leaned back on his heels, studying him. "And where do we find her?"

The priest laughed again. It was a broken, wet sound, like something already dead trying to breathe. "Did you not hear me boy? You don't find a goddess," he said. "She has made us to walk in her stead until she can grace us once more with her physical form." His hollow eyes gleamed.

Silence pressed in until Kain began to approach him, a smile ghosting his face. "Good," he said quietly as steel slid free of its sheath. "Then I don't have to hunt a god." He leaned in close, voice low enough to belong to the dark itself. "I just have to remind her children they can die."

The priest never finished his next breath.

Day Three. Then Four. Then the end of the week. They did not strike every night. They could not. Even Antonin bodies needed rest, and Bartoria's city would notice patterns. So they did it smart. They listened in taverns where soldiers talked too loose. They watched carts roll toward the docks at dawn, guarded by black-veined men whose wounds closed too fast. They took one man, then another, always alone, always quiet, always away from women.

They already knew one truth. They had learned it nights earlier, in the chaos with the priests, when steel had parted flesh and the rot had finally stilled. Beheading severed it. Not just the body, but the corruption itself. The realm was spared only when the head was taken from the thing the rot had claimed. But knowing what ended it was not enough. They needed to know if anything else worked. And more than that, if there was a way to strip the rot from a living body and leave the man behind. So they tested.

Fire made the black veins writhe and recoil. Salt burned them raw. Powder scraped from shrine stone sent the corruption shuddering beneath the skin, shrinking as if in pain. For a moment, it almost looked hopeful. Almost. But nothing held. A cut throat did not stop them. A blade through the heart only slowed the inevitable. Even steel driven cleanly through the eye bought no more than seconds. The Blessed would fall, twitch, and then drag breath back into ruined lungs, rising again with wet, wrong persistence. It seemed that once it took hold, it did not release.

"Seems like there's only one option to rid the rot," Kain said.

Sparrow's voice was flat as he nodded. "Beheading." Kain wiped blood from his knuckles. "Simple. Brutal. Honest."

On the seventh and final night, they hit the northern yard. Not to raze it. Not to play hero. To simply make Bartoria flinch. The yard was a wide training ground behind the tannery sheds, lit by lanterns hung from poles, the ground packed down into mud and blood. Men moved in lines, drilling with spears, their motions too synchronized. Too perfect. Like someone else was pulling the strings.

Kain and Sparrow approached in their stolen uniforms, heads down, walking in with the other guards. A captain shouted orders. Kain's stomach tightened at the sound. It sounded like the kind of man who believed he owned bodies.

Kain waited until they were close enough to see the captain's throat. Thick black veins. *Good.*

Sparrow murmured, "Now." Kain moved instantly. He drove his dagger into the captain's side, yanked him in close, and whispered into his ear. "This is for every hand you thought you could lay where ever you wanted." Then he took the captain's head clean off with one swing of his sword. The yard froze for only a heartbeat before chaos erupted. Men shouted. Blades came up. Black veined soldiers surged forward like wolves.

Kain laughed, low and mean. "Finally."

Sparrow's blade flashed beside him, precise and ruthless. They fought back to back, moving through the yard like a single machine. Kain took heads. Sparrow took legs, then finished with the neck. Steel met steel. Mud sprayed. Blood steamed faintly in lantern light. A Blessed soldier slammed into Kain, stronger than any normal man. Kain skidded back, boots digging into muck. The soldier grinned, mouth too wide. Kain spat blood and smiled back. "You are going to hate what I do next." He feinted left, stepped right, hooked the man's knee with his boot, and as the soldier stumbled, Kain drove his sword up under the jaw and ripped it through. The head tumbled into mud. The body dropped. Silence in that small pocket. Kain breathed hard. Pain sang in his ribs. He welcomed it. Pain meant he was still human.

Sparrow's voice cut through. "Kain, left." Kain ducked a spear, twisted, and took another head.

The lanterns rocked from the force of bodies slamming into poles. Somewhere near the fence, Kain saw movement that did not fit. Not soldiers. Not priests. Men tied to posts. Bare arms, bruised wrists. Recruits. Or captives. Sparrow saw them too.

He shouted, "Cut them free."

Kain's instincts screamed to finish the yard, to leave nothing standing. Then he thought of the dockhand's eyes. The woman in the alley. The princess who had crawled out of hell and still found the nerve to stand up straight. He made a choice.

"Two minutes," Kain barked. "Then we are gone." Sparrow nodded and sprinted for the posts. Kain held the line. He stood in the mud, sword dripping, and let the Blessed come to him. He took heads until his arms burned and his chest ached with the effort. He did not let them touch Sparrow. He did not let them reach the captives. He did not let them win. Bells began to ring in the distance. Real alarm now. He was certain more would be coming. Kain turned and saw Sparrow dragging two men toward the fence, the captives stumbling, half-blind with fear.

Sparrow shouted, "Now."

Kain backed toward them, still fighting. A Blessed soldier lunged. Kain sidestepped and hacked the head off in one clean stroke. Then he grabbed the fence, kicked a loose board free, and shoved the captives through. "Go," he snapped. "Run. Do not stop." One of the men stared at him, shaking. Kain bared his teeth. "Move!"

Precious seconds burned. Then they broke, scrambling into the dark. Sparrow slipped through the gap after them, blood streaked across his jaw. Kain followed last. He slammed the board back into place just as shouts rose beyond the yard. Boots thundered. Lantern light flared. But he didn't run yet. Instead, Kain turned, already reaching for his bow. One arrow came free. He struck the steel tip hard against the stone until sparks caught, then dragged it through the lantern oil spilled across the ground. The shaft flared to life in his hand, fire crawling up the fletching. With ease he drew back. Aiming not at men, but at the stacked barrels lining the tannery wall. Rendered fat. Lime. Pitch soaked hides. Everything that made the place reek and burn. The arrow flew and swiftly struck true. For half a heartbeat, nothing happened. Then the yard erupted.

Fire tore through the tannery in a violent roar, the blast hurling bodies and boards alike as flame climbed the walls and split the night. The ground shuddered. Heat slammed into Kain's back as he turned and ran. They vanished into the dark as the tannery burned behind them, smoke boiling into the sky like a warning.

Bartoria would wake to fire and fury. *Good.*

On the road out of the city, Sparrow rode in silence, wiping his blade clean with a strip of cloth already stiff with blood. Kain rode ahead, shoulders tight, eyes tracking every shadow along the broken road. Bartoria fell away behind them in layers of smoke and stone. They had taken what they could. They had proven what needed proving. In Kain's pack lay stolen prayer cloths marked with rot sigils, a ledger Sparrow had ripped from a priest's belt, names and payments scrawled in a tight, deliberate hand. Routes. Ports. Shrines. Proof that this sickness was not chance or curse. It was business.

They still did not have Theron's body. Kain had searched the yards, the shrines, the pits, the docks. Nothing. No bones to bring home. He locked that grief away where it belonged. Later. When his hands were not needed for war.

Sparrow broke the silence at last. "We did not finish it."

Kain's mouth curved, humorless. "No. But we cut it deep enough to bleed."

Sparrow nodded once. "Do you believe him? That they have priests across the realm?"

"Yes," Kain said. "And that means this isn't a border problem. It's a realm problem."

Sparrow exhaled slowly. "Okteria will want to burn it out."

"She will," Kain agreed. "The question is whether her hatred for Yssra outweighs her hatred for the southern kingdoms."

Sparrow glanced at him. "You mean Graystonia."

Kain did not deny it. "If this rot spreads the way they claim, alliances stop being optional."

Silence stretched again, heavier this time. The kind that came when both men were thinking the same thing and neither wanted to say it first. Sparrow finally did. "They'll think the war is over."

Kain's jaw set. "Because a king died."

"Because banners fell," Sparrow added. "Because people like to believe blood buys peace."

Kain let out a short breath. "It buys time. Nothing more."

"And Layla?" Sparrow asked, careful now.

Kain's grip tightened on the reins. Not to cause pain, but focus. "She's standing in the path of this," he said. "Whether she knows it yet or not." Sparrow waited. "When the rot reaches Graystonia," Kain continued, voice lower, colder, "those council men will die in their chairs still arguing about tradition. And she'll be left standing in a room full of corpses."

"A queen without an army," Sparrow said quietly.

"No," Kain shook his head once. "A weapon they were too blind to realize they already had."

Sparrow looked at him then, something unreadable flickering through his eyes. "You care."

Kain didn't turn. "I pay attention."

The Antonin forest rose ahead of them, dark and waiting. Home. Kain tightened his grip on the reins. "This is a start."

Sparrow nodded. "A start."

Kain's grin came slow and predatory, the familiar edge settling back into place. "Good," he said. "Then we raise something big enough to cut rot out by the root."

He rode on beneath the trees, the road narrowing, the night closing around them like a vow. Behind them, Bartoria kept burning.

# Chapter Eight

**PART II**

*When paths converge once more, is it by choice... or by destiny's hand?*

# Chapter Nine

*L*<sup>ayla.</sup>

Days after her talk with her mother, Layla found herself walking beside Ciana through the streets of Drelith. The city was rebuilding, slowly and stubbornly, as though it refused to remain broken. Scaffolding climbed the faces of stone once blackened by fire. Smiths worked in the open, their hammers ringing steady against anvils, sparks flashing like brief stars where flames had once devoured entire streets. Merchants had returned to the market square with cautious optimism, stalls half full, voices still low, as if the city remembered how easily sound had once carried screams.

People watched her as she passed. Not with awe. Not with fear. But with need. Layla felt it settle beneath her ribs, steady and insistent. She stopped near a toppled cart, its wheel cracked clean through. An older woman struggled beside it, tugging at a bundle of warped boards.

"Here," Layla said, already bending. She braced the cart while the woman slid the boards free.

"Thank you," the woman breathed, surprise flickering across her face when she looked up and truly saw her. "I didn't think..." She stopped herself, shaking her head. "It doesn't matter. Thank you."

Layla smiled, warm and easy. "It does. And you're welcome." They worked together in quiet rhythm. Another woman joined them. Then a man. Someone laughed when the cart finally righted, crooked but usable. Layla felt it then, the small lift in her chest. The ease of it. Hands doing something useful. Real. Nearby, Ciana knelt with a group of women repairing torn awnings, needle flashing as canvas was drawn tight again. She worked quickly, efficiently, seemingly focused and saying little.

A young mother hovered near Layla, a toddler balanced on her hip. "Are you staying long?" she asked, tentative but hopeful.

Layla wiped her hands on her skirts. "As long as we can."

The woman nodded, relief softening her features. "It helps. Seeing you here." She hesitated. "It reminds us we weren't forgotten."

Something warm and aching bloomed in Layla's chest. "We remember," she said, and meant it.

They moved on. Layla lifted stones slick with mortar, passed water to laboring hands, steadied beams while others hammered them into place. Sweat dampened her hair. Dust streaked her sleeves. She did not notice the time passing. Only the work. Only the way her breath slowed. The way the noise around her became something like harmony. For the first time in weeks, she felt quiet inside.

At the edge of the square, she found Ciana tying off the final knot of an awning. Layla stepped closer. "You're good at this," she said lightly.

Ciana's mouth curved, just barely. "I had to be."

Layla waited. "I'm glad we're here," she said, softer now. "Together."

Ciana did not look at her. She tugged the knot once more, then stood. "It's good for them." Not *us.* Layla heard the unspoken words as Ciana moved away to help someone else, the distance settling back into place like a door quietly closed. Layla watched her go, the ache returning, but it did not undo the peace she had found. She turned back to the square, to the work still waiting. This, she realized, was where she belonged. Not on a dais. Not behind sitting quietly and idly, but here. Helping. Listening. Holding the weight with them. And for now, that was enough.

The days and weeks that followed settled into a rhythm Layla came to treasure. Her favorite hours were spent in Drelith, sleeves rolled, hands aching, working beside the people who had lost the most. She helped clear rubble, carried water, listened to grievances that had no easy answers. She learned which families needed grain, which roofs still leaked, which streets grew quiet too early at dusk. There were no speeches. No titles spoken. Only trust built slowly, honestly, in the shared weight of effort. Those days grounded her. Gave her something solid to stand on. And when she was not there, she worked just as carefully.

Back within Graystonia's walls, Layla returned to her role with practiced precision. Lessons by day. Silence by choice. She listened when doors were left ajar. Remembered names, numbers, patterns. She studied the way power moved through rooms, unseen but absolute. The contrast sharpened her resolve. Drelith taught her what leadership required. The castle taught her how it was denied.

Between the two, her plan took shape.

One morning, Layla finally mustered the courage she had been gathering for weeks. She had watched the library long enough to know its habits. The way the librarians gathered near the front desk during midmorning, arguing softly over ledgers and catalogues. The moments when the back corridors emptied, when footsteps faded and vigilance dulled beneath routine. She knew she would have minutes at best. Enough for a gamble. Not enough for regret.

She entered the library as she always did, posture perfect, expression mild, a harmless volume tucked beneath her arm as camouflage. The air smelled of dust and ink and polished stone. She offered a polite nod to the nearest librarian and drifted toward the shelves, her pulse steady, her steps unhurried. At the far end of the room, half hidden between towering bookcases, lay the narrow corridor she had never been permitted to enter. No sign marked it. No warning was needed. Women simply did not go there.

Layla waited until the last clerk disappeared into a side alcove, then turned. She slipped into the corridor and did not look back. The restricted archives were different. The air was thicker, older, layered with the scent of leather and parchment and something faintly metallic beneath it. Shelves stretched from floor to ceiling, crowded with volumes worn thin by generations of hands. These were not books meant for display. These were books meant to be used. War journals. Campaign records. Border disputes scrawled in ink that had bled through time. She reached for the first book without hesitation, then another, then a third, stacking them carefully against her chest.

She did not read the titles. There was no time. Her arms were full when the voice cut through the stillness.

"Princess." The word cracked like a lash and Layla froze. Finally, she turned slowly to find a librarian standing at the mouth of the corridor, his expression already twisted with disdain. His gaze flicked to the books in her arms, then back to her face.

"You do not belong here," he said coldly.

Layla straightened, tightening her hold. "I was only..."

"Only overstepping," he interrupted coldly. His voice carried now, edged enough to draw attention. "These texts are restricted for a reason. They are not meant for you."

Heat surged up her spine, hot and furious. "They are records of our kingdom," she said carefully. "I only wished to learn..."

"To learn what?" he snapped. "To play at war?" His mouth curled. "These books are for men trained to understand them. Not for girls indulging foolish fantasies." The words struck hard, precise. "Knowledge like this," he continued, stepping closer, "is not suited to a woman's mind. You may be the king's daughter, but that does not grant you the right to trespass where you have no place."

Layla's jaw locked. Every instinct screamed at her to fight back. To remind him who she was. To demand what had been denied to her since birth. But reluctantly, she swallowed it all. Then slowly, deliberately, she turned and returned each book to its place. The weight leaving her arms felt heavier than carrying it. "I understand," she said evenly.

The librarian sniffed, satisfaction settling into his features. "See that you do."

Layla lifted her chin and walked out of the archives with her pace unbroken, her expression serene, every inch the obedient princess they expected. Yet inside, something shattered. She did not slow until she reached the main aisle. Her hands trembled faintly at her sides, fury roaring beneath her skin, hot and helpless and contained. This was the truth of the castle. This was how it still stood. Power wrapped in tradition and knowledge barred by silence.

"Princess Layla."

Her breath left her in a sharp gasp as the voice reached her ears and her mind caught up with the present. It was familiar... Deep...

She righted herself quickly and peered up. To her shock, there he stood: Sir Ryker Jameson. He looked carved from the same marble that lined the castle walls: tall, formidable, every inch polished perfection. If she hadn't seen him broken and bleeding in the wreckage of the ballroom, his lifeblood soaking the marble...She would never have believed this was the same man. There was no trace of ruin now. No scar. No weakness. He looked reborn, sanctified, as if the Gods themselves had remade him to fit her mother's design. Whole. Regal. Every inch the future king that Queen Raynera so desperately wanted.

He looked at her with the calm certainty of a man who believed the world already belonged to him. Each step was measured, controlled, deliberate. The faint gleam of his armor caught the light as though it too bowed to him. He swiftly stepped back and placed a hand over his heart, bending at the waist in a bow deep enough to show respect, but not so deep as to forget his rank. Layla inclined her head in return, graceful, precise. The movement was small, the kind born of years of training, enough to acknowledge his courtesy without surrendering her place. Their gazes met when he straightened, and for a moment, she saw warmth in his eyes. Relief. Even joy. The kind that expected to be echoed. But Layla felt nothing. Still, she stood taller. Shoulders square. Chin lifted. Her fingers folded neatly at her waist, her expression a portrait of poise. The mask slipped into place with the ease of habit, its edges seamless, unbreakable.

"It is wonderful to see you again. As it always is," Ryker said, voice steady but full of feeling.

"And you, Sir Jameson," she replied, smiling the way a princess should.

"Ryker," he corrected gently. "Please. Always call me Ryker."

"As you wish... Ryker." The name tasted like ash, but her smile was flawless.

He studied her, and for a moment, his composure cracked into something brighter. "I was overjoyed by the news," he said, that sincerity flickering like a candle through his formal tone. "To be chosen, it is the greatest honor. That you would find me a suitable husband, a suitable king... and one day, father."

Layla inclined her head, polite, practiced. "The honor is shared." The words came easily, though they rang hollow in her chest.

He smiled, clearly heartened, and continued, "Your mother informed me of the plans. The wedding will be held in two weeks' time. Enough notice for the lords to gather and witness both the crowning and the vows."

*Two weeks.* The air left her lungs in a quiet, invisible rush. There would be no time to think. No time to breathe. The crown, the vows, the throne. All decided before the next moon. Still, she nodded. Graystonia needed a king. And if Ryker could be that, strong, decisive, commanding, then she would not stand in the way of what the kingdom required. As for her place beside him. She would earn it.

He seemed to study her again, his gaze softening. "I know our wedding will follow my return from service," he said, "but I would like to spend time with you before then. To know you better, if you'll allow it." There was gentleness in his voice, honest and without guile. He meant what he said. That should have mattered. That should have stirred something. But all Layla felt was the faint echo of gratitude. Gratitude that he was kind, that he was good, that he was trying at least.

"Of course," she said automatically, because it was expected. Ryker's smile deepened, warm and approving. He truly meant to do right by her. She could see it in the sincerity of his eyes, in the careful way he spoke, as though every word were weighed for her comfort. He was an honorable man. Loyal. The kind who would never raise his voice, never stray, never shame her name.

And somehow, that made it worse.

She wanted more than loyalty and politeness. She wanted partnership. She wanted someone who saw her not as a symbol of grace to stand beside, but as an equal who could fight, decide, and lead in her own right. She was tired of shadows, tired of watching men move the world while she was expected to smile and watch it turn. Ryker would do right by her it seemed. But would he let her do right by their kingdom?

So, she tested the waters. "Have there been any updates on Sir Charles?"

The change was immediate. His jaw flexed, his shoulders tightening ever so slightly beneath his uniform. "Regrettably, he has not yet been captured," Ryker said, his tone even, though thinner now, strained. "Another search party has already been dispatched. We will not cease until he is found, and when he is, judgment will be swift." His gaze remained steady. "You needn't concern yourself with such matters, Princess. Especially not ones like this."

It was a measured response. Respectful. Controlled. But beneath it, Layla heard what he didn't say: *This isn't your place.* Layla's fingers curled slightly in her skirts, though her smile didn't falter. "Of course," she murmured sweetly, though her teeth itched to grind.

He had answered her, at least. That was something. A concession measured in inches, not miles.

When he looked at her again, his expression held sincerity and purpose, the kind forged by duty and worn with conviction It was an expression another woman might have treasured. Layla felt only the quiet closing of a door.

Devotion shaped by obligation was not what she wanted. She wanted fire. Challenge. A partner who did not shield her from the weight of the world, but trusted her to carry it beside him. Someone who saw her not as a princess to be preserved, but as a queen in the making.

The thought landed heavy and final... but before she could bury it, something inside her shifted. The abyss she had lived with, silent, endless, unfeeling, began to stir. Not a jolt. Not a spark. A slow awakening, like something ancient deep within her bones had begun to stir. It wasn't for Ryker, not for his honor or his vows. This was older. Wilder. A pull that defied reason. Her body knew before her mind did. Instinct straightened her spine, her breath stilling as if the world had suddenly gone too quiet. She turned, drawn to the sight waiting down the hall that shattered everything she thought she'd buried.

Sparrow walked with his familiar measured composure, dark hair tied back, the perfect soldier in stride. But it was the man beside him who unraveled her. Broader now. Harder. Every inch of him forged by survival. Brutal. Beautiful. Unmistakable.

Kain.

Alive.

Here.

Her chest tightened, her pulse stumbling as the world seemed to tilt toward him. Gods, he was different. The same man who'd bled for her, who'd held her when she thought she might shatter, was remade now into something sharper, deadlier. The unruly mane of golden hair that had once brushed his shoulders was gone. The sides of his head were shaved clean, the top bound into a tight braid that fell down his back, revealing the cut of his jaw and the promise of a scar she knew too well.

The mark of their fall. His eyes were the same, though. Wicked, bright, and alive. The kind that saw too much.

Her mind betrayed her first, flashing images she had buried a hundred times over. The sound of his laugh. The weight of his arm pulling her close. The way her heart had pounded against his chest as he breathed, barely alive, and she had prayed, begged, the Gods not to take him from her. And now here he was. Alive. Whole. Infuriatingly so. Layla forced her spine straighter. Every muscle locked into royal poise. She needed to smother this. Whatever this was. The pull in her chest, the heat creeping up her throat. She could *not* afford it, not for him, not for anyone. Not when she was engaged to the future king. Not when her sisters and her mother needed her. Not when the memory of Theron still haunted her in the quiet hours of the night.

She inhaled slowly, steadying her voice before it could tremble. She would be proper. Composed. Professional. The perfect princess. Because if she slipped, if she even looked at him the way her body wanted to, she'd never recover.

So, when Sparrow and Kain drew closer, she smiled the way queens were meant to smile: soft, measured, untouchable. Her hands folded neatly before her, the picture of grace and poise. But then he looked at her. Those piercing emerald eyes found hers and held. And for one traitorous heartbeat, she swore the world forgot how to breathe. That slow, knowing glance that seemed to strip past the titles and the silk, reaching for the woman beneath it all. The one she'd sworn no one would ever see again. Layla's throat tightened. She would not falter. Not here. Not now.

So she smiled wider, too wide, too polished, and dipped her head in perfect greeting, even as something deep within her twisted in defiance.

"Hello, Dove."

That name. Soft. Dangerous. Intimate. Her composure slipped, barely, but enough to feel the tremor ripple beneath her skin before she snapped it back into place. She summoned every ounce of poise drilled into her since birth, each muscle locking into the polished façade her mother demanded.

"Hello... Prince Drakaren." The title burned like acid on her tongue. And the instant it left her lips, she saw it hit. His brow arched, the muscle in his jaw ticking like he'd been struck. For one heartbeat too long, she met his eyes, emerald and unreadable, and it was a mistake. A terrible, exhilarating mistake.

She tore her gaze away, forcing her voice into calm diplomacy. "And hello, Sparrow. It is wonderful to see you both again." Sparrow inclined his head, every inch the soldier, but something in his eyes flickered, unease, discomfort, maybe even pity. It made her stomach twist. Before she could ask why they were here, a pointed cough shattered the silence. *Gods. Ryker!* She'd forgotten he was standing beside her.

"Oh my, forgive me. Where are my manners?" Her voice brightened instantly, smooth and brittle all at once. She turned slightly, the mask snapping neatly back into place. "Ryker, this is Sparrow of the Antonin tribe, and Prince Kain Drakaren, son of Queen Okteria. Formidable warriors, both. They saved Queen Raynera and the princesses." Her gaze slid back, inevitably, to the men before her. To *him*. "This," she continued, her tone controlled though her throat had tightened, "is Sir

Ryker Jameson. A member of our royal guard and... soon to be King of Graystonia. My betrothed."

The words landed like a blade between them. The corridor seemed to draw in on itself until the sound of her pulse drowned out everything else. Kain's head tilted, that wolfish angle she remembered all too well. Calculating. Assessing. Predatory. An instinctive reaction, unguarded and immediate.

For a heartbeat, it looked as though he might speak. Then he didn't. His jaw set. Something dark and volatile flickered behind his eyes before vanishing beneath iron control. The shift was subtle, but she felt it all the same. Rage, leashed tight enough to vibrate. The kind that did not need volume to be heard.

His gaze locked onto hers, unwavering, and it was as if the rest of the world fell away. The guards. The hall. Even Ryker beside her ceased to exist. Layla's breath stilled. Her spine stiffened. She could feel the faint tremor in her hands and laced them tighter together to hide it. Under that stare, the mask she wore felt paper-thin, fragile enough to tear with a single word. And he was still saying nothing. Which somehow made it worse.

Then, mercifully, footsteps whispered down the corridor. The queen's handmaid appeared, immaculate and composed. She bowed slightly to the Antonin warriors, her tone carrying all the authority of her mistress. "Prince Drakaren. Sparrow," she said, smooth as silk. "Her Majesty awaits you in our council room and requests your presence immediately."

The handmaid stepped aside. And for a moment, no one moved. Layla looked to Kain and realized he was still watching her. Not the queen's summons. Not the guards. Just her. Sparrow reached out and clapped a hand to Kain's shoulder, a quiet prompt to follow. But Kain's gaze never left Layla.

"Aren't you coming?"

The question hit harder than it should have. For one perilous second, she forgot how to breathe. Her pulse skittered, traitorous, but her mother's voice, iron-clad and unforgiving, cut through the noise. *Know your place. Remember your duty.* Layla straightened, folding her hands before her skirts. Her smile was soft but practiced, her tone the very picture of composure. "It is not my place to attend such meetings. I have lessons to see to."

"It was wonderful to see you both again," she added, voice honeyed and hollow. She inclined her head in graceful farewell, the perfect princess, the dutiful daughter, every line of her body trained in obedience.

Before leaving, she turned slightly to Ryker. Her expression gentled, polite and poised, and he met her with that quiet, honorable warmth. Steady, respectful, the kind of devotion that expected nothing but duty in return. But when her gaze, despite herself, flicked back to Kain, the air itself shifted. His stare wasn't warm or steady. It was raw. Untamed. The look of a man who remembered *exactly* who she was underneath the mask.

For a single heartbeat, she felt everything. His touch, his laughter, the spark of heat that had once tangled between them. Then she blinked it away. Spine straight, chin high, smile serene. A princess. A future queen. But deep down, she knew. Whatever burned behind those emerald eyes wasn't courtly or kind. It was the promise of chaos. The call of a wolf that had found her scent again. And wolves... were nothing but trouble.

THE BLOOM OF THE BLESSED
IS BORN IN DECAY

"Let every household yield one,
that all may rise."

It is commanded that each household
offer at least one soul to the Path of
Blessing. For every child given, every
mother surrendered, every kin devoted to
divine service, so too shall the family
ascend in favor. A home that offers none
shall find itself withering under the
weight of its own selfishness.

-BY THE SACRED LAW OF LUMIREN-

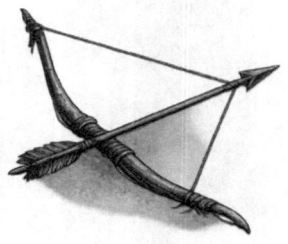

# Chapter Ten

*K*ain.

Kain watched her walk away, chin high, every step neat and measured, the perfect little princess gliding across the hall as if she were carved from polished marble.

*Betrothed.* The word struck fast and hard, a flare of heat igniting low in his chest before he could stop it. His first instinct was rage. It came on sudden and ugly. Then sense cut in, just as quickly. Layla did not bend easily. She did not submit without reason. If she stood bound to another man's future, it was most likely not by choice. Not truly. The thought cooled some of the fire, forced it down into something tighter, more controlled. But it did not extinguish it.

Because understanding *why* she endured it did nothing to soften the fact that she had been claimed. Decided for. Boxed into silk and ceremony by hands that had probably never seen her fight, never heard her snarl, never watched her stand unbroken in the dark.

It had taken him only a heartbeat to see the mask. Too perfect. Too careful. The stiffness in her shoulders. The precise placement of her hands. That wasn't poise. It was survival. Why was she being made to wear it? What was she angling for? Or had the choice already been stripped from her entirely?

The questions only fed the heat curling in his chest. Whatever the truth was, he would find it. He would pry it loose piece by piece if he had to. Logic continued to tell him this was not her doing. But instinct told him it was still wrong. And the rage that had flared at the word *betrothed* refused to be quieted.

Sparrow nudged his shoulder again, murmuring something about the queen waiting. Diplomacy. Duty. Kain barely registered the words. His eyes remained fixed on the corner where Layla had disappeared, the echo of her footsteps still etched into the marble like a challenge. She wanted distance. *Fine. She could try.* But she would learn soon enough. Kain Drakaren did not do distance. Not with her.

A slow, feral grin tugged at his mouth as he finally turned to follow Sparrow. He would find out what she was hiding. And when he did... Gods help anyone foolish enough to stand in his way.

The war room of Graystonia was every bit as polished and pompous as Kain expected. Gilded trim chased the walls, the table long enough to seat two dozen self-important bastards, and a map of Caeleria stretched across the center like a battlefield waiting to be spilled on. The air smelled of beeswax, old parchment, and men who had been sitting too long in their power.

Kain waited, expecting Queen Raynera to take her seat at the head of the table. But when they entered, it wasn't her who claimed it. It was *him*. Ryker.

The polished knight, clean-shaven, perfect posture, shoulders squared like he'd been born to the throne, sat himself in the high-backed chair at the head of the table without hesitation. And the queen... the queen *stood* beside him. Kain blinked once, slow and deliberate, as his mind caught up with what his eyes were seeing. The queen of Graystonia. Cold and unflinching. Raynera Eradellian reduced to standing at her own war council while her would-be son-in-law played king.

Most of the councilmen, lords, advisors, overfed soldiers, had already sat, muttering among themselves like hens in silk. Only Kain and Sparrow remained standing, the Antonin way demanding they wait for the highest rank to sit first. Apparently, Graystonia had forgotten that lesson.

Raynera finally turned to them and gestured with a graceful hand. "Please," she said, voice cool and measured. Kain's jaw ticked, but he obeyed. The carved chair creaked beneath his weight as he sat, Sparrow following silently at his side. But the moment he saw that the queen *remained standing*, hands clasped lightly before her, posture immaculate, expression unreadable, something hot and acrid curled in his gut. This wasn't subservience. It was politics. Control, quiet and absolute, wrapped in silk and ceremony. And it set his teeth on edge.

Then *Ryker* spoke first.

"So," the man began smoothly, voice even, professional. "To what do we owe the honor of your visit, Prince Drakaren?"

Kain's jaw flexed once, the only crack in his composure before he leaned back, folding his arms, gaze sliding right past him to the queen. "You look better," he said conversationally. "Health suits you. I'm glad to see it." Raynera inclined her head with a faint, practiced smile. The compliment was not lost, but neither was the challenge in ignoring her future son-in-law.

Ryker's jaw tightened. "You didn't answer my question," he said evenly. Still trying for diplomacy, *poor bastard.* "Why are you here?"

Kain didn't even glance at him this time. He tipped his chair back a fraction, boots planted wide, and gestured to Sparrow. Sparrow's tone was smooth, formal, the perfect balance between soldier and emissary. "We come on behalf of Queen Okteria of Antonin," he began. "To discuss an alliance between our kingdoms. The situation in the north has worsened."

Kain instinctively leaned forward, elbows on the table, voice cutting through the low hum of council whispers. "Like your daughter once asked of my people," he said, his gaze locking with Raynera's. "She wanted unity long before any of us were ready to hear it. Seems she was born a leader even then." The room went still. The queen's face didn't move, but the faintest flicker passed behind her eyes.

Ryker cleared his throat, shifting in his chair. "Princess Layla is wise beyond her years, certainly," he said stiffly, "but matters of state are decided by..."

Kain's eyes slid toward him, a slow, predatory drag that silenced the man mid-sentence. "By men?" he asked mildly. "I noticed there aren't any other women in this room. Not a one." A beat of silence. Only Sparrow's eyes flicked toward him in warning. Kain grinned, lazy and lethal. "Strange. In Antonin, we let the ones with sense speak too."

That earned a murmur around the table, half-scandalized, half-entertained. Raynera raised a hand and the noise died instantly. "You'll forgive our customs, Prince Drakaren," she said evenly. "In Graystonia, women do not take seats in councils of war. We serve the realm in other ways."

Kain tilted his head. "Then you might want to fix that," he murmured. "Because from what I've seen, your daughter's already done more for this kingdom than half the men in it." That landed. Raynera didn't respond. What she withheld spoke louder than any retort. The air held tight, brittle, waiting for someone to breathe first.

Sparrow was the one who did. His voice cut through the tension, steady but worn at the edges. "The north is deteriorating faster than predicted," he said, the faint rasp betraying his exhaustion. "Bartoria is not the only threat pressing south, perhaps not even the worst one." That stilled the council's quiet rustling. A few men looked up from their notes; others went pale. Even Raynera's polished composure shifted, subtle but there.

Sparrow went on, measured and precise, the words dropping like stones into still water. "You may think Bartoria's injured, broken after the siege here, after their army fell in this very castle, after their king's head rolled across his own chamber floor. But they're not broken. If anything, they've become indestructible. And that's because of Lumiren and in turn, Yssra." A ripple of disbelief ran through the council chamber, low voices, sharp scoffs, muttered prayers. One man's quill snapped in his fingers. Sparrow didn't raise his voice, but the weight of it filled the room. "When Bartoria's king fell, Lumiren moved fast. Within days, their banners replaced Bartoria's. Their priests took command of what was left of the army. Now, Bartoria kneels to Lumiren and Lumiren kneels to Yssra. They call her their divine queen, their living god. And she's given them power no mortal has carried in centuries." He let the words settle. The fire popped once, startlingly loud in the stillness.

Sparrow continued quietly. "She's gone beyond the small gifts the gods sometimes scatter among us. Yssra's priests claim she has *chosen* them, filled them with her magic, her corruption. Their ranks are full of men and creatures bearing what they call *Yssra's Blessings*. We've seen it up close. Men laced with black veins, stripped of thought and feeling. It's not disease, it's magic. Corruption disguised as endurance. They heal too fast. Die too slow. And every time they survive, they lose another piece of what made them human." Someone cursed under his breath. Another made the sign of warding against the gods.

Sparrow pressed on, unflinching. "Her priests call themselves her hands in this world. They burn villages that refuse her mark. They take prisoners not for ransom, but for worship. And they are coming south."

He straightened then, meeting the queen's eyes, voice dropping to a final, unyielding note. "They're coming soon."

Kain watched the faces in the room carefully. The queen's stillness. Ryker's attempt to look thoughtful while clearly struggling to keep up. The councilmen whispering behind rings and wine cups. It was all theater, and he hated theater. Ryker finally spoke again. "Graystonia will, of course, consider the matter carefully. There is much to think about...supplies, treaties, rebuilding efforts..."

Kain nearly rolled his eyes. "Take all the time you need," he deadpanned. His voice low but audible enough to slice through the table. "Meanwhile, the world burns."

Raynera's gaze snapped to his, cool and commanding. For a heartbeat, the air thickened between them, two predators measuring the distance between diplomacy and war. Then she smiled, small and decisive. "You will both be given rooms here at the castle. We will resume this discussion tomorrow, once my council has reviewed your proposal in full." Translation: *dismissed*.

Sparrow inclined his head respectfully. "We thank you, Your Majesty."

Kain didn't move immediately. His gaze lingered across the men all in their seats. Firmly believing the one of them should have been filled by Layla. And gods, the thought of her standing somewhere in this very castle pretending to be small made something sharp twist in his chest.

He finally rose, chair scraping back, his smirk returning like armor. "Appreciate the hospitality," he said. "And the conversation." His eyes cut briefly toward Ryker. "Some of it, anyway." The man's jaw tightened, but Kain didn't wait for a retort. He turned, cloak snapping behind him as he followed Sparrow from the room.

Once the heavy doors shut, Sparrow exhaled. "You couldn't just behave for one meeting, could you?"

Kain's grin was all teeth. "I did behave," he said. "Didn't kill anyone. Yet."

He cast one last glance down the corridor, toward where he knew Layla would be, swallowed by etiquette and lessons and expectations. He told himself he was here for alliances. For negotiations. For the future of Antonin and the balance of power that followed war. And perhaps some of that was true. But deep down, beneath reason and restraint, he knew there was another pull at work. One he was not yet ready to name. One that had far more to do with her than he would ever admit.

THE BLOOM OF THE BLESSED
IS BORN IN DECAY

"Let silence be the fate of those who poison the air with doubt."

Any speech that contradicts the sanctified decrees, questions divine selection, or disrupts unity among the faithful is deemed a corruption of the holy tongue. Whispers of heresy or unblessed philosophy shall be cleansed through binding silence. Be it gag, branding, or the surgical removal of the offending tongue.

-BY THE SACRED LAW OF LUMIREN-

# Chapter Eleven

*L* *ayla.*

Layla could not sit still. Afternoon light spilled across the study table, warm and golden, glinting off polished glass and stacked scrolls. Ink pooled on the parchment before her, a dark, uneven blot where her quill had stilled mid-sentence. Somewhere behind her, a tutor droned on about proper seating arrangements and ceremonial precedence, but the words slid past unheard.

Kain Drakaren and Sparrow are here. In Graystonia. That alone was enough to set the castle on edge. Antonin did not send warriors like that without cause. Not after Bartoria. Not after victory was supposed to be certain. Their king dead. Their armies scattered. If Antonin's finest had crossed borders, then something had gone wrong. Something dangerous. Layla felt it in her bones, the way one felt a storm before the first thunder cracked. That low, vibrating certainty beneath the skin that the world was about to shift.

The council chambers had been sealed since dawn. Guards lined the corridors thick as brambles, and servants moved through the halls with their heads down, voices hushed. Her mother had not summoned her. Of course she hadn't. She would not be allowed in that room. Her knee bounced beneath the table, tension coiling tighter with every passing minute.

"Stop fidgeting," Ciana murmured without lifting her eyes from her embroidery, her tone as sharp as the needle flashing between her fingers.

Layla stilled instantly. Spine straight. Shoulders back. She folded her hands neatly in her lap and smoothed her skirts. A perfect princess. A perfect lie, she reminded herself, as her thoughts began to spiral once more.

Ryker was back. Which meant this was it. The only path Graystonia would ever accept. She would never rule in her own right. That truth had been made brutally clear. But if she could stand beside him, if she could prove her worth slowly and carefully, then perhaps she could still lead. Not openly. Not alone. But through him. With him. It was not the future she had once imagined. It was the only one left.

*Two weeks.*

In two weeks, she would be crowned. And in two weeks, she would be bound for life to a man she barely knew. A necessary union. A political solution. The price of peace. Her mind understood it. Her body recoiled. The thought settled heavy in her stomach, stealing the air from her lungs. She had accepted duty. She had chosen her kingdom. But somewhere deep and private, something in her still broke at the idea of being forever shackled to a life she had not chosen for herself. And that crack...that weakness she despised... was where her thoughts betrayed her and shifted to the very man it shouldn't. Kain Drakaren.

Layla couldn't help but grind her teeth and shake her head. *Of course* he would return like a storm she wasn't ready for. Arrogant. Reckless. Infuriating. *Alive.* She had seen him only briefly, rough-edged and unrepentant, his presence filling the space like it always had. His hair shorn now, his posture harder, as if the past month had honed him into something even more dangerous.

Her pulse betrayed her. It always did. No. This was not about him, she reminded herself. It couldn't be. She was getting flustered because if Kain was here, demanding council time alongside Sparrow, then something was wrong. Very wrong. Something that would affect Antonin. Graystonia. The fragile balance holding the realm together. And she would not be allowed to hear a word of it.

She was not at all frustrated by whatever confusion had once existed between her and Kain. Whatever it was didn't matter. It *could not* matter. She had accepted Ryker's hand. She had chosen duty. She had chosen her kingdom. Plus, this was not about want, she convinced herself. It was about knowing. About protecting her people. About refusing to sit idle while men decided the fate of the world beyond her walls.

She pressed her palms flat to the desk, grounding herself. "It's nothing," she murmured, more to herself than to Ciana. "Just tired."

But even as she said it, her gaze drifted to the window overlooking the courtyard below, where guards shifted their posts and the echo of armored footsteps carried upward. Her pulse quickened again. She would not go to him. She would not seek him out. She would not make another mistake. And yet, beneath the porcelain stillness she wore so well, something wild and treacherous refused to stay buried. A memory of laughter in the dark. A steady hand at her back. A presence that had never asked her to be smaller.

Layla pushed to her feet. "I need air," she said, already moving.

Ciana looked up then, her needle pausing mid-stitch, brows knitting in quiet curiosity as Layla crossed the room with more haste than grace. Layla did not slow. Did not look back. She told herself it was nothing more than restlessness. A need to calm her thoughts. To reclaim her poise.

The garden received her in silence. Cool air filled her lungs as she stepped onto the gravel path, crisp and clean, carrying the scent of damp leaves and distant smoke. Autumn had settled deep into the grounds, all burnished gold and quiet decay. She had always loved this season. The pause between endings and beginnings. The moment where the world seemed to hold its breath. She tried to do the same. Her steps slowed. Her shoulders eased. The chill kissed her cheeks, grounding her, pulling her back into herself. For a few heartbeats, she focused only on the sound of her boots against stone, the whisper of leaves stirring overhead. But her thoughts would not be stilled.

Every time she closed her eyes, she saw the council doors. Shut tight. Guards standing watch. Voices murmuring beyond her reach. She could almost hear Ryker's measured tone as he spoke of borders and defenses and futures she was not allowed to shape. It set her teeth on edge. Ryker was brave. Loyal. A devoted soldier. But ruling was not the same as fighting. Her father had known that. He had understood the weight of power, the cost of choosing wrong. Could Ryker? Could he carry a kingdom on his shoulders when war loomed again, when peace proved fragile and thin? She needed to be sure. For Graystonia. For Antonin. For the realm itself.

Her pace quickened, leaves crunching beneath her boots. The motion helped. The cold helped. Her thoughts began to align, focused and purposeful, ideas taking shape. Until she saw him.

A tall figure leaned against the marble pillar near the fountain, half-drenched in sunlight and shadow. His stance was lazy, but nothing about him was idle. Confidence rolled off him in quiet waves, infuriating and unmistakable. The wind tugged at the shortened strands of his golden hair as he turned. Emerald eyes met hers. Alive with mischief. With danger. Her breath instantly caught. *Gods. No.*

One glance, and the fragile calm she'd built cracked apart. Her pulse stumbled, tripping over itself as heat and memory tangled in her chest. She told herself it was only the surprise of seeing him here in the one place she'd sought peace. That it was frustration, not the sudden flip in her belly or the spark racing up her spine. She told herself all those things. And not one of them was true.

Every instinct screamed at her to turn, to walk the other way, to flee before he said a word. Because she knew what happened when Kain Drakaren looked at her like that. The last time, it had left her breathless, reckless, and far too close to forgetting who she was supposed to be. But she couldn't run. Not this time. Not here, in her mother's garden, where composure was her only armor. So she lifted her chin, smoothing the tremor from her hands. She would nod, greet him politely, and glide away as if her heart weren't pounding hard enough to bruise her ribs. *Yes.*

*That was what she would do.* Then his gaze caught hers, direct, knowing, predatory, and every bit of that plan went straight to hell.

"Good evening, Prince Drakaren," she said, her voice soft but perfectly measured as she dipped her head and tried to move past. But Kain moved too, stepping directly into her path. The air shifted with him, heavy, charged, swallowing her composure whole. She stopped short, forced to look almost straight up at him. His arrogance rolled off him like thunder.

"Aren't you going to ask why I'm here, little Dove?" His voice was low and threaded with mockery.

Layla's throat tightened. "No," she said, steady but faint. "It is none of my business."

Kain's smirk deepened, infuriating, deliberate. "None of your business," he echoed softly, as if tasting the absurdity of it. His gaze flicked over her, the polished posture, the folded hands, the flawless mask she'd rebuilt brick by brick since her last breathless memory of him. He reached out and caught a loose strand of her hair, winding it lazily around his finger, studying it like a question he already knew the answer to.

Her stomach flipped traitorously before she jerked back, pulling the strand free. "If you'll excuse me..." He moved again, matching her retreat with a step forward. Every inch of him radiated command, not of rank, but of presence. His shadow spilled over hers.

"Funny," he murmured. "I half-expected the girl I knew to be beating down that council door, demanding to be heard. To my surprise..." He tilted his head, eyes sparking with wicked amusement. "...you're hiding instead. Tsk, tsk, tsk."

Her breath stuttered. "I am not hiding," she snapped before she could stop herself.

That grin. Gods, that grin cut sharper than any blade. "Oh, Dove," he said, the word thick with mock sympathy. "Then where, I wonder, did you go? The wild thing I grew so fond of. The woman who snarled instead of curtsied. The woman who looked at me like she might bite."

Layla's heart pounded against her ribs, her composure slipping with every word. "Perhaps I learned restraint," she managed. "Something you clearly haven't."

Kain laughed, low and unhurried, a sound that slid over her skin like smoke. He leaned in close enough for his breath to brush her ear. "Restraint's overrated," he whispered. "And don't worry," he went on, his voice softening into something far more intimate than it had any right to be. "You'll be happy to know I'm not going anywhere for a while." His smile turned predatory, slow and certain. "And while I'm here, I'm going to enjoy every damned second of dragging the real you back out to play."

She couldn't move. Couldn't breathe. The scent of him, pine and leather and the faint metallic bite of steel, filled her lungs until she swayed. For a moment, the garden spun, narrowing to nothing but his eyes. And then just as suddenly, he stepped back. The heat broke. The distance returned. His gaze lingered on her a heartbeat longer. Something unreadable glinting beneath the smirk before he turned away. Only then did she notice Sparrow waiting in the archway's shadow, silent and watchful as ever. The two men exchanged a look, a wordless signal, and then they were gone. Swallowed by the mist curling through the garden paths.

Layla stood there long after he'd gone, the air still trembling faintly where his presence had been. The garden had gone still. All cool wind and the rustle of dying leaves. Her pulse refused to settle. *He didn't understand. Of course he didn't.* Kain came from a world that glorified defiance. Where power was shouted, and women who roared were crowned for it. But this was Graystonia. Here, a woman who roared was dismissed. She had already learned that once by interrupting the war council and asking to be heard. Kain just didn't understand that if she was *that* woman again, the one he remembered, fierce and unyielding, they wouldn't listen to her. They would destroy her. They would call her hysterical, unfit, unbecoming of a queen.

No. To survive here, to lead at all, she had to become exactly what they expected of her. Calm. Composed. Patient. She would let them believe her gentle, let them mistake restraint for obedience and patience for weakness. She would wait. She would watch. She would learn. Time was the only weapon she had been allowed to keep. She would be cunning where she could not be bold. Careful where she could not command. She would wear the role they demanded of her while quietly becoming what they truly needed.

She drew a breath, the cold air biting her lungs as her eyes rose to the castle beyond the gardens. Its towers gleamed pale against the dusk, proud and ancient, a monument to tradition, to obedience, and to every rule she was trying so hard to master.

"Fine," she whispered to the wind, her voice steady, regal, convincing even to herself. "Let him watch. He'll see soon enough how power works in Graystonia." The words rang like iron in her chest. But beneath that polished certainty, something restless stirred. A faint spark refusing to die, a whisper of the woman who would one day set this court ablaze. Layla ignored it. Straightened her spine. Lifted her chin. Because for now, she still believed that she could change Graystonia by playing its game. That to earn her throne, she had to master their rules. And that one day, it would be Kain Drakaren, not her, who would have to learn how wrong he was.

Layla sat at breakfast as she always did, still reeling from a night claimed by that relentless nightmare, pushing food around her plate with no appetite to speak of. Raising a piece of fruit to her lips only because she knew eyes would notice if she didn't. The fork slipped suddenly from her hand, plucked away as though she were a child fumbling at the table. By the time her gaze snapped up, Kain Drakaren was already leaning over her shoulder, his grin wolfish as the crush of his teeth sinking into the fruit she had just had.

"Thanks, Dove," he said through the mouthful, voice low and mocking. Though intimate enough to turn her stomach. "Delicious."

Her jaw nearly hit the plate. *Here? At her table? In the royal dining room, as if he belonged?* Before she could recover, he slid into the chair beside her. He was the epitome of casual, and infuriatingly at ease, as though it had always been his place. Sparrow followed without a word, seating himself neatly beside Ciana across from them. Layla's chest tightened. This was madness! Absolutely inappropriate and unacceptable. *How in the hell had the guards allowed this?* Her fingers twitched against her napkin, but no. She would not ask. She would not give him the satisfaction of seeing her rattled. If they were here, then they were here with permission. It was not her business. She drew a slow breath, spine straightening until it could've been carved from marble. *Do not react,* she ordered herself. *Do not give him anything.*

She reached for her bread, carefully breaking off a piece, but Kain's hand was quicker. Stealing grapes, figs, anything from her plate, chewing loudly beside her. Every crunch of his teeth rattled her composure.

"You know, Dove," he drawled, deliberately loud enough to cut through Sparrow's quiet attempt at conversation with Ciana, "I was really hoping you'd wear that little sheer thing you paraded around Antonin in. That was a nightdress, wasn't it? I thought perhaps you wore it to breakfast every morning. Gods, I wouldn't mind seeing it again."

Her body went rigid before she could think to stop it as heat pricked at her cheeks. Ciana's eyes shot wide, darting toward her with raised brows. Layla swallowed hard. She would not react. She *would not*. He was prodding her, playing his favorite game, trying to make her crack. So she stayed silent and took another small bite. But of course, Kain wouldn't ever dream of letting her ignore him.

He chuckled, low and taunting. "Oh, come on, Dove. Talk to me." He murmured, voice pitched just for her, playful and sharp as a blade. "I know you're dying to ask how we got in here. Drop your polite little charade and yell at me. Glare at me. Ask me... I dare you."

Her lips curved into the perfect, polished smile. "I am sorry to disappoint you, *Prince Drakaren,* but I will be doing no such thing." The title landed like a stone and she felt a tiny victory in staying appropriate and giving him a jab that clearly unsettled him.

Kain's head tilted, his jaw tightening, that wolfish-smirk tugging across his damned lips as he leaned close. So close she felt the whisper of his breath against her ear. "Call me that again," he murmured, taunting and sure, "and I'll show you just how breathy my *first* name can sound on your lips."

Her breath caught as her gaze flicked to his, meeting emerald fire blazing with merciless amusement. He bit into an apple without looking away. Layla's chair scraped as she abruptly stood, her hands trembling only slightly as she smoothed her skirts down her thighs. "If you'll excuse me Prince...." She caught herself just in time, nearly tripping over that cursed title again. She drew a slow, steady breath, forcing the words into place. Her smile was serene, practiced, untouchable. "Have a wonderful day, gentlemen. I will see you shortly, Ciana." And with that, Layla almost ran out of the room.

Layla stepped into the corridor and let out a ragged breath, desperate for space, for air. But before her lungs could fully expand, he was there. Pine and leather wrapped around her like smoke, thick and inescapable. His warmth pressed close, a shadow that clung to her skin, made her nerves hum. Then his arm swung easily over her shoulders, heavy and claiming. Pulling her flush to his side as though the guards, the walls, propriety itself simply didn't exist. He engulfed her. His scent, his heat, his very annoying and continuous presence sank into her bones until she could hardly tell where she ended and he began. *Of course it was him. Of course Kain Drakaren had no sense of boundaries!*

Layla instantly ducked out from under his arm, the motion so instinctive it nearly jolted her. Too close. Too much. Too familiar. He only chuckled, low and amused, as though her rejection were a game he intended to win.

"So," he drawled, matching her pace without effort, "where are we off to in such a rush?"

She tightened her grip on her skirts. "*We* are not off anywhere. *I* am going to my lessons."

"Ah," he hummed, his tone a lazy taunt. "And what lessons would those be?"

She flicked a glance at him, expecting mockery but catching the faintest edge of genuine curiosity instead. Against her better judgment, she answered. "Daily lessons in etiquette, manners, the noble families of Graystonia, social relevance, norms, royal expectations, and roles." Her voice was smooth, practiced, a list she had uttered countless times throughout her life.

The silence that followed stretched long enough that she turned her head fully to meet his gaze. He was staring at her like she'd just told him she sharpened spoons for fun. His lip curled, the humor draining into something darker. Something cutting. "You've got to be *fucking* kidding me." The words started like a joke, but the way his voice dipped, serious and incredulous, made her spine prickle. "This," he gestured vaguely with a hand, like he could scoop all of her composure and lessons and masks into one word, "this is what you do every day? Sit there and get force-fed rules about how to smile, how to sit, which fork to pick up first?"

Her hands instantly clasped before her, posture snapping into place, the drilled instincts of a lifetime. Chin lifted, back straight, perfect as glass.

"Yes."

A single word. Cool. Regal. Dutiful. The exact answer her mother would want. And Kain laughed. Not politely, not softly, but a raw, unrestrained laugh that echoed down the corridor. The sound of his laugh jolted through her, wild and reckless in the polished silence of the corridor. It felt wrong here, in these halls of measured words and hushed voices. Wrong, and far too loud.

Layla's jaw tightened. "It is not a jest," she said evenly, willing her voice not to waver. "It is my duty."

"Duty?" he echoed, still grinning. His eyes swept her, head to toe, as though every inch of her composure were some absurd costume. "Dove, they've caged you in lace and manners and convinced you it's iron."

Her throat closed, heat rising in her cheeks once again. *No,* she reminded herself. *Do not let him rattle you.* He wanted this, her slipping. Her roaring and reckless. She would not give him the satisfaction. So, she lifted her chin higher. "And what would you know of duty, *Kain*?" The prod was deliberate. Intentional. Meant to put him on the defense for a second. But instead of retreating, his smile widened. The glint in his eyes said he'd caught it. The spark beneath her calm, the flash of fire under her skin, and gods, he looked pleased to have found it. Kain leaned in, the scent of pine and smoke engulfing her completely, drowning thought and leaving only breathless awareness behind.

Kain's voice dropped, low and razor-smooth. "You can lie to them all you want, Dove. Sit there and play the perfect little heir, bow when they say bow." His gaze cut through her composure with effortless precision. "But don't lie to me. You're not built for silence. You're not meant to serve. You're meant to lead and you know it."

The air between them tightened, heavy and thick with restraint. Her jaw flexed. "I'm doing what's necessary," she said evenly, every word measured, controlled. "You don't understand how this court works."

His mouth curved, slow and knowing. "No, you don't understand. You think if you keep your head down long enough, they'll let you rise. But you weren't made to wait your turn, Layla." He leaned closer, voice softening into something that sent a shiver straight through her. "You were made to take it."

She held her breath. Not trusting it for a second before he forced her chin higher, masking the tremor beneath her calm. "I'll do what I must for my kingdom."

Kain's smirk vanished for the first time since she met him. "Then gods help your kingdom," he murmured, "when it learns what you become to save it."

For three days, there was no escaping him. Whenever Kain wasn't behind the barred doors of her mother's war councils, discussing gods-knew-what with Graystonia's commanders, he was there. At her lessons, leaning lazily against the back of her chair, close enough that she could feel the warmth of his breath when he spoke. In the corridors, where the walls themselves seemed to bend to make room for him as he brushed past. In the gardens, waiting with that wolfish grin, as though the earth tilted solely to bring him into her path. *It was so damned frustrating!*

She was supposed to be focusing on other things. Important things. Her betrothed, for one. Ryker had yet to request even a moment of her time since their engagement was announced, too busy shadowing the queen and her council to spare his future wife a glance. While men debated borders and war and alliances behind locked doors, she was expected to wait. To be patient. To be grateful.

Night became her only reprieve. Sleep offered no mercy. The nightmare continued to claw into her, leaving her waking already braced for pain. So she stopped fighting them. Instead, she slipped from her chambers more often than not, trading restless hours for movement, thought for muscle. The courtyards became her refuge, the sword her answer.

Tonight, she didn't want quiet. She wanted that burn yet again. The weight. The kind of physical chaos that could drown out the war raging in her mind.

The courtyard was empty when Layla slipped into it, lanternlight pooling soft and gold across stone worn smooth by centuries of feet. The castle loomed above, dark and watchful, but here the night breathed. Cool air skimmed her skin. The fountain murmured low and steady, a sound she could almost pretend was peace. She set her slippers aside and lifted the hem of her nightgown just enough to move. The sword had felt wrong in her hands at first. Heavier than her daggers. Slower. Demanding. But she was trying, unwilling to fail at this.

Layla planted her feet anyway. One breath. Then another before she swung. The blade cut a clean arc through the air. Too wide. Too stiff. The weight dragged her shoulder forward, tugging her off balance. She hissed softly and adjusted her grip. Again and again. Her arms burned.

Sweat gathered at her temples. Her lungs pulled deep, anchoring breaths. *Good. This was real.* This was hers.

"Tsk tsk. Still fighting the sword instead of letting it work with you."

Her heart jumped as Layla spun, blade snapping up on instinct, breath tight. He stood a few paces back, half caught between lanternlight and shadow, arms crossed like he'd been there all along.

"Kain," she hissed.

He grinned. "Dove?"

She lowered the sword a fraction, jaw tight. "You're not supposed to be here."

"And yet," he said lightly, stepping closer, "here I am." His gaze flicked to the blade. "That's new."

"Go away. I don't have the energy for you. Not tonight."

He laughed, low and unbothered. "Not a chance." She turned back to her practice space, refusing to look at him, and swung again. The blade wobbled at the end of the arc. She was too mentally exhausted to hold her mask in place tonight. Too worn to pretend composure mattered while she held a sword in her hands. The pretense slipped with the weight of the blade, leaving only frustration and muscle and breath.

"Told you," he said. "You're muscling it."

"I did not ask for your help."

"No," he agreed. "You never do." He moved before she could stop him. One moment she was alone with the blade, the next his presence filled the space behind her, close enough she felt every firm muscle ripple beneath his tunic as he pressed against her back. Causing her breath to hitch without permission.

"Don't," she warned.

He didn't put his hands on her. Not yet.

"Your stance," he murmured near her ear. "Too narrow." She shifted, irritated. "Wider. Trust the ground." She adjusted again, reluctantly.

"Better," he said. "Now breathe."

"I am breathing."

"Not enough."

His hands came to her hips then, firm and deliberate, turning her just slightly. Electricity skittered up her spine. "Kain," she said through clenched teeth.

He chuckled, then she felt his breath on her ear, the faintest hint of his lips as he whispered, "Gods, I love it when you say my name."

Before she could process any of the thousand emotions that he just caused, she swung the blade out of pure frustration, pivoting sharply. But he was already moving, stepping back with an easy laugh as the sword sliced through empty air.

"Careful, Dove," he said. "Someone might think you're trying to kill me."

"Get out of my way."

"Never been my strength."

He stepped in again, catching her wrist gently this time, guiding her arm down. "You don't fight a longsword like a dagger," he said, quieter now. "You let your body carry the weight." He positioned himself behind her once more, closer this time. His abs fully against her back. His hands slid to her forearms, adjusting the angle. "Feel it," he murmured. "Don't force it. Let the blade follow."

Her breath came uneven despite herself. She moved with him. The next swing was smoother. Cleaner. "There," he said softly. "You're learning."

She twisted out of his hold, turning on him, eyes blazing. "You enjoy this far too much."

His smile softened, just a touch. "You don't?" She hesitated. Just long enough. He saw it. Of course he did. That wolfish grin returned. "Thought so."

She shoved past him, lifting the sword again, defenses snapping back into place. "You've made your point. Now leave."

He studied her for a moment, then inclined his head, a smile curving slow and knowing. "Fine. For tonight, little Dove."

Layla knew better. With him, it wasn't surrender. It was patience.

The very next morning, Ryker stopped her to request a stroll through the courtyard after dinner. To her own surprise, Layla found herself mildly looking forward to it. His presence seemed to be easy, predictable. The sort of thing she should have wanted. But it was Kain who unsettled her world. She continued to run into him everywhere. Or rather, he made sure she did. Whenever he wasn't locked away in meetings, he appeared. Leaning against a pillar as she walked to her lessons. Waiting outside the dining hall. Slipping into her path with that infuriating smirk. He was relentless. But tonight wasn't about him. It was about finally getting time with her future husband and starting on her plan.

As Layla slipped on her cloak and gloves just after dinner, Ryker appeared right on time. His face lit the moment he saw her, a boyish beam that seemed a little too earnest for a man training to be king. He strode forward and took her cloak ties gently in his hands, fastening them with careful precision.

"Allow me," he said warmly.

She offered him a polite smile, tilting her chin as he smoothed the clasp into place. Then he extended his arm, formal and practiced, and she rested her gloved fingers upon it.

"I know it's brisk," Ryker said as they stepped into the chill evening air, their breath rising in faint white clouds. "But I was told you favor fresh air, that you often come out here to walk. Is that true?"

Layla's brow arched faintly at that. *He asked about me.* It shouldn't have surprised her, but somehow it did. "Yes, I do," she admitted softly. "Thank you."

His smile warmed, as though relieved his information was correct. They strolled down the gravel path in silence for a moment before he glanced at her again, expression earnest. "I wish to know the little things about you, Princess. Not matters of state. *You.* The things that truly matter." She tilted her head, caught off guard by the sincerity in his tone.

"What is your favorite holiday?" he asked gently. "The one that makes you happiest."

"Lammas," she replied without much thought. "When the fields are golden and everyone feasts."

He nodded, pleased. "And of all the dresses you've sewn, which is your most treasured?"

Layla felt her lips twitch. "A pale green one. I made it myself when I was twelve. The stitches are uneven, but I've never parted with it."

Ryker chuckled quietly. "I hope you'll show it to me one day." Then, with a little more daring: "And your favorite meal? If I asked the kitchens to prepare something only for you?"

"Beef stew," she answered with a small shrug. "Thick bread to soak it."

He looked at her as though each answer was worth far more than it should have been. "Perfect," he said simply. "That's all I wanted, Layla. The small, important things."

As they continued their stroll, faint noises broke the quiet. Low grunts, the sharp ring of steel meeting steel. Layla's steps slowed, curiosity pulling her forward until they rounded the corner and her jaw fell agape.

Kain and Sparrow stood in the courtyard, swords drawn, locked in a spar that was more war than practice. Both men were stripped to the waist, their bodies sheened with sweat despite the chill of the fading sun. Steam rose from their skin like smoke curling into the evening air, the cold biting against the heat radiating from them.

Sparrow was a wall of lean, hard muscle, every movement precise, efficient. Impressive. But her eyes, those traitorous things. Wouldn't stay looking at him for long. They drifted back to Kain. Always to Kain. Her gaze followed the ripple of his abdomen as he twisted to parry, the flex of his shoulders as he drove forward, the bead of sweat rolling down his throat. Each swipe of his blade was savage grace, each grunt a low thunder she could feel echoing in her own chest. The forbidden thought stole through her before she could stop it: what would it feel like to lean in and taste the salt from his skin, to follow that trail of sweat down his stomach with her lips...

A cough snapped her from the thought.

Layla startled, eyes tearing away from the spectacle as if caught in sin. Ryker stood beside her, politely clearing his throat, though his expression betrayed nothing. Gods, please let her cheeks only look flushed from the cold. She forced herself to inhale, spine straightening, face tilting up toward the brisk evening air as though it were the view she'd been admiring all along.

"The Antonins are something else," Ryker muttered, exhaling heavily as he shook his head. His gaze lingered on the courtyard where Kain and Sparrow sparred, steel flashing in the fading light. "They've dragged out these negotiations long enough. Especially that one, Kain. I'll be glad when all this is finalized and they're gone."

Layla's eyes flicked to Ryker, then back to the warriors he dismissed so easily. The clash of their blades rang louder in her ears than his words. "Ryker," she said carefully, choosing her tone as much as her words. "I was wondering... hoping, really. What exactly is being finalized? Why are they here? Is something wrong?"

For a moment, he only studied her. His expression gave nothing away. Then his lips curved into a polished, reassuring smile, and he reached for her hand, squeezing gently. "Don't trouble yourself with such matters, my Layla," he said. "I will keep our kingdom safe, that is all you need to know."

The words were meant to soothe. Instead, they hollowed her out. The dismissal was gentle. Courteous. Absolute. And in that quiet certainty, the truth settled heavy in her chest. This was what awaited her. A life lived on the edges of power. Close enough to hear the decisions, never close enough to shape them. Smiling. Nodding. Being reassured while men spoke of war and fate as if her blood did not run in the same soil they claimed to protect.

Ryker would be no different from the kings before him. He would see his queen as something to shield, not something to stand beside. And with that realization, something in Layla finally gave way. Not loudly. Not dramatically. Just a soft, aching collapse inward. Defeated. Hollow. But of course, still smiling.

Ryker escorted her back through the quiet halls with practiced ease, his hand resting lightly at the small of her back. It was a gentleman's touch. Correct. Careful. When they reached her chamber door, he paused only long enough to offer a polite goodnight, his smile warm and distant all at once. Layla returned it automatically. Then door clicked shut behind him.

As she turned around, she found Kain waiting. He leaned against the stone across from her chamber, arms crossed, posture loose and infuriatingly at ease. Sweat still darkened the collar of his shirt, his hair damp and tousled from training, the faint scent of pine and iron clinging to him like a second skin. He looked like he belonged nowhere near silk corridors and polite conversations. Her stomach instantly dropped. Not with anger. Not with heat. But with humiliation.

After Ryker's gentle dismissal. After realizing just how neatly she had been set aside. Seeing Kain like this, unbothered, observant, *seeing too much*...It made her want to crawl out of her own skin. For a heartbeat, she considered retreating. Slipping into her washroom. Pretending exhaustion. Pretending she hadn't just been quietly, irrevocably reminded of her place. But she knew it was too late.

"Well," Kain drawled, pushing off the wall with lazy confidence. "That was... painfully formal."

She stiffened. Her chin lifted on instinct, but the mask didn't settle the way it usually did. It felt crooked tonight. Thin. "You shouldn't be here," she said, the words lacking their usual bite.

Something in him shifted immediately. "Funny," he said softly. "You don't sound like you mean that."

Her fingers curled at her sides. She hated that he noticed. Hated that he always noticed. "It's late. I'm tired."

Kain's gaze narrowed, the teasing dimming. "That's not what this is."

She stiffened. "You don't know what this is."

"I know what it looks like," he said, stepping closer. Not crowding her. Just enough that retreat felt like a choice she'd have to consciously make. "You look like someone who just realized the ground beneath her feet isn't solid anymore." Her breath hitched. Damn him.

"You shouldn't be here," she said again, quieter this time.

"And you shouldn't look like you're about to fold in on yourself," he replied flatly. "Yet here we both are."

Her jaw tightened. "You enjoy this? Watching me unravel?"

"No," he said. "I enjoy watching you *stop pretending*." That did it.

Her composure slipped, just enough to betray her. "I am doing what is required of me."

Kain let out a short, humorless laugh. "That's what they tell people right before they erase them." She flinched. "Say it again," he pressed. "Say you're fine. Say this is all part of the plan." She opened her mouth but nothing came out. Kain's expression hardened, whatever softness had crept in burning away. "That's what I thought."

"As I've said, you don't understand this court," she snapped, the words cracking despite her effort to keep them honed. "You don't understand what it costs to survive here."

"I understand exactly what it costs," he shot back. "And I also understand what it costs to *lose yourself*."

She shook her head, breath coming faster now. "I don't have a choice."

He stepped closer again. This time, there was no gentleness in it. "That's the lie they want you to believe."

Her throat burned. "You think I don't know that?"

"Then why are you letting them do it?" he demanded.

The question hit her like a shove. She staggered back half a step, shoulders slumping, the fight draining out of her all at once. Gods, she was so tired. Tired of holding herself together. Tired of being strong in all the wrong ways. "I can't fight them," she whispered in defeat. "I can't win their game when they won't even let me on the board."

Kain went still. For a heartbeat, she thought he might soften. Might step back. Might say something comforting. Instead, his voice came out low and leveled. "Then you're already losing."

Her knees felt weak. She pressed a hand to the wall beside her door, steadying herself, breath shallow and uneven. The mask was gone now. There was no strength left to hold it in place. "I am trying," she said, the words barely audible.

"I know," he said. "That's the problem."

She looked up at him then, eyes bright with unshed tears she would never allow to fall. "What do you want from me?"

Kain's jaw clenched. "I want you to stop waiting for permission."

She laughed, broken and bitter. "From who? My mother? The council? My future husband?"

"All of them," he said. "And yourself."

Silence crashed between them. Layla's shoulders sagged. Whatever resolve she'd been clinging to finally gave way, and she slid down against her wall, sitting hard on the stone floor, arms wrapping around herself like it was the only thing holding her together. She didn't look at him. "I can't...," she said quietly. "Kain... I just can't..."

The words settled between them. Kain didn't answer right away. When she finally looked up at him, he wasn't looking at her with frustration. Or fire. Or even anger. It was something worse. He studied her as though seeing her clearly for the first time and finding something missing. Something in his expression shifted then, slow and unmistakable. The tension that always lived in him, coiled and ready, went slack. Not relief but resignation.

"Right," he said quietly. The word hit harder than a shout ever could.

Layla's breath stuttered. "Kain..."

He shook his head once, decisively, cutting her off. "No." And gods, the finality in it...

He straightened, putting distance between them without a single step. His jaw tightened, eyes hard now, distant in a way she had never seen before, and he walked to her door. She pressed her palm harder to the stone, steadying herself. "You don't understand what happens if I fail."

"I understand exactly what happens," he said. "I just thought you did too." Silence fell once again, heavy and suffocating. When he reached for the door and glanced at her one last time, there was no anger in it. No teasing. No fire. Just disappointment. And gods, that broke her more than anything else could have.

"Goodnight, Layla," he said, his voice distant now. Formal. Closed. Then he opened the door and walked away.

She didn't move. Didn't breathe. Didn't even realize tears had slipped free until they hit the back of her hand. Because somewhere deep inside, beneath all the fear and planning and patience, she had believed, just a little, that he wouldn't stop believing in her. And now he had. And tomorrow, she knew, he wouldn't come to challenge her. He would come to **end this**.

THE BLOOM OF THE BLESSED
IS BORN IN DECAY

## "Pain sanctifies; death absolves nothing"

Execution is forbidden within the kingdom's blessed bounds. Instead, those who stray must walk the Path of Atonement. Rituals of penance, bloodletting, starvation, or rotfast confinement, until the divine deems them restored. Only the crown's seers may determine when a soul is once again worthy of belonging.

-BY THE SACRED LAW OF LUMIREN-

# Chapter Twelve

*K*<sup>*ain.*</sup>

      Kain did not slow until he was out of the corridor. Not because he feared turning back.Because if he did, he would break something. The stone beneath his boots felt too solid for the rage that had opened in his chest. Her voice still echoed there, fractured and small in a way he had never heard before. *I just can't.* The words lodged beneath his ribs like a blade left buried, twisting with every breath. Not defiance. Not stubbornness. But surrender. That was what cut deepest.

He had gone to her hoping to see the fire again. Hoping for teeth. For that untamed, defiant snarl she had given him in flashes before, brief and brilliant. He could have fought that. Gods, he would have fought

160

beside it. Instead, she had folded in on herself, arms wrapped tight as if she were trying to disappear before the world finished breaking her. And the worst part was not that she was afraid. It was that she was right.

The council would not listen. Her mother would not yield. Her future husband would smile and speak gently while shutting her out piece by piece. Kain's jaw locked, fury pressing hot and relentless behind his eyes. He had spent days watching men congratulate themselves on victories they had not earned, pretending the north was no longer their concern. While warnings were dressed up as inconveniences. While the one person in that castle who could see what was coming was being trained to sit quietly and pour tea. She was the only one who would be willing to acknowledge the storm. The only one with the instinct to recognize it and the spine to face it. And even she was being taught to doubt herself.

That realization burned hotter than anger. It truly baffled him. Baffled him that none of these men could see her. Not her title. Not her usefulness. *Her.* The mind that tracked patterns before others noticed them. The stubborn resolve that did not bend when things turned ugly. The quiet courage to stand when the ground shifted beneath her feet. And gods help him, it baffled him that *she* could not see it anymore either. Every time he had leaned close enough to make her breath hitch, every time she had snapped his name like a warning, something dark and electric had coiled tight in his gut. Not obsession. No. He knew obsession. This was recognition. The dangerous kind. He saw all of her. The sass. The stubbornness. The beauty and the brilliance. How could they not? How could *she* not?

She was a leader. Through and through. The kind he would trust beside him when blood started flowing. If she could not step into that truth herself... Kain exhaled hard, the sound rough, stripped bare. The truth tasted bitter. There just wasn't enough time...

So he decided that tonight, he would give her this. The space. The silence. The chance to break where no one could see her do it. Gods knew he wanted her in his arms instead. Wanted to haul her up from the stone floor and remind her what strength felt like when it wasn't carried alone. But if this was how she survived. If she needed distance to breathe, he would grant it. Just this once.

His jaw tightened. Because tomorrow, there would be no more room for doubt. Tomorrow, he would push her harder than he ever had. Strip away the patience she had been taught to mistake for virtue. Tear through the fear, the careful obedience, the belief that waiting would save her. Not because he wanted to hurt her, but because the world would not hesitate to. He knew she was still in there. The fire. The spine. The woman who had stared death down and refused to bow. She had not vanished. She was buried. And buried things could be unearthed. She would see it again. Soon enough.

Kain straightened, resolve settling into his bones like iron. Tomorrow, he would force the truth into the light. Even if it cost him everything.

Morning light poured through the high windows of the council chamber, gilding polished wood and the steel of ceremonial armor. The room smelled of ink and oil and something smug. Men seated comfortably behind tables spoke of borders and rebuilding and peace as if those things could be declared into existence. Kain leaned back in his chair, arms crossed, jaw tight. He had heard this all before.

"And so," one of the Graystonian lords concluded, fingers steepled, "with Bartoria's king dead and their forces scattered, we see no reason to extend Graystonia's concern beyond our own borders."

Kain exhaled slowly through his nose. Sparrow shifted beside him, a warning glance flicking his way.

Another voice joined in, confident, dismissive. "Our scouts have yet to report any organized threat in the north. Whatever unrest Antonin believes it senses will surely be clarified in time."

That was when Kain straightened. "We've been through this," he said, voice cutting clean through the chamber. Several heads turned at once. "We have told you," Kain continued, rising to his feet, "again and again, what we saw in the north. What we felt. What our scouts confirmed before yours ever left your borders."

He stepped forward, boots striking stone with deliberate force. "While you sit and wait for your own men to return with the same damned information, likely less of it, we are doing nothing but separating ourselves."

A lord scoffed. "Prince Drakaren, Antonin has always been quick to cry war…"

Kain's head snapped toward him. "Because Antonin has always been the first to bleed when others refuse to prepare." Silence rippled. "You are sitting ducks," Kain went on, voice rising now, tight with frustration. "Divided. Comfortable. Congratulating yourselves on a victory that has not been secured."

Ryker finally spoke, calm and measured. "Graystonia cannot commit to another war without proof."

"Then stop thinking in terms of war and start thinking in terms of survival," Kain shot back. "What we are asking for is not conquest. It is unity." He planted his hands on the table. "An alliance. Reach out to the southern territories with us. Gather all of our strength now, before fear fractures it. Stand as one front."

A murmur spread.

"That is unnecessary," Ryker said firmly. "A treaty of peace is sufficient."

Kain laughed, harsh and incredulous. "Peace?" He turned fully to Ryker then, emerald eyes hard. "You know what? Your princess would understand this…" The room went still. "You would think her so-called future husband could too."

Ryker stiffened, jaw setting. "Layla is not part of this discussion."

"And that," Kain said coldly, "is precisely the problem."

Ryker stepped forward, posture rigid. "Graystonia will not be drawn into fear-driven alliances. We will draft a treaty of peace. No obligations beyond our borders. That is the only agreement we are prepared to offer."

Kain's gaze flicked around the room, searching faces. Lords who would not meet his eyes. Men who had already decided comfort was worth the risk. At last, his eyes found Queen Raynera. She stood apart from the table, regal and unreadable, hands folded loosely before her. Watching. "Are you truly going to do nothing?" Kain demanded. "You see what's coming. You know what this will cost."

For a long moment, she said nothing. Then, slowly, deliberately, Queen Raynera lifted her chin... and turned her gaze to Ryker. Ryker met it with a faint smirk before looking back to Kain. "The treaty will be drafted," Ryker said. "You may sign it or refuse it. But it is the only offer on this table."

Something in Kain snapped. "Then enjoy your peace," he said, voice low and lethal. "I hope it keeps you warm when the rot reaches your gates." With that, he turned on his heel and strode for the doors, boots echoing through the chamber. Behind him, no one stopped him. And that silence told him everything.

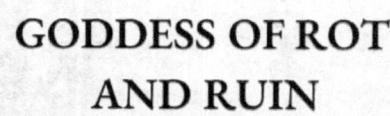

## YSSRA

### GODDESS OF ROT
### AND RUIN

# Chapter Thirteen

*Layla.*

That morning at breakfast, every scrape of a chair, every whisper of boots across stone had Layla's head tilting, her eyes darting to the doorway. Waiting. Expecting that shadow to stalk through. But Kain never came. Neither did Sparrow. That pit in her stomach began to ache once more. The sadness in his tone as he walked away from her last night had been gnawing at her. For the first time all week, she found herself searching for his presence, needing to know they were okay...

However, instead of the two warriors joining for breakfast like they had the past few days, the surprise was Aerilynn. Her sister's pale form appeared in the dining hall at last. Dark shadows bruising her eyes but here, *finally here,* and Layla's heart lurched with quiet relief.

Aerilynn gave her a small smile as she lowered herself beside her, picking half-heartedly at the food. It wasn't much. But it was something.

"Walk with me to lessons?" Layla asked softly after watching Aerilynn finish her plate. Aerilynn hesitated, then nodded. That alone was enough to put a flicker of warmth in Layla's chest as they rose together, skirts brushing in unison down the corridor. But as they rounded the bend, Layla saw them.

Sparrow emerged first, broad and silent as ever, his expression carved into its usual unreadable calm. Then Kain stepped into view beside him, and Layla's breath caught. He didn't see her at first. His gaze was fixed ahead, jaw locked so tightly it looked painful, green eyes burning with a fury that had nothing of his usual careless smirk. Whatever fire lived in him now was cold and vicious, the kind that consumed everything in its path. Rage clung to him like smoke, thick and suffocating, and for a heartbeat, it was clear his thoughts were nowhere near this corridor at all. And still, her chest tightened.

The delay felt intentional, even if it wasn't. No teasing glance. No immediate recognition. No sign that he had registered her presence at all. Layla's stomach dropped. Last night's hollow fear surged back to life, sudden and merciless. This wasn't anger turned toward her. It was worse. It was a man so deep inside his own fury that there was no room left for anything else. Something had gone wrong. Terribly wrong.

Aerilynn faltered only slightly before smoothing her expression and offering Sparrow a polite smile as they drew closer. With a soft greeting, the two slipped into fragile, careful conversation about the morning, voices light and measured, as though the air around them wasn't humming with tension. But Layla did not stop with them.

Her feet carried her forward before her better judgment could intervene, instinct sparking hot in her veins. Part foolish need to reassure herself. Part reckless urge to step into the storm and see if it would finally turn. She closed the distance between herself and Kain, stopping at the exact space propriety demanded. Not too close. Not distant enough to be ignored.

"Good morning," she said, her tone smooth, regal, perfectly composed. "I hope you had a pleasant night's sleep." She wanted a reaction. Any sign that before last night still existed. That whatever had broken hadn't gone irreversibly silent. But nothing could have prepared her for his response.

Kain stopped dead, staring at her like she'd just spit in his face. Then he laughed. It was short, bitter, and absolutely dangerous. "A pleasant night of sleep...," he repeated, mocking the words like they tasted foul. "That's what you've got for me? That's who you are now?" He stalked closer, voice cutting deeper with every step. "Gods, look at you." He shook his head. "Your spine's gone. Your fire's gone. You're exactly what your mother wants, huh? Silent, smiling, obedient, a doll in a dress. A fucking ornament with a crown waiting for the right man to pick you up and sit you on his shelf."

Layla stiffened, but Kain didn't stop. She didn't know what she expected after last night, expected walking up to him now. But not this.

His lip curled, venom dripping. "And the most insane part? Your mother, the queen of this fucking place, is the same. A porcelain mask. Standing next to her throne while a boy who hasn't even *finished his training* plays king in her stead. Decisions falling from his mouth while she stays mute. Pathetic. My mother would burn the ground before she let someone else speak for her. But yours? She lets this kingdom rot while she smooths her skirts."

His eyes blazed, his words brutal. "And you, you're worse. You're letting it happen when I know you know better. You, who should burn the hottest for vengeance. For your father. For your sisters. For *Theron.*" His jaw tightened. "But last night, you didn't fight. You didn't push back. You folded." The word landed like a blow. "You gave up," he said flatly. "I saw it."

His gaze hardened, disappointment sharp and unmistakable. "You, who clawed your way out of hell. You, who survived when everyone else fell. And now you stand here smiling, playing their game, pretending you aren't breaking yourself to fit it." A beat. His voice quieted, cold and final. "Gods, Layla. You make me sick."

The silence between them cracked like ice. His chest heaved, fury barely leashed as he took a deep breath. Then his voice dropped low, more lethal somehow, like a blade sliding home. "So here's the truth." His voice was flat and final. "I could walk away right now. Take my tribe with me. Walk away from these negotiations you haven't asked a damn thing about, haven't cared a single breath for. I could let centuries of blood feud stand, let the Antonin and Graystonians keep hating each other until we're both ash. All it takes is me walking away." The corridor went silent, the weight of his words suffocating. Layla's heart thudded painfully in her chest, her body trembling as she searched his face, confused but understanding the weight of this conversation.

"Or..." His voice darkened further, daring her. "You open your fucking mouth. Prove that some royal in this kingdom actually gives a damn. Convince me that Graystonia is worth an alliance. Worth bleeding for. Worth saving."

Layla's chest constricted, her heart hammering against her ribs, every word battering through the fragile walls she'd built. But Kain wasn't done.

"And let me make something clear, Dove. I'm not here just so that our two kingdoms can become allies. I'm not here so we can align to seek vengeance against Bartoria. No. While you've sat pretty and silent, I'm here because a force greater than you can even imagine is rising in the north and doesn't give a damn about your polished manners or your puppet kings. And when it comes, and it will. Your kingdom won't just bleed. It will vanish and you all will have done nothing."

Layla stared at him, breath caught, shock reverberating through every bone in her body. The mention of negotiations, of alliances, this mighty force in the north. It all struck like lightning, too much, too fast, and yet not nearly enough information. But most of all, it was the way he said he could leave. That he would leave. She swallowed hard, her voice breaking when it finally escaped. "What... what do you want from me?"

Kain's voice thundered, desperation seeping into every line of his expression. "To prove to me you care Layla! That someone with royal blood fucking cares in this castle! That you're all not just shells anymore and actually have an opinion on what you think we should do. Show me that fire." The words hit harder than steel. Layla's chest constricted, her breath caught against the weight of his stare. Her hands twitched at her sides, desperate to fold into something neat and proper, the last defense she had left.

"I want to help," she said quietly, the words cracking despite her effort to steady them. "I want to know what's happening. Gods, I want to *do* something. But you don't understand, Kain...That isn't how it works here." He said nothing, but the intensity in his eyes dared her to go on. "I can't just storm into the council chamber and demand answers," she continued, frustration bleeding into her tone. "My mother would have me exiled from court before I crossed the threshold. That isn't how Graystonia rules. We build trust. We earn favor. Influence takes time. That's how things change here... carefully and quietly." Her voice trembled with conviction she didn't fully feel. "If I barge in shouting, they'll never take me seriously again. I'll lose any chance of being heard when it matters."

Kain scoffed, low and bitter. "And while you're busy earning favor, how much time do you think you have left? You think the gods or the armies waiting at your borders care about your mother's politics?"

She stiffened, chin lifting. "You think I don't see the flaws in this court? I do. But I have to work *within* it. I can't burn it all down just because it's slow."

"You could," he said simply, stepping closer. "You just won't."

His words landed like a blow. Not cruel, but ruthlessly true. He looked her over, jaw tight. "You're playing a long game in a world that's already burning. You can't afford to whisper at men who won't listen when the walls start to fall."

Her throat closed. "That's not fair," she whispered.

"No," he said, softer now but no less fierce. "It's not. But neither is this damned court of yours."

The silence that followed was heavier than his accusations. Layla's gaze dropped to the stone between them, to her own reflection warped in the morning light. She wanted to scream at him that he was wrong, that she was doing what she *had* to do. That patience was strategy, not cowardice. But the words wouldn't come. Because somewhere deep inside, the part of her that still burned knew he was right, and that terrified her more than anything.

He leaned closer, eyes burning into hers, every word a strike meant to crack her open. "Look at me, Layla." She did. "We don't have the fucking time for your precious Ryker and his war council to keep sitting on their asses, talking in circles while the north moves like a poison," he said, each word low and deliberate. "The world isn't waiting for Graystonia to make up its mind." His jaw flexed. "You think the enemy's going to pause and let your lords debate proper strategy over wine?" Her pulse stumbled, heat flaring in her chest. "I know you're in there," he said quietly as his shoulders sagged and his expression dropped. "The woman who thinks. Who fights. I would never give up on her. I just wish I had the time to draw her out." He exhaled hard, dragging a hand through his hair. "But I don't. So I'll make this simple." His tone shifted back to that lethal calm. "I can get you answers. Real ones. All the truths your court keeps pretending don't exist. All you have to do is ask."

Layla blinked. "Answers?"

He stepped closer. "Everything you're not being told...about the north, the alliances, what's coming next. You want to save your people? Then stop hiding behind etiquette."

"I'm not hiding," she snapped, even as her hands trembled.

His mouth curved, not in mockery but in quiet certainty. "You are. You're just calling it patience." The brutal truth of it was another blow she wasn't ready for. "So tell me, Dove. Do you want answers, or do you want to keep pretending you're powerless?"

Silence stretched taut between them, her composure fraying thread by thread as she warred within herself. But Kain saw it, the flicker in her eyes, the fracture in her mask, and his grin turned slow, wolfish. "There she is," he murmured. "The woman I remember." He stepped close enough that she felt the heat of his words against her ear. "Here's my offer. I'll get you every answer you seek. About your kingdom, this war, our enemies, all of it. But in return, I want the truth from you. No masks. No titles. Just you."

Her throat tightened, but she started to find herself. Standing straighter now, she leaned back to look him in the eye as she challenged him. "And if you fail to answer every single question I have about *anything*?"

His grin deepened. "If you agree to this little deal. Then not only will I *not* leave right now. But if I fail to answer every single one of your little questions. Then I'll march back inside, sit my ass down, and listen to your would-be king. Hell, I'll even tell my mother to do the same. Play your court's ridiculous games and be a good little prince."

Layla's breath left her as she looked at him utterly shocked at his boldness. But the reality of this was at the forefront of her mind and she needed to know every possible outcome of this so-called 'deal'. "And if you *don't* fail?"

He leaned back in, his lips brushing her ear as his voice was both soft and lethal. "Then you owe me. Because nothing's free, Dove. Not even the truth."

She swallowed hard. "I owe you what, exactly?"

"We'll see," he said, the words brushing against her like a promise. "So now you know, Dove. What do you say?"

The challenge lingered in the air between them, heat, danger, temptation, all twisted together. Her heart thundered. Her mother's voice screamed in her head to walk away. But if he wasn't bluffing, if he actually walked away, if every word about the north was true, then she would never know. She would remain blind while her kingdom burned. And gods help her, she wanted to know. Wanted answers. Wanted to help, no matter that this wasn't the *right* way. That hunger gnawed at her, raw and undeniable, even as shame told her to stay silent. So, before reason could cage her again, she heard herself say it, soft, certain, and completely defiant.

"Okay."

Kain's smile beamed. Victory flickered behind his eyes like flame catching dry wood.

"Okay."

## YSSRA

**The Black Vein. The Whispering Decay. The Sickness Beneath All Things.**

Once, when the gods and goddesses walked freely among mortals, every divine gift had purpose. Abundance, valor, fate... and even rot. Yssra's corruption was not always feared. Her touch broke down what had grown stagnant, clearing way for renewal. For a time, she was revered as necessary as rain and nightfall.

But with every blessing she bestowed—every crop she allowed to wither so that new ones might grow, every illness she eased only to reclaim again Yssra felt the immense, intoxicating power coiling within her. And soon she no longer tended decay... she indulged in it.
Her rot began to spread beyond what was natural.
It burrowed into the soil, the bones of the land, and the very essence of humanity. Left unchecked, her power threatened to grow so vast that no god or goddess could oppose her.

Not even Eliryn, King of the Gods.

# Chapter Fourteen

*K*<sup>*ain.*</sup>

Victory hit like a surge of heat through his veins. He'd laid it all on the line, a desperate gamble, a knife-edge shot to force her hand. And it had worked. The Dove had said *yes*. Not because she wanted to, but because she had no other choice. Exactly as he'd planned it. Not because it was easy. But because she'd finally seen there was no other way.

The knot that had been cinched tight in his chest for days loosened all at once, breath rushing free as something bright and fierce surged through him. Relief, yes, but more than that. Satisfaction. Vindication. A pulse of wild, reckless joy that lit him from the inside out. He felt lighter. Charged. Alive again.

That familiar grin broke loose, the one Sparrow always muttered was more ruinous than any blade, and it curved across his mouth as he turned back to the others. Easy confidence settling over him like a second skin, the weight he'd been carrying finally gone.

"Sparrow," Kain drawled, rolling his shoulders as if he hadn't just upended the princess's world. "Cover for me in the rest of those dreary meetings today. I've got more important things to do." Sparrow's jaw ticked, but he didn't argue. He never did when Kain got that tone in his voice, the one that revealed the line had already been crossed, and there was no going back.

Then Kain turned his wolf's smile on Aerilynn. "And Aerilynn... good to see you again. I'm going to borrow your sister for a little while. Can you cover for her?"

Her eyes widened, startled at the audacity, he was sure. But Kain could see the wheels spinning in her head; she was analyzing and plotting away. The look was the same as her big sister. *Interesting.* He'd heard misery had carved shadows across her face since Bartoria, but for the briefest moment, mischief danced there instead. Like she *wanted* this. Like she wanted her sister to be defiant, even if it was him making it happen.

Aerilynn glanced at Layla, then back at him, and gave the smallest, most loaded nod. *Permission.* That was all he needed. Kain's hand shot out, rough and sure, his fingers closing around Layla's like a chain forged in fire. Her gasp was soft, startled, but he didn't give her the chance to argue. He tugged, pulling her from the safety of polished stone halls, dragging her into the chaos he carried with him.

"Let's go, Dove," he murmured, low and unapologetic, like a promise and a threat wrapped into one.

And just like that, the game began.

**YSSRA**

### Continued...

The Great War ended only when Eliryn created the Veil, a vast barrier separating the divine from the mortal realm. It severed Yssra's reach before she consumed too much power, forcing her into a realm where her decay could no longer feed on mortal life. Yet whispered tales speak of a foothold she left behind a fissure in the Veil, small but pulsing, where her rot still seeps through like a sickness that refuses to die.

### The Nature of Her Rot

Yssra's rot is not simple decay.
It twists what it touches, warping it into a mockery of life—flesh hardened and darkened by branching black veins, eyes turned hollow, emotions stripped away. A person overtaken becomes a Rotted, a vessel that obeys only the whispers of Yssra.

# Chapter Fifteen

*L* *ayla.*

Kain stopped before the door to his chambers and pushed it open, guiding her inside. The moment Layla crossed the threshold, her steps faltered.

It wasn't messy, not like she expected from him. The room was neat, ordered, yet stamped with his presence in every corner. A bow rested polished against the wall, its string taut as if ready at a moment's notice. A quiver leaned beside it, each arrow fletched in dark feathers. Maps stretched across the small table, not scattered but weighted in place with daggers, their points driven cleanly into the wood. A single wolf pelt hung across the back of a chair, worn smooth where his hand had clearly brushed it countless times.

The air smelled faintly of pine and leather, that same essence of him that seemed to follow her everywhere. The bed was made with exacting precision, though the coverlet bore the faint crease of a man who never truly rested. Every inch was purposeful yet chaotic. Every inch was *Kain*. Layla's throat tightened. The chamber wasn't just a room. It was an extension of him. Disciplined, dangerous, and impossible to ignore.

Her voice came quieter than she intended. "What are we doing... *here*?"

Kain leaned lazily against the edge of the table, his hand brushing the map as if it belonged to him as much as the air he breathed. His emerald eyes gleamed, clearly elated by watching her struggle with the intimacy of being here. "A safe place," he said, smooth and deliberate. He gestured to the maps, to the inked lines stretching across Graystonia and beyond. "To answer your questions. Every single one as promised... To show you what's hidden from you, Dove. To give you the truths they'll never hand over in your pretty little lessons."

Layla's fingers twisted in her skirts, her throat dry as stone. She still felt like she shouldn't be here, yet she so desperately wanted this. Wanted to *know*. So the words clawed their way up before she could stop them. "You said... a greater threat is coming from the north." Her voice trembled but held. "What is it, Kain? Tell me what we're truly facing." The silence that followed was suffocating. For a moment, she wished she could swallow the question back down, lock it in the hollow where she kept all the others. But Kain stilled, his eyes burning into her like he'd been waiting for that exact moment.

His head dropped for a brief second before he looked at her with a brilliant grin that lit up his entire face. Relief seeming to radiate off him.

He took a breath to compose himself. "You want the truth, Dove? Here it is. It's worse than Bartoria. Worse than Ivar. What's coming from the north isn't a king or an army you can outwit with politics and porcelain smiles. It's rot. It's ruin. And if you sit here pretty and silent while Ryker plays dress-up at your council table, your kingdom won't just bleed, it'll choke."

His words struck like daggers, brutal and unflinching. And yet, underneath the bite, there was no mockery. Only conviction. "What do you mean, rot and ruin?" Layla pressed, her voice unsteady but clear. "Like... the Goddess Yssra?"

Kain's eyes flashed, surprise cutting through his scowl. Then, slow and wolfish, a grin spread back across his face. "Well, look at that. Still sharp beneath all that polish. Took you half a breath to put it together."

He straightened, pacing a step, then turned back, his voice dark and deliberate. "Yeah, Dove. Yssra. The Goddess of Rot and Ruin. And it's not whispers anymore, it's fact. Wherever Lumiren goes, the land dies. I've seen it. Sparrow's seen it. Black earth, hollow trees, silence in the air. The rot follows them like a shadow." He leaned in, lowering his tone until it burned. "And here's the truth your council won't admit: Bartoria was never steering their own ship. Not really. Lumiren had strings in them long before we split off Ivar's skull. They're the puppeteers, always were I bet. And now?" He spread his hands wide, mock laughter twisting from his throat. "Now they've claimed Bartoria outright. What's left of it anyway. One kingdom falls, another swallows it whole. It was too quick, too controlled to be anything else." Layla's stomach twisted as she tried to process his words, but Kain wasn't finished. His attention locked on her, leaving no room to retreat.

"They're not hiding anymore," he said, his voice low and edged with disgust. "Yssra's priests are marching under her banner now, blessing villages one week and burning them the next. Taking any kingdom in their sights. They call it salvation, but it's corruption, Dove. People are changing. The priests touch them, pray over them, and what's left afterward..." His jaw tightened. "They call them Blessed. Mindless, hollow things that move when she wills it. An army of her own design."

Her breath hitched. "You mean..."

"I mean," Kain cut in, "she's expanding. And she isn't subtle about it. Every mile she claims, the land rots a little more, and her followers call it holy ground. She plans to take the entire realm."

Layla's pulse quickened, the words scraping raw through her chest. She could see it then. Fields blackened under false light. Villages hollowed out and renamed sanctuaries. Rot dressed up as divinity. "But why?" she whispered. "Why take everything?"

Kain's jaw tightened. For a moment, he looked away, as if weighing how much truth she could bear. Then his gaze returned to hers, steady and unforgiving. "Because she doesn't want kingdoms," he said quietly. "She wants ownership." He drew a slow breath. "She rots the land until it belongs to her. Soil. Stone. Blood. Everything living becomes part of her power. And when there's nothing left untouched, nothing left that isn't hers..." His voice dropped. "She uses it."

Layla felt cold spread through her veins. "For what?"

"To tear the veil," Kain said. "To walk this realm herself." He paused with a sigh. "And the rest of us? We don't die. Not cleanly I might add. We become what feeds her. Slaves. Vessels. Offerings." Silence fell heavy between them. "Gods don't need reasons, Dove," he said at last, voice rough. "Only enough worship. And enough rot to make them strong."

Her thoughts spun faster than her tongue could keep pace. "If she's moving this fast, why isn't the council doing anything? What are they doing? What's your kingdom's plan? Assuming Queen Okteria knows? Is she coming? What if they strike sooner... what if..." Kain's laugh cut through her spiraling. Deep, easy, and seemingly amused. He leaned back against the wall, hands spreading wide as if to steady her with nothing more than the weight of his grin.

"Whoa, whoa, Dove. I can only answer the questions if I hear them...one at a time." His brow arched, emerald eyes sparking with mischief as though her desperation was the best entertainment he'd had in weeks. "So slow down... or I'll start thinking you actually like the sound of my voice."

Heat burned in her cheeks at his taunt, but she clenched her hands in her skirts, forcing herself to still. Forcing herself to *listen*.

Kain sobered, though the smirk still tugged faintly at his mouth. "Yes, our kingdom has a plan, which can easily be described as we seek vengeance. For Bartoria trespassing on our soil. For Lumiren playing their games in the shadows. For Yssra thinking she has any right to take a human's soul and warp it to do her own bidding." His eyes burned, the words rough with conviction. He took a steadying breath before staring her down with that wolfish intensity. "But we also fight because survival isn't something you wait for someone else to hand you. You take it. You bleed for it. You guard it with teeth bared."

## SERRELAI

### GODDESS OF ADUNDANCE AND RENEWAL

# Chapter Sixteen

*K*ain.

He shifted, leaning closer, voice dropping into something almost conspiratorial. "And yes. My mother knows. She always knows." A flash of teeth, equal parts pride and bitterness. "But she's not here yet. She wanted me to handle the... what did she call it?" His grin widened. "Ah, yes. The bullshit. The haggling and posturing. Soooo, when she arrives at the end of the week, all she'll have to do is nod, shake hands, and put her stamp on whatever I've already tied up."

He sat back again, studying her. "So if you've got more questions, Dove, breathe first. Because I've got all day."

Kain watched her as he spoke, and for once, *thank the gods*, she wasn't retreating behind that polished mask. She was absorbing. Every word, every truth, settling into her like drops of rain soaking through stone. Her eyes brightened with focus, her lips parted in thought, and he could almost hear the gears of that clever mind grinding.

Without a word, she drifted toward the table he'd been leaning over. His maps lay spread across it, scarred parchment inked with every detail the Antonins had scraped together. Their borders, every known Bartorian outpost, towns reduced to ruin, the creeping line of rot spilling from Lumiren. Her fingertips skimmed the edges, tracing lines and notations as though they might whisper the answers she craved.

And then, without even seeming to realize it, she leaned closer. Not just to the map, but to him. Her shoulder brushed near his, her hand hovering close enough to graze his on the table. The princess who had spent weeks locking herself in glass walls was now standing within his storm, unthinking, unguarded. Kain didn't move. Didn't dare break the spell just yet. He only let a slow knowing smile curl across his mouth, victory humming low in his chest as he took in the moment before cracking it.

"Careful, Dove," he murmured, velvet and mocking. "Keep leaning like that and people will start thinking you enjoy my company again."

Her gaze snapped up, flustered. "I don't."

His grin widened. "Good. I'd hate to think I was losing my touch."

Her lips pressed tight to smother the retort, but it slipped anyway. "You never had a touch."

Kain pressed a hand to his chest, mock gasp and all. "Blasphemy. And here I thought I'd aged like fine wine."

Minutes bled into hours. At first, her questions came careful, measured. *Why Lumiren, why now? What did Yssra gain from rot?* He answered, his voice steady but precise, breaking the truths down as though carving them into her. When she pressed too hard, his sarcasm lashed again, and when she glared, he grinned like he'd been waiting for it. Loving every reaction he was getting from her.

The questions came quicker after that. Her lips curled once at one of his jabs. Barely a ghost of a smile, but enough to make his chest tighten. She rolled her eyes at his needling, muttering he'd run out of metaphors if he kept on. He leaned closer, voice low and smug. "Don't worry. I've got plenty more where that came from." And so it went. She poked, he prodded. She asked, he answered. She bristled, he smirked. Slowly, without either of them naming it, the air between them shifted back into the cadence they'd once shared, when she wasn't hiding and he wasn't holding back.

By the time two hours had passed, she was bent over the map, eyes narrowed, her shoulder brushing his with no thought of distance. She was alive again, bold, reckless, hungry, and Kain sat back, letting himself soak in the sight.

He waited, patient as the predator he was, for the next question to fall from her lips. And gods, he hoped she never stopped asking.

Her lips parted, a question rising more urgently than the rest. "The Great War. Why did it start? Truly? Was Yssra part of it then? Has she always been..." She faltered, swallowing. "...watching us more closely than the others?"

Kain tilted his head, studying her, the smile tugging at his mouth, not wolfish this time but edged with something darker. "Keep asking things like that and people will forget you're supposed to be just a pretty smile on a throne." Her glare was answer enough. He chuckled low in his throat, then pushed off the table. "Come on."

She blinked at him. "Come on...where?"

"The library." He flashed her a grin that promised trouble. "You want history? Answers? Let's dig them out. See if the ghosts of the Great War want to whisper us a few secrets."

He watched as that hesitation, that timid princess she had been the last few days start to creep back in. "I'm not permitted..."

"I figured." His tone was casual, but the glint in his eye was lethal. "Lucky for you, I don't give a shit about permits."

And before he would let her retreat into herself anymore, his hand closed around hers and he tugged her toward the door with that infuriating confidence. Tossing a wicked look over his shoulder while catching the shock and comfort flash back at him.

"You're with me today, Dove. And I always get what I want."

The library loomed ahead, its carved doors heavy with history, the air around them quiet as a tomb. Layla's hand tightened around his just as Kain pushed the doors open with casual irreverence, the sound echoing too loudly in the solemn space. It smelled of dust and old parchment, of candles long snuffed out but never forgotten. Rows upon rows of shelves rose high as battlements, each stacked with brittle scrolls and thick leather tomes. Knowledge, forbidden to her.

The librarian was waiting near the archives entrance. An elderly man with thin lips and a spine stiff as the shelves he guarded. His gaze snapped to Layla at once, heavy with disapproval. The old man shuffled forward, bowing low, voice trembling with decrees that had probably been rotting for centuries.

"Forgive me, Princess, but as you well know... women are not permitted in the archives."

Layla froze but Kain didn't. A slow grin spread across his face, all teeth and intent. "Not permitted," he repeated softly, like he was tasting the words. "Now that's interesting. Because where I come from, Dove, anyone stupid enough to keep knowledge from a royal usually ends up decorating a spear."

The librarian stiffened. "It is decree. Tradition..."

Kain held up a hand, laughing under his breath as though the whole thing amused him. "Tradition. Right." He leaned in, his grin never slipping. "Your tradition makes her ignorant. Mine makes corpses. Care to guess which one I respect more?"

The man faltered, paling as Kain tapped a lazy rhythm against the hilt of the dagger at his hip. "Here's how this goes. She walks in. She reads what she wants. You smile, nod, and pray to your gods you never look at her the wrong way again. Because the second you agitate her, I'll gut you in these pretty little halls, stack your bones with the scrolls, and call it redecorating."

The librarian's lips worked soundlessly before he finally stammered, "O-of course... the archives are open to the princess."

Kain clapped him on the shoulder, cheerful as if they were old friends. "See? That wasn't hard. Now run along before I decide I want to test how flammable that beard of yours looks."

As the man scrambled off, Kain turned to Layla, his grin softening into something wicked, deliberate, his tone maddeningly casual. "So Dove, where should we start? Great War? Yssra? Or maybe the bit where they keep pretending you're safer not knowing a damned thing?" And then it happened. She laughed. Bright. Sudden. And completely unpolished. It slipped out before she could smother it, and Kain's chest went tight with the sound. Gods, he hadn't realized how starved he was for it until now. He'd missed that sound. Missed her.

She shook her head, trying to smother it, but the corners of her lips curved anyway. "Storming libraries, terrifying old men... what's next, Kain? Do you plan to interrogate the kitchens for their recipes, too?"

The words were harmless, sarcastic even. But the laugh behind them was what wrecked him. And he couldn't help himself. He tilted his head, grinning slow. "Only if you're on the menu, Dove." Her eyes narrowed, but the color in her cheeks betrayed her. And Kain sat back, satisfaction humming low in his chest. He'd take that laugh again. He'd take that blush. He'd drag every last piece of her back from the ashes, even if he had to scandalize her into remembering she was still alive.

Deep in the archives after what felt like an endless search, Layla lifted a scroll carefully, the parchment brittle beneath her fingers. Dust rose as she unrolled it across the table, the ink dark despite its age. "This is older than the fracture," she murmured. "Before the seven kingdoms."

Kain leaned in, gaze narrowing. "Read it."

She drew a slow breath and began aloud.

## THE GREAT DIVIDE

*In the Age of Union, when the realm stood whole beneath one crown and the gods still walked among mortals, the world was governed by balance. The gods ruled beside men then, not above them. Strength was given freely. Harvest answered prayer. Valor was rewarded. Death was honored. Endings gave way to beginnings. But balance is fragile.*

*Among the gods, one hungered for more. Yssra, Goddess of Rot and Ruin, turned her gaze upon the mortal realm and sought to claim it as her own. Where her influence spread, the land blackened. Soil curdled. Stone softened. Blood fouled. Those who bent their knee to her were granted power through decay, and they named it holiness.*

*The gods were divided. Mortals were caught between them. Eliryn, God of Endings and New Beginnings, turned against his own when the woman he loved was slain by Yssra. In his grief, he saw what the others would not: that gods and mortals were never meant to share the same plane forever. To preserve the realm, the veil was conceived. Yssra was torn from the land and bound beyond it. Her influence severed. Her worship forbidden.*

*The war ended not in victory, but in fracture. The realm that had stood united beneath one king was broken. Borders were drawn. Power was hoarded. Unity became memory.*

*The kingdom who ruled during the Great War...*

Layla's voice faltered. She stared at the parchment. The line ended abruptly, the fibers beneath it shredded, as though the name itself had been scraped from existence. She swallowed and continued, quieter now.

*... stood at the center of the realm's fall. The name has been stricken from record, bloodline erased. Let none speak it.*

Silence pressed in around them. Layla lowered the scroll slowly. "Someone didn't just forget him," she said. "They erased the original king of our land."

Kain's jaw tightened. "Which means they were afraid of what remembering him would do."

Layla's gaze dropped back to the ruined line. A united realm. A war among Gods. A king deliberately unmade by history itself. And now Yssra was stirring again. Whatever had ended the world once had not been finished. It had only been delayed...

After hours buried in maps and ink-stained histories, their stomachs finally reminded them they were mortal. Layla had laughed under her breath when Kain actually made good on his earlier joke. He drug her down into the kitchens like they were a pair of thieves instead of a princess and a savage diplomat. By the time they slipped back into the courtyard, plates in hand, the air had cooled with the brisk bite of autumn. Leaves skittered across the stone, gold and crimson in the wind, while the faint hum of the castle seemed far away.

They settled on a low bench beneath the ivy-clad wall. Kain tore into his food with the easy satisfaction of a man who never wasted a meal, but his eyes kept sliding sideways. Layla sat beside him, the breeze tugging at her hair, picking delicately at the edge of a roll as though eating were some kind of chore. He'd noticed it at every meal. How she barely touched the food, how her frame seemed slighter than when he last held her. It gnawed at him, so he went for the taunt. Kain smirked, eyes flicking to her plate.

"You ate more when you were our prisoner," he said, while popping another grape into his mouth.

Layla arched a brow, her voice dry. "Well, nearly starving me to death might've had something to do with that."

Kain tilted his head as if he were giving it serious thought. Then his mouth curved into a slow grin. "Ah, so I just have to nearly kill you to get you to finish a meal. Good to know."

A startled giggle slipped out of her before she could stop it, quickly smothered by a hand against her lips. Her cheeks warmed. "That's not funny."

"Sure it is," he said, eyes flashing with mischief. "You laughed."

Kain leaned back on one elbow, watching with quiet satisfaction as she actually took another bite, then another. For once, she wasn't just picking at crumbs. The sight settled something deep inside him. That same rare, bone-deep peace he'd only ever found in her presence every time before, and in every damned dream since.

Gathering his thoughts, he smirked. "So... the questions have slowed. Don't tell me I've already won?"

Her gaze drifted from the half-eaten bread in her hand to the leaves tumbling across the courtyard stones. She hesitated before asking, softly, "Theron. Did you ever... find his body?"

Kain's chest tightened. He shook his head once. "No. But when one of ours falls, we don't need a body to know where he's gone. We drink. We cheer. We raise our mugs to Ondurin, welcoming him to the warriors' hall. It was a grand night in honor of him." His lips curved faintly. "He would've liked it. Loud, bloody, chaotic. Just like him."

To his surprise, Layla smiled at the sarcastic quip. It was small, fleeting even, but real. The sight hit him harder than he'd admit. She leaned back against the cold stone wall, exhaling. "My mind's so full, I don't even know what else to ask anymore." Silence settled between them then. But it wasn't strained. It was... comfortable. The kind of quiet that let the breeze speak, carrying the scent of fallen leaves and autumn earth as the branches overhead whispered against the sky. They sat like that for a long while, side by side, watching the gold and crimson leaves spiral down.

And then, he heard her exhale, and with a dry laugh, Layla asked, "Do you know how to get rid of nightmares?"

**SERRELAI**

**The Golden Bloom. The Ever-Spring. Keeper of the Flourishing Realms.**

Serelai's presence is the promise of life renewed. Her hair, bright as golden straw, carries the warmth of summer fields, and the crown of flowers she wears drips gold as though shaped by sunlight itself. Once, her blessings stretched across every corner of the realm. Fields thrived, rivers overflowed with clarity, and the earth pulsed with her generous touch.

But as the kingdoms slowly ceased their gratitude, turning their hearts from the old ways and their thanks from the gods, Serelai's gifts began to dwindle. Through the veil, all power is give and take, gratitude and grace intertwined. Now, her blessings reach only those who still honor her name, and even then, her touch is faint, softened by distance and the world's forgetting.

Yet where true thanks is given, even softly, Serelai answers as best she can, coaxing life to bloom again.

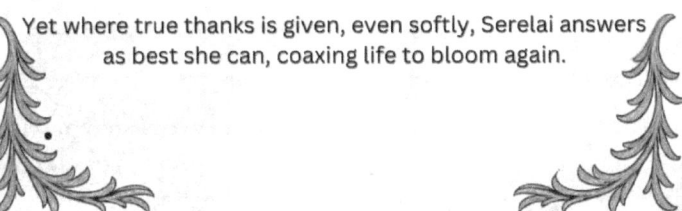

# Chapter Seventeen

*L* *ayla.*

Layla peered at him through her lashes, catching the faint lift of his brows. A smirk tugged at her lips before he could speak. "Like some secret tonic Eir whipped up just for you all? Dreamless sleep in a cup, you know, nightmare-proof, perfectly blissful?" She knew such a thing didn't exist. *Of course it didn't*. But if anyone could conjure something close, it would be Eir. And if anyone would know, it would be Kain. A ridiculous question, but she had to ask, even knowing the answer. She glanced at him then, lips quirking. "Because if you do, I'd like to formally accuse you of withholding vital information and might just have to strangle you."

Kain didn't answer right away. Not long enough to be obvious. Just long enough for her to notice. His fingers stilled where they rested against his knee. His head tilted, eyes narrowing slightly, not in amusement but consideration. The firelight caught along the edge of his jaw as if he'd gone suddenly still.

Layla's smile wavered. She rushed to fill the space. "I'm kidding," she added quickly. "Mostly."

A corner of his mouth lifted at last, slow and familiar. "If Eir's got something like that," he said, "she hasn't shared it with me."

There it was. The answer she'd expected. A flicker of disappointment brushed through her, sudden and irrational. Some foolish part of her had hoped for anything at all. Something that might make the nights less traumatic. Help her to endure them easier. But Layla wouldn't let the knowledge dimmish the day.

So she exhaled softly and shrugged, forcing lightness back into her tone. "Figures." But she didn't miss the way his gaze lingered on her a moment longer than necessary. The way his expression shifted, not quite concern, not quite anything she could name. As if he were weighing words he chose not to speak. And somehow, that was worse. And better.

The moment eased, sliding back into that easy rhythm they'd found again today. The one that didn't ask questions or demand answers. Just space. Just presence. Layla hadn't realized how heavy she'd been until that weight lifted, just a fraction. She was still a princess. Still bound by duty, expectation, and the quiet ache of what she couldn't say. But here, with the wind whipping and Kain close enough to ground her, she felt lighter. And for now, that was enough.

As she popped another grape into her mouth, a small hum escaped her lips. Her whole body seemed to uncoil, her soul loosening in a way it hadn't in weeks. She just... smiled. *Content* she realized. That was the word that came to mind. Strange and foreign, but true. She wondered, not for the first time, if she had pushed Kain away too hard these past few days. Not because he unsettled her, but because he didn't. He was a storm, yes, but he was calm water too. He made her laugh when she'd forgotten how. Made her remember she was more than a princess begging to be seen or approved of. Reckless. Infuriating. And yet... steady, in his own chaotic way. She had felt it then, that heat she refused to name, the pull that had made her retreat before it could take hold. That was why she'd drawn the line. Why she'd kept him at a distance. But friendship didn't have to mean surrender. Friendship could be safe. Controlled. He was a friend. A disruptive one, perhaps, but a friend all the same. And if she kept it there, firmly and carefully, then surely nothing else could grow between them.

The thought lingered, soft as the autumn breeze, as she reached for another grape, the fruit just shy of her lips when Kain's hand closed around her wrist, firm and immovable. Her eyes whipped to his as her breath stuttered. He guided her hand toward his mouth, slow enough that she could have pulled away. She didn't. Couldn't. His gaze held hers, unwavering, until the world narrowed to the space between them. He leaned in with infuriating patience, taking the fruit from her fingers one careful inch at a time. He lingered long enough for her to feel the warmth of his breath and the faintest sweep of his tongue against her fingertips, before finally pulling back. His lips curved as the tip of her finger slid out. As though the taste had been something far more intoxicating than a grape.

Layla's chest constricted. Her lips parted uselessly. Her pulse pounded so hard she swore he could hear it. And then, low and velvet, his voice coiled around her in its most suffocating and entrancing way.

"Now... what was that you said about strangling me?" His grin curled infuriatingly smug. "I'd love to see you try. Though..." His tongue flicked out, catching the bead of juice clinging to his lip. "...there are far more interesting places I can think of for those hands to wrap around."

Heat roared through her so fast she nearly reeled. Her body betrayed her, cheeks burning, breath shallow, mouth open in stunned silence. Somehow, instinct saved her. She swatted his shoulder, her gasp cracking into a flustered laugh, desperate to smother the fire.

"You're such an *ass*!"

He barked a laugh, warm and delighted, leaning in as though she hadn't just tried to put distance between them. His breath was hot against her ear now, his words intimate, possessive. "So happy to have you back, Dove."

Layla shook her head at him, the motion almost absentminded. Fury and annoyance tangled with something far more volatile, waging a quiet war low in her belly as he effortlessly reminded her why his friendship *wasn't* a good idea. And still, she could feel it. That reckless warmth of her true self returning, dragged out by him whether she wanted it or not.

The chill of the courtyard clung to them as they slipped back inside, stone swallowing the wind. The corridor stretched ahead, torches sputtering against the walls, and for a while they walked in silence. The sound of their footsteps echoing together was almost peaceful. Layla let herself breathe, the quiet wrapping around her like a balm. And then Kain shattered the silence.

"Five years ago," he said abruptly, his voice low, even. "That's when Lumiren made their first move. They crept into Antonin lands like rats, thought they could slink past unnoticed. My father was there at the border. He happened to be out on a scouting trip. He saw them cross. He didn't let them take a step further into our lands." Layla's eyes snapped to him. "They fought," Kain continued, almost clinically. "One Lumiren cut him down. Theron saw it. He saw our father's last breath leave him." A muscle ticked in his jaw, but he didn't falter. "None of them lived to crawl back across the border."

Layla stopped mid-step, her heart stalling in her chest. He didn't slow.

"My mother gave me the vengeance," he went on, voice low, relentless. "She put their heir in my sights. She knew I could end it quick, clean, blood for blood, before anyone else even knew what had happened. And I did. One arrow. Straight through his skull." His mouth curved faintly, though it was nothing like a smile. "But it wasn't enough. She knew it. I knew it. Nothing about it was enough."

The weight of his words pressed into her bones. Layla swallowed hard, sorrow burning low in her chest. Not fear, not horror, but the ache of his loss, the pride that he had avenged his father with his own hand.

Kain finally looked at her then, eyes gleaming with something wild, something that belonged to the storm itself. "This..." he said, a dark edge in his tone, "...all of this with Lumiren, with Bartoria, with Yssra's rot choking the land? Don't think it started last month. This has been building. This has been coming for years. And my mother will not stop.

Not this time. She will burn them to ash before she lets them take a single step further."

Layla's mind spun, trying to piece it together. *Yssra. Lumiren. A five-year shadow creeping longer than anyone in Graystonia had realized.* Her voice was barely a whisper. "Does Sir Edwin and the council know?"

Kain's smirk curved, slow and mocking. "No. Haven't told a soul. You're the first."

Her breath caught at the admission, at the vulnerability, at what he was giving her. "Then...then may I? Please. They need to know this, Kain. If the alliance is to work...if Yssra's hand has been in this longer than we thought, they must."

For a moment, he only studied her. Then that wicked grin deepened, enough to make her pulse jump. "Why do you think I just told you?" He said with a wink. "They haven't believed a damned word I've said. I hope they listen to you." He sighed and crossed his arms. "Now run along, Dove. Tell them Antonin's queen isn't backing down. Tell them Yssra's been rotting at our door for years. Let them chew on it, twist it, use it however they please. All I care about is that they remember this: when my mother arrives, she isn't coming to negotiate. She's coming to finish the war they started."

Something inside her broke at the rawness of it, the honesty. She didn't think, she simply threw her arms around him. Hugging him fiercely. "Thank you," she whispered, though the words felt pitiful compared to what she meant. Thank you for the truth. For this entire day. For more than she could say. His arms tightened instantly, iron and fire banding her to him. When she pulled back to meet his eyes, he was staring down at her. His gaze unflinching, dropping slowly, deliberately, to her lips. Their breath tangled. Her own gaze fell to his mouth. And gods, she leaned...

"My lady?"

The voice shattered the moment like glass.

Layla turned to find Sir Edwin standing at the far end of the corridor. His expression betrayed only the barest flicker of surprise, quickly schooled back into neutrality, but it was enough to send her pulse roaring. She should have been terrified. Caught like this. Too close. Too exposed. She went to pull away, but Kain's grip only tightened, holding her in place as though daring Edwin to speak. She shot him a wide-eyed, almost comical look of disbelief, silently begging him to let go.

He only smirked down at her, wolfish and shameless, utterly unconcerned. Worse, utterly confident. The way his gaze slid to Edwin wasn't confrontational, but it wasn't careless either. It was knowing. As if he already understood exactly how this would end. And just like that, the fear ebbed. Not gone, but quieted. She realized, with a strange certainty, that she had nothing to worry about. That whatever unspoken exchange passed between those two men had happened long before this moment.

Finally, Kain released her, slow and deliberate, like a blade being sheathed.

Layla drew a steadying breath and gathered her composure, lifting her chin as she crossed the distance toward Sir Edwin. "Sir Edwin," she said smoothly. "I have something important to share with you."

When she glanced back over her shoulder, Kain was already gone.

LAPETIC

**GOD OF DEATH**

# Chapter Eighteen

*L*<sup>*ayla*.</sup>

The brush slid through her damp hair, each stroke slow, deliberate, as though she could tame not only her curls but the chaos of her thoughts. Marilla had just left her chambers, leaving behind the faint scent of lavender oil and the warm hush of the dying day. The sunset spilled through her window, soft orange bleeding into violet, gilding her in light. For the first time in weeks, she didn't look away from her reflection. She didn't flinch from her own eyes. The girl in the mirror wasn't polished, wasn't wearing a façade. Not tonight. And she was so relieved.

Her blue shift clung lightly to her shoulders, simple and unadorned, but she didn't hate what she saw. She didn't dread tomorrow. She didn't think of who she would have to perform as then. Instead, she lingered in the weightless quiet of now. Reflecting on peace, on joy, and on knowledge. Kain had kept his word. Gods, he had kept it to the letter. Every question answered. Even the forbidden ones. He had gotten her into the library archives, into the heart of Graystonia's history itself. It had felt so good, intoxicatingly good, to be treated as more. To be seen, heard, challenged, instead of hushed into silence.

And when she'd told Sir Edwin everything... her heart had braced for dismissal, for a cold reminder of her place. But instead, he'd listened. Truly listened. No judgment in his eyes. Only intent, steady weight. He'd told her it mattered. That he would bring it to the others, press for more, use it. He'd thanked her. *Thanked her!* She'd felt... worthy.

A smile curved across her lips as she brushed through another tangle, her reflection softened by the last streaks of sunset. And then, unbidden, a different memory slipped in. The heat of Kain's mouth closing around her fingers, a merciless heat in his eyes. The solid wall of him when his arms had caged her, his gaze dropping to her lips until her breath caught. Her own lips parted now, and she bit them lightly, foolishly, as if her body remembered before her mind could stop it. Her heart thudded, heavy and painful, because gods help her, for one reckless moment it hadn't felt wrong. The brush stilled in her hand as the memories engulfed her. But a quiet *click* instantly broke the onslaught. The latch turned and her door eased open. Kain slipped into her chambers without a word, shutting the door behind him with deliberate finality. Layla's breath faltered, not just from the intrusion but from the cruel timing of it. She'd been thinking of him only moments ago, his lips, his eyes, the memory of being pressed against him, and now here he was. Gods, she prayed he couldn't read it on her face.

But when she turned fully to him, her embarrassment faded to unease. His brows were drawn, his jaw taut. Frustration radiated off him like heat from a forge.

"Is everything... alright?" she asked carefully, setting her brush aside.

He didn't answer at first, only walked to her fireplace and gripped the mantle tightly, bowing his head as though wrestling with himself. The sight of him, this untouchable force suddenly weighted, made her chest tighten. Then, voice low and raw, he said, "I didn't answer all your questions, Dove."

Her surprise spilled out in a startled laugh, though nerves made it brittle. "Kain, I don't know what you're talking about. You did answer them. All of them. Honestly, I didn't think you could...but you did." Her shoulders loosened as she taunted him lightly, hoping to tease him out of whatever was brewing within.

But when he lifted his gaze to hers, her stomach dropped. His eyes weren't playful. They were relentless. "Tell me about the nightmare, Dove."

The smile fell from her lips. Her throat closed, her breath catching painfully in her chest. *Gods, no. Not that.* She tried to deflect, her voice quick and too bright. "It's nothing... no big deal. I'm used to it.... Really, Kain. That question didn't count earlier. Seriously, you won."

He straightened, crossing the room in two strides. His hand rose, warm and calloused, cupping her cheek with a gentleness that clashed with the raw intensity in his eyes. Pine, leather, and heat... He encompassed all her senses as he bent close. "Tell me."

She trembled, every instinct warring to run, deny, hide. But ultimately she dropped her gaze, shame dragging her down, her voice breaking as she whispered, "It's always the same. That night in Bartoria. What King Ivar did...to me..." Layla dared a glance back up at him. Kain's jaw clenched hard enough to crack bone. But he didn't speak. He only waited, silent and implacable, until the rest spilled from her lips. "Hands pawing at me, all over my body, then the sound of my slip being torn...." She gulped, staring at nothing on the ground. Her voice quivered as she forced the memories into words. "Then his face, him forcing me onto my back. A blade pressed to my throat. I can't move, can't scream, can't fight..." Her hands were shaking, but she forced herself to finish. "Then he...violates me...I endure the pain until I finally wake up." She took a deep breath, preparing herself, steadying her mind.

A finger slid beneath her chin firm and unrelenting. Forcing her gaze back up to his. Kain's face was a thunderhead waiting to break. His emerald gaze burned, not with mockery, not with pity, but with something far more bare. *Pain*. Sheer violence straining against its chains. And beneath it, something raw that undid her completely. She watched him ponder something then finally, his voice dropped, lethal and intimate, every word a dagger pressed to her skin. "Do you trust me?"

The answer was simple. "Yes."

He searched her eyes for what felt like an eternity, and she felt helpless beneath the weight of it. He was looking for something...*doubt? Hesitation?* But she honestly had none. She trusted him completely. She had since what he did for her mother, for her kingdom,... for her. He gave the smallest nod, and before she could ask what it meant, his hands guided her gently to stand and turn toward her mirror.

Layla drew in a deep breath as she took in the sight of them within: Her pale and trembling in her shift, and him, a shadow at her back, storm, fire, and something unreadable coiled beneath his skin. She didn't understand. Her fingers strained at the sides of her shift as panic pressed in.

"Kain...what are you doing?" she whispered.

He bent close, so close she felt his breath sweep against her ear, low and velvety smooth. "At any point you want me to stop," he murmured, "just say the word." Her eyes widened, locking on his in the mirror. Confusion twisted sharp inside her chest. *What was he doing?* But his gaze in the glass held her steady, pinning her where she stood. She'd never seen him like this. Not mocking. Not teasing. Just... fierce. Raw. Her pulse pounded so loud she thought he could hear it.

"Close your eyes, Dove," his voice was like steel wrapped in silk.

Her lips parted, breath shaky as her eyes darted between his reflection and her own. She didn't understand... but she closed them anyway.

Her entire body snapped to high alert instantly, nerves lit like tinder. His breath brushed the side of her neck, low and steady as he whispered again, "Think about the nightmare, Dove. I know it's hard, but I need you to picture it for me."

Layla swallowed, the sound loud in her own ears. But she forced herself back into the memory. The unseen hands clawing at her, faceless, ruthless, and terrifying. Her chest tightened. Then she felt him. Kain's fingers, feather-light, sliding up the length of her arms. The touch knocked the breath from her, a soft, involuntary gasp slipping free.

"Keep thinking," he murmured, velvet edged with command. "Stay with it, Dove."

She forced herself back into the memory. *The faceless hands tearing at her*, just as Kain's slid from her arms to ghosting down her hips. One hand stopped and pressed firmly. Now squeezing the inside of her thigh, grounding her in heat and strength, while the other began to trace a slow path up her stomach, lingering just below her sternum. Her breath hitched. She was nothing but sensation now, eyes shut, trapped between the nightmare she was trying to recall and the reality of his touch. His hands were everywhere, circling closer, hovering at the edges of forbidden places but never crossing. He was teasing, tormenting, and completely undoing her inch by inch.

Her breathing quickened, chest rising rapidly as heat flooded her. Her breasts ached with fullness, her nipples tightening. She couldn't summon Ivar's hands anymore, only Kain's. Everywhere at once, alternating between feather-light caresses that made her shiver and demanding squeezes that stole her breath. Her back pressed into his solid chest, his presence surrounding her, filling every space where fear had lived.

His voice came low against her ear, "Okay, Dove... now what happens next? You said your shift rips, didn't you?" She gulped, mustering just enough courage to nod. His hands moved at once, strong and deliberate. As he slid up her sides, fingers grazing the curve of her waist before gliding higher. They swept over her breasts, full and aching beneath his touch, lingering only an instant before... *rip!*. The sound tore through the air, the same sound that haunted her nightmares. Her shift split, and the cool night rushed in to kiss her bared skin. Goosebumps scattered across her body, a tremor of shock and want colliding all at once. Heat poured from Kain at her back, his presence swallowing her whole.

She gasped, the sound raw and unguarded. His hands roamed without pause, down her hips, back to her breasts. Now confidently squeezing, kneading, and claiming. She was all sensation and no thought. Every nerve in her body burned alive, every part of her pressed tight against him as though he could anchor her in place by touch alone.

"His face torments your nightmares. But I want you to open your eyes Dove." And she did, opening her now hooded eyes and what she saw was surreal. It was Kain's hands on her naked body, her shift hanging on either side of her. And the look of raw hunger as Kain stared into her soul in the mirror. His hands never stopping. Kneading, roaming. He was everywhere, but his eye were on hers. Kain's hand then slid up, cupping her jaw, tilting her face toward his with a deliberate gentleness that still left her breathless. Then he turned her, guiding her body with sure hands on her ribs. Step by step he pressed forward, her feet retreating until the back of her knees met the edge of the mattress. She toppled softly onto it, the shift torn and useless around her, leaving her bare and open beneath his shadow.

He loomed between her thighs, the heat of him searing, his focus unwavering. "You felt helpless, didn't you? No control. A blade at your throat?" His voice was low, dangerous, but steady. Forcing her to meet the memory, not flee it. Her teeth caught her lower lip, trembling, and she gave the faintest nod. So lost in this with him.

He drew a dagger from his belt, slipping it between his teeth as his hands went to the hem of his shirt. Her mouth fell open as he pulled it over his head, tossing it aside. Then maddeningly slow, he worked the ties of his pants loose. Inch by inch, the fabric slid down, pooling at his feet. Layla's gaze raked over him, her throat tightening. Lean, sculpted muscle carved in sharp planes and shadows, every line honed to perfection. He stood before her like something forged for war and sin alike, and the only thought in her head was a raw, breathless *holy gods*.

She looked back up at him, no longer even bothering to hide the desire burning through her. Kain climbed on top of her and leaned down until their noses nearly brushed, emerald eyes locked to hers as he drew the dagger from between his teeth and let its cold edge whisper against her throat. Before she could react, overthink, he dipped his head and pressed his mouth to the curve of her neck beside the blade, danger and desire now entwined. Her eyes fluttered shut, ultimately savoring the contrast: the sting of the blade, the worship of his lips.

When his hips shifted, she gasped, awareness snapping back to every inch of him. He pulled back just enough to look into her eyes as he aligned himself, his stare unrelenting, daring her to look away. She didn't. Couldn't. And then, so achingly slow, he pushed inside her. Her back arched helplessly, body straining to take him, to mold around him. She didn't know how he could possibly fit but gods, every part of her wanted him to.

Immediately his arm slid beneath her lower back, arching her deeper against him before suddenly, he moved. With effortless strength, he rolled them, the world tilting until she found herself straddling him, seated fully down on his cock. The gasp that tore from her lips was helpless and unguarded, her body stretched around him, owned by the fullness of him. Before she could even catch her breath, he caught her hand, guiding it upward with deliberate care. The cold weight of the dagger pressed into her palm, and then higher, until the tip hovered at his own throat.

His voice was low, rough, reverent. "You are in control."

The words slammed into her harder than any thrust. Shock. Awe. A flicker of adoration she hadn't known she could feel in this moment, all tangled together as she realized what he'd just given her. *Freedom. Power. Choice.* Her hand trembled, but he released her wrist, leaving the blade poised where *she* held it. She could end this. She could run. She could draw the dagger across his throat and feel his blood spill warm and certain. Or she could stay. Ride him. Claim this moment as her own. It was hers to decide. *Her choice.*

And with that, she kept the dagger steady at his throat and began to move. Slowly, deliberately, testing the edge of her control. His hands clamped around her hips, fingers biting into her skin as his head fell back, emerald eyes half-glazed with hunger.

She rode him slow at first, then faster. Every shift of her body sending fire lancing through her veins, the blade glinting between them, trembling with each rise and fall. His gaze locked on hers, unwavering even as his breath grew ragged, even as she pressed him harder, faster. Her need consumed her, flooding her body until there was no space for thought, only him beneath her, the danger in her hand, the storm in his eyes. The heat built overwhelming and merciless, cresting too fast, too hard, until she broke. A cry tore from her lips as release crashed through her, her body clenching around him, rippling, gripping him tight as if she could drag him under with her. And even with the dagger still poised at his throat, he smiled. It was hungry, wicked, and victorious.

Once her body finally stilled, shaking from the storm he'd pulled her through, his hands steadied her hips. With a gentleness that didn't match the rawness of what they'd just shared, he lifted her and eased her down beside him on the bed. If she hadn't already been stunned, she was now.

Without a word, he rose, bare skin gilded by the faint glow of the lamplight. He bent to snatch the throw blanket, draping it over her shoulders with a sure, deliberate touch. Not as though she might break, but as though she was worth guarding. Worth being wrapped in something more than heat and hunger. The gesture was unexpected and unnecessary. Not grand, not loud. But gods, it undid her more than any of it. Because it was comfort, it was Kain, and it was exactly what she hadn't known she craved until now. His strength had stripped her bare, but this quiet tenderness wrapped her whole.

Yet a single thought pressed at her. He hadn't finished. Hadn't taken the release he'd so freely given her. He'd carried her through the chaos and left himself in the wreckage, as though her pleasure alone had been the point.

She found her voice at last, broken and unsure. "Umm... you didn't... we could..."

But he only shook his head, a wry smile ghosting across his lips as he tugged his shirt back over his shoulders. "No, Dove. This was about you."

With his pants only half-laced, he crossed back to her, bending low until his mouth brushed the crown of her head. Her lashes fluttered as he pulled back just enough for their eyes to meet, his gaze was a molten blend that burned and soothed all at once.

"Come find me if you have another nightmare," he murmured. And with a grin that seemed half-wicked, half-promise. He winked, slid out the door, and was gone. Only then did she notice it. The dagger he had pressed into her palm was still there, glinting in the low light, abandoned on the coverlet beside her. A reminder. A choice. A mark of trust she hadn't asked for but couldn't ignore. She sat wrapped in the blanket, stunned, the maelstrom of him still pressed into her skin.

LAPETIC

### The Final Veil. The Hollow King. Keeper of All That Ends.

Lapetic is the stillness that follows the last breath, the silence that swallows all mortal echoes. Where Eliryn governs the turning of fate, Lapetic rules what waits after it. Cloaked in shadow and moonless cold, he walks unseen among the dying, guiding souls across the threshold only he may open. His touch is neither cruel nor kind, merely inevitable.

Long ago, mortals offered him reverence for peaceful passage, but as the kingdoms turned from the gods, fear replaced devotion. Through the veil, fear feeds him little, and so his presence has grown darker, hungrier, more restless. Now, he answers only those who face death without trembling, for only courage can meet the Hollow King without being devoured by his shadow.

# Chapter Nineteen

*L* *ayla.*

Layla woke from her first full night of sleep in longer than she could remember. No jolting awake in a cold sweat. No silent screams clawing at her throat. Just quiet stillness and rest. Gods, real rest. For a blissful moment, she simply lay there, staring at the morning light filtering through her window, her lips curving faintly before she realized why her body felt loose, why her limbs hummed as though she were boneless. *Kain.*

Heat rushed up her neck, and she bit her lip as flashes of the night before tangled in her mind. His hands, his voice, the dagger cool against her throat while his mouth... She squeezed her eyes shut as she groaned into the pillow. *Absolutely not. She would not think about it again.* She was betrothed! Promised to Ryker Jameson, a good and honorable man.

What had happened last night was wrong. Reckless. A mistake she could not, would not, repeat. But then the thought struck, cold and unforgiving. Theron. *Gods, Theron!* This was his brother. His blood. The man he'd bled beside, been raised beside. And she had let him touch her, had wanted him to do so much more... Layla's stomach twisted violently. What kind of person did that make her? What kind of woman did that make her? And if anyone in the castle would have seen them! *Gods!* Layla buried her face in her pillow as she let out a frustrated scream at herself.

And still, no matter how many times she scolded herself, the memory slithered back, unbidden and relentless. While she bathed, the warm water only betrayed her, coaxing her skin to remember the ghost of his touch. She hissed a curse and plunged beneath the surface, as if she could drown the sin clinging to her like heat.

And later, when she stood before the mirror, Marilla's fingers tugging and tightening the laces of her gown, Layla's breath caught. For one treacherous heartbeat, she didn't see herself alone with Marilla assisting her gown. She saw the memory of him behind her in the glass...Those eyes heavy with desire, his body pressed against hers, his hands roaming her as if she were something he had every right to claim. The flash of it burned so hot and consuming she had to shift her legs just to steady herself.

Her reflection stared back at her, and she knew she would never see it the same way again. She straightened abruptly, willing the heat away, forcing her shoulders back as though posture alone could cage what he had awakened. But no more. She would not let Kain undo her. Not again.

Breakfast was painfully quiet. Aerilynn sat across from Layla, pale but present, while Ciana pushed bits of food around her plate. Layla herself stared down at her porridge, her spoon stirring in idle circles as her mind betrayed her again and again. *Not here. Not now.* She bit her lip, willing herself not to think about last night. Not his hands, not his mouth, not the way her body still ached from the memory of him inside her. *Gods, stop.* She repeated the words like a commandment, but her treacherous mind disobeyed, conjuring the ghost of his heat, the scrape of his teeth, the press of his breath...

"How did you sleep, Dove?" The voice purred at her ear. Warm. Low. And darkly amused.

Layla jolted so violently her spoon clattered from her fingers, ricocheting across the table and landing in Ciana's lap. She froze, mortified, heat blazing up her neck. Behind her, a laugh quietly erupted. It was deep, sinful, and utterly unrepentant. The sound curled over her skin like smoke. And then he appeared, sliding into the chair beside her with the kind of casual arrogance that made her want to scream. His presence swallowing the air between them as though he had been sitting there all along.

Layla forced her spine straight, hands rigid in her lap, but her pulse thundered in her ears. She couldn't look at him. Wouldn't. Not with Ciana's eyes flicking curiously between them. Not with Aerilynn staring, half-shocked, half-amused. But she could feel him. Smirking. Watching. Reveling in her unraveling.

Not a minute later, her body betrayed her commands as she glanced at him. He was the picture of arrogant ease. Lounging back in his chair, broad shoulders relaxed, one boot propped casually against the table leg. Every so often, he'd reach across her plate, stealing something: a fig, a slice of bread, everything on her plate without asking like he had done each day. Each theft deliberate and annoying.

"Hungry?" Layla muttered through clenched teeth as he plucked a strawberry from her bowl.

"Starving." The word dripped with suggestion, his tone low enough that only she could hear as he devoured the strawberry. Her hand tightened around her fork. She refused to rise to it. *He wants a reaction. Don't give him one.* She kept her eyes down, pretending to focus on her porridge. But every sense seemed attuned and tangled in him. And then, as if sensing the crack in her resolve, he picked up a grape, rolled it lazily between his fingers, and popped it into his mouth. His gaze slid to hers, slow and deliberate, as he chewed. Heat rushed to her cheeks. Her stomach flipped. *Gods, no.*

She pushed back her chair, rising so abruptly the legs scraped against the marble floor. "Excuse me," she said tightly, forcing a polite smile toward her sisters. "I need some air." Ciana blinked, startled. Aerilynn's brows lifted ever so slightly. But before anyone could question her, Layla turned and walked briskly toward the door, ignoring the quiet chuff of laughter that followed her out.

She barely made it five feet down the corridor before a hand caught her wrist. The world tilted momentarily before her back hit a wall, hard but not painful, the cool stone biting through her gown. Kain stood before her, caging her with one arm above her and one on her waist. He was so close the air between them trembled.

"What are you doing!?" she hissed, eyes wide as saucers. "Someone could see!"

He only raised a brow, utterly unbothered. Then, with infuriating calm, he lifted his hand. She now noticed an apple resting in his palm. "Didn't want you skipping breakfast just because you're trying to avoid me again."

"I'm *not* trying to avoid you," she snapped, though her voice betrayed her with its breathless edge. "I just...we just..."

Something in his expression shifted. The smirk faltered, his jaw tightening. "Did I..." His voice lowered, almost hesitant now. "Did I do something wrong last night?"

Her pulse stuttered. The change in him was so sudden, so sincere. It unraveled her composure in an instant. She shook her head quickly, the words tumbling out. "No, of course not." Kain's shoulders eased a fraction, but the heat in his eyes didn't fade, it deepened. "I just..." Layla swallowed hard, struggling to find the words. "We can't do this, Kain. You can't act like this. We can't...Theron! Gods, he was your brother! And I'm engaged! Kain we *can't* be anything!" Her excuses came out ragged, stacked on top of each other like a desperate barricade.

Kain's smirk never faltered, but his eyes hardened to sharp, cutting emeralds. He dropped his arm and stepped back just enough to lean his shoulder against the wall beside her, arms folding across his chest, the picture of lazy indifference. As if her trembling confession hadn't so much as grazed him.

"Feel better now?" he asked softly, one brow lifting. "Got that all out?"

Layla's lips parted, her pulse still skittering. "Don't mock me, Kain. I mean it."

"Oh, I know you do." His voice was deceptively calm. "You always mean it when you're trying to convince yourself of something." Her throat tightened at his jab as he tilted his head. "So last night didn't satisfy you?" His voice dripped with mockery now. "Is that what I'm hearing? Because I could've sworn that sweet heat flooding around my cock told a very different story. And that sound you made..." His smirk deepened into something wicked. "Gods, Dove, that didn't sound like a woman who *wasn't* enjoying herself."

Layla's mouth fell open. *The audacity!* Heat rushed to her cheeks. "Kain," she hissed, her voice dropping to a frantic whisper. "That's not... ugh, that's not what I'm saying. I mean... we cannot..." she stumbled over the words, mortified, "we cannot have sex again."

In a blink, he shoved off the wall and closed the space she'd tried to create. His presence hit her like thunder rolling over the mountains. "First of all, Dove," he murmured, voice silk over a razor's edge, "that wasn't sex. That was ...a *release*. A tonic for your nightmares you could even call it. But Dove, when I have sex with you, when I *fuck* you...you'll be screaming my name so loud the gods themselves will hear." Her breath caught as heat immediately coiled low and merciless in her belly.

"Second..." His hand rose, brushing a stray lock of hair from her cheek, his tone roughening. "Theron is dead. He's feasting in Ondurin's halls, drinking and laughing with the warriors. He has no place in a discussion about *my cock inside you.*" Her entire body jolted at the bluntness, shame and hunger tangling like thorns inside her chest. "And third," Kain went on, lips curving into that wolfish grin, "I'm not here to ruin your ridiculous betrothal. But you're not married yet. And until that crown shackles you, you've got choices." He leaned close, his breath brushing her ear. "So if you want another release. Or better, a *royal fucking*...friends can do that. I can be your friend in any form you want, Dove."

Her mouth dried at the raw truth he was laying out. It was sinful, brutal, and deliciously honest. He wasn't even hiding it. Offering her something she knew if she dared, would be the most devastatingly exquisite pleasure she'd ever taste. For the longest heartbeat of her life, she actually thought about it. Contemplated saying yes. The pure ecstasy that could await her. And then she snapped herself back. *Hard.*

"No, Kain." Her voice shook, but she forced steel into it. "Just friends. No se—" She broke off, flustered, waving her hand as if to swat the very word from the air. "No." His smirk said he'd heard exactly what she hadn't said.

"Now," she pressed on quickly, straightening her spine, forcing composure, "as my *friend*. Why don't you tell me how your meetings are going now that the council has more information?"

Kain studied her for a moment, then gave a decisive nod, stepping back. His voice was flat at first, but edged in that cutting humor of his. "Nothing's being decided until Mother arrives in two days. But last we talked, we were trying to convince your almighty Ryker to pull his head out of his ass long enough to seek alliances with Myriamis and Elarith. Get all the southern kingdoms on the same side."

Layla nodded slowly. "That would be the smartest move. And Ryker?"

"He's saying it wouldn't be necessary. Defending each of our own kingdoms will be enough like it *always has*." Kain's lip curled. "Naïve dumbass." Layla's head snapped toward him, a warning glare narrowing her eyes. Kain only shrugged, utterly unbothered. "What? Friends are supposed to be honest with one another."

He turned, striding a few steps down the corridor before pausing. His voice carried back over his shoulder, silken and cutting all at once. "Run along, Dove. You've got porcelain to polish." And then, with a glance that made her chest tighten and a wicked grin tugging at his mouth, he added, "Oh... and the offer still stands. Next nightmare, come find me. I'll be right here."

The wink he threw her before disappearing left her standing there breathless, her pulse far too wild to pretend she hadn't considered saying yes.

"Sooo, are you going to tell me what all that was about?"

Layla nearly jumped out of her skin, startled by Aerilynn slipping around the corner and looping her arm through hers. "I..." Layla faltered, words dying on her tongue. What *could* she say? What he told her yesterday, what he did last night... it wasn't something she could just hand over, even to Aerilynn. Everything they had done was inappropriate. Improper in their kingdom. Improper of a woman betrothed. Improper for a woman in general. Not something to be voiced out loud, let alone ever actually occur.

Aerilynn squeezed her arm, her voice gentle. "It's okay. You don't have to tell me. Just answer this: Do we trust him?"

The tension eased from Layla's shoulders. She looked at her sister, and a small, content smile curved her lips. "Yes. We trust him." Aerilynn nodded firmly, as if that was all she needed. She gave Layla another squeeze, grounding and warm. "You seem... better," Layla said, narrowing her eyes, suspicion soft but curious.

"I am." Aerilynn's smile was faint, but it carried a weight of truth Layla hadn't seen on her in months. "I feel better, actually."

Relief bloomed through Layla's chest, loosening something she hadn't realized was tight. "I'm so glad. Truly."

"I've been... talking to someone." Aerilynn's cheeks colored, her smile turning sheepish. "It's helped."

Layla blinked in surprise. The confession was small, but it carried a world within it. Aerilynn clearly wasn't about to say more, and Layla knew better than to press. Or to even go so far as to lecture her about who she could and couldn't trust. Instead, Layla squeezed her back. "I'm glad, too. Whoever it is... I'm grateful they're helping you find peace. Helping you find yourself again."

"Me too." Aerilynn's voice was soft but steady.

And together, the sisters walked on, arm in arm, toward another day of lessons and expectations. The same gilded cage, the same careful script. But something in Layla had changed. The doubt that had once silenced her was giving way to something far more dangerous: conviction. Her confidence wasn't just returning; it was rebuilding itself stronger, steadier, forged in frustration and quiet defiance.

For the first time in weeks, she didn't feel small. She didn't feel forgotten. She felt inevitable.

The next two days blurred together, heavy with anticipation. Not only was Queen Okteria's arrival looming, but Aerilynn's eighteenth birthday pressed close as well. Queen Raynera insisted on a grand ball in her honor now that she was up and about. A spectacle meant to reassure Graystonia's people that nothing had changed, that their kingdom still stood firm and stable. But Layla knew better. The celebration was as much for politics as for her sister. A performance staged for the court, for the people, and most of all, for Queen Okteria's eyes.

Preparations swallowed their days whole. Seamstresses, musicians, and cooks filled the castle with constant noise. Lessons doubled. Dresses were fitted. Hair was styled and restyled until Layla's scalp ached. And still, the weight of expectation pressed down like iron.

It was during one of the few stolen hours between fittings that Ryker finally asked for her company again.

That evening, Ryker chose the upper east terrace overlooking the gardens, quiet and tasteful, just as he was. Lanterns glowed along the stone balustrade, their soft light catching in his dark hair and the clean lines of his tailored coat. He looked every inch what Graystonia wanted him to be. A future king.

He drew out her chair before she could reach for it herself, his touch careful, respectful. "I thought you might like the quiet," he said. "It's been a long week."

She smiled, genuinely this time. "That was thoughtful of you."

He returned the smile easily, warm and disarming. "You deserve peace, Layla. Gods know you've carried enough already." And for a moment, Layla let herself hope this could work. I mean this was still what she wanted, wasn't it? A chance to know the man she was to marry. To build something that could grow into partnership. Another opportunity to see exactly where he stands on their future together.

The tea arrived, fragrant and steaming. He poured for her first, as etiquette demanded, then for himself. His movements were practiced, elegant without arrogance. He asked about her lessons. About Aerilynn's excitement for the upcoming ball. About her favorite books. He remembered the small things. The human things. She watched him listen and he was completely at ease. Serene and comfortable in this space. In this castle. In this moment.

"This," Ryker said softly, gesturing to the lantern-lit terrace, "this is what I want for you. Calm. Safety. No more fear. No more bloodshed. You've lost enough."

She wrapped her hands around the warm porcelain cup. "And what about you?"

He chuckled lightly. "I'll worry about the rest. That's my duty." There it was again. That word. "I'll take care of the council," he continued, voice confident, reassuring. "The borders. The alliances. Keeping all of Graystonia safe and secure. You'll never have to burden yourself with those things. You can focus on what truly matters."

She lifted her gaze, doing her best to remain calm, collected, a porcelain princess. "And what is that?"

"You," he said without hesitation. "Us. Our family. You'll be an incredible queen, Layla. Beloved. Admired. The people already adore you. You'll host. You'll inspire. You'll give Graystonia heirs who ensure stability for generations." Her fingers tightened around the cup. He leaned forward slightly, smiling as if sharing a kindness. "You'll never have to worry again."

The words should have soothed her. But instead, it was like he lit a fuse. Layla lifted the cup to her lips, buying herself a breath. Then another. When she set it down, her smile remained perfectly intact even with the flame beginning to burn throughout her body.

"And what if I want more?" she asked lightly.

Ryker blinked. Just once. Then laughed, gentle and indulgent. "More?"

"Yes," she said, keeping her tone calm. "What if I want to understand the council's decisions. To be involved. To help guide the kingdom alongside you."

He studied her now, still smiling. "Layla, that isn't necessary."

"I didn't ask if it was," she replied softly. "I asked if it was possible."

There was a pause. A small one. The kind most people wouldn't notice. Then he nodded, as though humoring a child. "Of course it's possible to *listen*. But involvement like that... it's complicated. And would simply be too emotional for you."

Her stomach tightened. "Emotional?"

"You've been through trauma," he said kindly. "Any woman would be affected. That doesn't make you weak. It makes you human."

She felt the shift then. The ground subtly tilting beneath her feet. "I survived war," she said. "I survived captivity. I survived losing my father. I invaded a foreign kingdom and rescued the remaining royals of this kingdom. If that doesn't qualify me to have an opinion, what does?"

Ryker's smile thinned. "Experience doesn't equal aptitude."

"And gender does?" she asked quietly.

His jaw set, though his voice remained smooth. "You're letting passion cloud reason."

Her pulse quickened. "Or maybe you're mistaking obedience for reason." That did it.

His smile returned, deliberate now. Controlled. "Listen to yourself. You sound... overwrought."

Her breath caught. "Overwrought."

"Yes," he said gently. "This need to *prove* yourself. It isn't dignified. Queens don't need to argue for authority. They inspire trust by knowing their place." The words landed like a slap.

"My place," she repeated, as grip on her cup became so tight she feared it might shatter within her grasp.

"At my side," he clarified. "Supporting. Advising privately when appropriate. Not challenging publicly. Not wading into matters of war like..." He stopped himself, then finished calmly, "like men."

Her chest burned. "So this is it, this is what you expect of me?" she said. "Smile. Bear children. Host dinners. And be grateful."

Ryker sighed, as though disappointed. "You're being dramatic."

Before Layla could respond, laughter spilled onto the terrace. A small cluster of lords approached, their steps purposeful, expressions bright with expectation. One of them inclined his head toward Ryker with an apologetic smile. "Forgive us, Sir Ryker. We were told you might be here. There are a few matters we hoped to discuss."

Ryker's face lit instantly, composure settling into his features as easily as a crown. He glanced at Layla, his smile widening just enough to suggest indulgence. "Of course," he said warmly. "I was just enjoying a wonderful evening with my betrothed, as I'm sure you noticed."

Several of the lords nodded at Layla in polite unison. Courteous. Brief. Their gazes slid past her almost immediately, attention snapping back to Ryker as though pulled by gravity. He stepped forward to meet them, posture immaculate, dark hair neatly combed, every movement confident and unhurried. Hands clasped his forearm. Voices overlapped with praise.

"Graystonia is fortunate indeed," one said

"A steady hand at last," another added, clapping Ryker's shoulder. *The future king.* The reassuring presence. The man who had survived the siege and emerged unbroken. Layla had heard it all many times now.

Ryker's arm settled lightly around Layla's waist, possessive without being crude, fingers warm through the silk of her gown. To anyone watching, they were a picture of unity. Stability wrapped in velvet and gold. The kingdom's grief made orderly. Presentable. "You look beautiful tonight," he murmured near her ear as one lord droned on about trade routes and rebuilding efforts. "They're reassured just seeing you smile." And Layla did smile. Soft. Perfect. Practiced. Just how she was raised. Though the familiar hollow feeling that typically came with it was gone. Replaced by a smoldering fire within her that was growing by the second.

"Come, my lords," he said, gesturing toward the balustrade. "Let's speak privately. I want your honest counsel." Ryker's hand slipped from her waist as he turned fully toward the men, laughter rising easily from his chest. They shifted at once, walking some feet away, voices lowering. Ryker moved with them without hesitation, already immersed, already essential. Layla remained where he left her, hands folded, smile still fixed in place. Decisions already taking shape just beyond her reach.

Her chest tightened as she strained to find her composure. Taking a shaky breath, steadying herself before she turned and froze.

Kain Drakaren sat in the chair Ryker had vacated. The epitome of casual. His long legs stretched out, one arm draped over the back like he owned the space. His blonde hair was tied back loosely in a large braid, a few strands escaping to brush his jaw. He looked utterly at odds with the polished nobles surrounding them. Like a wolf that had wandered into a parlor and decided to stay.

His gaze lifted to hers and her heartbeat betrayed her instantly. A slow, knowing smirk curved his mouth, green eyes bright with amusement and intent, as though he'd caught her mid-thought. "You've been avoiding me again, little Dove."

A forbidden sweep of butterflies ransacked her stomach as her mind was flooded with memories of the other night. Before she could respond, deny that she's been busy, she felt Ryker step close to her.

"Prince Drakaren," he said smoothly. "I didn't see you there."

Kain's eyes never left Layla. "Funny," he replied. "I had the same thought." A couple of the lords chuckled uncertainly.

Ryker recovered fast. "We were just discussing funding for the southern roads," he said, stepping even closer, reclaiming the space. "Important matters."

"Of course," Kain said lightly. "Wouldn't want to trouble your betrothed with that." Shock and awe lit up inside Layla at his boldness. At the truth of the innuendo.

Ryker laughed, good-natured. "Layla has had a long day. No need to burden her with dry politics."

Kain's brows lifted, slow and deliberate. "Ah," he said. "Of course. Best not to burden her." His gaze finally flicked to Ryker then, openly unrepentant. "Wouldn't want her thinking too much."

The air tightened around them. One of the lords cleared his throat, trying to ease the tension. "Prince Drakaren," he said jovially, "you Antonins certainly have... opinions."

Kain grinned. "We do tend to survive by them."

Layla finally turned to look at her betrothed and noticed Ryker's jaw flex. He stepped closer towards Kain, voice lowering. "Careful," he said pleasantly. "This is Graystonia."

"And she is its future queen," Kain replied, eyes sliding back to Layla. "Or so I'm told." Layla fought to hide her smile. She felt amused and vindicated.

She reached for her tea with practiced calm, lifting the cup just in time to hide the flicker of betrayal that crossed her face. She may have been annoyed with Kain and how he was treating her future husband if Ryker hadn't just shed light on her biggest fears and dimished her to a silent womb.

Kain leaned back, utterly at ease. "I was just admiring how quickly you left her unattended," he added. "Bold move. I'd have thought you'd want to keep her close."

Ryker bristled. "Layla knows her place."

*Oh.* Layla's smile grew saccharine. She turned fully to Ryker, tilting her head sweetly. "Of course I do," she said. "A lady would never wander where she shouldn't. You needn't worry." Before she glanced back at

Kain. Just in time to see his smirk deepen. To everyone else, she seemed the humble future wife. The tamed woman. But Kain knew her better than that. Which made it all the funnier in her head.

Ryker nodded, entirely missing the edge. "Good," he said. "I'm glad you understand."

When Kain finally rose, it was with lazy grace. He passed Layla close enough that his arm brushed hers. "See you around, Dove," he murmured. He didn't bow. Didn't acknowledge the lords. Didn't spare Ryker another glance. And gods help her, Layla fully smiled into her cup. Just for a second.

Layla then noticed something in Ryker's posture tighten, just for a heartbeat, before he turned back to the lords with that effortless smile that had already won half the court. He adjusted his cuffs, relaxed his shoulders, and became the future king again. "Gentlemen," he said smoothly, "forgive me. I've neglected my manners long enough this evening." His gaze slid to Layla, warm and deliberate, his arm settling around her waist as if to display her. "I promised my betrothed my full attention." They approved at once. She felt it in the murmured praise, the satisfied nods. A king who remembered his bride. A union worth admiring.

Ryker waited until the lords drifted away before leaning closer to her. His voice softened, almost tender. "I should apologize," he murmured. "I was short with you earlier. The weight of everything you asked... it caught me off guard." Layla inclined her head. The motion came easily now. Years of practice. "I didn't expect it," he continued, clearly encouraged by her silence. "Most women want safety. Stability. A man who takes the burden from them so they never have to worry."

His thumb brushed lightly against her wrist, a gesture meant to reassure. "Not a voice, when it isn't necessary."

Her smile stayed in place as she spoke. "But we won't actually be safe, will we?" she asked gently. "Not if Lumiren invades." The words landed, and she felt it the moment they struck. Ryker stilled. He looked at her as if seeing her for the first time that evening. Not as something charming or agreeable, but as something unexpected. His jaw tightened, the warmth in his eyes cooling by degrees.

"That's a curious concern," he said at last. "One might think you've been spending time with the Antonins." His gaze turned assessing, searching her face. "It certainly sounds like it."

Layla kept her expression serene, innocent. "Of course not," she said lightly. "I know my place." She folded her hands, perfect and composed. "Though I would listen, if Graystonia's heroes ever chose to speak with me." She saw the flicker then. Irritation, swift and involuntary, before he buried it beneath practiced calm.

Before he could respond, soft footsteps approached. A maid appeared at the edge of the lanternlight and dipped into a respectful curtsy. "Princess Layla," she said quietly, eyes lowered. "Her Majesty requests your presence in her chambers."

Ryker's irritation vanished as if it had never existed. He straightened, all poise and authority, and offered her his arm. "Of course," he said. "Allow me to escort you." Layla slid her hand into the crook of his elbow, her posture flawless, her smile intact. And as they turned back toward the castle, she wondered which of them the court was truly meant to see.

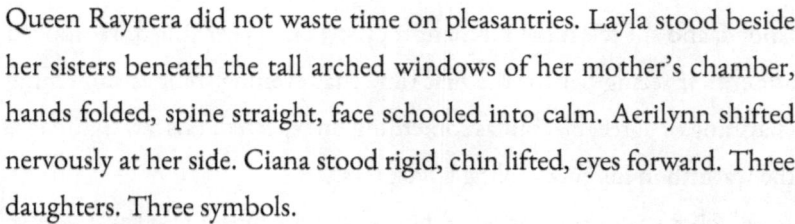

Queen Raynera did not waste time on pleasantries. Layla stood beside her sisters beneath the tall arched windows of her mother's chamber, hands folded, spine straight, face schooled into calm. Aerilynn shifted nervously at her side. Ciana stood rigid, chin lifted, eyes forward. Three daughters. Three symbols.

"The ball tomorrow night is not a celebration," Queen Raynera said coolly. "It is a statement." Her gaze moved between them, cool and assessing, lingering longest on Layla. "The people will be watching. The court will be watching. And Queen Okteria will be watching most of all. It has been centuries since a foreign king or queen has stepped foot within these walls. It is imperative that they will see unity. Strength. Stability." Her lips thinned. "They will see a family unshaken by loss."

Layla listened as she always did. She absorbed the instructions about posture and smiles, about laughter timed just so. About gratitude. About grace. About how Aerilynn's birthday would be framed as hope renewed, not grief remembered. About how Ciana was to be soft and radiant. And about how Layla was to act with Ryker.

"You," Queen Raynera said, "will look happy." The words pressed harder than any blade. Layla's thoughts drifted, unbidden, to earlier that evening. To Ryker's gentle smile. His careful words. The way his kindness folded into dismissal the moment she asked for more than safety. The way he had spoken of her future as though it were already decided. Children. Silk. Silence. Her jaw tightened. "And you will remember," her mother continued, "that Ryker Jameson is not merely your betrothed. He is the future King of Graystonia. You will support him accordingly."

"Yes, Mother," Aerilynn murmured.

"Yes, Your Majesty," Ciana added, voice clipped but steady.

Layla said nothing and Queen Raynera noticed.

When the lecture finally ended, when the expectations had been laid like chains across the floor, Layla inhaled slowly. "Mother," she said. Her voice did not shake. That alone felt like a victory. "May I speak with you privately?"

Aerilynn's fingers brushed Layla's hand in silent encouragement. Ciana met her gaze, something unreadable passing between them before she gave a single, curt nod. The sisters excused themselves without protest, the door closing softly behind them. The silence that followed was heavy. But Layla mustered her strength as she turned fully to her mother. "I don't think Ryker is the right choice." Queen Raynera did not blink. "For me," Layla continued, pulse roaring in her ears, "or for the kingdom." That did it.

Her mother's expression hardened, disappointment flashing like a strike of lightning. "You are tired," she said coldly. "And speaking from emotion, not sense."

"He does not see me as an equal," Layla pressed. "He does not listen. He does not question. He will rule, and I will be expected to smile beside him while decisions are made without me."

"And that," Queen Raynera snapped, "is precisely how it must be." Layla flinched despite herself. "You think you are unique in this?" her mother continued, voice rising just enough to sting. "You think you are the first woman to feel overlooked, to feel constrained? Duty is not a punishment, Layla. It is a necessity. Your father understood that. I understand it. You would do well to remember it."

The guilt came swift and punishing, as it always did when her father was invoked. Layla swallowed, steadying herself. "We don't have time for uncertainty," Queen Raynera went on. "We don't have time for your doubts. The decision has been made. It is above your head."

Layla's hands clenched. "And if it's wrong?" she asked quietly. "If this choice weakens us instead of strengthening us? If it ends in our demise?"

Her mother's eyes narrowed, the warmth draining from them entirely. "Then you will carry it anyway." The words were not raised. They did not need to be. "He is the future king," Queen Raynera continued, voice precise and final. "The council has decided. The military has agreed. And I have sanctioned it." Her gaze cut like glass. "You forfeited the right to question this long ago." Layla felt the weight of it settle, crushing and absolute. "This is for the kingdom," Raynera said coolly. "For the people. For this castle." She stepped closer, presence looming. "And you will not fail us tomorrow night." Her tone turned steely, each word a command. "You will convince every eye watching that you are happy. That you are honored. That you are grateful, thrilled even, to welcome Ryker Jameson into this family."

Silence stretched between them. Layla did not look away. Instead she lifted her chin, slow and deliberate, meeting her mother's gaze head-on. Not pleading. Not shrinking. Just steady. Unyielding in a way that made something tighten in the room.

For the first time, she saw Queen Raynera hesitate. It was brief. Barely there. A flicker of recognition she did not allow to settle into her face. Her expression smoothed, regal and unreadable once more, but the challenge had landed. She felt it. Layla let the moment linger just long enough to be unmistakable. Then, with practiced precision, she lowered her eyes. The porcelain smile slid effortlessly into place, flawless and serene. She bowed, deep and formal, every inch the dutiful daughter, the obedient princess.

"Yes, Your Majesty." When she turned and walked out, her spine remained straight, her steps measured and calm. Not defiant. Not submissive. Something new. And behind her, Queen Raynera stood very still, watching the door long after it had closed.

# FEYRIC

## GOD OF LUCK

# Chapter Twenty

*L* *ayla.*

"How was your evening with the future king?" Aerilynn asked lightly at breakfast the next morning, breaking the silence between the sisters.

"It was... delightful," Layla replied with practiced ease. The word slid out polished, proper, just as it was meant to. But she knew it was a lie, and she was tired of it. *Why did she have to be proper around her own sisters? Why keep pretending? Why lie to them?* She was starting to question everything when it came to their expectations as princesses, as women.

She had just opened her mouth to say more when Kain and Sparrow plopped down at the table like they owned the place. Kain immediately reached across and plucked a piece of fruit from her plate once again. "You know you have your own plate. It's right there in front of you." Layla dramatically pointed out the plate in front of Kain before she could stop herself. Her patience with everything simply fried.

"Layla!" Ciana chastised, scandalized by her rudeness.

But Kain only grinned, ignoring the rebuke. "But your fruit is so much sweeter." He winked, deliberately slow.

Layla glared at him, cheeks warming despite herself. "Does your mother know how vulgar you are?"

"Layla!" Ciana hissed again, exasperated.

Kain leaned lazily on the table, unfazed. "What's wrong, Dove? Are you going to run and tell mommy dearest on me?"

"I should," she shot back. "Maybe she could force you to shut your mouth for once."

"Layla! By the Gods!" Ciana rasped, half in horror.

Layla rolled her eyes and waved her spoon dismissively, officially unbothered by expectations right now. "Ciana, they eat with us every morning. The guards let them wander our halls freely, be near us freely. I think that allows us to drop the *decorum* for once. Besides..." her voice took on a sardonic tone, "these are the same men who held me captive in a pit and found you imprisoned in Bartoria. I think we're well past feigned politeness at this point." Ciana's jaw fell open in shock, while Aerilynn giggled behind her hand. Even Sparrow cracked the faintest of smiles around a mouthful of porridge.

But when Layla turned back to Kain, he was already watching her. Pride radiated from him, so intense and unguarded she flushed under it. Quickly she looked back at her plate, forcing a small chuckle. "How on earth did you convince the guards to allow you both free rein of our castle anyway?" She asked, trying to sound casual as she glanced back up to meet his stare.

Kain's grin widened, pure mischief. "That's a secret I'll never tell."

She narrowed her eyes at him, head shaking as a quiet laugh slipped free. The sound felt easy, unforced, as comfort and contentment settled around her. For once, she didn't overthink, didn't posture, she simply was herself. A small smile lingered on her lips as she turned back to her plate, letting the warmth of the moment carry her through breakfast.

The five of them rose from breakfast together, for once moving in step. Her sisters, Sparrow, Kain, and her, were in an odd sort of unity Layla couldn't help but enjoy. The warmth of it still clung to her chest as they crossed into the main hall, her smile lingering as though she couldn't quite let it go.

That was when Marilla appeared, gliding down the corridor with purpose, her voice calm but urgent. "Your Highnesses," she said, eyes sweeping over the group, "an Antonin woman has just arrived at the gates."

Kain's smirk was instant, crooked and wolfish. "That'll be Mother," he drawled, rolling his shoulders as though bracing for impact. "Here we go."

Layla's stomach dropped. Nerves turned hot in her veins, twisting with fury. The last time she had seen Queen Okteria, the woman had sentenced her entire family to death, had looked at Layla as though she were nothing more than a chain to be shackled and broken. Rage pressed taut beneath her skin, but so did the cold, inescapable truth: Graystonia needed this alliance. She needed Okteria. So, she followed anyway and pushed her negative feelings down. Her steps clipped, determined to face the queen and get it over with.

But when they reached the great doors, it was not Okteria waiting on the threshold. It was Frea.

Layla froze at the sight of her. Tall for a woman, towering even in the soft morning light, she stood framed by the carved archway like a portrait of Antonin strength. Her dark olive skin caught the sun, warm against the deep blacks and browns of her Antonin leathers. A thick fur cloak draped her shoulders, the pelt shifting with each subtle breath. Long, ink–black hair spilled in a glossy curtain down her back, and her watchful brown eyes, keen as any hawk's, brightened the moment she saw them. She was just as breathtaking as Layla remembered. A warrior sculpted by the gods themselves.

Frea's face broke into a brilliant, delighted grin. Before Layla could blink, she let out a joyful cry and sprinted forward, launching herself straight into Kain's arms. He caught her effortlessly, lifting her off the ground as she giggled into his chest.

"Did you miss me?" Frea purred, tilting her face up to his. Her voice dripped with seduction. Layla's shock turned instantly, violently, into a raging fire.

Sparrow's tone cut through the tension, flat and impatient as Kain put her down. "What are you doing here, Frea? Where's the queen?"

Frea slid her eyes lazily to him, smirking. "She was... occupied. So, she sent me in her stead to attend this apparently important little ball. She'll be along in a few days." She lifted a hand and waved it dismissively, as though Graystonia's walls and all within them were beneath her notice. Then her smirk turned sly, her gaze flicking back to Kain.

"Speaking of balls... where do yours sleep? I traveled all night. Could really use some... *rest*." She winked, brazen and unashamed.

Layla's teeth ground together so hard her jaw ached. Her mind betrayed her, conjuring the memory of Kain slipping out of Frea's tent one morning in Antonin lands, hair mussed and eyes bright with the aftermath of passion. Layla's stomach twisted. But before she could spit words that burned her tongue, Marilla stepped forward, face the picture of cool control. "I will show you to your chambers, Miss."

Frea looked at Marilla with open disdain, her lips parting as if to protest, but her eyes cut to Kain, waiting... expecting him to intervene. To offer her his room, no doubt. But he didn't. He didn't say a word... Relief flickered through Layla, a fleeting balm. But it barely touched the blaze still roaring in her chest as she watched Frea finally step back, letting Marilla lead her away. And gods help her, Layla already knew this was far from over.

Layla spun on Kain, fury and urgency lacing her words. "Why the hell is she here, and where is your mother? These negotiations cannot keep getting pushed aside, Kain. Yssra could strike at any moment. What the hell is going on?"

He stood there as he always did. Calm, infuriatingly steady, as though her fury couldn't touch him. "If my mother couldn't be here today, there's a reason," he said, voice even and maddeningly reasonable. "She has no desire to drag this on any longer than necessary, nor give Lumiren the upper hand. I'm sure Frea will explain everything to me in private later."

Layla's teeth clenched so hard she thought they might crack. "Oh, I'm sure you two won't be doing much talking. But fine. Do let me know if her mouth manages to form anything useful afterward." And with that, she turned on her heel, skirts snapping as she stormed off down the corridor. Behind her, she could have sworn she heard Sparrow covered a laugh with a cough.

Layla slammed another pastry onto the silver tray, the poor thing collapsing into a puff of crumbs and jam that sprayed across the linen. She groaned and brushed her hands down her skirts in frustration, only succeeding in smearing a streak of sugar across the fabric. Exasperated, she turned toward Aerilynn, who was serenely trimming stems from a bouquet, slotting each bloom neatly into place.

"Do you want any help with that?" Layla asked, voice edged with sarcasm and desperation both.

Aerilynn didn't even look up, just flicked her eyes from the battlefield of broken pastries to her pristine arrangement. "Uh... no. I'm okay. Thanks though."

That was enough. With a huff, Layla dropped the serving tongs and stalked out of the ballroom before she destroyed anything else.

Later in her chambers, Marilla tugged the laces of Layla's gown tight, making her shift uncomfortably before the mirror. The gown had been made specially for the occasion. A sweeping creation of deep emerald silk, threaded through with veins of gold embroidery that caught the light like turning leaves. It fit close through the bodice and hips before spilling into layered skirts that shimmered when she moved, the colors a careful marriage of Graystonia's pride and the season's slow decay. The neckline swept wide, baring her shoulders and collarbones to candlelight. Gold filigree traced the sleeves like curling vines, delicate and undeniably regal. And yet, as Layla stared at her reflection, her stomach twisted. Emerald. Of all colors. She couldn't help but let out a frustrated huff as her mind betrayed her. Those eyes. Green and unrelenting. The way they had burned into her yesterday, seeing too much, asking too much. And just as quickly, the memory shifted to Frea's laughter, her hands fisting in his tunic as she had thrown herself into his arms without hesitation, without consequence. The image struck hot and brutal, a jealous surge rising fast and unbidden. Layla's fingers curled until her knuckles blanched. *No! Not tonight. Not now.*

She forced the feeling down, burying it beneath discipline and silk and spine. This night demanded composure, not longing. It demanded a princess, not the weakness he tempted loose. Still, she tugged at seams that did not need adjusting, fingers restless against silk. "It pinches here," she muttered. "And pulls there. Why does it feel like a cage?"

Marilla smacked her hands lightly away and cinched the final tie with a sharp tug that forced the air from Layla's lungs. "Stop fidgeting. Truly. What has gotten into you?" She stepped back, sweeping her gaze over the gown with brisk satisfaction before smoothing her apron. "You look beautiful, Layla. Perfect. Ryker will swoon at the sight of you."

*Ryker.* The name landed like a weight dropped into still water. But this time, something else sparked with it. Not dread. Not hope. A quiet flame, steady and resolute. Layla stilled, her restless hands falling slack against her skirts as she met her own gaze in the mirror. Marilla's words cut through the noise, grounding her in the truth she could no longer avoid. Tonight was not about Kain. Not about Frea. Not about the mess of feelings she would have to master later. Not even about Ryker himself. Tonight was about her.

After last night's conversation with Ryker, and after the colder clarity of her mother's dismissal, Layla was done hoping. Done imagining futures that required permission. If this was the path laid before her, then she would walk it exactly as expected. But she would not vanish into it. She would stand at Ryker's side as the kingdom's future queen, not as an ornament or a shadow, but as a presence impossible to ignore. She would not ask to be seen. She would make herself seen. Let Ryker's crown place her in rooms she had been barred from. Let his authority lend weight to her voice until it no longer needed lending at all.

Let them see her smile and mistake it for compliance if they wished. Let them believe she was content, softened, satisfied by the role chosen for her. They would not realize until it was too late that she was using the very expectations meant to contain her as the means to rise. They could not stop her from shining.

Layla lifted her chin, shoulders settling back as if the gown itself had become armor rather than restraint. The woman staring back at her looked calm. Confident. Almost luminous. And in that moment, Layla believed it.

The ballroom breathed to life. Light spilled from chandeliers in molten gold, glinting off polished marble and silk and jewels until the space felt alive with movement and sound. Music swelled, laughter echoed, and the court of Graystonia gathered in its finest finery, hungry for reassurance, spectacle, and something to believe in. Layla gave them all three.

She entered at Ryker's side with her head high and her spine straight, emerald silk catching every flicker of candlelight as though the gown itself were alive. She felt it immediately, the shift in the room. Eyes turning. Conversations faltering. Interest gathering. Not because she demanded it, but because she radiated something impossible to ignore. *Confidence.* Not the quiet, obedient kind her mother prized. This was something warmer. Charismatic. Commanding in its ease. Ryker noticed too. His hand settled at the small of her back, possessive and deliberate, guiding her forward as though to display her. Each touch sent a quiet recoil through her that she kept carefully buried beneath her smile. She did not flinch. Did not pull away. If anything, she leaned in just enough to sell the illusion.

Around them, lords and ladies flocked easily. Praise came readily to Ryker, admiration stacking thick around his shoulders, but Layla did not fade into the background as she once might have. When Ryker spoke, she listened. When the lords spoke, she answered. She asked questions. Clever ones. Insightful ones. She laughed at the right moments, redirected conversations with grace, and spoke of rebuilding with a clarity that drew people in before they realized they were listening to her. She did not bask in it. She owned it.

She could tell that Ryker felt the shift too, though he masked it well. His hand tightened occasionally, fingers lingering a moment longer at her waist, at her arm, as if reminding the room and perhaps himself that she was his. There was a faint edge to his smile now, a subtle competitiveness beneath the polish. Almost as though he were trying to outshine her. No one else seemed to notice. They were too busy watching Layla.

Across the room, Queen Raynera observed it all with a carefully neutral expression. Her gaze never left Layla for long, cool and assessing, tracking every movement, every smile. When a break in the crowd finally appeared, her mother seized it. She caught Layla's arm gently and steered her aside, her smile still fixed perfectly in place for the watching court. "What are you doing?" Queen Raynera murmured through clenched teeth, her tone pleasant enough to fool anyone nearby.

Layla met her gaze calmly. Unflinching. Her own smile never wavered. "Being a future queen," she replied softly. "Just as you instructed."

Something flickered behind her mother's eyes. Surprise, perhaps. Or irritation. But Raynera said nothing more, only released her and returned to her place among the court. Layla exhaled slowly and turned back to the crowd, slipping seamlessly once more into conversation as though nothing had happened. And yet, beneath it all, her attention kept drifting. She scanned the room without meaning to. Over shoulders. Between clusters of nobles. Near the edges where shadows gathered thickest. He was not there. The absence tugged at her more insistently with every passing minute. She told herself it did not matter. That it was foolish. That this was exactly what she had chosen.

Still, jealousy coiled low in her stomach, hot and unwelcome. A vivid image surfaced unbidden, Frea's hands in his tunic, her laughter unrestrained, the ease with which she had claimed space beside him. Layla forced the thought down, schooling her expression into serene composure. Ryker leaned close, murmuring something meant only for her, his hand warm and steady at her back. She smiled. Laughed softly. Played her part.

But as the music swelled and the night wore on, one truth pressed heavier than the silk against her skin. She was shining. And she was still searching the room for a man who was nowhere to be found.

**FEYRIC**

Feyric walks where fortune tilts and chaos laughs. Neither wholly benevolent nor cruel, he is the golden edge between triumph and disaster. His smile is the promise of possibility, his shadow the warning that luck is never free.

Those who follow him speak of sudden windfalls, narrow escapes, impossible victories... and ruin just as swift. Feyric gives generously and takes without apology, for chance is a balance he alone commands.

His presence is marked by a glint of gold, a fox's cunning, and eyes that shimmer like spinning coins. Many pray to him in taverns and battlefields alike, but only fools believe they can ever truly predict him.

Where Feyric walks, destiny stumbles and fate dances to his laugh.

# Chapter Twenty-One

*K*<sup>*ain.*</sup>

Tailcoats. Fucking tailcoats. The thing strangled his shoulders, pinched at his ribs, and made it damn near impossible to breathe. And worse, there was barely enough room to hide more than three knives. He'd managed it anyway, slipping one flat against his spine, another inside his boot, and a third sheathed up his sleeve. A man had to have standards.

He tugged at the collar with mock solemnity, muttering under his breath, "If I survive this night without stabbing someone, it'll be a miracle." He was just about to shove the ballroom doors open when the air shifted. Not perfume, never perfume. But a familiar presence. *Frea.*

She leaned against the wall like she owned it, her leathers traded for something cut to flatter and distract, though the way she carried herself screamed steel more than silk. A curve of her hip, a slow drag of her eyes over him, she knew exactly the effect her body could have, and she used it like a weapon.

"My prince," she purred, eyes dragging over him, "You clean up well," she admitted. "Shame about the setting."

Kain barked a laugh, dragging his thumb along the line of his collar. "Careful, Frea. If you start sounding like you're impressed, people might mistake you for civil. Can't have that ruining your reputation." Her lips quirked, sultry and knowing all at once, as she slid her arm into his. But before she could continue Kain jumped in. "What the hell is going on Frea?"

"Later," she promised in a low voice, "when ears aren't listening, I'll tell you what I actually came here for."

He side-eyed her, grinning like a wolf. "Later. Sure. Because dangling secrets is so very unlike you."

Her nails traced a deliberate line down his sleeve, lingering just long enough to be noticed. "And yet... you'll wait."

"Only because stabbing you in front of the entire Graystonian court might cause a scene." His grin widened as he shoved the ballroom doors open, dragging her along with him. Light and music spilled over them, a flood of nobles and silk, of empty chatter and false smiles.

"Fantastic," he muttered. "All this pomp just to celebrate an eighteen-year-old who'd probably rather be anywhere else. Remind me again why diplomacy doesn't involve more blood?"

Frea only laughed at his muttered complaint, draping herself across his arm as if they'd been paired for this ridiculous charade. Together they swept into the ballroom, greeted instantly by a flock of nobles he didn't know and didn't care to. Men with too much oil in their hair, women with smiles stretched thin as daggers. Every one of them hungry for something. Whether that be curiosity, gossip, power or all three. But the titles, pleasantries, desperate smiles, all of it slid right past him like piss in the mud. He gave them nothing but a grunt, maybe a nod if Sparrow's elbow dug into his ribs, but mostly he let Frea handle them. She knew how to wield her beauty. She was constantly laughing, leaning close, touching just enough to make a man stumble over his words. Lethal with steel, lethal with her body, *let her have her fun*. But Kain? He had no fun here. Not when he was trussed up in a gods-damned tailcoat that hid half the daggers he normally carried. Not when every word in this room dripped with fake honey and poison. He had no patience for courtiers. He wanted blood, not banter.

And then he saw her.

The room seemed to bend around her without realizing it had done so. Emerald silk caught the light with every movement, gold threading glinting like something alive, but it was her that held him. The lift of her chin. The quiet confidence in her posture. The way she stood as though the space belonged to her rather than the other way around. She wasn't fading tonight. She wasn't shrinking. She was radiating.

Kain felt a low, fierce pull in his chest. Vindication. Awe. Gods, relief. *There you are Dove.* Then he noticed the rest of it. The way the lords angled themselves toward her. The subtle shift in conversation when she spoke. She wore the court's polish, yes, but she wasn't hiding behind it. She was using it. Letting them see her brilliance through the veil they'd forced on her. *About damned time they noticed.*

His gaze slid, inevitably, to Ryker fucking Jameson. To the man's satisfied posture. The easy confidence of someone who thought the attention in the room belonged to him by right. Who thought her presence was an extension of his own. Kain's fist flexed and then tightened. Ryker wasn't seeing it. Wasn't seeing *her*. He was sure that Ryker thought the glow was his reflection.

And when Ryker's hand settled at her waist, casual and claiming, like a habit already formed, something in Kain went very still. *No. Not fucking happening.* Kain forced himself to let it go once. Barely. But when Ryker did it the second time, when that polished future king reached for her again like she was a prize meant to be displayed, something cold and exact snapped into place and Kain moved. He crossed the room with deliberate ease, boots striking the marble in time with the music, silk and lace parting as nobles stumbled out of his way. Conversations faltered. Heads turned. He did not slow. Ryker noticed him just in time to school his expression into polite surprise.

"Prince Drakaren," Ryker greeted smoothly, offering a measured nod as though this were all perfectly expected. "Enjoying the celebration?"

Layla turned at the sound of Kain's title and he watched her breath stumble. He couldn't help but gaze at her. Her beauty, her shock, her clear anger starting to seep into her eyes. For half a heartbeat, he said nothing. Just took her in. Then his gaze flicked, briefly, to Ryker. Amusement curved his mouth.

"Princess," Kain said, returning his attention fully to her, as though the man beside her were no more than furniture. "You look like you're being tragically underused." Her eyes widened just a fraction as she shot a quick glance at Ryker. Kain caught it. Of course he did. He extended his hand anyway.

"Dance with me, Dove," he said lightly, staring directly into her soul now. The irritation flickering behind her eyes was unmistakable, and he had to bite back a laugh. Then, as if something had only just occurred to him, his attention slid lazily to Ryker, his courtesy suddenly deliberate. "It is a ball, after all. Cultural exchange, diplomatic goodwill, and whatnot," he added, voice smooth, almost courteous. "Wouldn't want the Antonins accused of poor manners." His eyes gleamed as Ryker's smile tightened, stretched thin with restraint.

Kain did not wait for permission. His hand settled at Layla's waist, firm and certain, prying her free with effortless confidence as though Ryker's touch had never existed at all. Gasps rippled through the court, silk whispering as she was pulled from one man's grasp into another's. Kain only smiled, already guiding her into motion.

The music caught them instantly. He moved like he fought. Precise. Controlled. Dangerous. He drew her in, spun her out, the silk of her gown flaring like emerald flame before hauling her back against his chest with a grin that promised trouble. The moment he looked down at her. Kain knew. Layla smiled up at him. It was perfect. Polished. Courtly. And furious.

"Kain," she said through a smile so flawless it should have been illegal. "This is highly inappropriate."

He laughed, low and unrepentant, already guiding her into the turn as though the floor had been built for them alone. "Is it?" he murmured. "Strange. I was under the impression balls were meant for dancing." She shot him a look full of warning as he spun her out again and right back in. He felt the heat of her through the fabric, the tension coiled tight beneath her composure.

"You are making a scene," she hissed.

"I walked into a room full of silk and egos," he replied easily, grinning down at her. "The scene was already made." Her fingers curled into his sleeve. Not to pull away. Never to pull away. Just to warn him. Oh, he felt that. He moved with her like it was instinct, every step precise, every turn timed to wring another reaction out of her. She followed despite herself, body answering his without hesitation, and gods, that alone was worth whatever trouble came next.

"This ends now," she muttered, lips barely moving.

"Mm," he said, leaning in close enough that his breath brushed her ear. "You say that like you mean it." Her glare flickered. Heated. Alive. Exactly what he'd come for. And then it changed. He saw her eyes slid past his shoulder. Just once, fast and unmistakable, irritation snapping as her gaze cut toward the edge of the crowd. *Toward Frea.* The realization hit him so cleanly he almost missed a step. Oh. *Oh, that's what this is.* His grin turned positively wicked.

He spun her again, skirts snapping around his boots, then pulled her closer than decorum would ever forgive, his voice dropping low, unmistakably pleased. "You can glare at her all you want," he said softly. "But right now, you're the one I'm holding in my arms."

Her spine stiffened instantly. "I have no idea what you're talking about."

"Funny," he murmured, dipping her just enough to steal her breath before lifting her smoothly back against him, "because you look like you're deciding whether to stab her or curse her."

She sucked in a sharp breath. "You are delusional."

"And you," he said lightly, delight curling hot and feral in his chest, "are jealous." Her eyes snapped to his. Wild. Furious. And devastatingly beautiful. She hissed his name like it was a threat in response and Kain only beamed. Gods, he lived for his name on her lips.

He guided her through the final turns with infuriating ease, smiling like a man who had just won a game she hadn't known she was playing. The music swelled, then began to fade.

When the final note rang out, she stepped back, breath uneven, cheeks flushed, fury and something far more dangerous sparking behind her eyes as the mask slid neatly back into place. She turned as if to return to her sisters, to Ryker, to the waiting court, but Kain caught her wrist. Just for a heartbeat. "They're finally seeing you shine," he murmured, gaze dark and unapologetic. "I can't wait for the day they see you ignite." Then he released her.

Layla took a few steps before she stopped and looked back. Their eyes met across the space between them. And he saw it. The moment she knew he meant it. Every word. He would always believe in her.

Kain watched her retreat, satisfaction thrumming deep and steady in his bones. Because now he knew. She could pretend all she wanted but tonight had cracked something open. And he would never unsee it.

The rest of the night was a blur of speeches, nobles, and endless posturing. Kain endured it with Sparrow at his side and Frea continuing to wield her beauty like a blade to pry loose secrets from fawning men. But he wasn't listening. His attention just kept drifting back to the emerald goddess in the crowd, smiling and laughing on command, playing her part and they were eating it up. He would've loved the sight if Ryker didn't continuously have his hands on her. By the time another toast was raised, his patience was gone. He caught Sparrow's glance, saw the same disinterest in his brother-in-arms eyes, and turned to Frea. "We're done here."

Her lips curved into that knowing, sultry grin as she slipped her arm through his. "Finally."

Together they strode out, Sparrow already ghosting through the doors ahead, leaving the hollow pageantry behind. Kain had stayed through enough of this farce. He needed answers. And he was going to get them, *now.*

Kain's chambers were dim, lit only by the low fire still clinging to the hearth. He had barely tugged off the suffocating tailcoat when Frea slipped inside behind him, closing the door with that usual feline grace. *At least she didn't waste time.*

"Your mother's in Myriamis," she said, sultry tone even when delivering war news. "She went straight there after you left for Graystonia. I went with her. She didn't trust those pompous heirs to agree to alliance in time, so she went herself. It's taking longer than she expected, but she's close. When she arrives here, she'll be bringing Myriamis with her."

Kain wasn't shocked, not really. His mother was lethal, but a strategist above all. Cutting through the bullshit with her own blade was exactly what she'd do. He gave a curt nod. "Smart move. Saves time. What else?" Frea's mouth curved, but her eyes flickered. There it was, the *more*.

"Myriamis had word from Elarith," she admitted. "The rot's spreading on their shores. Slowly at first, now like a plague. It's moving fast, Kain. Yssra is coming south, and we're not ready. Everything I heard from those idiotic nobles tonight made that painfully clear."

At the table, Sparrow muttered a curse, his broad frame hunched over the map as he jabbed a finger at the ink-stained coastlines. "We can't do this without Graystonia. It's obvious now. This is what Yssra wants, whether we know why or not. It ends here. One way or another. So we need them. Even if it means letting that ball-less fool sit on the throne."

Kain's jaw locked at that. *Ryker. Always Ryker.*

His voice came out low, cutting. "Anything else?"

Frea's gaze lingered on him, too long, too familiar. "No. Your mother will be here in a day or two. Three at most. Stall until then on whatever you're doing. And pray to whatever gods you've got that Yssra slows down. Because we don't have our own god or an army big enough to stand against her yet."

Sparrow grunted, shoving back from the table. Without a word, he slipped out, leaving only the crackle of the fire and the map stretched between them. But Frea lingered. *Of course she did.* She trailed her fingers across Kain's shoulders, nails grazing skin through his shirt. "You look tense," she purred.

"Not tonight, Frea." His tone was iron. His arms pressed hard against the table, head bowed as he glared at the map.

She gave a little shrug, showing her indifference, and sashayed to the door. "Suit yourself."

And then he was alone. The fire popping. The map beneath his hands. And the weight of every truth that had just been dropped at his feet. He let his head sag farther. Processing. Planning. *Raging.*

A soft knock interrupted his turmoil. Kain's jaw locked, his patience shot to hell. *It better not be fucking Frea again. Gods, if she thought batting her lashes was going to get her what she wanted tonight, she'd learn fucking quick.* He was in no mood, not after the shit news she'd just dropped. He wrenched the door open, ready to bite and froze. *Layla.* Not Frea. Not Sparrow. *Her.* Her shoulders squared, chin held high, and those honeyed eyes were blazing with something he couldn't name. *Fury? Nerves? Desire? Maybe all three.* Whatever it was, it had his pulse thundering before either of them said a word.

"Dove," he drawled, leaning his shoulder to the doorframe, masking the sudden spike in his blood with practiced ease. "To what do I owe this little midnight visit?" She didn't answer. Didn't even blink. Just swept past him like she owned the room, her shoulder grazing his chest like she hadn't just lit every nerve in him on fire.

He shut the door slowly, eyes narrowing as he watched her pace his chambers. She moved like a storm barely contained, scanning every corner, slipping right into his bath chamber before he could fully understand. "Well," he called after her, "if you're planning to soap me up, Dove, I expect a thorough job." Though no bite came back. Instead, she returned to his bedchambers, scowl gone, though her spine still held that coiled tension. Kain cocked his head, studying her in silence. She drifted past him again without a word, the sweep of her skirts whispering over the floor as though she hadn't just barged into a wolf's den. Her steps carried her to the table where his maps sprawled, ink and parchment scarred by endless hours of planning. She stood there, studying, her fingers hovering near the edges but never touching. Kain still didn't move. He just tracked her every shift, every shallow breath, every flick of her lashes like a predator watching prey wander too close to the snare. Then she turned. Those lashes lifted, her teeth catching her lower lip as though the words might tear her apart if she let them out. Her lips parted, the smallest tremor tugging at them before the words spilled out, quiet and devastating: "I had another nightmare."

Kain stilled. The world stilled. For a heartbeat, he thought he'd misheard. But no, he saw it in her eyes, wide and glinting, that storm breaking inside her. Then slowly, deliberately, he moved. A predator's prowl. She matched him without seeming to mean to. Step for step, retreating until her back found the far wall. The candlelight threw her in gold and shadow, every shallow breath, every flick of her lashes a silent plea and challenge all at once.

Kain planted a hand above her head, caging her in. Not so she couldn't escape, but because gods, he wanted her to try. His other hand hovered, then toyed lazily with the bow that tied her gown, knuckles grazing the swell of her breasts.

"A nightmare," he echoed, voice low, dangerous, mocking even as desire thickened every word. He leaned closer, drinking in her scent, her tension, her want. "Just now?" Her teeth caught her lip again, damn near driving him mad, and she gave the smallest nod. His jaw clenched, his pulse a drumbeat in his ears. He bent lower, mouth brushing the shell of her ear, his voice velvet and knives all at once. "Hm. Funny thing, Dove." His thumb dragged slowly across that bow, tugging the ribbon loose. "I've never heard of someone having a nightmare while they were awake."

He pulled back just enough to trap her with his stare. "Could it be," he drawled, lips curving into a knowing grin, "that you're lying to me? Using a nightmare as an excuse to slip into my room... into my bed?" The ribbon slid free. Her breath stuttered in response. And for one razor-sharp moment, all he could think was how badly he wanted to ruin her and how much sweeter it would be if she asked him to.

The ribbon slipped free in his hand, her bodice loosening just enough to bare the faintest hint of skin. He didn't touch further. Not yet. He wanted her trembling. "Look at you," he murmured, voice pitched low enough to scrape down her spine. "Lip caught between your teeth, chest rising like you're already out of breath... tell me, Dove, does this look like a nightmare to you?"

He watched her throat bob, but no words came. He let his mouth hover just above hers, not kissing, not touching, just close enough for his breath to feather over her lips. His free hand dragged slowly down her arm until his knuckles brushed her hip. He felt the shiver she tried to hide.

"Say it," he whispered, a predator's order wrapped in silk. "Don't nod. Don't hide behind silence. Say what you came here for."

"I..." Her voice broke. She shook her head as if the word lodged in her throat.

Kain chuckled darkly, though his cock strained against his trousers, his own restraint fraying. "You're killing me, Dove. And gods, I think you know it. That's why you're here...why you're in my room, staring at me like I'm the only thing keeping you breathing." He caught her jaw, thumb brushing over her lips. Watching them part beneath his touch was its own kind of torment. "You don't get my cock inside you until you say it," he taunted, the words harsh against her ear as he nipped her lobe. "Say how bad you want me to fuck you. Say it, and I'll give it to you until you can't walk straight. Until you forget every nightmare." Her breath came ragged and shallow. He pulled back just enough to see her close her eyes, chest heaving, and when she opened them again, there was no hesitation left, only raw need.

"I want you to fuck me, Kain. Here. Now."

The world went silent. His heart slammed once, hard, then everything inside him snapped. He crushed his mouth to hers, savage and starving, no space left between them as his tongue claimed hers in a fierce rhythm. One arm wrapped tight around her back, the other slid under her thighs, lifting her as though she weighed nothing. He pinned her against the wall, already unknowingly grinding his hips against her. Every kiss deeper, hungrier, a war waged in lips and teeth and gasps. He couldn't get enough. Would never get enough. Her words still echoed in his skull, wrapping around every pulse in his body. *I want you to fuck me, Kain. Here. Now.* Gods, he'd never forget the sound of it.

His lips crushed hers again, rough and unrelenting, tongues tangling until he nearly lost himself in her taste. She was fire and velvet, everything he'd dreamed and denied. His hand slid down, gripping the back of her thigh, hauling her higher against the wall so her skirts bunched between them.

"Greedy little Dove," he rasped against her mouth, his cock straining as he pressed into the heat of her through the thin barrier of her shift. "You barge into my chambers, you lie about nightmares, and then you demand me like this? Gods, I should punish you." But his hips were grinding hard now, betraying his threat. He caught the laces at her bodice and yanked, letting them fall loose under his hand. Inch by inch, pale skin revealed itself, and he bared his teeth in a wolfish grin. "Say it again."

Her breath hitched. "Kain..."

"Say. It." He dragged his lips down her jaw, biting lightly at her throat as his thumb swept dangerously close to her clit through the thin silk.

Her head thunked back against the stone. Her voice broke on the words: "I want you to fuck me."

His groan was guttural and raw. He spun, carrying her across the room, her legs wrapping tight around his waist. He slammed her down onto the table where his maps lay scattered, parchment crumpling beneath her back. "Let the world burn," he growled, yanking the fabric from her shoulders until she lay bare before him. "I want you screaming my name loud enough for your whole fucking castle to hear." He freed himself with an impatient tug, the thick length of him slapping heavy against her thigh. Her eyes widened, pupils blown, chest heaving.

He smirked, merciless and amused. "Too much for a little porcelain princess now? You handled it so well the other night."

Her glare sparked, lips trembling but defiant. "Try me."

"Gods, Dove," he whispered, lining himself up, teasing the head against her soaked folds until she writhed. "I think I'll die before I'm done with you." And with one fierce thrust, he buried himself inside her.

The sound she made when he filled her, half gasp, half moan, nearly unmade him. Tight, hot, perfect. His fingers dug into her hips as he drove in deep, savoring the way her back arched and her lips parted in silent shock.

"Gods above, Dove," he rasped, teeth gritted as he held himself there, buried to the hilt, forcing her to feel every inch. Her nails clawed at the table, maps tearing beneath her grasp, but he wasn't about to let her drift anywhere but with him. He caught her chin, forcing her eyes open. "Look at me. I said *look*." The hazel eyes found his as he pulled out slowly, torturously slow. Before slamming forward again, the table groaning under the force. Her cry ripped through the chamber, raw and desperate.

"That's it," he growled, setting a brutal rhythm, every thrust claiming, marking, daring her to deny him. "Scream for me, Dove. Let every damned man in this castle hear who has your soul on fire."

Her shift slid uselessly down her arms, breasts bouncing with each pounding stroke, and he seized one in his palm, kneading it, rolling her nipple between his fingers until she gasped again. He bent low, biting it lightly, sucking until she writhed. He loved watching how she reacted to him. "Dove, you're drowning me," he groaned against her skin, her walls tightening, gripping him like a vice. His cock twitched deep inside her, begging for release, but he wasn't finished. Not even close. He hooked her leg over his shoulder, driving into her at an angle that made her cry out louder, raw and broken. Sweat slicked his back, his hair falling loose around his face, but all he saw was her flushed, quivering, and undone.

"Beg me," he snarled, dragging his lips up her throat to her ear, his breath hot and ragged. "Beg me to let you fall apart. Beg me to ruin you."

And when she whispered *please*, he nearly lost it. His hand flew to her clit, ruthless circles over the swollen bundle of nerves while his cock pounded harder, deeper. Her whole body arched, convulsed, then shattered. A scream tearing from her throat as she came around him, pulsing so tight it dragged his climax with hers. Kain's roar echoed off the stone, low and guttural as he spilled into her. His hips still grinding, chasing every last spasm of release.

When the haze ebbed, he was still there, pressed deep inside her, forehead against hers, chest heaving. "Gods damn you, Dove," he whispered, voice rough and reverent. "I'll never stop wanting to fuck you." He didn't give her time to collapse. The table rattled under them, maps torn and curling at the edges, but Kain was already scooping her up into his arms. She gasped, arms tightening around his neck, but he only grinned against her lips as a giggle escaped her.

"Careful, Dove. Someone might think you like being carried around like this."

Her nails dug into his shoulder in response, but her legs stayed wrapped around him. He stalked across the room, boots heavy against the stone, and when the bed hit the back of her knees, he tossed her onto it with absolutely no ceremony. She bounced once on the mattress, glaring up at him, flushed and wrecked. And gods above, he'd never seen anything more perfect.

"You look furious," he said, stripping his shirt over his head with one hand. "Don't worry. I can fix that." Her retort died the second he climbed over her, pinning her wrists to the bed as his mouth devoured hers again. His cock ground against her slick heat, deliberately slow, and he groaned into her lips. "Mm. Still soaked. Guess I'm not completely useless after all."

Her cheeks burned, her glare sharper now, but she couldn't stop the whimper that slipped free as his hips snapped forward. "That's it," he rasped, thrusting harder, deeper, forcing every sound out of her throat. "Scream for me again, Dove. Let me know how much you *hate* this."

She tried to turn her head, tried to hide the moans tearing out of her, but his hand was already on her jaw, forcing her eyes back to his. "Nope. Don't look away. Don't you dare rob me of the view." His grin split wide, wicked and hungry. "Fuck, you're beautiful when you're ruined."

He set a ruthless rhythm again. He was punishing and relentless until she shattered around him again. He laughed low, breath ragged against her ear. "Twice already? Gods, Dove. At this rate, you're going to start expecting effort from Ryker. Poor bastard won't survive it." Her nails raked his back, her lips caught between moans and curses, and he reveled in it. He could give her no reprieve, no escape. Because this was his storm, his fire, and he wanted her burning in it with him.

When he finally spilled into her, growling her name like a curse and a prayer, he didn't collapse. He stayed pressed to her, shallow thrusts dragging her through every tremor. His lips brushed her temple, teeth scraping lightly before he murmured, smug and breathless: "Hope you weren't expecting sleep tonight, Dove. I'm just getting started."

BY THE TIDE'S GRACE AND THE WIND'S
COMMAND, OUR STRENGTH MAY FLOW

 **MYRIAMIS**

# Chapter Twenty-Two

*L* *ayla.*

Layla drifted awake to a haze of warmth and pleasure. Half-dreaming, half-aware, she found herself moving. Her hips rolling lazily, seeking friction against the heat at her back. A fierce jolt of pleasure tore through her, snapping her closer to consciousness, and that was when she realized Kain's hand was on her. His touch deliberate, ruthless, coaxing her body awake while his hard length pressed against her from behind.

Her breath caught, a startled gasp muffled as his voice slid low against her ear, velvet, and commanding. "That's it, Dove. Take your pleasure from me."

The words ignited something reckless inside her, and before she could stop herself, a smile tugged at her lips. She bit down on it, unable to smother the rush of heat that followed. Slowly, she turned her head over her shoulder, and Kain was already there, watching her with those knowing green eyes. His free hand came up to cup her face, strong and steady, tilting her toward him. The kiss that followed stole what little air she had left, deep, unrelenting, and intimate. His mouth consumed hers, and she melted into it, surrendering to the storm she'd sworn she would never let pull her under again. Without thought, without hesitation, she shifted, rolling fully into him, into the fire that was already burning her alive.

Her body moved before her mind could catch up, pressing flush to him, her leg sliding between his as his arm wrapped firmly around her waist, anchoring her. His kiss deepened, consuming, pulling her under like a current too strong to resist. Every brush of his lips, every flicker of his tongue, made her ache with a hunger that had lain dormant too long. Her hips betrayed her, bucking forward with instinct, desperate for friction. The hard ridge of him met her movement, and a moan tore free from her throat before she could stop it. Heat flooded her cheeks, but Kain only chuckled darkly against her mouth, his lips curling in dark satisfaction.

"So demanding," he murmured, his breath hot, his words sliding over her skin like sin itself.

She pulled back just enough to whisper, half-defiant, half-breathless, "You're one to speak." His eyes flashed, that familiar glint of mischief sparking to life even as his hand roamed lower, ruthless and skilled, circling her clit with maddening precision. She gasped, her nails digging into his bare shoulder as pleasure coiled tight and relentless.

Her control shattered. There was no porcelain mask, no princess, no duty. Only her writhing under his hand, savoring every merciless stroke, every whispered taunt. And when his mouth found hers again, swallowing her cries as she got closer to oblivion once more. She thought just for that moment, that maybe this was what it meant to truly breathe.

Her body arched into his touch, her breath coming ragged, when suddenly he shifted beneath her. In a blur of strength, Kain flipped her around as he rolled on top of her, pinning her beneath him as he began to kiss down her spine. She gasped, her hair spilling across the pillows as his weight pressed her into the mattress. His hands roamed boldly, mapping every curve like he'd been starved for her.

"Kain..." she started, though she had no idea what she meant to say.

"Shh, Dove." His voice was a growl, laced with heat and command. "I've let you take your pleasure... now it's my turn."

Before she could catch her breath, his hands slid down her waist, gripping firmly as he hiked her hips up to him. She squealed, a half-giggle breaking through her shock.

"So eager," he drawled, lowering his mouth to her ear as his thumb teased circles over her thigh. "Grinding on me before you were even awake... Tell me, were you dreaming about me again?" Her cheeks burned, her lips parting soundlessly, but she knew he didn't need her answer. He laughed darkly, as though her silence was confession enough. His mouth blazed a trail down her spine, biting her hip, squeezing her ass. She was ready for him to sink into her. *Needing it.* But when his tongue found her core, hot and relentless, she buried her face in the pillows and gasped his name like a prayer. Shock and vulnerability at the angle of this.

"You're so wet, Dove," he murmured between strokes, the words vibrating through her until she thought she'd shatter. "So fucking sweet."

Her thighs trembled, every part of her unraveling under his ruthless mouth. She buried her face in the pillow, clawing at it, pleading without words, and he only chuckled against her. He was wicked, patient, and entirely in control.

Her scream tore into the pillow, muffled and wild, as his mouth held her captive. Kain's grip was iron on her hips, pinning her against him, dragging every last tremor from her body as his tongue worked her mercilessly. She came hard, back arched, thighs trembling, his hold unyielding as he forced her to ride it out, to give him everything. And just as her climax began to ebb, when she thought she might finally breathe, he shifted. A growl rumbled against her skin, and then he drove into her in one swift, relentless stroke. A whole new scream ripped out of her throat, raw and helpless, her nails clawing at the sheets as pleasure and shock collided into something unbearable. His hand caught her waist, yanking her back against him, deeper, harder, until she was lost in the rhythm of him.

"Fuck, Dove," he hissed against her ear, his thrusts brutal and sure, "you're going to kill me like this."

Her body convulsed around him, still reeling from the first wave, already burning toward another. His pace was savage, his body unrelenting, and she could do nothing but sob with her head back against his shoulder as another climax clawed its way up her spine. He was everywhere. His hands, his breath, his cock driving her higher and higher until she thought she might actually explode. But then, just when she thought he would consume her whole, he slowed. His hand slid from her hip to her stomach, flattening there, grounding her. His lips brushed her shoulder softly. So at odds with the way he was still inside her, deep and pulsing.

"Easy," he murmured, dragging his mouth up to her ear. "Breathe, Dove. Let me feel you. All of you." The shift undid her more than the savagery had. His thrusts were still strong, but measured now, every roll of his hips deliberate, coaxing, pulling her down from the storm instead of hurling her deeper into it. She turned her head, desperate to see him, and he met her halfway. His mouth slanting over hers in a kiss that was slower, deeper, and unbearably tender. Her body melted into it, into him, her trembling easing against him. His hand laced with hers against her stomach, fingers tightening as if to anchor her there. As he held her back tight against his chest, Kain's mouth devoured hers between each driving thrust. His growl broke against her lips as he spilled inside her, and her gasp melted into his kiss until they both collapsed into a slower rhythm. Breathing, smiling, tasting each other in the aftershock. For one blissful heartbeat, there was nothing but warmth and quiet. But then, as her thoughts drifted beyond the bed, reality seeped in like a draft beneath the door.

"Kain," she whispered, her lips brushing his, "I didn't mean to stay here all night. I need to get back before someone notices I'm gone." His forehead dropped against hers, eyes closed, as if he could will her words away. Then seemingly reluctantly, he gave a single nod. He slipped free of her, and the absence made her shiver. Layla sheepishly climbed from the sheets, cheeks flushed as she gathered the silken layers of her gown. Before she could lace it herself, he strode to her, clearly unbothered, utterly unashamed in his nakedness, and took the ribbons in his hands. His gaze never left her as he cinched them tight, the heat in his eyes making it impossible to breathe.

"Kain..." Her voice faltered, softer now. "I have to go."

He tied the last lace, fingers lingering at her waist, and that wolf's grin carved across his mouth. "You can run, Dove," he murmured, leaning close enough that his breath teased her ear, "but I'll find you. I'm nowhere near done with you."

Her teeth sank into her lower lip, failing miserably to hide the smile that tugged at her mouth. She peeked into the corridor, nerves hammering, then slipped into the shadows of the hall. Behind her, she swore she still felt his eyes on her skin.

Layla slipped back into her chambers, thanking the gods no one had caught her wandering the corridors at such an hour. The door clicked shut behind her, and she sagged against it, forehead pressed to the cool wood as if it might ground her. Last night's fire still burned beneath her skin, images flashing too vividly throughout her thoughts. His mouth, his hands, his voice... A soft *ahem* echoed throughout her chamber. Her eyes flew open to see that Marilla stood in the doorway of the bathing chamber, arms folded across her chest, brows arched with the unmistakable knowing of a hawk.

"Shit," Layla muttered under her breath, scrambling upright.

"No need to lie," Marilla said crisply, her tone half-scold, half-affection. "I can see it all over your face. Now get in that bath and wash whomever off you." She gestured to the steaming tub she'd clearly just drawn. Heat flooded Layla's cheeks, her body betraying her guilt as she shuffled forward like a child caught sneaking pastries. She could almost *feel* Kain on her skin still, trailing down her thighs. Gods, if Marilla noticed.... She did. She definitely did.

"Don't bristle, young lady," Marilla continued, setting a towel neatly on the counter, her voice brisk but not unkind. "But I'm going to ask, and you will answer. Was this...suitor...your betrothed?" Layla's head snapped up, eyes wide. Words tangled uselessly in her throat. "I'm not here to judge," Marilla pressed on matter-of-factly. "But if it was not, then there's a tea I'll need to brew. We can't have an unwanted heir brewing in that belly."

Layla nearly choked. Mortified, she shook her head, mouth opening, closing, but no sound emerged.

"Just nod if I should fetch the tea." Her pride screamed to refuse. But her head dipped, reluctant, betraying her. Marilla gave a firm nod of her own, all business, and slipped toward the door. "Stay in the bath until the water cools. You'll want every trace of him gone before the maids start whispering." Then the latch clicked shut behind her. Layla sank onto the stool, head in her hands. *Holy hells. What was she doing?* Her first instinct was to blame Kain. His grin, his touch, the way he pulled that side of her out. But the truth burned clearer than any shame. *That* part of her. The reckless, passionate, confident part, wasn't his doing. It was hers. And she had no idea what that meant for the girl she was supposed to be.

Layla tried to appear calm, spooning porridge as though she weren't sitting on the edge of ruin. Under the table, Kain's hand rested warm and heavy on her thigh, thumb tracing lazy, maddening circles.

"As I've told you before," she murmured, her voice steady despite the heat crawling up her neck, "you have fruit on your *own* plate."

He didn't even glance at her. Just plucked a slice of pear from hers and bit into it, eyes twinkling. His fingers squeezed her thigh deliberately, making her pulse stutter. "And as I've also told you before, yours is so much sweeter."

The doors to the hall burst open, the air itself shifting. Frea swept in like an infestation that expected the world to bend around it, leathers molded to her body, hair shining like raven feathers under the morning light. She didn't ask before sliding into the empty chair beside Kain, one arm draped casually on the table, her smirk bold and insolent.

"Well," Frea purred, voice carrying, "I see I'm just in time. You couldn't possibly start breakfast without me, could you, Kain?"

Kain arched a brow, utterly unbothered. "Actually, I was just enjoying Dove's fruit." He reached for another grape, thumb still circling Layla's thigh as though daring her to flinch. Layla stiffened, but before she could speak, Ciana set down her spoon with a deliberate *clink*. As she lifted her gaze, smiling so sweetly it could've been carved from sugar.

"Strange," Ciana mused, "I don't recall anyone inviting you to this table." Layla blinked at her. *What in the gods' names?*

Frea tilted her chin, eyes flashing. "I don't wait for invitations."

Ciana's smile held, stripped of sweetness and pretense. "No, I suppose you don't. You strike me as the type who mistakes arrogance for charm. And unfortunately, no one's corrected you yet." The silence that followed seemed to ripple outward across the table. Even Sparrow glanced up from his bowl, a brow cocked in quiet surprise.

Frea leaned forward, lips curving. "Careful, princess. You don't want to spar with me."

"Oh, I'm not worried," Ciana countered smoothly, her tone silk over steel. "You see, within these walls, battles aren't won with blades. They're won with minds. And from what I can tell..." her smile sharpened into something vicious, "you won't be of much use in that regard." Frea froze. Just for a beat, but it was enough. The great warrior, silenced. Layla's stomach flipped, not from Kain's thumb this time, but from the sudden, vivid spark that lit inside her chest. This was Ciana. Not the hollow, broken sister who had been dragged back from Bartoria. This was the girl who once laughed until she cried, who could cut someone to ribbons with a smile. Layla didn't know why Ciana was doing it now. She couldn't place if it was on her behalf or, gods help her, because of Kain. But she didn't care. She only knew that for the first time in weeks, her sister looked alive. And that was enough.

Layla sat straighter, warmth curling in her chest as she let herself savor the moment. Appreciating it. Appreciating her. Appreciating anything that brought the old Ciana back to them even if it came from an unexpected place.

Frea's jaw worked, lips parting as if to craft some retort, but nothing came. The silence stretched taut. Then Sparrow coughed loud and deliberate. Poorly disguising the twitch of his mouth that betrayed amusement. "Well," he drawled, pushing back from the table with a scrape of his chair, "as entertaining as this is, it's time we head to the council. Someone's got to explain why our queen isn't here yet."

The tension fractured. Frea leaned back, face composed but her eyes still sparking, and Ciana returned serenely to her spoon as if she hadn't just gutted a woman with words. The entire time Kain's thumb never stopped moving against Layla's thigh. But Layla barely noticed now. She was too busy watching her sister. Ciana's smile lingered, unrestrained and alive. Aerilynn's gaze flickered too, bright with some hidden thought. Layla's breath caught. *Did they want to know too?*

All this time she had thought Ciana was nothing more than their mother's mirror image: perfected porcelain, untouchable. That Aerilynn was simply the baby to protect. *But what if they carried the same hunger she did?* The same fire that had been smothered beneath expectation and silence? Her pulse quickened. And for once, she didn't swallow it down.

She straightened, feeling Kain's quiet squeeze like a dare beneath the table, and let the words tumble out into the open. "Do you... want to know? What's really happening in those council chambers? What threats we're actually facing?"

The air seemed to shift, thick and heavy. Aerilynn's fork stilled midway to her mouth. Ciana's brows arched, cool but curious. And Layla realized she had just broken every rule her mother had ever carved into her bones. For a moment, silence. The clatter of spoons, the murmur of servants clearing dishes, even Sparrow's steady scrape of chair legs, all of it dimmed.

Ciana's spoon stilled in her hand. She tilted her head, assessing Layla like one might a rival across the battlefield. A measured smile curved her lips. "Well. Finally, you've decided to ask." Layla's jaw dropped.

Aerilynn leaned forward, her hands clasped together tight in her lap. Her wide eyes flickered between them, uncertainty warring with eagerness. "I... I *do* want to know. More than anything. But Mother..." She faltered, lowering her voice as if Queen Raynera might materialize behind her. "If she ever found out..."

"Then she'll find out," Ciana cut in, firm and decisive. Her gaze locked on Layla, not Aerilynn. "But I'm done with silence. Done with smiling while the world burns. So, sister..." she leaned back in her chair, lips curving with challenge, "...if you have something worth saying, say it." Heat rushed through Layla's veins, fire and terror tangled so tightly she couldn't tell them apart. Her whole life she'd been told to swallow words, to smooth edges, to keep the porcelain mask in place. But here, here were her sisters, looking at her not as the dutiful princess but as *something more*. Kain's thumb pressed firmly into her thigh beneath the table, a grounding, goading pressure that said: *do it*. And for once, Layla did not hesitate.

Layla drew a long breath, then began. The words tumbled faster than she expected, but none of them faltered. She spoke of Lumiren, of Yssra's creeping rot, of Bartoria being nothing more than a puppet, of Queen Okteria's vengeance. She gave them everything Kain had given her. Every secret whispered, every map detail burned into her mind. Her sisters did not interrupt. Aerilynn leaned in, wide-eyed, as though drinking in every syllable. Ciana's expression was intent and thoughtful, her spoon abandoned as she watched Layla with the kind of intensity that made her spine tingle. Even Sparrow, across the table, listened without a word.

Though Kain's fingers tracing idle circles on her thigh nearly unraveled her focus with each pass. He didn't speak, didn't intrude. Just sat there like the wolf he was, reminding her silently that she wasn't alone anymore.

Frea opened her mouth once, lips curving for some cutting remark, but before she could form it, Ciana lifted her hand. Not harsh, not loud. Just a simple gesture. *Enough.* The silence that followed was razor-sharp. Frea scoffed, muttered something under her breath, and Layla, gods help her, giggled. The sound slipped out, light and startled, before she pressed her hand to her lips and kept going. By the time she finished, she felt... emptied. Yet lighter too, like speaking the truth had pulled air back into her lungs.

Ciana sat back slowly, her smile tight, but her eyes glittering. "So now what?"

Layla turned instinctively to Kain. Kain leaned forward, his tone steady but edged with steel. "Now we keep Lord Jameson from scattering your armies like frightened birds. We stall him, calm these alliance negotiations just a little longer. Hold the line until my mother arrives, and with any luck, the royals of Myriamis too. Then together, we convince him that going to war with us is the only sane choice." The weight of his words settled over the table. And yet Kain never let go of her, his light caress never stopping. It was steady, grounding, and impossible to ignore.

Sparrow cleared his throat, already rising. "Speaking of, time for that council meeting."

With one last squeeze to her thigh, Kain stood. Sparrow and, of course, Frea followed, her sway deliberate as ever. Layla's stomach twisted. Gods, the injustice of it. The woman who wasn't even Graystonian would sit at that table, hear every word, while she, a princess of this kingdom, was expected to smile and wait in ignorance. Even now, with everything she'd learned, everything she'd dared to ask, she was still locked out of her own future. Her jaw tightened as she turned back to her sisters, determined to smother the bitter heat rising in her chest. And then Ciana shocked her again.

Ciana leaned forward, eyes fixed with certainty, voice low but sure. "You should be in there, Layla. Not her."

The words punched the air from her lungs. Layla blinked, caught off guard, searching her sister's face for mockery but there was none. Only conviction. For a moment, Layla could only stare. Ciana, of all people. Ciana, who had mirrored their mother's silence for so long. And now she was saying the very thing Layla had never dared to voice aloud. Something inside her shifted. Things were changing. That much was undeniable. For the first time in what felt like forever, the silence that had pressed on her chest like a cage was cracking open. She had dared to question, dared to want more, and instead of pulling her back into place, her sisters were stepping with her. It was empowering. Terrifying, yes. But gods, empowering. And the best part? She wasn't alone. Ciana's resolute smile, Aerilynn's steady presence, their voices different from her own, yet echoing the same hunger proved it. They were changing too. Not just survivors. Not just pawns of their mother and this kingdom's will. But women who wanted to know, to decide, to fight.

"Let no mind remain idle where wisdom may swell. To deny the pursuit of knowledge is to betray the tide itself."

All citizens are required to dedicate time each moon cycle to study, reflection, or teaching. Libraries and scroll sanctums are maintained as sacred ground.

-IN ACCORDANCE WITH THE
HARMONIOUS ACCORD OF MyRIAMIS

# Chapter Twenty-Three

*L* *ayla.*

    Layla spent the rest of the morning with her sisters. Not lessons. Not at embroidery or etiquette or learning all the useless refinements meant to shape her into something smaller. They talked instead. Really talked. Around half-finished plates and cooling tea, voices low and earnest. Layla spoke of her fears, her doubts, the weight of everything she now carried. Aerilynn listened with quiet steadiness, asking questions that cut cleanly to the heart of things. Ciana challenged her. Not unkindly, but with intention, forcing Layla to consider angles she hadn't before. It was strange. Exhilarating even, to not be alone in her thoughts.

    By midday, when the girls finally went their separate ways, Layla's mind had turned elsewhere. She wanted to know how the meeting had gone. Each corridor she passed deepened that need, every brush of shadow across stone pulling her attention forward. She found herself scanning faces, doorways, listening for a familiar cadence of footsteps. Not Ryker's. The thought came with unexpected clarity. Not him. Not the man she was meant to marry, whose presence now felt less like reassurance and more like a looming question mark.

No, she searched for Kain. For his certainty. His confidence in her. For the unquestionable way he spoke of fighting and saving their future as though it were already his to defend. For the unwavering answers he gave when she asked questions, never once dismissing her need to understand. But also for him. And that realization alone told her how much had changed.

As she continued on down the corridor, a hand clamped over her mouth and yanked her backward into darkness. Her heart slammed violently in her chest. She barely had time to gasp before her spine struck shelving, linen shifting beneath her fingers as she was caged in by rough wood and shadow. Panic flared fast and wild, then died just as fast when a familiar scent wrapped around her. Heat. Steel. *Him.*

His breath brushed the shell of her ear, searing and intimate, sending a shiver straight down her spine. "I told you I'd find you," he murmured, low and unrepentant.

Layla's pulse skidded, then raced, caught between shock, disorientation, and seduction. The pressure over her mouth eased, not rushed, not apologetic. But confident and knowing. He turned her before she could form a thought, and in the narrow spill of light, she caught his eyes, dark with intent, just before his mouth crashed into hers, stealing the rest of her breath and every protest she had already lost.

Gods, she melted. Her body betraying her, hands clutching desperately at his shoulders, pulling him closer, needing him. It had been mere hours since she'd left his bed, since his mouth had ruined her in ways she couldn't forget, and yet it felt like years. And most importantly, there were far too many layers between them.

"These cursed clothes," she breathed against his lips, tugging at the layers between them with frantic fingers.

Kain chuckled darkly, his teeth grazing her bottom lip as his hands roamed possessively down her waist. "Oh, Dove," he drawled, cocky even as his hips pinned her to the wall. "Say things like that, and I'll tear every stitch off you right here, right now." Her laugh caught between a gasp and a moan, and gods help her, she didn't doubt for a second that he meant it. Then his mouth claimed hers again, rougher, hungrier. His hand slid under her skirts, dragging the fabric high until his palm was at her thigh, thumb circling with devastating intent.

"Kain..." she whispered, though it was less protest and more plea.

"Gods, I love the way you say my name when you're trying not to want me," he rasped, lips trailing down her jaw, grazing the tender hollow of her throat. His teeth nipped, just enough to make her gasp, just enough to remind her exactly who had her caged between linen shelves and his body.

Her cheeks flamed, but her body arched into his hand, craving, unthinking. "You're insufferable."

"Mm." His grin ghosted across her mouth, wicked and sure. "And yet here you are, grinding against me like I'm your salvation."

Heat shot through her at the truth of it, at how easily he unraveled her. She was betrothed, a princess, a daughter of Graystonia, and still she couldn't stop herself from melting into him. Still, she couldn't stop her breathless laugh as his fingers found her slick center and teased.

"Quiet now, Dove," he murmured, sealing his mouth over hers again. "Or the whole damned castle's going to know exactly how sweet you sound when I touch you."

She tried, gods help her, she tried to swallow the moan that tore out of her when he pushed two fingers deep inside her. Her hand tangled in his hair, tugging desperately, her hips bucking against his palm. He swallowed her cries with his mouth, every kiss rough, frantic, like he wanted to devour her whole. The door rattled as voices passed right outside. It sounded like two guards trading jokes, their boots echoing against the stone. Layla went rigid, panic blazing hot in her chest. But Kain didn't stop. His thumb circled her clit harder, his grin pressed against her mouth. "Don't freeze up now, Dove." Her eyes squeezed shut, her breath breaking against his shoulder as she fought to stay silent. The footsteps lingered, slowed even it seemed. One of the men laughed, far too close. *Gods, if they were caught....* Her mind at war with the logic and desire fighting to win.

"Kain..." she whispered, begging him for more, begging him to stop.

"Almost there," he rasped, thrusting his fingers faster. "Give it to me."

And gods, she did. The climax hit her so hard she nearly screamed, but his mouth crashed down on hers at the same moment, stealing the sound, swallowing it whole. Her body trembled violently against him, the linen shelves rattling behind her back. But the guards moved on and silence fell.

Her chest heaved, her legs weak, but Kain only grinned, his breath ragged against her ear. "See? Nothing to worry about."

She smacked his chest weakly, still shaking. "You...are impossible."

"Impossible," he echoed, pressing a final kiss to her swollen lips. "And irresistible. Don't forget that part." Kain drew his fingers from her slowly, and in the faint darkness, she watched as he slipped them past his lips. He hummed low in his throat as though savoring something divine, his eyes burning her through the shadows. "Gods, Dove... I love the taste of you." Her cheeks flamed so hot she swore they'd light the whole closet, and then he caught her mouth in another deep kiss. She gasped when she tasted herself on him, her body betraying her, grinding against his hardness without even thinking. He chuckled darkly against her lips, the sound deliciously and annoyingly smug. "So needy." His teeth grazed her bottom lip, tugging before he drew back just enough to whisper, hot and lethal, "And here I thought you wanted to know about the meeting."

Her breath hitched, torn in two. "So which is it, Dove?" His hand slid firmly over her hip, squeezing, anchoring her against him. "You want to ride my cock right here, in this little closet? Don't get me wrong, I'll make it work. Or..." his grin twisted, all confidence and intent, "do you want your answers?" Every nerve was alive by the way his hand squeezed her hip, by the promise in his voice. For half a heartbeat, she almost caved. Almost begged him to take her right there among the linens, reckless and wild. But no. Not this time. She forced her body to still, though every nerve burned for him. "The meeting, Kain," she whispered, low but steady. "Tell me."

His grin curved with predatory certainty, a hunter scenting weakness. He leaned closer, his breath hot against her ear. He expected her to fold. To yield. To beg. But when she didn't, when she met his eyes in the dark and held, something shifted. That cocky humor faded, leaving only the cut of respect. "Fine," he drawled at last in mock disappointment, though his thumb dragged one last slow circle into her hip before pulling back. "The meeting."

His voice was velvet edged with iron as he told her. Ryker furious, slamming fists, spitting outrage that Antonin refused to bend to sign the peace agreement. The council restless, whispering. And Frea, gods-damned Frea, smiling that serpent's smile, whispering poison and silk until Ryker agreed to stall. For now.

The words should have cut her. They should have cracked her composure. Maybe Kain wanted them to. Maybe he wanted to watch her squirm. But if she was being honest with herself, it didn't matter if Frea straddled Ryker on the council table itself, not if it kept Ryker reined in. Not if it bought Graystonia time. At least, that was what she told herself. The real truth throbbed hotter deep down. That as long as it wasn't Kain beneath Frea, as long as he still came to *her* in these stolen shadows, she could survive anything else.

Kain's lips curved, smug and knowing, like he'd pulled the thought straight from her chest. "There it is," he murmured, voice silken, lethal. His thumb slid higher, daring her pulse to betray her. "That flicker. You tell yourself you don't care, but you do."

"I don't," she hissed, cheeks burning.

"Oh, you do." His mouth brushed hers, the smirk bleeding through every word. "You don't give a damn who Frea flirts with or fucks... so long as it isn't me. Admit it, Dove, you want me all to yourself. Even while you play the dutiful princess. Even while you wear another man's claim." Her body betrayed her, shuddering under his touch. "Truth tastes sweet, doesn't it?" His teeth grazed her jaw, dragging her desire out further "Now tell me...do you want the council's dull little plans? Or do you want me to fuck you right here, until you can't lie to yourself anymore about who you are....and who you really want?"

Her breath stuttered. Her body wanting to admit something she was determined to keep denying. Thankfully her mind snapped like a blade drawn clean. Finding herself, not falling for his goading. *Not this time.* She caught his wrist, stilling his hand. Her lips curved slow, deliberate, into a smile that mirrored his own. It was wicked, knowing, and triumphant. "That's enough." Kain froze. Surprise flickered. Then hunger. She leaned up, close enough that her breath ghosted hot against *his* ear, her voice silk and steel all at once. "I got all I needed from you." And with that, she slipped past him, skirts whispering like a dare. At the threshold she glanced back, just once. A thin line of light carved across his face, illuminating emerald eyes wide with shock before narrowing into blazing hunger. He leaned against the wall, shaking his head with a low, disbelieving laugh.

The grin that spread across his mouth was pure wolf. "Fuck Dove," he murmured to the empty dark. "You're going to ruin me."

Layla was still smiling, still basking in the triumph of leaving Kain undone in the dark closet, when she turned the corner and nearly collided with Ryker. He steadied her out of reflex, his hand closing briefly at her elbow before withdrawing. His smile followed, smooth and familiar, as though nothing stood between them.

"There you are," he said. "I was hoping to find you. With the wedding so close, I wanted to be certain you were well."

"I am," Layla replied. Her tone was polite and even. But beneath it, something steadier had taken root. "I need to speak with you." That drew a flicker of caution to his eyes. She did not soften. "I know we discussed this briefly the other night," she said, "but I'm afraid I must insist. I intend to sit in on the next council meeting."

Ryker blinked. Then he laughed. Not cruelly. A short, incredulous sound, as though she had misjudged the moment entirely. "Layla," he said, smiling, "there's no need for that. Especially now. I have everything handled."

"I'm aware," she replied calmly. And for once, she did not temper the words that followed. "That does not change my request."

His smile thinned. "This is not something you need to involve yourself in. With the wedding days away, your focus should be else-where."

"My focus," she said carefully, feeling the unfamiliar strength of saying it aloud, "is Graystonia."

That caught him. He studied her as though reassessing something he had long ago decided. Layla held his gaze, heart steadying rather than racing. This was new. Speaking without shrinking. Without apologizing for the space her words took. "You're letting nerves speak," he said at last. "Once we're married, these concerns will no longer fall to you."

She lifted her chin. Just slightly. "I am not asking out of fear," she said. "I am asking because I intend to rule."

The silence was immediate. Ryker stared at her, genuine shock breaking through his composure. For a heartbeat, he seemed to wait for her to smile. To retreat. To make it lighter. She did not. "That's...," he began, then stopped, a short breath leaving him. "Layla, that's absurd."

Her expression did not change. "You will be queen," he continued, incredulous now. "Beloved. Influential. But ruling is not what this marriage is for."

"And what is it for?" she asked quietly.

"For stability," he said, irritation bleeding through. "For order. The council answers to a king. Not a symbol." She absorbed that without flinching.

"I will ask again," Layla said. "Formally, if I must."

Ryker's jaw tightened. "You will not," he said flatly. "This is not the time to challenge tradition. Certainly not on the eve of our wedding."

"Because it would embarrass you," she said, still calm.

"Because it would undermine everything we are about to secure." Silence stretched between them, taut and fragile.

"I see," Layla said at last.

Ryker stepped closer, lowering his voice. "Trust me," he said. "Let me carry this burden. That is what you're marrying me for."

The words landed heavy and final. Layla inclined her head, every inch the dutiful princess. But inside, something had shifted for good. She was done shrinking to fit the future others had decided for her. "Of course," she said.

He pressed a kiss to her temple and stepped away, already finished with the conversation. Layla remained where she was. She did not know when it had begun. Whether it was Kain's certainty, the way he spoke of her strength as though it were already real. Or her sisters at the table, leaning in instead of urging silence, reinforcing every truth she had once been taught to swallow. Perhaps it was all of it, layering slowly until something inside her had begun to stir. She felt it now. Not fully formed.

Not yet defined. But present. Her voice no longer felt fragile. No longer something to guard or ration. It hovered just beneath her breath, steadying instead of shaking, waiting instead of retreating.

BY THE TIDES GRACE AND THE WIND'S
COMMAND. OUR STRENGTH MAY FLOW

"The sea provides to those who serve it.
What is taken must be honored; what is
gifted must be earned."

Fishing, harvesting, and use of
sea-born goods must follow
ancient sustainable rites. No net is
cast without blessing, no catch
consumed without gratitude.

-IN ACCORDANCE WITH THE
HARMONIOUS ACCORD OF MyRIAMIS

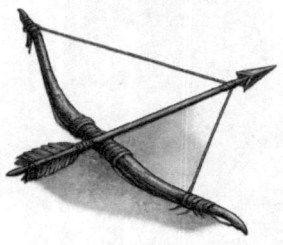

# Chapter Twenty-Four

*K*<sup>*ain.*</sup>

Steel rang through the courtyard, clean and satisfying. Kain pivoted, sweat dripping down his temple as Sparrow's blade met his again with a shower of sparks. It felt good, gods, it felt *needed*. To work the frustration out of his system one strike at a time.

"You're getting sloppy," Sparrow grunted, circling him.

"Sloppy?" Kain sneered, baring his teeth as he pressed forward with a brutal strike that sent Sparrow stumbling back a step. "You're the one on your ass every third bout."

"Yeah," Sparrow said, catching his breath, "but at least I know what's got me distracted." Kain froze for just a fraction of a second. He didn't like Sparrow's tone. It was too knowing, too careful. Sparrow rested his blade across his shoulders and gave him a look, flat and unamused. "I've seen the way you look at her, Kain. Hell, I've seen you *with* her. You're helping her find her fire again, good. Gods know she needs it. But..." He hesitated, and that hesitation made Kain's grip tighten on his sword.

"But what?" Kain snarled.

"But she's already been through enough," Sparrow said evenly. "You know that. And she's getting married. *This weekend.*" Kain's jaw flexed, the reminder hitting like a strike to the gut. Sparrow didn't flinch. "Even if it's to that mindless soldier who couldn't lead a wolf to meat if you painted his boots in blood, he's still going to be king. And if he finds out you're fucking her? All of this..." he gestured vaguely toward the castle, toward the halls where negotiations were happening, "goes to hell. Our alliance, the southern line, everything. We lose her kingdom's army. We lose our chance against Lumiren and Yssra."

Kain turned away, sword point digging into the dirt as his chest heaved. He hated that Sparrow was right. Hated that the truth felt like chains, wrapping tighter with every word. "She deserves better than being some man's pawn," Kain bit out at last, voice low, rough.

Sparrow's expression softened, but only slightly. "Yeah. She does. But that includes you thinking with more than just your cock."

Kain barked a harsh laugh, humorless and clipped. Sparrow truly had no idea what was going on in his head. "You done lecturing me?"

"For now." Sparrow's mouth curved into the faintest grin. "But think about it. You may not be afraid of much, but if this blows up, it's not just your heart on the line. It's hers. And maybe the whole damned realm." Kain didn't answer. He just lifted his blade again, jaw set, and Sparrow took the hint. Swiftly coming at him hard enough to keep them both from thinking too much about what had just been said. Steel rang against steel as Kain and Sparrow circled each other, sweat slicking their skin in the autumn sun. The rhythmic clang was almost enough to drown out the gnawing thoughts left by Sparrow's warning. Layla, the wedding, the noose tightening around her neck and his. Only to be annoyingly distracting by incoming footsteps.

"Real fucking party out here today, huh?" Kain called as the crunch of boots neared. He didn't even glance over his shoulder to know who it was. "Don't remember sending out invites."

Frea's laugh cut through the air, low and knowing. "Relax, Kain. I came to save Sparrow from your bruised ego when he finally bests you." She stepped into view, twirling a dagger idly, her lethal grace enough to make most men sweat. But not him. Kain rolled his shoulders and tipped her a half-smile. "You want a turn? Or are you just here to watch me sweat?"

Her answering smirk was pure sin. "Maybe both." Her gaze drifted past him, landing on the figure now striding across the courtyard from his other side. Ryker. *Of course.* Kain held back a groan.

Frea's smile shifted, turning coy as she straightened and greeted him. "Your Highness." Her tone was honey and steel, her eyes bright with mischief. Ryker, ever the picture of control, inclined his head politely. Though Kain didn't miss the glint in his eyes, the faint twitch at the corner of his mouth. The man was mesmerized, just like every other idiot who'd ever stood too close to Frea. Then Ryker turned, fixing Kain with a look that was all business. "We need to talk. Now."

Kain bared his teeth in a wolfish grin. "We're already in the ring, Kingling. Let's talk while we spar."

To his mild surprise, Ryker drew his sword. "Fine."

Their first clash rang like thunder. Ryker was better than Kain expected. He was measured, efficient, and not afraid to press hard. "You're wasting time," Ryker gritted out between strikes. "Every day you stall puts my kingdom in greater danger."

Kain parried hard, forcing him to pivot. "Better to waste time than waste soldiers. You scatter the armies now, Lumiren will carve through you before you can whistle them back."

Ryker advanced, fast enough that Kain had to dig deep to keep up. "My first act as king will not be plunging this kingdom into war."

Kain laughed, a rough bark that echoed across the yard. "Then your first act will be delivering it straight to the pyre." Their blades locked, ringing with the clash of steel, faces so close Kain could see the sweat dripping down Ryker's temple. The man's chest heaved, but his voice came low and hard as hammered iron.

"Easy words, Kain, when you don't wear the crown," Ryker bit out. "When you're not the man who has to look his people in the eye and decide which of them won't see another sunrise." The blade between them caught the light, trembling with their breath. Kain's grin vanished, replaced by something darker: raw conviction.

"You think I want your fucking crown?" he snarled, driving Ryker back with a vicious twist of steel. "I don't even want my own. But you know what? While you sit on your throne and *protect* everyone, the world burns and I'll be the one out there stopping it. Hopefully before it takes your entire precious kingdom."

Ryker didn't flinch. His own sword came up again, the strike clean and decisive, forcing Kain back a step. "And that's exactly the problem. You want to lead without ever carrying the cost. You want to play at being the savage prince, give orders, take the glory. But not the crown, not the burden that comes with it." Their blades clashed again, a brutal, echoing strike. "One day you won't have the choice," Ryker snarled, bearing down until Kain's boots scraped the dirt. "And until you know what it's like to have the weight of a kingdom on your shoulders. Until you've stood there knowing every wrong move will damn your people, don't you dare lecture me on what my first act as king should be." The words settled into the silence.

"Agree to the alliance or get out of my way." Ryker stepped closer as he said it, his voice dropping just enough that only Kain could hear the threat beneath it. "And stay the fuck away from Layla," he added under his breath. "She's not your concern." Kain didn't move for a second. His rage a tangible thing at the comment. Before he finally stepped closer. Just enough to make the space between them nonexistent as he looked down at Ryker.

"Men who need to stake claims are afraid of what they can't control," he said quietly. "That's why you think you own her. But you don't. You're just standing in her way." The words landed heavier than the steel between them. Ryker's jaw tightened, irritation flashing before he smothered it. He sheathed his sword in one fluid motion, turned, and strode off across the yard, leaving silence in his wake, the smell of steel and sweat hanging thick.

Kain stood there, chest heaving, fingers white knuckled around the hilt of his sword. Every muscle screamed to chase him down, to force him to understand. Instead, with a snarl, he rammed the blade point first into the dirt and let it stand quivering.

Sparrow's voice was little more than a whisper, but it lit Kain's blood like a match. "She's here." That was all he needed. His sword was sheathed before Sparrow finished the breath, boots already eating up the corridor stone as he strode for the front of the castle. They arrived just as the massive doors swung open. The autumn air spilled in, cold and bracing, but nothing compared to the figure framed by the waning light beyond.

Queen Okteria stood there, still as a drawn bow. Her eyes found her son first, locking on like a hunter sighting prey. Emerald, the mirror of Kain's, but colder and far more dangerous. Her eyes were glittering with that relentless, assessing spark he knew too well. Her dark hair loosely braided behind her. Then, the viper smiled.

"Kain." No bow, no waiting for formal welcomes. She crossed the threshold and tugged him into her arms before the guards could even announce her arrival. Her embrace was firm, armor and muscle pressing into him, but brief. She pulled back just as quickly, her gaze already searching his. "Did you handle it?"

Kain exhaled, lips quirking in that half-smile he knew she hated because it meant bad news. "You're not going to like it." One brow arched, waiting. "They want an alliance, yes. War? No. They'd rather hide behind their walls, wave a treaty like a prayer, and hope their gods handle the rest. The future of their kingdom is being decided by a council of men too scared to bleed, and the one who calls the shots? A kin-gling with no true leadership instincts. He's crowned in two days."

Something flared in her gaze. Not rage but something colder, more calculating. "And the women?" she asked, though her voice was already bitter with the answer.

Kain's mouth twisted. "They don't speak here. You remember."

She nodded once, decisively, as though sealing away the infor-mation. Then her lips curved, a knowing smile sliding into place. "We'll fix that problem. Quickly. And they will learn exactly what a woman's voice sounds like."

Footsteps echoed behind them, crisp and deliberate. Queen Raynera appeared at the top of the stairs, her presence as regal and commanding as ever. Her pale gown was gold thread and iron dig-nity, her face unreadable but Kain saw the tension in her jaw.

"Queen Okteria," Raynera said, her voice cool, even. "Welcome. We have been expecting you."

The two women inclined their heads, nothing more. No smiles, no courtesies beyond what tradition demanded. "We had... an un-expected delay," Okteria replied smoothly, stepping aside as she ges-tured toward the man entering behind her. King Malrik of Myriamis climbed the steps with a gait that spoke of years in the field rather than the throne room. His silver-streaked beard was braided neatly, his glasses caught the firelight as he bowed low. Despite his age, there was nothing frail about him. He radiated measured strength. Knowledge, yes, but the kind that had been forged in books, not battle.

"Queen Raynera," Malrik said warmly. "It has been too long."

If she was surprised, Raynera hid it well. Her own bow was precise, her smile faint but practiced. "King Malrik. What a pleasant surprise. I did not know Myriamis would also be joining us."

As the pleasantries were exchanged, Kain noticed Okteria's smile tighten, her entire posture coiling like a striking snake as she interrupted. "We are here to finalize the alliance of the South and to plan for war. Where can we speak?" Raynera did not flinch, though her hands clasped more tightly before her.

"Our military dignitaries and the future king are currently engaged with drills outside the city walls," she said. "They will return in the morning. I suggest we dine first and meet at dawn, when all are present."

Okteria's scowl came instantly, a calculated display she wore like war paint. "I do not see why we must wait," she said coldly. "The leaders stand here now, do they not? War does not wait."

Raynera's voice stayed smooth, silk covering steel. "I am sure your journey has been exhausting. My ladies will show you to your rooms so you may refresh yourselves before dinner." For a moment, the air itself seemed to still. Then Okteria inclined her head, a slow and deliberate movement, and turned on her heel without another word. Kain caught the faintest curl at the corner of her mouth as she passed him. His mother's private smile, the one that promised she was already plotting her strike. He bit back his own grin as he fell into step behind her.

Gods help them all. By morning, this castle would know what it meant to have a viper in its halls.

The moment Kain crossed the threshold of the dining hall, his path was decided. He went straight for the seat beside Layla. The one she never would have expected him to claim. Not with the entire table watching. Not with the Eradellian queen seated at the head, her jaw set like stone at the quiet breach of etiquette.

Sparrow's earlier warning brushed the edge of his awareness then. A reminder of what they all stood to be lost if he mis-stepped. But Kain acknowledged it only long enough to dismiss it. Whatever the risk, whatever the cost, it meant nothing in the face of her. He did not slow. Did not hesitate. He had long since learned that no warning could keep him from her once she was within reach. He was simply helpless in her presence.

As he reached her and plopped down, he couldn't help but taunt her. "Relax, Dove," he murmured low enough for her alone, a grin tugging at the corner of his mouth. "If you stab me under the table, I'll only enjoy it." Her mouth snapped shut and she turned forward, every inch the princess again, but not before he caught the way her fingers dug into her napkin, knuckles white. Then the door opened behind them. Ciana and Aerilynn swept in together, silent as ghosts. Ciana's expression didn't flicker when she saw him in her usual seat. No raised brow, no cutting remark. She simply crossed to the empty chair Kain had abandoned at the far end of the table and sat gracefully, her little sister following suit.

If the shift in seating rankled anyone, they didn't show it. But Kain felt Layla's awareness of him like a live current between them, thrumming under her skin. And he couldn't resist letting his knee brush hers under the table. A deliberate, slow press of contact that made her inhale too suddenly for it to be mistaken for anything but what it was. Kain smiled and leaned back in his stolen chair, his arm still draped behind her like he owned the space. He heard the great doors at the end of the hall swing open, and the hush that followed was instant. Boots struck marble. Silks whispered. Servants scrambled into formation, their voices echoing faintly against the vaulted ceilings. But Kain didn't look up. His attention stayed locked on Layla. He leaned in, close enough that his breath brushed the shell of her ear, his words a dark whisper meant for her alone. "Showtime, Dove," he murmured, voice rich with mischief. "The viper's here. Let the fun begin."

Her spine snapped straight, every muscle taut beneath his proximity. Her fingers tightened around her napkin until the linen wrinkled, but she didn't turn. *Couldn't,* he was sure. Not with half the court's eyes already flicking toward them. Kain's grin only deepened, lazy and satisfied before he reluctantly glanced up. Then the air shifted into something cool, taut, and electric as Queen Okteria entered. The sound of her steps was soft, but the silence they commanded was absolute. She glided into the hall as though she'd been carved from the same stone that built it, and every head bowed in her wake. Emerald eyes, bright and merciless, found Kain instantly. Approval blazed there, predatory, proud, and calculating. Before sweeping across the table, assessing every soul present like pieces on a board. Kain only grinned wider, leaning back as though entirely at ease. *This was going to be fun.*

Queen Okteria and King Malrik took their seats flanking Queen Raynera at the head of the table, Malrik ending up on Layla's other side, the Queen directly across. Kain didn't miss the look his mother gave Layla. That razor-edged, calculating glint she reserved for adversaries worth her attention. But what truly made his chest heat with something dangerously close to reverent satisfaction was the look Layla gave back. No fear. No flinch. Gods, she held Okteria's gaze like she'd been born to do it. Just like she had the very first time they met. *That's my girl*, he thought savagely, barely hiding the smirk tugging at his mouth.

He lounged in his chair, letting the formal greetings and stiff pleasantries wash over him like a tide he had no intention of getting swept up in. King Malrik began politely engaging Queen Raynera in talk of the happenings in Myriamis, his children, and the growth of his kingdom.

Kain's eyes, however, stayed fixed on Layla. On the set of her shoulders, the graceful line of her throat as she lifted her goblet. And without breaking the rhythm of his meal, he let his hand slip beneath the tablecloth, settling warm and firm on her thigh. He felt her jolt and he forced himself not to smile. With his left hand, he speared another bite of venison as though nothing at all was amiss, while his right hand began idly stroking slow, deliberate circles higher and higher until he felt the tension coil through her like a bowstring.

Across the table, Okteria finally spoke. Her voice smooth, absolute, every syllable crafted to command attention. Queen Okteria's goblet clicked firmly against the table as she set it down. "Enough of this small talk," she said, her voice smooth but edged. "We did not ride this far to discuss weather and crops. The war will not wait for your courtesies."

Queen Raynera's smile did not falter, though her fingers stilled on the stem of her wineglass. "And yet, Queen Okteria, we will wait until morning, when all parties are present."

Okteria's brow arched. "And who, exactly, are we waiting on?"

Raynera's gaze slid, deliberate as a blade, to Layla. "My son-in-law to be. Ryker will be king within two days time. After his wedding to my daughter that is."

Kain felt his mother's attention pivot, sudden and absolute, until it landed on Layla like the tip of a spear. Queen Okteria's gaze was a blade as sharp as any dagger. "My, how things have changed since last we met. Once, you would have snarled and snapped. Now you sit silent, letting the men speak for you it seems."

He took in how Layla didn't shrink. She instead met that green-eyed stare head-on, her expression calm, her voice steady but laced with steel. "Those who are silent," she said softly, "are often the most dangerous at the table. Like a viper, Your Majesty. You never hear it before it strikes." The air went utterly still. Queen Raynera's spine stiffened at her daughter's boldness, a flicker of disapproval flashing in her eyes. It was subtle, but enough to be noticed. Yet Layla didn't look away, didn't wither, and that refusal sent pride flooding Kain's chest, so fierce it almost hurt. *Gods, she was perfect. Beautiful, brilliant, and lethal.*

Kain's hand was still under the table on her inner thigh. With an entirely new wave of desire he already didn't need to amp him up. He slowly began inching Layla's gown up higher and higher on her thigh. He stopped looking at her, not wanting to give anything away as he took on his own mask of detached civility. Admiration, awe, and hunger braided together until his cock strained against the confinement of his trousers.

Beside him, Layla didn't flinch. She kept her smile poised and serene, but Kain felt the faintest tremor run through her thigh as his fingers stroked deliberate, teasing patterns higher and higher. Gods damn, he thought, she was going to undo him right here in front of every royal in the room.

Queen Okteria's lips curved, faintly amused. "Then perhaps tomorrow, Princess, we will see if your strike lands as well as your words."

Queen Raynera's tone was crisp, formal. "Layla will not be present tomorrow," she said, her jaw tight. "Within our kingdom, council meetings are attended by men only. I will sit as a royal presence, but Ryker will make the decisions."

Kain watched as Queen Okteria's gaze stayed locked on Layla, testing her, weighing her, daring her to flinch. Layla didn't. Her shoulders stayed square, her chin high, even as the air between them thrummed like a bowstring. Finally, Okteria's head tilted toward King Malrik. "And in Myriamis?" she asked, her voice silk over steel. "How are women treated in *your* council chambers?"

Kain barely heard Malrik's answer. All his senses but his eyes were pinned to Layla. To the way her breath hitched, slow and shallow, as his hand slid higher under the table. To the warmth of her body as he continued his approach. He let his fingers trail the barest path up to her center, slow enough to make her want to squirm, slow enough to make her jaw tighten. Gods, she was wet. He gave her thigh a firm squeeze before letting one finger glide up her slick heat. He heard her breath stutter and spared a glance. She kept her face carved from porcelain, only her throat working as he saw her swallow hard. He hid his smirk, tearing a piece of bread with his free hand while his other worked deliberately between her legs. Long, slow strokes, enough to make her shift in her chair, until he couldn't resist pressing his middle finger directly against her clit. Circling, dragging, teasing until he felt the faintest tremor run through her thigh.

She reached for her goblet, hand shaking almost imperceptibly. Kain's grin was pure wolf. He slowed just enough to keep her on edge, tracing slick paths up and down her slit before bringing his fingers back to her clit, rubbing harder now.

Layla abruptly cleared her throat, her voice steady but tight with tension. "I do apologize," she said smoothly, slamming her thighs together as she turned in her chair, "but I find I'm not feeling well. I need some air."

Her mother's glare was severe and unmistakable, but she gave a short, regal nod. Kain released her at the last possible second, letting her skirt fall back into place before she rose to leave. He didn't miss the way her hand brushed the table for balance as she passed, or the quickness of her steps as she slipped out. Kain bit back a laugh, hiding his smirk behind his goblet as he drank. Gods, she was going to kill him one day.

BY THE TIDES GRACE AND THE WIND'S
COMMAND, OUR STRENGTH MAY FLOW

"The strength of Myriamis lies not in
conquest, but in our own hand. Depend
not on the tide of another's mercy."

Each household must maintain its
own means of sustenance. Be it
trade, craft, or farming, to prevent
reliance on foreign powers.

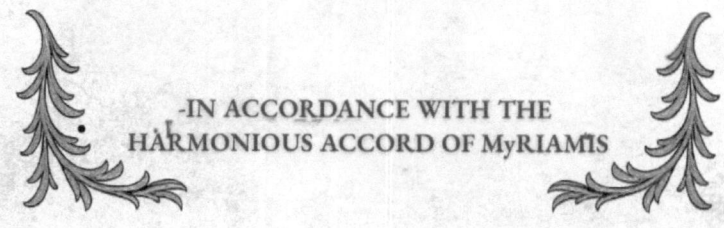

-IN ACCORDANCE WITH THE
HARMONIOUS ACCORD OF MyRIAMIS

# Chapter Twenty-Five

*L*<sup>ayla.</sup>

*What in the seven hells was he thinking?* The thought screamed through her skull as she shoved open the heavy doors and burst into the crisp night air. Fall leaves swirled across the courtyard, the wind snapping at her skirts. Her skin felt too hot, too tight, like she was simmering under the moonlight. She gripped the stone railing, chest rising and falling as she dragged in deep, unsteady lungfuls of air. Gods, why had she let him do that? Why had she liked it? The sinful drag of his fingers, the risk of being caught, the way he smirked like he owned her?

Her jaw clenched. Queen Okteria's challenge hadn't confused her or awakened anything new. It had burned through the last of her restraint. The laws. The rules. The endless, suffocating chains dressed up as duty and protection. Every expectation that she smile, endure, wait her turn while men decided her fate. She was so goddamn tired of it she could barely breathe. Tired of being managed. Tired of being silenced. Tired of being told to be grateful for the cage they'd locked around her since birth. She was done.

She tipped her head back, the night wind cooling the flush on her cheeks, but it did nothing to calm the riot inside her. Her pulse still pounded in her ears, a battle drum she couldn't ignore. She wasn't sure what burned hotter: the memory of Kain's hand under the table, or the hunger to finally, truly break free. Layla's chest was still heaving when the courtyard door creaked open behind her.

"Well, well," Kain drawled, the lazy edge of his voice dripping with provocation. "Couldn't even last five minutes at dinner before running off to brood?"

She spun on him, fury sparking in her blood. "I am not brooding."

His grin was bold and unapologetic. "Then what are you doing out here, Dove? Praying to the gods? Plotting my murder? Or just wishing you'd let me finish what I started under the table?"

Heat flared up her neck with anger or embarrassment. She couldn't tell. "You're vile."

"And you're lying." He stalked closer, each step deliberate and predatory. "Go on. Hit me if you're so angry. Might do you some good." She didn't think. She moved. A lunge, a feint, and before he could react she swiped his dagger clean from his belt.

"Atta girl," he purred, grinning like the devil himself. She slashed at his side, fast and vicious, but he caught her wrist before she could break skin and twisted, sweeping her feet out from under her and sending her crashing to the ground.

She scrambled back up, hair wild, dress askew. Her blood was roaring now, fury mixing with something hotter. "Wipe that damned smile off your face, Kain. This is your fault!"

"My fault?" He was laughing, gods damn him. "What, for putting a little fire back in you? For making you remember you've still got claws?"

She lunged again, and this time she grazed his shirt, the blade catching and tearing the fabric. "Careful, Dove," he teased, circling her, loose and ready. "Or do you need Ryker to fight this battle for you too?"

That tore the last thread of her control. With a cry that was half-growl, half-scream, she launched herself at him, dagger flashing. "I do not need a man to fight for me! Or speak for me! Or run this gods-damned kingdom for me. Not if they're going to fuck it up and get us all killed!"

He parried, grinning wide enough to bare teeth. "Then don't!"

Something inside her snapped, no, *ignited*. She slammed into him, tackling him to the ground. They rolled through the grass, her hair spilling like flames across his chest, her fists colliding against him with every word she couldn't contain. He caught her wrists, pinning them easily above her head, but there was no mockery in his grin this time, only awe. Only reverence.

"There she is," he breathed, voice low, reverent despite the chaos.

"Let me go," she snarled, struggling beneath him, eyes flashing with fury.

Kain shook his head slowly, the corner of his mouth curling as his thumb brushed her pulse. "Not yet. Not when you're finally awake."

Her chest heaved, breaths coming fast and wild. "You think this is funny? That I'm angry?"

"I think it's *you*," he said simply. "The woman who doesn't wait to be invited to lead. The one who terrifies every man too stupid to see what she's capable of." Her words faltered before they formed. The air between them burned, thick and heavy with everything unspoken.

"Stop looking at me like that," she whispered.

"Like what?"

"Like...like I'm..."

"Exactly who you're meant to be?"

That stopped her cold. His tone wasn't mocking now. It was soft. Proud. The kind of pride that settled under the skin and ached. His gaze traced her face as if he were memorizing proof of what he'd always believed and her heart stuttered. The swell of feelings she'd been trying to bury surged all at once, threatening to drown her. And before she could say something she could never take back, she kissed him. It wasn't gentle. It wasn't pretty. It was demanding and molten. Every ounce of her defiance, her hunger, her unspoken truth poured into that kiss. Kain responded in kind, intent and fierce, keeping her arms pinned as if afraid she might vanish if he let go. He took everything she gave and gave it back tenfold, until there was no breath, no thought, no divide left between them. They melted into each other, a perfect storm of fire and devotion, power and surrender, two forces colliding not to destroy, but to finally be seen.

When she finally tore away, both were trembling and breathless. The world had gone utterly still. Kain's eyes continued to trace her face as if memorizing something sacred before he finally let her wrists go. When he spoke, his voice came rough and unsteady. "There," he said softly. "Now you remember what power feels like."

Layla's pulse fluttered in her throat. She didn't trust her voice. Didn't trust herself. So she laughed instead. It was shaky and breathless. Before she smacked him square in the chest now that her hands were free. He caught her wrist mid-retreat, grinning wide, and in one smooth motion rolled, scooping her into his arms. Layla gasped, her protest lost against his chest as he held her there. Tight and unyielding, like she was something precious. Something worth holding onto.

Layla let herself be carried, hidden in his arms as they slipped back through the servant's corridor and into the quiet, shadowed halls. When they reached her rooms, he didn't bother with words. Kain just set her down only long enough to shove the door closed and press her against it, his mouth crashing into hers, ravenous once more. The moonlight spilled across the floor as he tore at her laces, her laughter turning to gasps as he devoured her all over again. Slow, hard, and kept going until she was boneless against him. This time, there was no fight left between them. Just fire.

Layla didn't know when it happened, but at some point she had fallen asleep wrapped in Kain's arms again. She woke warm, sore, and completely satiated as her cheek pillowed on his chest. For a blissful moment, she just lay there, listening to the slow, steady beat of his heart. Gods, he was peaceful like this. *Silent.* She almost laughed aloud at the thought. Of course the only time Kain Drakaren ever shut up was when he was asleep.

She was still smiling when she carefully sat up, pulling the sheet with her, and allowed herself a long, unguarded look at him. His hair was a mess, his jaw shadowed with stubble, one arm slung carelessly over where her waist had been. He looked infuriatingly perfect, even in sleep. Then her door burst open.

Layla yelped, instinctively yanking the sheet tight against her chest just as Kain moved like lightning. One second he was sprawled in bed, the next he was on his feet, dagger in hand, emerald eyes blazing and every muscle coiled.

A beat later, Aerilynn stood frozen in the doorway. "Oh...oh gods!" Aerilynn's hands flew up to cover her eyes, but not before Layla saw her younger sister's expression. Wide-eyed horror, crimson cheeks, and suspiciously close to amusement.

Layla's entire face burned. "Aerilynn!" she hissed, voice strangled.

Aerilynn peeked through her fingers, immediately regretted it, and whipped back toward the hallway. "I, um, I'll be right outside!" She squeaked, before darting out and slamming the door behind her. Layla's jaw was on the floor as she turned to glance back at the naked warrior behind her.

Kain lowered his dagger, grinning with lazy satisfaction. "Well," he drawled, utterly unbothered by his nudity, "I think that went well."

Layla groaned and buried her face in the sheet. "I am never leaving this room again."

He laughed, stalking back toward the bed, still gloriously, infuriatingly naked. "Oh, you're leaving," he said, tossing the dagger aside before pulling the sheet out of her grip. "But not until I've ruined you all over again."

Aerilynn's voice still echoed in her ears, *"I'll wait right outside."* Layla's cheeks flamed hotter as Kain prowled over her, gloriously nude and wearing that wolfish grin that made her stomach flutter and her thighs clench. His gaze raked over her with shameless hunger, and gods help her, she wanted him all over again. But reality slammed back into her. Aerilynn was *literally* on the other side of the door. "Oh, hell no!" Layla squeaked, shoving at Kain's chest with her heel.

He caught her ankle, laughing, and let her go with a mock wince. "Ow. Savage little Dove."

"Get some clothes on!" she hissed, scrambling to grab the nearest dress. "She's right outside!"

"One second, Aerilynn!" Layla called toward the door, voice strained as she dragged the gown over her head.

Before she could tie the laces, Kain was suddenly behind her, big hands capturing the ribbons. She had a faint flash of a memory of Theron doing that exact same thing... But before she could think more of it...."You're going to leave me over here naked and wanting?" he drawled as he cinched the dress tighter than necessary, tugging her back against his chest.

"I don't have time for...ah!" she yelped as his teeth grazed her ear.

Kain chuckled, clearly pleased with himself. "You're adorable when you panic."

"Damn it, Kain!" she swatted at him and darted for the door before he could distract her further. When she opened it, Aerilynn was standing there stiffly, her lips pressed together, shoulders shaking with the effort not to laugh.

"Not. A. Word," Layla warned, stepping aside to let her in. Aerilynn nodded solemnly. Then ruined it with a tiny snort of laughter that she tried to hide behind her hand. Behind Layla, Kain just leaned lazily against the bedpost, very much clothed now but still smirking like a man who'd just gotten away with murder. Layla just shook her head at Kain, cheeks still flushed. Aerilynn, to her credit, finally stopped grinning and sobered.

"Sorry for the interruption," she said, glancing between them before her expression turned grave. "But I overheard something you need to know. Aid was requested from Elarith. They're under attack from Lumiren."

Layla's breath caught, whipping her head toward Kain. His entire expression shifted. Gone was the lazy wolfish grin and it was replaced with a hunter's focus. He crossed the room in two strides, his hand finding her elbow, a grounding squeeze.

"I have to find my mother," he said, low and certain. "I'll find you right after, before I go to the meeting. I promise." Layla nodded, heart pounding, trusting him without question. When he turned to leave, Aerilynn's gaze shamelessly followed him out, lingering a moment too long.

Layla narrowed her eyes. "Aerilynn!"

Her sister clapped a hand over her mouth, shoulders shaking with barely contained laughter. "Sorry! I know it's not the time but Layla, oh *wow. I SAW...Just wow.*" She gestured vaguely toward the door. "Really, I mean good for you!"

Layla smacked her arm, heat rushing to her face. "Really not the time, Aerilynn!" Aerilynn just giggled again, clearly pleased with herself.

With an exasperated groan, Layla snatched her cloak from its peg and swept out the door, determination burning hot in her chest.

Running through the castle, Layla had one goal: to find Ryker. Her skirts snapped against her legs as she tore through the corridors, breath coming fast, heart hammering harder with every step. The torches along the walls cast leaping shadows across the stone, but she barely saw them. All she could think about was Aerilynn's words, the look on Kain's face when he left, the heat still simmering low in her belly from his hands, his mouth, his voice. *By the gods*, she needed to focus.

She skidded to a stop outside the council chamber, shoving the doors wide only to find the room empty. Curses bit the tip of her tongue. *If he wasn't here, he'd be...*She spun and ran again, this time toward the training yards. The air grew thicker with noise the closer she came, the sound of shouting and clashing steel reaching her ears. And there he was. Ryker. Sword in hand, sweat glinting on his brow, barking orders as soldiers obeyed without hesitation. For a beat she hesitated, watching him. This was the man she was supposed to marry tomorrow. The man meant to lead Graystonia. The man who would make choices for her kingdom while she stood at his side, silent. Not anymore.

Layla squared her shoulders and marched across the yard, ignoring the curious stares of the soldiers as she approached. "Ryker," she called, her voice slicing through the din.

He turned, surprise flashing across his face before softening into that practiced, pleasant smile he always gave her. "Layla," he said, lowering his sword. "What brings you out here?"

She didn't slow, didn't soften. "We need to talk. Now." The soldiers exchanged wary looks. Ryker studied her for a long moment, then nodded and dismissed his men. Layla didn't wait for pleasantries. "Elarith sent an aid request," she said, voice sharp enough to cut through the clang of the training yard.

Ryker stilled, turning to face her fully, brows knitting. "What?"

"They're under attack," Layla pressed, stepping closer until she was almost chest to chest with him. "From Lumiren. And if we don't move, if we don't help them now, the south will fracture before it even unites. We need to finalize the alliance today, Ryker. We need to march."

Shock flashed in his eyes, then suspicion. "How do you even know this?"

"It doesn't matter," she snapped. "What matters is that we have the chance to do the right thing before it's too late." For a moment, he just looked at her. Weighed her words. Then he exhaled slowly, shook his head, and gave her a faint, patronizing smile that made her blood boil.

Layla," he said, exhaling hard. "Enough." Her chin lifted, heat flaring behind her ribs. "You do not understand what you are asking," he went on, his voice no longer gentle. "You are a princess. Not a commander. Not a soldier. You do not get to decide when men march to their deaths." His hand dragged through his hair, frustration written plainly across his face. "You have no idea what it means to carry that kind of weight."

She opened her mouth, but he spoke over her.

"And after everything that has happened," he continued, his tone tightening, "after what Bartoria did to you, do not pretend this is not personal." His gaze hardened. "You are the last person who should be pushing for war." The words struck hard and fast. "You are acting out of fear," he said flatly. "Out of grief. You are angry. And I understand that.

320

But anger does not make a ruler. It makes a liability." His jaw clenched. "You would burn this kingdom just to quiet what is eating at you."

The words knocked the air from her lungs, fury and humiliation crashing together in her chest. But before she could speak, before she could draw another breath, there was a blur of movement.

***CRACK.***

Ryker's head snapped to the side, blood beading at the corner of his lip. Kain stood there, chest heaving, fist still raised. "You don't get to say that," he snarled, low and lethal. "Not to her." The entire training yard went dead silent. Even the wind seemed to stop.

Ryker straightened slowly, wiping the blood from his mouth with the back of his hand. His eyes were ice as they locked on Kain. "Careful, Antonin. You're a guest in this kingdom."

Kain didn't flinch, didn't blink. "Then throw me out. But speak to her like that again, and I won't stop at one hit." Layla's heart was hammering. Not just from the shock of the strike, but from the way Kain looked. Like a wolf finally baring its teeth. Like he'd been waiting for someone to cross this line so he could show exactly what he was capable of.

Ryker turned his head, blood dripping from his mouth, and leveled Kain with a glare that could have cut stone. Then he turned that fury back on Layla, his voice cold and precise. "Your little Antonin will be cozy in the castle dungeons by nightfall," Ryker said, tone clipped but icily calm. "Assaulting the future king comes with consequences, even for him." For a moment, the words rang in Layla's ears like a death knell. Kain stood motionless at her side, jaw clenched, shoulders coiled as though ready to strike again. But Layla stepped forward instead.

"No." Her voice cracked like a whip, carrying across the training yard. "He will not." Ryker blinked, startled by her steel. "I pardon him," she said, louder this time, every syllable ringing with authority. "By order of the royal princess of Graystonia, Kain Drakaren is absolved of any crime committed here today." The silence that followed was suffocating. The soldiers in the yard exchanged glances, the air tense with the weight of what had just happened. This wasn't Layla the dutiful princess, the quiet shadow. This was Layla the ruler, her words not a plea but a decree.

Ryker's nostrils flared. "You're overstepping."

"No," Layla cut him off, her voice firm enough to halt him mid-thought. Her chest was still rising and falling, but her spine straightened, fury settling into something far more dangerous. Control. "I am not overstepping," she said clearly. "I am stepping into my place. The place this kingdom needs me to be in."

She moved closer, skirts brushing the dirt between them, her gaze unflinching. "You forget yourself," she continued, each word deliberate. "You are a soldier. I am the future Queen of Graystonia by birthright. We are not wed. You hold no authority over me." His jaw tightened. "I am the royal here," she said, voice low and absolute. "And you will not speak to me as though I am a liability to be managed."

Her eyes burned, not wild now but focused. Certain. "If you will not fight for this kingdom and what's right, then I will," she said. "I will not let Graystonia cower behind stone walls and parchment while the south burns." She held his gaze, unblinking. "Now fall in line," she said, "or shall I remind you of the oath you swore to this crown?"

Ryker stood there, blood streaking down his face, every soldier watching him. And Layla turned on her heel, skirts snapping as she strode toward the castle. Kain followed, his presence a solid comfort at her back even with her rage. When they reached the shadowed archway, she spun on him, her breath still ragged from the fury boiling in her veins.

"I didn't need you to do that," she hissed.

"I know," Kain said, simply. No grin. No quip. Just the truth. Rough, raw, and honest. His eyes devoured her, pride and hunger burning bright. And gods help her, before she could stop herself, she grabbed his face and kissed him. It was a clash more than a kiss. Fury and need intwining once again. Kain pinned her to the wall, claiming her mouth, his hands locking around her hips as though he'd never let her go. When they broke apart, both of them were breathing hard, lips swollen. Kain's forehead rested against hers.

"What did your mother say?" she asked, voice barely above a whisper.

"That she and Myriamis are marching either way," he informed. "This is Graystonia's last chance to stand with them." Layla nodded once, resolve crystallizing in her chest. She stepped back, straightened her skirts, and strode down the hall.

"Find Sir Edwin," she told Marilla when she reached the breakfast hall. "Tell him to summon the war council immediately. We don't wait until later. Not anymore."

The last of the lords had taken their seats when Queen Raynera swept in, her frosted gaze landing on her daughter already standing at the head of the table.

"Layla," her mother said, voice clipped, "what is the meaning of this?"

Layla's pulse roared in her ears, but she didn't move. Didn't bow. Didn't flinch as she spoke. "I know I am not recognized here as anything but a future bride," she began, her voice cutting through the chamber like steel on stone. "I know I have no vote, no sanctioned voice. But I am Layla Eradellian, blood of the line that built this kingdom, the rightful heir to this throne. And today," her shoulders rolled back, her chin lifted, "you will hear me." Silence fell, so thick it felt like the air itself was holding its breath. "Our allies are under attack," Layla continued, her voice gaining strength with every word. "And we sit here, safe behind our walls, pretending parchment will protect us. That silence will save us." Her gaze cut to the council, one lord after another wilting under it. "But that is not how my father ruled. That is not how any Eradellian has ever ruled."

Her words struck like arrows loosed into still air. No one dared move. Layla took a step forward, each syllable ringing with the conviction that had lived caged in her chest for too long. "My father taught me that duty does not wait for permission. That the blood of Graystonia does not hide behind closed doors while the world burns. We are protectors, not cowards. Leaders, not ornaments." Her eyes flashed toward the table, toward the men who had whispered behind her back and dismissed her with polite smiles. "If our allies fall, Elarith burns, then Graystonia will be next. And when history speaks of this council, I will not have it said that we sat idle while the realm turned to ash." She lifted her chin, her voice steady now. A queen's voice, not a daughter's. "So let it be written in this hall, before every god who dares to listen: I will not wait for the crown to tell me when to fight. I will not wait for permission to protect my people. I *am* Graystonia's blood and I will act like it."

Her final words cracked like thunder. "Now I ask you." The room trembled under the weight of her gaze as she turned to face him. The commander who had once stood at her side only weeks ago in Bartoria. "Sir Edwin," she said, her voice soft but unyielding, "You swore your loyalty to this kingdom, not to its silence." A pause, the whole chamber hanging in it, watching, waiting. "Will you follow me, Sir Edwin?"

Sir Edwin didn't hesitate. He bowed his head, his voice ringing firm and proud. "Always, my lady." The words struck the room like a rung bell. And then chaos erupted.

Lords surged to their feet, their voices colliding in a storm of protest.

"Outrageous!"

"She has no right!"

"This is unprecedented!"

Queen Raynera's voice cut through the clamor. "Enough!" She stepped forward, her expression controlled but tight. "Layla, this is not your place. You are not queen. You are not wed. You will stop this!"

But Queen Okteria's laugh sliced through the room like a knife. It was low and unapologetically amused. "Why?" she asked, her tone silken, coiling. "I see no problem with a woman leading an army. In Antonin, we do not wait for permission to defend what is ours." The room fell into stunned silence. Layla's chest heaved, but she didn't look away. Her eyes met Okteria's, that lethal green gaze sparking with something that looked almost like respect.

"Then let it be heard," Layla said, voice steady, even as her pulse thundered, "Graystonia will march. If no man here will claim this choice, then I will." A wave of muttering rolled across the table, but it was too late. The words were loose in the world, and nothing could call them back.

From his place against the wall, Kain caught her eye. Pride blazed in him like wildfire, lighting him from the inside out, his mouth curving into the faintest wolfish grin. And finally, Layla felt it too. The familiar burn of purpose, the fierce exhilaration of choosing her own path. Layla's words still hung in the air, her chest heaving, her palms pressed to the table as though she could will every man here to feel the fire running through her veins. And then the doors opened. Ryker strode in, his boots ringing loud against the stone, his face still flushed from the training yard. His brows furrowed as he took in the sight: Layla standing at the head of the table, the council seated, Queen Okteria watching with a faintly feral smile.

One of the older lords seized the moment like a man drowning spotting a lifeboat. "Ryker," he said, his voice thin with relief. "Please handle her." The words hit Layla like a slap. Slowly, she turned to him.

Not Ryker, the lord who had dared, her voice cutting through the air like a drawn blade.

"Handle me?" she said, softly, lethally. "You forget yourself, my lord." The room went still. Layla straightened, her spine a rod of iron as she met every pair of eyes around the table. "I am Layla Eradellian. The rightful heir to this throne. And while my betrothed may one day share my crown, *today* he is merely an officer of the Graystonian army. He does not outrank me here. *None of you do.*"

She turned, locking her gaze on Ryker at last. His surprise plain, his mouth half-open as though unsure if he should be angry or impressed. "Graystonia defends. Graystonia fights. And for the first time since the Great Southern War, the South will unite against a greater threat. Politics, pride, fear, they are luxuries we no longer have. We act now, or we fall divided." The council chamber was silent. Only the crackle of the torches filled the air.

Queen Raynera rose, her tone clipped, almost pleading. "Enough of this, Layla. You are out of line. This is not your place..."

"It is *exactly* her place." Queen Okteria's voice cut through the chamber, cool and absolute. Her undeniable gaze burned as she leaned forward in her chair. "I see no problem with a woman leading an army, only a problem with a kingdom too foolish to let her." That silenced even Raynera. Layla stood frozen for a beat, heart hammering. Then she inclined her head toward the Antonin queen in wordless thanks before turning to Ryker. Daring him to challenge her. For a long, tense moment after Layla's speech, no one moved. The weight of her words still seemed to vibrate in the stone of the council chamber. Then Ryker's boots echoed against the floor as he stepped forward into the circle of torchlight. His jaw was tight, but his posture, gods, his posture, was that of a man reporting for duty.

He didn't argue.

He didn't roar.

He didn't command the room back under his control.

Instead, Ryker's gaze swept from Layla to the council, to Queen Raynera, and finally rested back on Layla again. "If this is your decision," he said quietly, voice steady, almost too steady, "then I will see it carried out." No anger. No defiance. Just obedience. He turned to Sir Edwin, his words clipped, efficient, as though issuing orders on the training field. "Begin readying the troops for movement. Have the captains prepare supply lists and routes before nightfall." And then, with nothing more than a curt nod to the council, Ryker stepped back, shoulders squared, awaiting his next set of orders.

The chamber was utterly still until Layla realized what had just happened. Her betrothed, the man about to be crowned, had just ceded command of the kingdom's army without a single fight. The lords shifted uncomfortably in their seats. Queen Raynera's lips pressed into a thin line. But Queen Okteria, gods help them all, smiled like a wolf scenting blood. And Layla? Layla stood taller. Straighter. Because for the first time in her life, she didn't just feel like the rightful heir. She felt like the one leading the kingdom.

BY THE TIDES GRACE AND THE WIND'S
COMMAND, OUR STRENGTH MAY FLOW

"In solitude, we endure. In unity, we thrive."

Disputes must be settled through
sanctioned Counsel Circles
before any martial action is
considered. The breaking of
communal trust is among the
gravest offenses.

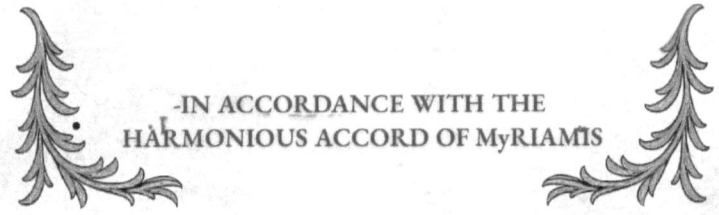

-IN ACCORDANCE WITH THE
HARMONIOUS ACCORD OF MyRIAMIS

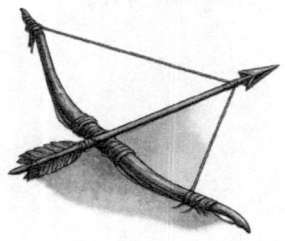

# Chapter Twenty-Six

*K*<sup>*ain.*</sup>

Kain leaned against the cool stone wall, arms crossed, looking every inch the relaxed warrior, but inside, his blood was singing. *Gods, look at her.* Layla stood in the center of the council chamber like she'd been born for it, shoulders squared, chin high, fire in her veins and on her tongue. Every word she spoke landed with precision and force, cutting through centuries of stale tradition. And Ryker? Ryker just stood there. No roar. No challenge. No command. Just a soldier's nod and the obedient click of orders leaving his mouth.

Kain had thought he would enjoy it, watching the pompous bastard take the blow, bend, and fall into line beneath her words. He had expected satisfaction. Vindication. What unfolded before him was something else entirely.

The entire council saw it. They saw a soldier bow where he had once stood rigid. They saw resistance crumble into obedience. And they saw Layla rise, not through spectacle or force, but with the quiet inevitability of something long denied finally claiming its shape. Something fierce and unyielding settled deep in Kain's chest. Not triumph. Not mere desire. Something older. Instinctive and inescapable.

Gods, she was radiant. Not adorned by titles or lifted by permission. She stood as she was, commanding simply by existing. Every line of her bearing declared what she had always been. A queen in all but name. And as she held the room, lords and soldiers alike caught in her gravity, Kain understood with brutal clarity what had always been true.

He did not just want her in his bed. He wanted her in every way that mattered, even though he knew it was impossible.

His jaw flexed as Layla finished speaking, her breath ragged, her body trembling from the sheer force of her conviction. When she turned, her gaze caught his for the briefest heartbeat. That was it. That was the look that undid him. The spark that said she knew exactly who she was now, and there was no putting her back in the cage they'd kept her in. Kain straightened from the wall, slow, deliberate, a grin tugging at his mouth like a wolf baring teeth. Ryker might have just given her the kingdom without even knowing it. But Kain? He would help her defend, and kill anyone who tried to take it from her.

Kain slipped out of the council chamber the second Sir Edwin dismissed them, grin tugging at the corner of his mouth. For once, the bastards had actually agreed on something. They were marching. *Final-*

*ly.* He rolled his shoulders as he strode down the hall, feeling lighter, sharper, more alive than he had in weeks. Gods, it felt good. Felt right. Layla, standing tall and glorious, had practically lit the room on fire with that speech. And Ryker the Righteous? Finally falling in line where he belonged. Not a king, not a leader, but a soldier who'd be marching under someone else's banner.

"About damn time," Kain muttered, smirking to himself. His bow would be back on his shoulder soon, where it belonged. No more standing around in these suffocating halls, listening to nobles wheeze about treaties and parchment. War was coming, and he could almost taste the iron and pine of it already.

He was so lost in the good mood radiating through him that he wasn't even watching where he was going. Which was the only reason he didn't dodge the wall of muscle that slammed into him head-on. Instinct had his dagger halfway unsheathed before the familiar, infuriatingly calm voice cut through the air.

"Well, look at you."

Kain's head snapped up and there he was. Xaden. Tall, broad, onyx muscle bundled up in controlled lethality. Wearing that easy grin that made Kain want to swing at him just for old time's sake.

"Son of a bitch," Kain barked a laugh, sliding the dagger back into place. "If it isn't Antonin's favorite golden boy. What, you get bored babysitting the tribe?"

Xaden just grinned wider. "Queen Okteria sent word. Figured someone needed to make sure you weren't getting too soft playing diplomat in this castle."

Kain's grin turned wicked. "Diplomat? Gods, you have no idea how ready I am to put an arrow through something that bleeds."

Xaden clapped him on the shoulder, nearly knocking him back a step. "Good. Just aim away from my beautiful face, please."

LET LIGHT BE OUR PATH,
AND GRACE BE OUR GUIDE

# ELARITH

# Chapter Twenty-Seven

*L* *ayla.*

The training grounds buzzed with life. The clang of steel on steel, the bark of commands, the steady rhythm of boots pounding the packed dirt. The air was thick with the scent of iron, sweat, and smoke from the nearby forges. Sunlight spilled over the ranks, glinting off shields and polished helms, turning the rising dust into drifting gold.

Layla stood at the center of it all, the pulse of the camp beating around her like a living heart. The Antonin war drums thudded from the far end of the field, their rhythm merging with the crisp shouts of Graystonian captains. Men and women moved in formation. Antonin warriors, Graystonian guards, and Myriamis soldiers, all marching together for the first time in generations.

For the first time since her father's death, Graystonia's army didn't look fractured. They moved with purpose instead of politics. Unity instead of suspicion. Shoulder to shoulder with those who had once been enemies, they looked ready to face the gods themselves if she asked it. The sight struck something deep in her chest with what she might guess as pride, fear, and an ache that felt dangerously close to hope. *This* was what she'd been fighting for. Not the council's empty debates. Not hollow promises wrapped in silk and etiquette. But this: the sound of courage being forged beneath the morning sun.

She rolled her shoulders back, feeling the weight of every gaze, every oath, every heartbeat that would soon follow her into battle. She lifted her chin, steady and unflinching. This was no longer theory. No longer politics. This was action.

Behind her, two sets of hurried footsteps pounded across the stone. Aerilynn and Ciana skidded to a stop, both dressed in riding leathers, faces set with determination.

"You're not coming," Layla said immediately, even as her heart stuttered.

"We are," Ciana said simply, like it was already decided.

Layla spun on them. "Absolutely not. This march will be brutal. There will be battles, bloodshed..."

"Then we will be there," Aerilynn cut in, eyes flashing. "If you can stand on that field, Layla, so can we. You're not leaving us behind again."

"You'll be a liability!" Layla snapped, the fear cracking through her composure. "I cannot protect both of you *and* lead an army. If anything happens..."

"We'll train on the march," Ciana interrupted, stepping closer until they were nose to nose. "We are not children, Layla. We survived Bartoria. We know what's at stake. You don't get to bear this alone." The words hit like a blow. Layla opened her mouth, then shut it again. They weren't wrong, gods, they weren't wrong, but the thought of losing them turned her stomach to ice. From the shadow of a pillar, Kain's low whistle cut through the tension.

"She's right, Dove," he said, his voice rough with approval. "They've got fight in them. You should see it for what it is: strength."

Layla's glare shot to him, but her chest eased the tiniest fraction. Her sisters were watching her like she held the sun in her hands. She exhaled slowly, rolling her shoulders once more. "Fine," she said at last, her voice steady. "But you stay near me. You do what I say when I say it. No heroics." Both sisters nodded, grim-faced, and Layla turned back toward the army.

Behind her, she heard Kain's quiet laugh, low and full of pride. "That's my girl," he murmured, too soft for anyone but her to hear, and heat licked up her neck. She swallowed deeply to try to regain her composure. But before Layla could fully smother that feeling and step into the courtyard, a pair of massive arms wrapped around her waist and lifted her clean off the ground.

"Well, hello, our little dagger-wielding badass," Xaden rumbled, spinning her once before setting her back on her feet. "Tell me, taken anyone's eye out today?"

A startled squeak escaped her before it turned into a laugh. An unrestrained, unroyal bark of sound that startled even her. She grinned as he set her down and immediately pulled him into a fierce hug, surprising herself with how natural it felt. When she looked up, Kain was watching. One dark brow arched in challenge, a single corner of his mouth twitching like he was trying not to smile. Layla shrugged, unapologetic, and Aerilynn's wide-eyed shock only made her giggle harder.

"No, not today, Xaden," she teased, smoothing her skirts back into place. "But the march is about to begin. Maybe I'll get lucky on the road."

"That's the spirit," Xaden said with a grin, falling into step beside her.

He started chattering about the march, about the Antonin warriors already preparing the rear line, about how Kain had apparently bullied the scouts into doubling their watch rotations and Layla found herself smiling more than she had all morning. "You're up front," Xaden said, matter-of-fact, as though there had never been a question. "If we're going to make decisions on the move, the leaders ride together. You'll see the land first, get reports first. That way when orders need giving, you give them." Something in her chest lifted at the words, so simple, so certain. He hadn't asked if she wanted to lead, he had assumed she would.

They reached the courtyard just as the horses were being led out. "Wait a damn minute," he blurted, staring at the tall, pawing beasts as if they'd personally offended him. "We're riding these damned beasts again?"

Layla's head whipped toward him brows climbing as she hid her laugh. "You don't have to," she said, as if humoring a stubborn child, "but we'll be riding slow enough for the foot soldiers to keep pace. This just saves your legs. Your strength." Her grin turned wry. "I was trying to be nice, oh mighty Antonin. Offer you a little comfort on this merry trip to war." Before he could retort, her gaze snagged on movement at the far end of the yard.

Queen Okteria swung astride a massive black warhorse, her cloak rippling like shadow. The sight hit Layla square in the chest. *Theron's horse*, the one he had ridden to Bartoria to help save her sisters. The beast stood tall and proud beneath Okteria, and she sat on him with the same casual confidence her son had. For one fleeting, breathless moment, Layla could almost picture them, Okteria and Theron, riding side by side into battle. Her chest squeezed. Then a voice cut through her thoughts.

"So much for the savage warrior," Ciana drawled behind her, "afraid of a little saddle?" Layla realized Ciana was referring to Xaden and his current protests about the horses. Xaden seemed to be frozen mid-grumble. His jaw dropped, whether at the sight of Ciana in all her golden-haired glory, or the barb itself, Layla couldn't tell. Either way, the corner of her mouth twitched, holding back a laugh.

A moment later, Xaden's grin returned, wide and irreverent, as though he had just remembered how to breathe. "Well, hello there, Princess Sunshine," he said smoothly, his voice rich with teasing charm. He gave a dramatic bow, one arm sweeping wide, before straightening and flashing Ciana a grin that was all teeth. "Didn't know the court was sending its most dangerous weapon to escort us." Ciana arched one perfect brow, utterly unimpressed, and stepped past him without breaking stride. Xaden straightened, mock-offended, before turning on his heel to fall into step beside her anyway. "No response? You wound me," he said, pressing a hand to his chest. "Here I am, risking life and limb to defend your kingdom, and you won't even grant me a smile?"

Ciana didn't even look at him, her golden braid swaying as she adjusted the gloves on her hands. "If you want a smile, try earning one." Layla bit her lip to hide her laugh as Xaden's grin only widened, clearly taking the dismissal as a challenge rather than a rejection.

"Oh, I'll earn one," he murmured under his breath as if promising it to himself, before glancing sidelong at Layla with a conspiratorial glint in his eye.

The castle gates yawned open with a groan, spilling sunlight across the courtyard like liquid gold. The air was crisp with the bite of coming winter, carrying the smell of leather, steel, and oiled fletching. Layla sat tall in her saddle, the reins tight in her grip, her pulse thrumming in time with the steady stamp of hooves. Around her, the column of warriors stretched like a living river. Graystonian banners snapping in the wind, Antonin warriors already formed into perfect lines, Myriamis riders slotting seamlessly into position.

Beside her, Kain adjusted the bow across his back with a grin that was all teeth, all trouble. "Gods, I missed this," he muttered, scanning the horizon. "Finally feels like I can breathe."

Xaden, a few feet away, barked orders to the Antonin scouts, his voice carrying easily over the courtyard. "Double the watch rotations on the outer flank. I want eyes everywhere before we hit the ridge. If anything moves out there, I want to know before it even thinks about breathing in our direction."

Layla's stomach tightened. Not with fear, but with grim determination. For the first time, she was not watching from the safety of castle walls. She was leading. Her sisters rode just behind her, Aerilynn barely keeping her excitement contained, Ciana stone-faced and unreadable. When Layla glanced over her shoulder, Ciana's cool nod told her all she needed to know: *they were with her.* Just beside them, Queen Okteria's black warhorse was moving to the head of the column, the Queen herself the picture of ruthless composure, every inch the woman who had commanded Antonin armies for decades. She turned briefly, her green eyes meeting Layla's. Something passed between them: approval maybe, or challenge?

"Sound the march," Okteria said, her voice carrying like a war horn. The drums began, deep and steady, setting the pace. Hooves thudded. Boots struck dirt. The gates behind them shut with a final, echoing boom, locking Graystonia behind them. And just like that, they were no longer a council of bickering nobles or factions barely united by treaties, they were an army. Layla's fingers tightened on the reins. She lifted her chin, her heart pounding in time with the drums. *This is it. We ride for Elarith. We ride for the South.*

Kain's horse shifted closer to hers until their knees brushed, his voice low enough for only her to hear. "You ready for this, Dove?"

Her lips curved into a dangerous smile. "I was born ready." Kain grinned, wolfish, and raised two fingers to his mouth. The sharp whistle rang out, and the entire Antonin line answered with a howl that rolled like thunder across the valley. Layla's breath caught, her pulse spiking. It was wild and unstoppable.

LET LIGHT BE OUR PATH,
AND GRACE BE OUR GUIDE

## Let No Sword  Be Drawn Without Cause.

The path of the righteous is one of peace. Only the Crown's decree or divine command may sanction the bearing of arms. To strike in anger is to fall into darkness.

-AS SET FORTH IN THE ILLUMINATED
DOCTRINE OF ELARITH.

# Chapter Twenty-Eight

*K*<sup>*ain.*</sup>

The camp stretched as far as the eye could see. A sea of flickering torches and canvas tents under the indigo sky. Graystonian and Myriamis banners rippled in the breeze, their soldiers working in practiced rhythm to set the sprawling encampment. Beyond them, Antonin warriors sprawled on bedrolls or lounged near the edges of the forest, laughing and passing skins of wine. They didn't need tents. The stars were roof enough for those who'd grown up with the wind and the trees for walls.

Kain slung the pair of rabbits he'd just hunted over one shoulder, the satisfaction of the kill buzzing faintly in his veins. His muscles were warm from the run, his senses still sharp from the chase, and for half a second, he thought about finding Layla, about teasing her until she smiled that knowing little smile, about watching the firelight catch in her hair as he stole another kiss. But the shadow that detached itself from the line of trees wasn't Layla.

"Kain." He froze, jaw tightening, as Queen Okteria stepped into the light of a nearby fire. Her green eyes caught like shards of glass, flickering with something between knowing and lethal calculation.

"Mother," he greeted warily, dropping the rabbits at his feet. "Didn't expect you to be prowling this far out."

Okteria regarded him in silence for a long moment. Not with anger. Not with accusation. With the calm certainty of someone who had already traced the shape of the truth. "Do not insult me by pretending I am blind," she said at last. "Or foolish." Kain straightened, instinctive as he quirked an eyebrow at her. "I knew something was different the moment you offered to cross into Graystonia to negotiate," she continued. "You do not volunteer for diplomacy. You do it only when something matters enough to change your instincts."

He said nothing. Though he had a nagging feeling he knew where this conversation was going.

"I know what brought you to that moment," Okteria went on. "Or rather, who." She lifted one brow. "I did not need Sparrow to confirm it, but I asked him anyway." Kain's jaw tightened as he began ripping the hide off the rabbit before him, not wanting to engage in this conversation any longer. "I do not care that it was for a woman," she said plainly. "That is not my concern." Her voice remained even. "What matters is that you did not act as a warrior seeking victory. You acted as a ruler seeking stability. You went to another kingdom to secure what was best for your people."

She stepped closer, forcing him to look up at her from his crouched position. "And it took me one glance when I arrived at this castle to know I had been right." Her eyes flicked briefly, meaningfully, toward the heart of the keep. "You are entangled," she said. "More than you should be. Enough to shape your choices." Kain's chest tightened. "But hear this clearly," Okteria continued, her tone firm now. "There is no future for you there." She met his gaze without flinching. "She is betrothed. Her path is set. Whatever feelings exist do not change that reality." The words landed clean and final.

"You did not come here to claim a woman," Okteria said. "You came here to learn what kind of leader you are becoming." She let that settle before continuing. "If we win this battle, and then this war, the south will press for unity. Borders will shift. Power will consolidate." Her voice lowered. "Graystonia will have its queen." Her gaze never left him. "And Antonin will need its king."

Kain frowned, the tension between his brows deepening. "I have never felt the call of the throne," he said plainly. "Not once. It was never something that spoke to me. Never something I was meant for."

"I know," Okteria replied without hesitation. "And I believe you." She held his gaze, studying him with the quiet intensity of someone weighing truth, not testing it. "But hear me now," she said, her tone taking on quiet gravity. "The fates do not always call when it is convenient. Sometimes they wait until a man has become capable of answering. You may not have felt it before," Okteria said. "But the world has shifted. The board has changed. And whether you recognize it yet or not, something is calling for you now." She stepped closer, lowering her voice. "You will have to listen harder than you ever have." With a deep sigh, she raked her hand over her face before continuing and then smiled once more. "You are already thinking beyond the next fight. Beyond glory. Beyond bloodshed. That is not the work of a man passing through another kingdom. That is the work of someone who must soon stand at the center of his own."

She turned away, finality in every step. "Layla showed you what it looks like to think beyond survival," Okteria said over her shoulder. "That lesson has served its purpose." Then she faced him once more. "Now it is time you start thinking about your own future," she said. "And the tribe that will depend on you when this is over." She paused, just long enough for the weight of it to settle. "Do not confuse the hand that guided you here with the throne you are meant to stand upon." Then she disappeared back in camp.

Kain stood rigid, fury coiling tight in his chest. Not at the crown. Not even at the fate she kept trying to press onto his shoulders. At her. At the way she had dragged the truth into the light and refused to let him look away. Because she was right. About the part he had been avoiding. There was no future for him and Layla. Not the way the world was shaped. Not with her betrothed, her throne waiting, her path already hardening into something immovable. And gods help him, he hated that his mother had named it. Hated that she had forced him to acknowledge what he had been pretending not to see.

His instincts screamed in the opposite direction. Find her. Stand near her. Guard her back while she carved her own future with bare hands. Not a throne. Not Antonin. *Her.*

He was so damned proud of her it hurt. Proud that she was fighting now. That she was claiming her voice and her future instead of letting men decide it for her. He wanted to be there for that. Wanted to witness it. Wanted, selfishly, to pretend that future did not end with distance. With duty. With crowns that would place them on opposite sides of a map. He wasn't ready to let that go. So he didn't.

Kain stalked back through camp, his bow slung over his shoulder, his hands clenched hard enough that his knuckles ached. His mother's words followed him like a curse he refused to answer. *"You will."* No. *Not fucking yet.*

He threw the rabbits to another Antonin and swiftly scanned the camp. Searching for the one presence that steadied the storm in his chest. And then he found her.

Layla stood near the fire, her head tilted as she spoke softly to Aerilynn and Ciana. The flames turned her hair to burnished copper, her skin to molten gold. She looked fierce even in stillness. Unbowed. Uncontained. For a heartbeat, Kain simply watched. The sight of her calm amid the chaos was both a balm and a torment. One he forever wanted to be wrapped up in.

Just beyond the glow, Sir Edwin stood at his post outside her tent, broad-shouldered and watchful. Kain crossed the distance with purpose, clasping a hand to the man's shoulder in silent acknowledgment before slipping inside. No one truly understood the bond between the two men. How much trust had been forged in blood and shadow. They'd nearly died beside one another in Bartoria and it had built something stronger than duty. Sir Edwin had never hesitated to follow Kain once

Layla had told him to trust him. And after Bartoria, Kain trusted the commander just as fiercely.

Few knew about their quiet meetings, the late-night councils under canvas and starlight, the whispered strategies that had nothing to do with rebellion and everything to do with readiness. Not against Ryker. Never treason. But preparation, for the moment they both knew would come. The moment Layla Eradellian would stop waiting for permission and step into the power she was born to wield. A faint smile tugged at Kain's lips as he glanced toward the tent's entrance. *Sir Edwin would've made a damned fine Antonin,* he thought, before his expression hardened again. The fire outside crackled, and the world held its breath. Layla's time was here and gods help anyone who tried to stop her.

Kain stood alone with his thoughts knotted tight, his mother's words still echoing through him like a blade struck against bone. Not accusations. Not warnings. Truths he had no defense against. Layla's future was no longer a fragile thing. It was forming now, solid and undeniable. A crown waiting for her. A throne she was finally reaching for with both hands. And ultimately a path that did not include him.

And gods, he wanted it for her. Her power. Her voice. Her becoming. He wanted to see her rise into everything the world had tried to deny her, and there was no jealousy in it, no fear. Only a pride so sharp it ached.

What he did not know was whether they would have tomorrow. He knew only that the world had already decided what came after. Crowns and distance. Duty dragging them in opposite directions until whatever this was could not survive the pull. The truth pressed in on him from every side, insisting he accept it, prepare for it, let go. He refused. So if now was all they had, it would have to be enough. This fragile, burning sliver of time before everything tore them apart. And he would cling to it like a starving man to a morsel of food, knowing it was actually not enough, knowing it would never satisfy, but unable to turn away from it all the same.The thought sent him pacing, restless and tight, the walls of her tent closing in until the air felt thick in his lungs. Duty waited beyond the canvas, patient and inevitable. He would face it when it came. But not yet.

His steps quickened, impatience clawing at his chest, his gaze snapping again and again to the tent flap, willing her to be done with her sisters. Willing her to come to him. Because now was all he had left to hold.

Then he felt her before she entered. The air shifted, subtle and unmistakable, like the space itself had learned her name. Layla stepped inside and stopped short. He saw it in her eyes immediately. The way her gaze traced the tension carved into his shoulders, the fury he hadn't bothered to hide. Her expression softened, the mischief fading into something gentler.

"Kain?" she asked quietly. "What's wrong?"

He swallowed hard, but only was able to shake his head. What could he possibly say? The truth that everyone seemed determined to remind him of. Or the truth he felt in his very core. The one he wanted to voice so bad he might explode. But how could he do that to her? Weigh her down with a truth that would only make things harder for her. Just as she was finally standing taller.

So he said nothing and Layla watched him for a long moment, searching his face like she might find the answer there. When he didn't give her one, she didn't push. Instead, she stepped closer, her voice warm, teasing just enough to coax him out of himself.

Her voice stayed warm, teasing just enough to coax him out of himself. "Well," she said softly, a glint lighting her eyes, "if you don't want to talk, then let me help you feel better. You've done that for me more times than I can count. It's time I returned the favor." Something in his chest loosened at that. Just a fraction. He watched as she moved around him slowly, deliberately, and felt every inch of her presence like a brand. Her fingers brushed his thigh as she passed behind him, stealing his breath despite his resolve. Gods, she always did this. Knew exactly how to undo him without even trying. And then, slowly, deliberately, she sank down before him.

His breath tore from his lungs in a sharp, guttural exhale. His hands fisted at his sides, every instinct screaming to reach for her, to anchor himself in the one thing that still felt right. Gods help him. If the world insisted on tearing them apart, he would take this moment anyway. Just a little longer. "Dove," he rasped, his body braced, tension biting deep.

Her eyes stayed locked on his, steady, full of purpose. "Teach me," she said simply. "Show me how to take what I want." For a moment, everything in him went still. The words hit him harder than any blow he'd ever taken. Then a laugh, low and hungry, rumbled out of his chest, and he reached down, threading his fingers through her hair and tilting her face up toward him.

"Oh, you have no idea what you just asked for," he growled, desire thick in his throat. The tension, the anger, the weight of his mother's words all burned off like fog under the sun, replaced with something far more magnificent. And for the first time that night, Kain felt like he could breathe as his other hand slid to her jaw, tilting her head just so. "You want to learn, little Dove?" His voice came out low, rough, almost reverent. "Then keep your eyes on me. Always on me. I want to see every thought on that face when you do this."

Her throat bobbed, but she nodded as she untied his laces and pulled his already aching cock free. And when she wrapped her hand fully around him and guided him in her mouth, he swore under his breath. "Good," he rasped, his hand stayed woven in her hair, guiding but never forcing. "Slow. Take your time. Let me feel how much you want it." She obeyed, tentative at first, then bolder as curses began to escape from his lips.

"That's it," he said, awe and hunger twining in his chest. "Wrap your lips around the head...yes, like that. Gods, yes." She hummed softly in satisfaction, and the vibration shot through him so hard he nearly lost his composure. He let out a low breathless laugh. "You're enjoying this," he tauntingly accused. Her answering glance was wicked, daring him to deny her power in this moment. "Then take me deeper," he instructed, his grip tightening just enough to keep her pace steady. "Not too fast, slow enough to drive me insane."

She did, hollowing her cheeks, and his head tipped back with a groan. He could feel her confidence in every deliberate motion, her control in the way she drew out his pleasure. "You feel that?" he growled, looking down at her again. "That's me about to lose every damned shred of patience I have left." Her mouth curved into the smallest, smug little smile around him and that did it. "Enough," he said, yanking her gently to her feet and crushing his mouth to hers, tasting himself on her lips. "Lesson's over. My turn."

He spun her, bent her over the cot, and tore her gown out of his way. She gasped, frantically finding something to brace her hands on, but she didn't tell him to stop. Didn't even hesitate. "You want to learn how to take what you want?" he murmured, pressing against her slick heat. "Then learn this, Dove, sometimes you don't ask. You just *take*." And then he thrust into her hard enough to drag a guttural moan from her throat, his hand fisting in her hair as he set a relentless and consuming pace.

When it was over, they stayed like that for a long moment. Kain bent over her, chest heaving against her back, his breath hot against the nape of her neck. He pressed a kiss there, soft and lingering, before slowly pulling out and easing her upright. Layla turned, her face flushed, her hair a glorious wreck. She looked devastating in the most stunning way. Exactly like the woman who had faced down an entire council that morning.

Kain couldn't stop the wolfish grin spreading across his mouth. "You look pleased with yourself," he said, leaning lazily against the cot, utterly unbothered by his nakedness.

Her lips curved into a small, lethal smile. "I am," she admitted. "I think I just learned exactly how easy you are to break."

He barked a laugh, dark and utterly amused, the sound rumbling in his chest. "Easy?" he repeated, stalking closer until she had to tilt her chin up to meet his gaze. "Sweetheart, I let you have control tonight. Don't get used to it."

Her cheeks flamed hotter, but she didn't back down. "Then next time," she said, voice daring and soft as sin, "you can just stand there and keep teaching and I'll stay on my knees until you beg me to stop." Gods. That went straight to his cock.

Kain's grin turned feral. He caught her chin between his fingers, tilting her face until she was forced to meet his gaze. "Careful, Dove," he murmured, his thumb brushing her swollen bottom lip. "Promises like that will keep me up all night imagining them."

Layla's laugh was breathless, but there was no fear in her eyes. No hesitation. "Good," she whispered, stepping past him toward the tent flap, her hips swaying deliberately. "Maybe you'll finally shut up for once." Kain threw his head back and laughed. A full, rough sound that he was sure startled a few guards outside.

"Oh no, little Dove," he called after her, his grin wicked as ever. "You keep that mouth of yours ready. Next time, I'm going to make sure it's too busy to sass me." Her answering laugh was light and teasing, and Kain sank down on her cot pulling her into him. She snuggled up instantly, their warmth and joy mingling into one in the same. As Kain stared up at the canvas ceiling, he couldn't stop smiling like a damned fool. For the first time since his mother's words, the weight on his chest didn't feel suffocating. Layla hadn't just distracted him, she'd given him fire again. And he'd be damned if he didn't stoke that fire until they both burned bright.

Kain was mindlessly caressing Layla's naked flesh, muscles loose, mind humming with the afterglow of her mouth and the way she'd taken control of him. When a voice outside froze them both.

"Sir Edwin," Ryker's tone was clipped, carrying just enough weight to remind everyone who he was still meant to be. "I need to speak with Lady Layla. Now." Kain's smirk vanished. Layla instantly scrambled upright, yanking her skirts into place. Kain rose slower, deliberately slow, rolling his shoulders as if shaking off the spell she'd just cast on him.

Sir Edwin's answer was cautious, but respectful. "She's... occupied at the moment, my lord."

"I'll wait," Ryker said, and the sound of his boots planted just outside the tent flap was like a gauntlet thrown.

Kain's emerald gaze slid to Layla's, hungry and unrepentant. "Occupied," he repeated under his breath, the word practically a purr. "Dove, that's the best compliment I've heard all week."

Layla swatted at his chest, panic and adrenaline sparking through her veins. "You have to go."

"Oh, I'm going," Kain said, but there was nothing obedient in his tone. He stepped in close, letting his fingers trail down the front of her gown, just enough to remind her what they'd been doing before their interruption. "But you owe me for this hasty exit, little Dove. And next time..." his grin turned feral, "I'm not letting you be the one on her knees first."

Layla's flush deepened, but her chin lifted in defiance. "Get out," she hissed, though her voice betrayed how wrecked he still had her.

Kain left without hurry, tugging the tent flap aside like he owned the place. For a single, delicious second, he locked eyes with Ryker and smiled. It was slow and knowing, before striding past him into the night.

## in Light, We Find Justice

Justice must never be swift with
fury nor clouded by vengeance. It
must be seen through the lens of
truth, mercy, and divine
guidance.

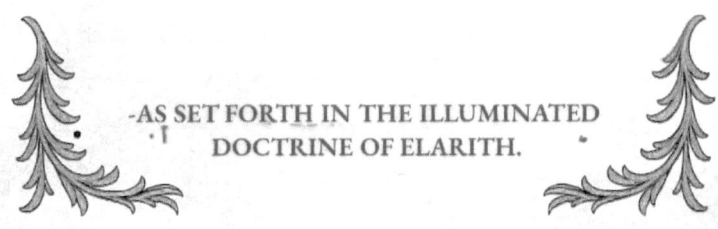

-AS SET FORTH IN THE ILLUMINATED
DOCTRINE OF ELARITH.

# Chapter Twenty-Nine

*L**ayla.*

Layla did not know what to expect when Sir Edwin announced Ryker was outside her tent. An apology, perhaps. Or a lecture softened by concern. Either way, she knew she could not refuse him. Not now. Not with the council still backing him whether they admitted it or not. Not with her position newly earned and painfully fragile. Ryker was still her betrothed. *For now.*

If she survived this march, this war, he was the future the realm expected her to accept. Her mother had chosen him. The council had approved. The nobles had nodded their agreement. Graystonia had already arranged itself around that certainty. Ending it now would cost her everything she had just claimed. So she stepped into the cool night air composed, her spine straight, her expression carefully neutral, to speak with her betrothed.

Ryker stood waiting, helm tucked beneath his arm, posture rigid as any soldier awaiting inspection. His face softened when he saw her, relief flickering through his expression. "I wanted to see you," he said gently. "After today. To make sure you were well."

"I am," Layla replied evenly.

He studied her for a moment, then nodded, reassured. "Good. It has been... a long day." His gaze drifted briefly toward the commanding officer tents and back. "And with everything moving so quickly, I thought it best we remain aligned. Especially with the wedding approaching." *There it was*. Layla did not flinch.

"Yes," she said calmly. "Alignment matters." Something in her tone gave him pause. She took a measured breath. "So let me allow you to understand something. Today was not a performance. What I said in that council chamber was necessary. For the kingdom. For morale. For what lies ahead."

His brow furrowed slightly. "No one is questioning your dedication."

"But they are questioning my authority," she said, her voice still controlled. "And I will not allow that. Not anymore, not again."

Ryker hesitated, clearly recalibrating. "Layla, you have always had influence. Respect. The people love you."

"That is not the same as being heard," she replied quietly.

He opened his mouth, then closed it again, choosing his words carefully. "You don't need to involve yourself so directly in matters of command. That is not what you were raised for."

She met his gaze steadily. "I was raised for Graystonia." The silence stretched. Layla softened her tone just enough to keep him from bristling. "I am not seeking to disrupt order," she said. "I am ensuring it survives."

Ryker exhaled, tension easing from his shoulders. "Safety is what keeps a kingdom standing."

"Stability," Layla corrected gently, "is what keeps it alive."

He studied her, unsettled but unwilling to challenge her outright. "This war will end," he said at last. "And when it does, we will return home. We will rebuild."

"Yes," Layla agreed. "We will." The words were deliberate. Neutral. Uncommitted. She stepped closer, just enough to remind him of the role he still believed awaited him. "Until then," she continued, "I need you to trust me. Publicly. Without hesitation. Any uncertainty will be noticed."

Ryker straightened instinctively. "Of course."

She inclined her head, accepting his compliance without gratitude. "Good." For a moment, neither of them spoke.

"I am proud of you," he said finally. "Even if I don't always understand this... fire in you."

Layla offered a small, practiced smile. "You will." She did not elaborate before she turned back toward her tent, signaling the end of the conversation without dismissal or defiance.

Inside her tent, something settled into place. She had not broken the betrothal. She had not surrendered her voice. She had done something far more dangerous. She had learned how to stand where the crown expected her to be and still move freely.

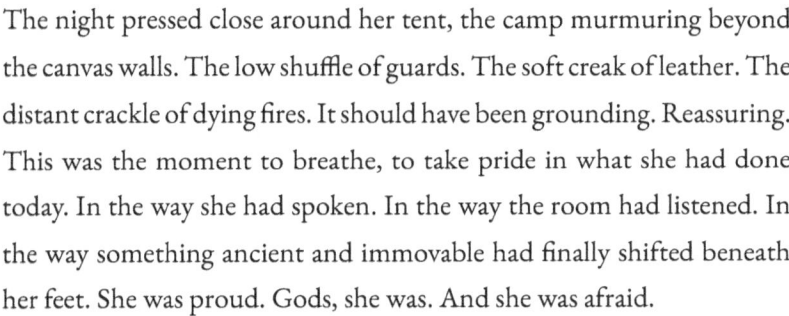

The night pressed close around her tent, the camp murmuring beyond the canvas walls. The low shuffle of guards. The soft creak of leather. The distant crackle of dying fires. It should have been grounding. Reassuring. This was the moment to breathe, to take pride in what she had done today. In the way she had spoken. In the way the room had listened. In the way something ancient and immovable had finally shifted beneath her feet. She was proud. Gods, she was. And she was afraid.

Tomorrow they would march. Soon there would be blood and smoke and the kind of decisions that never stopped echoing once they were made. This was what she should be holding onto. The war ahead. The lives depending on her choices. The weight of becoming someone her kingdom could not afford to lose. But her mind refused to stay where it belonged. The day replayed itself in fragments she could not quiet. The council chamber. The fire in her chest. The way Kain had looked at her like he already knew what she was capable of. Every stolen glance, every charged silence followed her now, humming beneath her skin. It shouldn't matter. None of it should. Not with death waiting so close, not with the road ahead soaked in uncertainty and blood. And yet it did.

She was not naïve. She knew exactly what Kain was supposed to be. A complication. A danger. A diplomat. A warrior tolerated for the sake of survival, nothing more. He was not her future. Not her duty. Not the man chosen by her mother and the council to stand beside her and rule. That place had already been filled, long before she had learned how to speak for herself within her own kingdom. But somewhere along the way, she had stopped pretending he was just a distraction. Somewhere between the first time he had challenged her instead of placating her, and the way his presence had steadied her when the council tried to press her back into silence, something had shifted. She did not just want his touch, or his grin, or the reckless way he pulled her back into herself. She wanted *him*. His fire. His certainty. His infuriating, unshakable belief that she was meant for more, long before she had dared to believe it herself.

Layla sank onto the cot, her pulse still racing, her chest tight. It was untenable. Foolish. Inconvenient in every way that mattered. Because if she lived. If they survived this march and the war that followed, she knew what waited on the other side. A wedding. A crown. Ryker. Her breath stalled at the thought, the weight of it pressing down until it was hard to breathe. What was she supposed to do with this? With him? With the knowledge that every day, every stolen moment, she felt herself leaning closer to something she had no right to reach for? Closer to wanting him in a way that could cost her everything. Closer to loving him. And knowing she might never be allowed to keep him.

The sound of the flap swishing brought her spiraling thoughts to a halt. Aerilynn slipped inside on quiet feet, her golden braid swinging loose over her shoulder. She didn't even ask permission, just padded across the tent and sat cross-legged at the foot of Layla's cot. "You're still awake," Layla whispered.

Aerilynn just shook her head. "Couldn't sleep."

Before Layla could reply, Ciana ducked inside too, her ever-perfect hair slightly mussed for once. She didn't say a word, simply lowered herself onto the cot and sat stiff-backed, as if trying to pretend she hadn't just broken a rule by coming here. Layla gave a small, breathless laugh and scooted over so the three of them could sit close, knees brushing like they used to as children. The silence stretched until it became heavy, waiting. Finally, Layla spoke.

"Aerilynn," she murmured, "Something has been nagging at me. How did you possibly know? About Elarith? You came to me before anyone in the castle knew. Before the council... Before Mother... How?" Aerilynn froze, then turned her face away, guilty. "Oh no you don't!" Layla said, catching her chin and forcing her to look at her. "You are not wriggling out of this. Tell me. Does this have something to do with that mystery man you've been sneaking off with?"

Ciana's brows shot up. "Wait. What mystery man?"

Aerilynn groaned and covered her face. "Please don't be mad."

Layla snorted softly. "Mad? Gods, I have no room to judge. I've been sneaking around with Kain of all people..."

"You and Kain?" Ciana blurted, her voice slicing through the tent. "I mean I saw the looks but, what?!"

Layla groaned, hiding her own face now. "Yes. Me and Kain. We've been... having fun."

Ciana's stare turned to stone. "Fun?" she asked, quiet and pointed.

"Of course it's just fun," Layla lied smoothly, even as something twisted hard and low in her chest. Ciana's lips pressed into a thin line, but she didn't push further. Instead, she turned back to Aerilynn expectantly, and Aerilynn sighed, shoulders drooping.

"It's Sir Edwin," she said softly. Both Layla and Ciana went still, eyes wide. Aerilynn kept going before either of them could speak. "I know he's a bit older...but he's just...ugh. He's perfect guys... When I couldn't get out of bed, when the world was just so dark... He kept checking on me! Every single day! At first, I thought it was just duty, but then he started hanging around, sitting off in a chair and just started...talking, telling me about his life, his years in the army, his family. He never asked for anything. He just... gave me something else to think about. To distract me with. Something outside my nightmares and spiraling thoughts." Her voice softened to a whisper. "He found me at the bottom of that dark hole and pulled me out. Then one day he asked me if I wanted to go for a walk. Then another day we were walking and I just couldn't take it anymore, so I kissed him. He tried to be formal about it, the stubborn idiot." She giggled. "So, I kissed him again. And then he kissed me back. It was...everything."

Aerilynn's face broke into a shy, radiant smile. One Layla hadn't seen in months. "We've been spending all our free time together since. I was with him when the scout came running in with the news about Elarith. I went straight to you."

Layla's throat tightened. She reached out, catching Aerilynn's hand and squeezing hard. "I'm glad he was there for you. Truly."

But Aerilynn wasn't done. Her voice steadied, gaining strength. "I don't want to sit back and wait anymore, Layla. Not this time. I don't want to hide in my room wondering if he's coming back alive. I want to be here, with him, for as long as we both still have." Layla nodded in understanding. Gods help her, she understood.

The three of them fell silent for a long moment before Ciana, shock still etched on her face, slowly reached out and linked her fingers with Aerilynn's. Layla covered both their hands with her own, letting the warmth of her sisters seep into her. For just one night, the war outside felt far away. As they curled together on the cot like they had when they were small, Layla stared into the darkness, her mind anything but still. Aerilynn had chosen. Chosen love, chosen life, chosen to step into danger because she refused to be a passive shadow anymore. But Layla's choice wasn't so simple.

She stared into the darkness, the canvas ceiling barely visible above them. Everything she had ever wanted was finally within reach. Her voice. Her purpose. The power to shape her own future instead of inheriting one decided by others. She had fought for it, clawed space for it, refused to be small when the world demanded she be. This was the life she had always wanted. And still, her heart ached. Not with doubt. But with grief. Because Aerilynn had been able to choose love without it costing her everything else. Layla could not. Not now. Not without risking the ground she had only just begun to stand on. Love, for her, came with weight and consequence and a price she was not yet willing to pay. It wasn't fair. She knew that. Power rarely was.

Layla turned slightly, careful not to wake her sisters, and let the ache settle where no one could see it. She did not resent Aerilynn's happiness. She envied the simplicity of it. The way love could be a beginning instead of a liability.

She closed her eyes. She would become what she was meant to be. She would claim her place, her future, her crown. But tonight, in the quiet dark, she allowed herself one small sorrow. That she could not choose love as easily as her sister had.

When sleep finally claimed her, it did not come as rest, but as revelation, thinning the veil just enough for her to glimpse the gods on the other side.

*The silver plain stretched forever, starlight rippling across it like water. Layla stood frozen beneath an oak so massive its roots felt as if they held the whole world together. Its leaves shimmered faintly, breathing with an otherworldly glow.*

*"Do you know where you are, child?"*

*The voice was deep, resonant. Not loud, but so vast it seemed to speak through her bones. Layla turned, and there he was. Eliryn. King of the Gods. The God of Beginnings and Endings. He sat with one knee bent beneath him, radiance spilling from his skin like molten gold. Her breath caught. She couldn't speak. Couldn't move. One heartbeat he was seated, the next he was before her, close enough that she could see galaxies swimming in his eyes. Reverently, he reached out and laid a hand on her shoulder. The world blazed. Her entire being lit from within, each fragment of her soul shining like the stars above them. It felt like recognition, like the moment when a flame finds its waiting wick. Layla's knees buckled and she dropped into a bow so deep her forehead nearly touched the starlit ground.*

*"I... I'm sorry," she breathed, mortified at her rudeness.*

*"Rise, child," Eliryn said, his voice gentling, though its power still thrummed through her. "You sought me out for a reason. What is it?"*

*"I..." Layla's words faltered. Had she sought him? Was this even real? And yet, she knew. Deep in her marrow, she knew this was realer than anything she had ever touched.*

*When she finally found her voice, it came out a whisper. "Am I... doing the right thing?"*

*Eliryn's expression softened, but his reply was grave. "I cannot choose your path for you. There are many roads, many futures. But there is one, one path that will not just save your kingdom, but all of Caeleria. Even us."*

*Layla's breath stilled. "The gods?"*

*"Yes." His hand dropped from her shoulder, but she still felt the heat of his touch. "The veil was meant to protect both mortals and gods, but Yssra's power gnaws at it, widening the tear. If it breaks completely, she will not just corrupt your world, she will corrupt ours as well."*

*Layla's heart pounded, but she clenched her fists, lifting her chin. "Then tell me what to do."*

*"I cannot," he said, a faint thread of sorrow in his tone. "The choice must be yours, every step of it. Fate can only guide. Choice is what gives it power."*

*Serelai appeared then, her presence like the smell of rain-soaked earth after a drought, warm and nurturing. She smiled at Layla with pride. "Trust yourself, little one. Trust what burns inside you. You have felt it, that pull, that fire that tells you that you were meant for more. This is your chance."*

*Eliryn's light brightened until she could feel its warmth on her face. "Lead. Choose. Love. That is all I can give you. When you doubt, reach through the veil again. You will find me." As he began to fade, she heard him whisper,* "you have always burned, Layla. Long before you knew what the fire was for." *Then he was completely gone, as if he had never been, leaving only the glimmer of starlight and the sense that she had been remade.*

Layla woke with a gasp, sitting upright in her bedroll. The tent was dark, the air cool and heavy with the scent of smoke and canvas. Outside, the camp murmured in half-sleep. Guards changing shifts, fires hissing and cracking low, horses snorting somewhere in the dark. Her sisters lay tangled together beside her, their breathing soft and even, untouched by the storm clawing through her chest.

Her heart raced, her lungs straining to catch up with the dream still echoing through her veins. It had felt so real. A warning, a calling, a truth whispered straight from the gods. Fear lingered in its wake, but beneath the fear was something else. Purpose. It wasn't slipping through her fingers anymore. It *burned* in her, bright, defiant, and alive. As if the stars themselves had poured their light into her blood. For the first time in what felt like years, she didn't feel like she was chasing fate. She was standing in its center.

## Prayer is Law

As the sun rises, so too must voices rise in gratitude. Daily prayer is the heart of the kingdom, binding all to the Light.

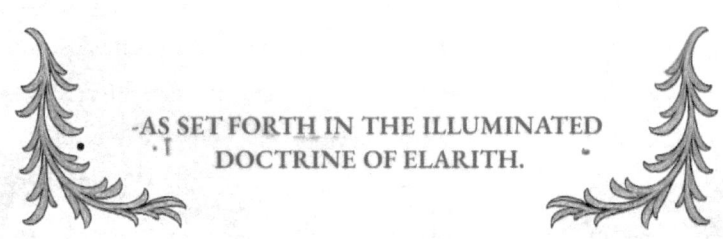

-AS SET FORTH IN THE ILLUMINATED DOCTRINE OF ELARITH.

# Chapter Thirty

*L*<sup>*ayla.*</sup>

The sky was still violet when Layla pushed free of her tent. The chill bit at her skin, brisk enough to remind her she was very much alive. All around her, the camp was waking. Fires glowed low, their smoke rising in thin, twisting columns. Soldiers moved quietly, checking tack, packing supplies, muttering in low voices as though not to disturb the weight of the morning. The tents of Graystonia stretched wide to her left, Myriamis' bright banners fluttered in the breeze, and the Antonin warriors lingered closer to the treeline, rolling bedrolls with the precision of men who had done this their entire lives.

But it was different now. The dream clung to her like the stars still faintly shimmering overhead. She could almost feel Eliryn's hand on her shoulder, the echo of his presence humming through her bones.

Layla straightened, rolling her shoulders back until the last trace of sleep slipped away. This was no longer about discovering who she was meant to be. She knew that now. This was about seeing it through.

The second day on the road felt different. Yesterday, she had followed and obeyed. Sat on her horse in silence and listened as others decided where the scouts would ride, how far to push the army, when to rest. But not this morning. This morning she mounted with her shoulders squared and her voice clear, issuing orders before anyone else could. When she had questions, she sought Sir Edwin's counsel, listening intently to his answers. When they discussed the march, she no longer merely nodded. She asked about supply lines, weather patterns, flanking options.

She also made certain of something else. Quietly, deliberately. That every unit understood how to fight what waited ahead. Whether they believed Yssra's Blessed existed or not, they would know how to kill them. Countermeasures were explained. Formations adjusted. No one dismissed her when she spoke of rot and corruption. They listened.

By noon she was riding side by side with Xaden, leaning close over her saddle as they spoke in low, steady voices about strategy, about what might wait for them in the north. And every time she asked a question, he answered without hesitation, treating her like any other commander. Even Myriamis' contingent, distant and wary since leaving their burned shores, began to take note. Their commander giving her longer glances, their soldiers falling in line with crisp precision whenever she spoke.

And Kain? Kain watched all of it from a few horses back, a wicked grin tugging at his mouth like he was watching the dawn break after a long night.

It wasn't until dusk that anyone put words to what they were all seeing. The campfires burned bright against the falling night, the smoke curling into the lavender dusk. Layla sat with her sisters, watching Aerilynn's fingers fumble with the dagger Xaden had given her earlier. While Ciana's stance was corrected for the third time by an Antonin soldier who didn't dare complain. Queen Okteria's shadow fell across the fire before she settled gracefully on a low log across from Layla. Her piercing green eyes flared in the firelight, assessing, measuring the way a predator watched something fascinating just before the pounce.

"You've changed," Okteria said at last, her tone neither approving nor accusing, just a simple fact laid bare. "Two days ago you followed. Now you command."

Layla felt every gaze around the fire turn toward her. She lifted her chin. "Maybe I finally realized what was expected of me."

Okteria's mouth curved into a slow, dangerous smile. "Expected? No. This isn't expectation, girl. This is choice. This is blood waking up." The words sent a shiver down Layla's spine. Then Okteria stood, brushing ash from her dark riding leathers, her shadow long and stark in the firelight. "If you're going to lead," she said, her voice cool as tempered steel, "then you'd better be able to defend the men you lead. On your feet, Eradellian. Let's see if your sword hand is as sharp as your tongue." Ciana and Aerilynn both looked up at once, but Layla was already rising, her shoulders back, the flames catching in her hair like a crown as she stepped into the circle Okteria was clearing.

Kain appeared like smoke, leaning against a tree with his arms crossed, that wolfish grin curving his mouth. "Oh, I'm not missing this."

Xaden dragged two practice swords from where they leaned against a cart and tossed one to Layla. She caught it without flinching, the weight grounding her, steadying the wild beat of her heart. Okteria's blade gleamed like molten fire as she saluted once. "Show me," she said.

Layla's grip tightened. Her sisters held their breath. And with the crack of steel meeting steel, the duel began.

Okteria was ruthless from the first strike, driving Layla back with brutal precision. "You're too stiff," she barked, her strikes a blur. "You fight like a man, heavy and clumsy. We don't have the luxury of brute strength. We survive because we're faster. Smarter. Use it." Layla gritted her teeth and pivoted, letting the next strike whistle past and coming back at an angle like Okteria had forced her to do. Steel glanced off leather with a hiss. "Better." Okteria's mouth curved, not quite a smile, but close enough to twist something hot and fierce in Layla's chest. "We are smaller, more flexible. That is not weakness, girl, that is an advantage. Slip under their guard. Get close. Put your blade where it hurts most and make them bleed for every inch they take." Layla ducked under Okteria's next swing, her braid whipping behind her, and landed a clean tap against the queen's ribs. The crack of it echoed like a challenge. For a heartbeat, silence stretched. Then Okteria's grin bared teeth. "Again."

Something wild unfurled in Layla's chest, bright as firelight. She pressed forward, this time meeting Okteria's strikes with her own. Not just defending, but driving back. And Okteria only pushed her harder, demanding more with every clash, every feint. From the tree line, Kain's chuckle was low and wicked. She knew if she looked, pride would be blazing in his eyes like emerald flame. When Layla finally managed to twist under Okteria's guard and tap her shoulder with the point of her blade, she was breathless, sweating, grinning despite herself.

Okteria lowered her sword, chest rising and falling, her expression fierce and approving. "Good," she said at last, and it wasn't just praise. It was permission. "Now again. This time, don't let me live." At first, Layla thought this was punishment, Queen Okteria's chance to make her bleed for every defiance, for every time she'd stood her ground, for being Eradellian, for daring to live when Theron had not. But as the duel wore on, as her muscles burned and the taste of iron filled her mouth, she began to see it. The precision of Okteria's strikes, the way she corrected Layla's stance with the flat of her blade instead of cutting her down, the near-imperceptible nod when Layla ducked under a swing and countered, it wasn't cruelty. It was instruction. It was recognition. And, gods help her, maybe even respect. Something warm uncoiled in Layla's chest at the thought. It wasn't her mother teaching her, wasn't Queen Raynera nodding in approval, but it was *a* queen. A deadly one, a warrior queen who commanded armies and men without hesitation. And it meant more than Layla wanted to admit.

By the time Okteria called an end, Layla was drenched in sweat, every strand of hair plastered to her neck. Her lungs burned, her arms trembled, but she stood tall as she saluted her opponent, refusing to show weakness. "Better," Okteria said simply, sheathing her blade. The single word landed heavier than praise, almost like an anointing.

Layla turned to her guards and ordered them back with a quick flick of her hand. They hesitated, but she repeated it, commanding and sure. And for the first time they obeyed her without looking to anyone else for permission.

She slipped away into the trees until she found a narrow stream, the moon catching silver in its ripples. Dropping to her knees, she splashed cold water over her face, gasping as it shocked her overheated skin. The stream's surface caught the moonlight like scattered glass, cool mist brushing over Layla's heated skin. She crouched, splashing more handfuls of water over her face, trying to cool the fire still simmering from Okteria's relentless duel. Then the air shifted. Kain's presence slid over her senses before she even heard him. That infuriating, intoxicating hum of pine and leather that made her stomach twist in the best possible way.

"Don't stop on my account," he drawled, stepping out of the shadows and crouching beside her. "Gods know you needed it. You were looking like a feral little cat out there."

"Shut up," she muttered, but there was no venom in it.

Kain reached past her, cupping his big hand in the stream and letting the cold water spill over her neck. Layla gasped at the shock, spinning to glare at him, only to find him grinning like the devil.

"You looked like you were about to combust, Dove. I was being helpful."

"You're insufferable."

He leaned closer, voice dipping into something darker. "And yet you keep letting me in your bed. Fascinating."

She snorted despite herself, splashing a bit of water at him. "Best friendship I've ever had," she teased, letting the words hang, testing him.

Kain's face twisted in mock offense, and for a heartbeat she thought she had misjudged him. Thought she had crossed a line he would laugh away. Then the mischief faded, replaced by something slower. Older. The kind of look that saw too much.

"I'll be whatever you need me to be, Dove," he said quietly, the words no longer a tease but a vow. His voice dropped, rough and certain. "Friend. Sinner. Salvation."

Her breath caught hard, her pulse roaring in her ears. Because he was right. Gods, he was right in every way that mattered. He had been all three already, whether she admitted it or not. The truth of it wrecked her, stripped her bare without ever touching skin. Before she could respond, Kain's mouth found hers with bruising certainty. The kiss fierce and claiming, as if he had waited too long already. She fell back against the earth, the cool ground biting through the heat racing under her skin, his weight anchoring her to the moment. To him. His hands were sure, unhesitating, mapping her like something precious and dangerous all at once. And Layla knew, with a clarity that terrified her, that there was no part of herself left untouched by him now.

"You think you can just make jest at our *friendship* and not pay the price?" he rasped against her mouth, his teeth grazing her bottom lip before he bit down just hard enough to make her gasp.

Her fingers fisted in his shirt, dragging him closer before she could think better of it. "Then take your price," she whispered, daring him, even as something in her chest trembled at the words. Kain growled, low and feral, the sound vibrating straight through her. After that there was no more talking. Only the rush of movement, the earth hard beneath her back, his mouth claiming hers with reckless hunger, as if dawn might never come and he would not waste a single breath pretending this was anything less than everything. She arched into him, nails biting into his shoulders, the world narrowing until there was only heat and pulse and the way he made her feel unbearably present.

"Say it," he demanded against her mouth, rough and unguarded. "Say you want this. Say you want me."

"I want you," she breathed, the words breaking free like a confession she had been holding back for far too long. There was no space left after that. No distance. Just the press of him, the raw urgency of it, earth and sweat and moonlight blurring together as he held her there like he meant to anchor her to the moment. He kissed her until thought burned away, until the only thing that existed was the way her body answered him without hesitation, without armor, without lies.

When it was over, she lay there panting, skin streaked with dirt, hair a wild tangle, her heart still racing. She had never felt so undone. Or so alive.

Kain lay back beside her, chest rising and falling, that familiar crooked grin pulling at his mouth as he stared up at the stars. "Best friendship you've ever had, huh?" The words were light. The returned joke meant to soften the edge. But her laugh never came.

Layla shifted, turning just enough to look at him. The stars glimmered faintly above them, reflected in his eyes, and for one fragile heartbeat she almost pretended she could play along. Almost let herself believe this was still something she could shrug off. Then her chest gave way. The tear slipped free before she could stop it, hot and sudden, betraying everything she had tried so hard to keep contained. She sucked in a sharp breath, mortified, but it was already too late. He saw it. Kain's grin vanished instantly.

"Dove..."

"What if I want more?" she asked. The words were barely louder than the night around them. Not an accusation. Not a demand. Just truth, laid bare. Kain went still beneath her. She felt it immediately, the way his body locked, the way his breath changed. For a moment, she thought he might reach for her face, wipe the tear away, pull her closer. Instead, he drew a slow breath, steadying himself like a man bracing for impact.

"You're going to be an incredible queen," he said softly. Her heart clenched. He met her gaze then, his expression resolute in a way that made her chest ache. "Everything you're becoming. Everything you're fighting for. I would never stand in the way of that. Never."

The words were meant to reassure her. Instead, they landed like a quiet surrender. Layla swallowed and nodded once, because she understood what he was not saying. That he was placing her future above his own wanting. That he would not claim her. That he would not ask her to choose, not when they both knew what that choice would demand of her. And gods help her, she knew it was a lie in the deepest part of her soul. Because if standing in her way meant keeping her safe, keeping her his, Kain would burn the world down without hesitation. If she asked him to choose her, truly asked, she had no doubt he would. But his kingdom needed him the way hers needed her. So she let the lie stand.

They sat there in the quiet after that, the warmth between them suddenly fragile, insufficient. Kain finally lifted a hand and brushed his thumb gently beneath her eye, wiping away the tear she hadn't even realized was still there. "I'll always find you," he murmured. This time, it sounded less like a promise. Layla closed her eyes and leaned into his touch anyway.

Eventually, they washed and dressed in silence. No teasing. No deflection. Just the soft rustle of fabric, the scrape of buckles, the night pressing close around them as if it knew better than to intrude. When he finished, Kain stepped toward her and cupped her face, pressing a kiss to her mouth that was slow and deep and devastatingly gentle. It carried every truth they could not say. Everything they would not dare to. She watched him walk away, his shape swallowed by shadow and trees, until there was nothing left of him but the echo of his presence and the ache in her chest. Only then did she turn toward her tent.

Layla drew in deep, steady breaths as she walked, forcing her shoulders to stay squared, her steps measured. She would not break here. Not now. Not where anyone could see. The tears burned anyway, threatening, held back only by sheer will. She was nearly there when a branch cracked behind her. Layla froze.

Frea stepped out of the trees like a shadow made flesh, her hair loose around her shoulders, that lethal curve of her lips making Layla's pulse spike. "Well," Frea purred, eyes flicking over Layla's flushed cheeks, her damp hair, the dirt still clinging to her skirts. "Looks like someone had fun. All... cleaned up, are we?" The barb landed, and Layla's spine straightened. She met Frea's smile with one of her own, sweet and poisonous.

"Why? Hoping for tips?"

Frea's laugh was a soft, dangerous thing. "Oh, I don't need tips. I know *exactly* what Kain likes. I just hope you understand there's no future here for you two, Princess."

Layla's jaw locked. Frea had no idea how close she stood to the truth. Layla smiled anyway and kept her tone honey-sweet. "Funny. He didn't seem to remember that when he had me screaming his name."

Frea's eyes flared, before she stepped closer. Until the space between them was nothing but fire. "Have your fun. Gods know he's good for it. But don't fool yourself, your precious little kingdom still sees Ryker as their king. You'll go back to your keep, marry your soldier-boy, and this..." she gestured vaguely between them, "this won't matter." Layla's stomach knotted, but she refused to step back. "And when you do," Frea went on, her voice smooth as a blade's edge, "I'll be where I was always meant to be. At Kain's side. Queen of the Antonin. He doesn't want to rule, but I do. I'll do what he won't, what he can't. And I'll be exactly what this tribe needs." She tilted her head, mock sympathy shining in her eyes. "You of all people should understand that, Princess. Kingdom first. Duty first. Don't fuck it up for him just because you want to play at being a wild little thing under the stars."

The words sank like a stone in Layla's gut. For the first time since she'd stepped into the clearing, she couldn't think of a retort. Couldn't find the bite of her usual reply.

Frea smiled slow and triumphant. "Sweet dreams," she murmured, then slipped back into the woods, leaving Layla alone with the echo of her own thundering heartbeat.

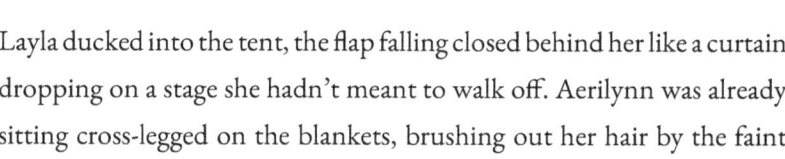

Layla ducked into the tent, the flap falling closed behind her like a curtain dropping on a stage she hadn't meant to walk off. Aerilynn was already sitting cross-legged on the blankets, brushing out her hair by the faint glow of the lantern. She took one look at Layla's face and immediately set the brush down.

"What happened?" she asked softly.

Layla dropped down beside her, the weight of Frea's words hitting her all over again. She didn't bother pretending she was fine. Didn't bother holding back. The first tear slipped hot and bitter down her cheek before she could stop it. "She found me," Layla whispered. "Frea. She said..." Her throat closed. She had to force the words out. "She said I'll go back to Graystonia and marry Ryker, and Kain will go back to Antonin, and she'll be there waiting for him. That it's always been the plan. That she's going to be queen."

Aerilynn's brows drew together, but she didn't look surprised. She just nodded slowly, thoughtfully. "I mean... that makes sense, doesn't it?"

Layla's stomach twisted. "Yeah," she said bitterly, with a shrug that felt heavier than her armor.

Her sister's voice stayed quiet, gentle, but it still cut through her like an arrow. "Ryker seems like he's... adjusting. Letting you lead. You'll rule Graystonia, Layla. He'll be the king at your side. And it sounds like Kain will be the same for Frea. She's like Okteria if I've ever seen one."

Aerilynn's gaze met hers, soft but searching. "It sounds like the best case for both kingdoms if we all live. Right?"

Layla opened her mouth and stopped. She didn't have an answer. Not one she could say aloud. The ache in her stomach spread, burning, twisting into something ugly and devastating. Then the tent flap burst open and Ciana stormed in like a hurricane, her cheeks flushed and her braid half undone.

"UGH. THAT. MAN!" she shouted, throwing her hands into the air.

Both Layla and Aerilynn stared at her. "What man?" Layla asked, blinking.

Ciana waved them off, scowling. "Never mind."

Aerilynn's mouth twitched, and then she grinned. "Men troubles all around, huh?"

Ciana shot her a look. "What's wrong with Sir Edwin, then?"

Aerilynn groaned, flopping onto her back dramatically. "We haven't had sex in *days*. DAYS. It's agonizing." The stunned silence lasted only a second before Layla and Ciana burst into laughter. Aerilynn joined them, giggling helplessly, and soon all three were leaning against one another, laughing until their ribs ached. The heaviness in Layla's chest didn't disappear entirely, but it loosened. The tent didn't feel so small anymore.

When the laughter finally died down, Layla lay back on the blankets, staring at the roof of the tent, her sisters pressed warm against her sides. Things were changing. She was changing. But this, this bond between them, was unshakable. It was the one thing she could count on, even as the rest of her world twisted out of shape. Still, as she closed her eyes, one truth lingered, heavy and inescapable. She was helplessly in love with Kain Drakaren, and she could never have him.

The next few days crawled by. They were long, grueling, and utterly agonizing. Every step brought them closer, every breath a reminder that by tomorrow, they would be there. They would see what was left of Elarith. Layla avoided Kain as best she could, throwing herself into every task that would keep her mind steady. At night, she reached for Eliryn in her dreams, begging silently for guidance, for anything, but the veil stayed quiet. No voice, no stars, no sign. So, she did the only thing left to do. She prepared. She trained until her muscles screamed, sparred with Sir Edwin or whichever Antonin would meet her blade, and dragged her sisters into the circle until they learned the same. She asked questions. She demanded answers. And for the first time in her life, the men around her did not hesitate, did not condescend. They answered her plainly, as if her voice carried as much weight as theirs. It was foreign. Strange. But gods, it felt right.

Tomorrow, they would see what awaited them. They didn't know the numbers. They didn't know what Yssra had truly given Lumiren, what kind of monsters her gifts had turned them into. But Layla knew one thing with absolute clarity: she would fight. She would bleed. She would die, if she had to. Because it was the right path. Because this was more than Graystonia, more than Antonin, more than Myriamis and Elarith. This was the South itself. And she would defend it.

BY THE TIDE'S GRACE AND THE WIND'S
COMMAND, OUR STRENGTH MAY FLOW

"The strength of Myriamis lies not in
conquest, but in our own hand. Depend
not on the tide of another's mercy."

Each household must maintain its
own means of sustenance. Be it
trade, craft, or farming, to prevent
reliance on foreign powers.

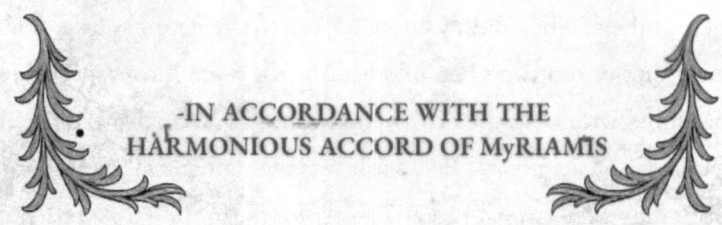

-IN ACCORDANCE WITH THE
HARMONIOUS ACCORD OF MyRIAMIS

# Chapter Thirty-One

*ayla.* The dawn broke blood-red. Layla tightened her grip on the reins as the first rays of sun bled over the horizon, revealing what the darkness had hidden. The land before them was no longer Elarith luscious and thriving; it was *rotted*. Black veins stretched like a spiderweb across the earth, leeching the life from grass, from trees, from everything it touched. The air smelled wrong. It was damp and metallic, like mold and iron. Even the wind felt heavier, carrying with it a weight that settled in Layla's chest. And then she saw them.

Across the open fields, where Elarith's villages should have been, stood ruin. Charred homes, toppled walls, smoke still curling from the remnants. And beyond that, the shoreline. Boats. Dozens of them. Dark hulls lined the water like teeth, their decks swarming with soldiers. The

Lumiren banners snapped in the brisk sea wind, black and gray, a sea of enemy forces stretching farther than Layla's eye could follow.

A hush rippled through their army as the sight registered, as every soldier, Antonin and Graystonian alike, realized the same thing: Elarith had fallen. Layla swallowed hard, her heart hammering against her ribs. They were too late to stop the invasion. Too late to save the kingdom as it had been. But not too late to *fight for what was left.* Even if there was only one survivor, they would find them. Even if every stone had to be turned over, every drop of blood spilled, they would take back this land. For Elarith. For the South. For Caeleria.

Kain's horse stepped up beside hers, his jaw set like iron, his bow slung and ready. "Looks like we found them, Dove," he said grimly, the green of his eyes catching the sunlight.

Layla's fingers tightened on her reins. "Good," she said, her voice steady despite the storm in her chest. "Then let's show them what happens when they bring ruin to our lands."

The ground shook as the drums began. Layla's fingers gripped her sword's hilt so tightly her knuckles ached, her breath ghosting white in the frigid morning air. All around her, the united armies of Graystonia, Antonin, and Myriamis stood in tense silence, a living wall of shields and steel. Across the blackened field, Lumiren's warhorns bellowed. A sound like something torn from the belly of a dying beast, and the enemy immediately surged forward. A sea of black and green and gold, armored boots slamming the ground in perfect, terrible rhythm.

"Hold!" Xaden's voice roared from the front, carrying over the clash of steel. Layla's heart pounded with every beat of the war drums, every step that brought the enemy closer. Her sisters stood somewhere behind her with the healers, but she could feel their presence like an anchor at her back. She drew a slow breath, steadying her pulse, and raised her blade when Xaden did.

"Archers, release!" Sir Edwin called, his deep voice steady as a drum. A deadly hum filled the air as arrows flew, a dark storm blotting the sky before raining down on the front lines. Screams split the air, bodies collapsing into the churned mud, but still they came, relentless and endless.

"Charge!" Xaden roared. Then the two tides collided and the world became chaos.

Almost immediately Layla was knocked from her horse. She rolled as she fell, instinctively swinging her sword up in defense as it met another with a crack that vibrated to her shoulder. The stench of sweat and blood filled her nose as she ducked, twisted, and struck. The Antonin training blazed through her veins. Every parry, every pivot sharper than it had ever been. She caught the glint of rot-blackened armor, one of Yssra's Blessed. Its eyes glowed faintly in its helm, and its grin was inhuman as it swung a blade nearly the size of Layla herself. She braced, blocked, the force rattled her bones. It shoved her back, boots skidding in the mud.

"Layla!" Kain's voice, rough as a growl, cut through the fray. And then he was there, arrow already loosed before she could blink. The creature dropped, its head snapping back with a sickening crack before Kain leapt forward and swung his sword, severing the head clean off.

Kain grinned back at her like a wolf. "Keep up, Dove!" Before she could retort, he was gone again, moving like shadow and fire through the battle, loosing arrow after arrow with deadly precision.

# ONDURIN

· I

# Chapter Thirty-Two

*K**ain.***
The field was hell. Kain's lungs burned as he loosed another arrow, the string biting his fingers raw. The enemy kept coming, wave after wave, their armor splattered with filth, their faces twisted in bloodlust. But worse than the soldiers were the ones with the black veins, crawling up their necks, shining faintly under their skin like molten rot. He'd already learned the hard way that they didn't go down like normal men. A shot to the chest only slowed them. A slice across the gut barely fazed them. You had to take the head clean off, and even then, they thrashed for a few seconds like dying snakes before going still.

"Fucking Yssra-spawn," he snarled, notching another arrow. The shot took one through the eye socket. It fell at last, twitching in the mud. He didn't stop to breathe. Couldn't. His eyes were already scanning for the one thing that mattered, her. *There she was.* She was a flash of green and steel ahead, fighting like a hellcat. Every block, every swing she made sent a jolt through his chest of feral admiration and terror and something too raw to name. Another shadow moved for her blind side. Kain growled and released. The arrow went through the throat. Layla spun and sliced the stumbling man. They were a good team.

The press of bodies surged, pushing him farther forward. He let it take him, let instinct rule, his bow singing death into the fray. When they got too close, the dagger was in his hand, hacking and tearing, blood spraying hot over his knuckles. He was a storm, and the storm would not break. But still he tracked her. Always her. A roar cut the din. Sparrow somewhere to his right, rallying a line of Antonin warriors. Good. The front was holding. For now. Then he saw it. A cluster of the black-veined ones, breaking through the shield wall, heading straight toward Layla.

"Fuck no." He was moving before he thought, shoving through men, loosing arrow after arrow until the quiver was nearly empty. He jumped over a fallen horse, landed hard, and ripped his dagger free again, barreling toward her. By the time he reached her side, two of the things were already down, their heads barely attached. Layla's chest heaved, her braid half-loose, but she didn't back up.

"That's my Dove," he muttered, grinning like a wolf even as he spun to slit the throat of the third attacker. "Keep up!" Her answering glare was pure fire and gods, he loved it.

The push toward Elarith's outer wall was brutal. Every foot of ground was bought with blood. The blackened grass sucked at their boots, turning the field into a grave. Kain's arm ached from drawing his bowstring, but he didn't stop. Not until the last arrow was gone. Then he switched back to twin daggers, slicing through anyone that got too close, his movements as smooth and implacable as a dancer's.

"Advance!" Xaden's roar cut through the chaos. Kain surged with the line, scanning, always scanning for that green figure. There, she was still there. Still fighting. Reverence bloomed in his chest even as sweat stung his eyes. She wasn't just keeping up anymore. She was leading. They were so close now he could see the ruined gates of Elarith. And then the enemy's horn sounded again, deeper, longer. And the earth shook in response.

From the shoreline, a full murder of shadows advanced. Towering shapes breaking free from the smoke. The sky bled red above them, and for a breathless moment, the battlefield went still. Then came the roar. The flood of monsters, Yssra's *Blessed*, poured forward. Hulking, bare-ly-man, total-abomination. Their bodies were so riddled with blackened veins that it even seemed to bleed and pulse across their armor as if alive. The Blessed from earlier were barely touched compared to these men. They moved in eerie unison, a single living tide, the goddess's will made flesh.

The first one struck their line like a hammer. Bones cracked. Men screamed. Spears shattered beneath the blow.

"Hold!" Xaden's voice tore through the chaos, but the line was already faltering, the ground slick with blood and mud. Kain cut one down, then another, the motion a blur of fury and precision but his instincts screamed at him. And then he saw her. Her sword flashing gold in the sunlight, her stance unyielding, defiance carved into every line of her. But she was too close to them. Too far ahead and completely surrounded. And behind her stepping from the smoke, came the largest of them all. For a heartbeat, Kain felt like time stopped as he fought his way to her. Watching the scene before him unravel like his worst nightmare made real. The creature's blade dragged across the dirt with a hiss. His armor was torn, scorched, the crest of Antonin still faintly visible beneath the rot. And when the beast lifted its head, Kain's world split open. Theron. Or what was left of him.

The face was his brother's, same hard jaw, same scar at the temple, but everything else was wrong. Black, spidery veins webbed up his throat, across his cheek, over his chest, writhing like they were alive beneath the skin. His eyes burned black, void of humanity, cold and endless. Yssra's mark. Yssra's claim.

"Theron..." Kain's voice cracked, disbelief and horror colliding. The Blessed thing that had once been his brother turned toward him, like he could hear him across the war-wrenched crowd. Then toward Layla. And when it smiled, it was all teeth and shadow. Kain's gut dropped. *No.* The monster moved.

"LAYLA!"

Kain sprinted harder somehow, boots digging deep into the blood-soaked earth, cutting down anything in his way. His heart slammed against his ribs, the sound deafening in his ears. He would reach her. He *had* to.

But he wasn't fast enough.

Layla met the first strike, her sword singing through the air as steel met steel. The force of it jolted her entire frame, her knees nearly buckling under the weight of his unnatural strength. Sparks burst between their blades, the sound like thunder.

Then Kain saw her eyes locked on the man's face. Recognition. Horror. Disbelief. And in that single moment, that heartbeat of hesitation, everything happened. Theron's blade twisted. The steel slid into her abdomen, deep and merciless. Her gasp was soft, strangled. For a second, she didn't seem to feel it. Then the warmth of blood spread down her stomach, and her sword slipped from her grasp.

"NO!" The world narrowed to only the crimson bloom spreading across her armor. His roar tore through the chaos, primal and broken. Blessed Theron ripped his sword free, raising it high for the killing blow but as it came down, Kain was there. Steel met steel. The clash exploded in a storm of sparks. Kain drove forward, rage and grief fusing into a single, savage force. He slammed his shoulder into Theron's chest, snarling.

"COME ON THEN!" he bellowed. "COME ON, BROTHER!" Theron's corrupted snarl was the only answer as the two locked blades, each strike harder than the last. Kain spared a single glance of Sparrow kneeling with Layla. *He would save her. He had too.* And with that, the ground quaked beneath the once brothers. Fire painted the edges of the world. Around them, men fought and died, but all Kain saw was *him*. The brother he'd loved. The brother he'd grieved. The monster who'd gutted the only woman he could not lose.

He fought like a man possessed, dodging a swing, countering with a slice that tore through corrupted flesh. Black blood hissed where it touched the ground. Still, the thing kept coming. Kain roared, parried, and drove his dagger deep beneath the breastplate. The impact sent a shudder through his arms. Theron staggered, fell to one knee, his inhuman glare searing through the dark. For a fleeting heartbeat, Kain swore he saw his brother again, a flicker of human pain beneath the ruin. Then it was gone, replaced by Yssra's hollow rage.

Kain buried his blade to the hilt. "Rest now, brother," he whispered through gritted teeth. "You've done enough." The creature crumpled. Kain barely heard it fall. He darted back to Layla, his knees hitting the mud as he grasped her face with both hands. Sparrow was pressing hard on her wound to attempt to stop the bleeding while a circle of warriors and guards alike surrounded them. Guarding them from the onslaught all around.

"No. No, no, no. Stay with me, Dove," he rasped. "You stay with me."

Her eyelids fluttered. Her lips parted, breath shallow. "Kain..."

"Don't," he choked out, leaning so close his forehead brushed hers. "Don't you dare give up. You stay."

"We need a healer!" Sparrow's voice cut through the din. "NOW!" A healer finally made their way to them. Sparrow and Xaden joined the makeshift wall around them as another wave of Blessed crashed against their flank. Kain refused to move.

He held her tighter, his blood mixing with hers, his voice breaking against her fading pulse. "Gods damn it, Dove," he whispered. "You can't leave me. Not now. Not ever." He didn't feel the tears burning down his face. Didn't see the chaos raging around him. All he saw was her, his light in the ruin, slipping away in his arms.

They say Ondurin waits only for warriors.
Not all who fall are chosen. Only the
bravest, those who meet death with steel
raised and fire still burning in their veins,
are called.

In Ondurin, the fallen rise unbroken. The
fires never dim. The steel never dulls. Every
name is remembered and every battle
honored.

To fall with your sword in hand is not an
ending.

It is how warriors are made eternal.

**-THE GREAT TALES OF ONDURIN**

# Chapter Thirty-Three

*L* *ayla.*
 Everything was noise. There was screaming, the sound of metal on metal, the copper taste of blood. Then silence. Layla suddenly felt weightless. She floated, the pain receding until there was nothing left but endless night and a sky full of stars.

"Do you know where you are, child?" The voice was everywhere at once. Soft and thunderous, gentle and commanding. Layla spun and there he was, rising from where he had been sitting in the grass. Eliryn. His hair glowed like starlight, his golden eyes piercing through her. She hadn't even realized she was kneeling until he stepped closer and laid a hand on her shoulder. Warmth flooded her once again, so bright she swore her body was burning, her soul unraveling like thread in his light.

"I... I don't know," she whispered. Her voice trembled.

"You are between," he said simply. "Not yet dead. Not fully alive. You are here because you sought me, because you are asking if it is time to rest."

Her throat closed. "Is it?"

Eliryn's gaze softened, but his words were iron. "That is not for me to say. I will not choose for you. Fate cannot choose for you. *You* must choose." The stars flared. Shapes emerged, silhouettes of gods surrounding her, their presence ancient and crushing. Serelai, crowned in flowers that dripped gold, smiled at her. Varyn stood like a wall of muscle and war paint, arms crossed. Tychic's hand rested on the hilt of his sword, Lapetic's black hood shadowed his face, Every god she had ever been taught about was here, except Yssra.

"You have the power to end this age," Eliryn said, his voice deep as the earth. "To burn away rot, to begin again. But each step will be your choice: your triumph or your ruin. Do you understand?" Layla's breath came quick, her heart hammering. "You were blessed with my power the moment you were born. And now..." He extended his hand, palm up, where a small glowing pebble of light shimmered. "...you may claim it fully. But doing so means choosing life. Choosing to fight. Choosing to bear what will come." She didn't think. She *couldn't*. Her hand shot out, fingers closing around the light. It burned, gods, it burned, stitching through every nerve, every bone, until she was whole again, blazing from the inside out. When she opened her eyes, Eliryn was smiling at her, pride in his divine face. "Then rise, Layla Eradellian, Child of the Oak. Blood of the first dawn. The time has come," he said, his voice soft and endless as time as it echoed through her. "Rise, and finish what we began."

The world of the living flickered before her eyes, the battlefield in total chaos, Kain's arms locked around her body, his face carved in anguish. She gasped, breath flooding back into her lungs as if the gods themselves demanded it.

*"Endings and Beginnings,"* the timeless voice murmured within her soul. *"Both dwell in you. Choose what must end. Choose what must begin."* And then light exploded. A blinding pulse erupted from her chest, hurling outward in all directions. A shockwave of divine fury and rebirth. Light poured from her body like molten gold, threads of it streaming into the sky. The air cracked open, vibrating with the sound of creation itself. She felt Kain's arms locked around her as the world seemingly erupted. The light swallowed everything, sky, ground, shadow, until nothing but brilliance remained. The wave struck the enemy lines first. The Blessed convulsed where they stood, black veins bursting into smoke. Their screams tore through the air, not of pain but release, as if the darkness itself was being exorcised from their flesh. The corruption sizzled away, dissolving into dust. And still the light spread.

Across the valley, it swept over the living and the dying alike. The war paused as every man was thrown to his knees on this shore. Weapons clattered to the ground. The cries of battle turned to gasps of awe. The light struck the trees, the kingdom of Elarith, the soil. Every inch of ground around them that had withered beneath Yssra's curse. And wherever it touched, life answered. Flowers burst through the mud. The trees groaned as new leaves unfurled in a single breath. The air filled with the scent of rain and renewal. It was the power of *Eliryn himself*, the God of Endings and Beginnings, unleashed through her mortal veins. Then, just as suddenly as it came, it began to fade.

The brilliance dimmed, softening into shimmering motes that drifted through the air like falling stars. The battlefield was silent, save for the hiss of cooling steel. Kain still held her. His breath came ragged, his arms shaking as he looked down at her. She felt no pain from where she had been wounded; glancing down she could see it was now gone. Her skin, luminous beneath the thin film of blood and ash, shimmered faintly like starlight under her flesh.

All around them, the armies stirred. Soldiers rose to their feet in disbelief. The Antonin warriors crossed themselves with trembling hands. Even the Lumirens, those who still lived, fell to their knees, gazing at her with wide, terrified eyes. And then...

"By the gods..." Xaden's voice carried over the field, raw and shaking. "She *healed* them."

It was true. Every Blessed lay motionless in the dirt, presumably knocked unconscious by the impact of the change, but the corruption was gone from their skin. The black veins had vanished. Their chests rose and fell, shallow but alive. The air was clean. No rot. No stench of death. Only silence and life. Layla had awareness of all of it, yet none of it at the same time.

Then sensation slammed back into her body. Heat burned beneath her skin, fierce and unrelenting, power thrumming through her veins like a living current. It was too vast to name, too new to grasp, and it left her breathless, disoriented, as though the world had split apart and sewn itself back together around her. The aftershock rattled her bones, hollowing her out even as it filled her.

She felt arms locked around her. Solid and unyielding. *Kain.* He was holding her so tightly it stole the air from her lungs, his body braced around hers as if the force that had torn through the battlefield might return at any moment. As if she might vanish again if he loosened his grip. She felt the tension coiled through him, the way his chest rose sharp and uneven beneath her cheek, the tremor in his hands despite the iron strength of his hold. With effort, she forced her eyes open and the first thing she saw was him. Blood streaked his jaw. Ash darkened his hair. His eyes were bright and wild and fixed entirely on her, as if she were the only thing left standing in a ruined world. His throat worked as he swallowed, hard, and when he spoke her name it sounded torn from somewhere deep and unguarded.

"Dove..."

The sound anchored her. For a heartbeat, there was nothing else. Just his arms. His warmth. The undeniable truth that he had not let go. Not when the light had erupted from her chest. Not when the ground had shaken beneath them. Not even when she had slipped beyond the veil of life itself. He had held her through all of it.

Her fingers twitched weakly against his chest. He gave her a broken smile, one that did not quite hold, then swallowed hard and glanced past her shoulder. With more willpower than strength, Layla turned her head to follow his gaze. A few feet away, among the fallen, lay Theron. Not twisted. Not monstrous. *Breathing*. For a heartbeat, she could not believe her eyes. Then she saw the rise and fall of his chest. Slow. Steady. The black corruption that had once consumed him was gone, wiped clean from his skin as if it had never existed at all. His sword lay beside him, the metal bright and unmarred in the sunlight. And then she truly saw the rest.

The battlefield around them had gone utterly still. Weapons lay abandoned in the dirt. Men knelt where they had fallen, staring in stunned silence at what stood before them. The air was clean. No rot. No stench of death. Only quiet. Only life. Layla tore her gaze away at last and looked back at Kain. He had gone completely rigid, his arms still locked around her as if letting go were unthinkable, impossible. As if she might die again the moment he did.

Layla swallowed hard, her voice trembling as the truth settled heavy in her chest. "What does this mean?"

The man who had always worn arrogance like armor looked stripped bare now, every defense gone, emotion raw and unreadable for the first time she had ever seen him. "...Everything."

# Chapter Thirty-Four

## EPILOGUE

The dungeons beneath Graystonia had never been so full. The air was thick with damp and iron, the flicker of torchlight casting uneasy shadows over rows of cells. Once, these halls had held traitors and thieves. Now, they held something far worse and far more tragic. The former Blessed. Men who had once fought for their homelands, now cleansed but not trusted. Their black veins had faded, their skin no longer stretched and burned by Yssra's rot, but their eyes... their eyes carried the weight of remembering. Some stared blankly at the walls, others whispered prayers that went unanswered. Each one a living reminder of what her light had undone and what it had cost.

As Layla approached the final door, the guards stepped aside without a word. Inside, the cell was dim. A single torch burned low in the bracketed wall, casting long shadows that stretched across the figure seated on the floor. Theron Drakaren. He was alive. Miraculously, impossibly alive. The black veins that had consumed him were gone, replaced by naturally tan, clean skin. His body bore scars, the kind only war and resurrection could leave, but the light in his eyes, gods... the blue of them was clear again. Familiar. He looked up the moment she appeared.

Layla froze in the doorway. Her pulse thundered. The sight of him almost stole the strength from her knees. For a long moment, neither spoke. The world outside felt impossibly distant. Then she drew in a slow breath and forced the word past her lips, soft but steady. "Hi."

Theron rose to his feet. The chains that once bound him had been removed. He stood tall, the flicker of torchlight catching in his hair, in the quiet curve of his mouth. The spark there, the one she thought she'd never see again, flared bright. He truly smiled then. The same warm, infuriating, heartbreakingly human smile she had once known. "Hi."

# Acknowledgments

To my husband- Yes, you're here again. And yes, you deserve it. You are an incredible dad, a steady partner, and the kind of support system every author secretly prays for. You believed in this dream long before it felt real, and you never once asked me to shrink it. Thank you for holding everything together while I disappeared into this world, for showing up every single day with patience and humor, and for being un-apologetically yourself. Your sarcasm, your sharp wit, and your expertly delivered asshole commentary have absolutely fueled the men in these pages. Whether you meant to or not. I couldn't do this without you, and I wouldn't want to.

To Alex Palmer- My sounding board, my hype woman, my emo-tional support human. You once again read this story more times than anyone should reasonably be asked to, and somehow remained enthu-siastic, invested, and suspiciously willing to keep going. You've endured voice memos, screenshots, unhinged theories, and last-minute "WAIT WHAT IF—" moments with grace and excitement. Your belief in this story and in me has never wavered, and that matters more than I can ever properly say. I'm endlessly grateful for you, for our shared chaos, and for every fantasy ball, dramatic gown, and story still waiting for us.

To my family- Mom, Dad, and my beautiful sisters—thank you for continuing to support me even after realizing this writing thing was not, in fact, a phase. You've encouraged me, listened patiently to my ramblings, and celebrated milestones that once felt impossible. To my mom, thank you for enduring the updates, the spoilers, and the moments I absolutely could not keep to myself. And Dad...yes. I know. This one is *also* not wholesome. And no, I still did not choose a pen name. At this point, we're committed. Try to stay strong.

To Bryanna Beverlin- Thank you for keeping my husband wrangled so I could continue working on this dream hobby of mine. Your patience, your flexibility, and your ability to manage both him and my chaos deserve recognition all on their own. Your support has given me space to create, and your kindness never goes unnoticed. Truly, thank you for everything you do.

To Mandi Ann- Thank you for your sharp eye, your thoughtful feedback, and your ability to see straight through the noise to the heart of the story. You helped shape this book into something stronger, deeper, and more honest than it would have been without you. Your guidance challenged me in the best ways, and I'm so grateful our paths crossed when they did.

To the feral women of Girls Night- Thank you for being my constant reprieve. For the laughter, the venting, the brutal honesty, and the nights that reminded me I wasn't carrying this alone. Thank you for listening through every phase of this book, helping me navigate each step, and showing up with exactly what I needed when I needed it. I am deeply grateful for every one of you.

And finally, to you-the reader. You came back. Knowing full well what kind of story this would be. That tells me everything I need to know about you, and I adore you for it. Thank you for trusting me again with your time, your heart, and your emotions. Whether you laughed, cursed, blushed, or fell a little in love along the way, I'm endlessly grateful you chose to continue this journey with me.

# About the Author

Alexia Gray is a lifelong lover of all things magical, romantic. And just a little dangerous. Raised on fairy tales and fantasy novel, she's spent years dreaming up enchanted worlds and star-crossed lovers. When she's not writing, Alexia can be found chugging coffee, getting lost in smutty books, or chasing her toddlers. She lives in a small town in Missouri with her novel-worthy husband and two wild boys.